MICHELLE RENE

Maud's Circus

First published by Michelle Rene 2020

First edition

ISBN: 978-1-63732-076-1

This book was professionally typeset on Reedsy.
Find out more at reedsy.com

Dedicated to my mother.

Contents

Part One   1

Part Two   25

Part Three   62

Part Four   94

Part Five   135

Part Six   167

Part Seven   206

Part Eight   237

Part Nine   263

Part Ten   289

Afterword   314

About the Author   317

Part One

1893

Maud retrieved the small, worn bible from the shelf in the pew in front of her. This had been her seat since she was six years old; and thus, the bible had become her own personal friend and confidant. When she opened its pages, there was the familiar sweetness of the flowers pressed inside. She breathed in deep the gentle nostalgia of one of the few things that felt totally her own.

To all the world, it looked as if she were reading her favorite passage, but Maud was really studying the dandelion that had dried in between the pages. Its yellow petals stained the thin paper, looking like little rays of sunlight made by God himself. Behind another page was a bit of blank paper she had stored away.

She made a gesture as if to brush a strand of hair from her neck. Such an inconspicuous move, but one that allowed her to pick the stick of pencil from behind her ear with ease. She palmed it, waiting for the prayer.

Heads bowed as the preacher began his recitation. Maud bowed too, letting her long hair act as a curtain around her—an auburn drape to hide behind. If anyone happened to be watching Maud, she looked as though she were intently praying.

While everyone else sat in quiet contemplation, she took out her pencil. With a gentle hand, she began to sketch the little dandelion, trying to capture its texture. Such small nuances. Such tiny detail. The minuscule lines of an edge or a fold. The pencil strokes had to be feather light, otherwise the scratching noise against the paper would rouse her mother's attention.

Suddenly, she felt a sting spread across her hand. Maud had misjudged the length of the prayer and hadn't noticed when it ended. She gazed up to see her mother's tight scowl; her face was hot with anger.

In one swift motion, Maud shut the bible and looked forward with everyone else. None of the other congregants had noticed her drawing, so that was a blessing. There would be much worse than a swat waiting for her at home if anyone had seen her indecency. Then again, it might not matter at all. Everything depended on the fickle mood of a sour woman.

There was a certain scent to the inside of their church on Sunday mornings. Musty, almost thick with the smell of human breath and wood. Maud always imagined it was like the inside of a coffin. So many people lined the pews, each pressed close to the person next to them; one could barely move an arm without rustling the fabric of their neighbor's dress. Perhaps not a coffin. Maybe a mausoleum would be a better likeness. Either way, death was death.

Of course, she would never say such things. Not ever. Thoughts like that would guarantee her the whipping of a lifetime.

The congregation was divided with men seated on one side and women on the other. Whole families split by their gender. Little children could sit with their mothers as long as they were too small to know the meaning of things, but as soon as that innocence was lost, they were mandated to their proper places. Exceptions were made for the infirmed or those missing a parent. Somehow, more often than not, the two ended up in the same category.

The men wore rough clothes and serious faces and sat in a haze of sweat and tobacco. Most looked to be miles away, thinking of all the chores that awaited them: the mule that needed tending for an injured leg, the cow that was due to give birth next week.

The women's side smelled of talcum powder. Dusty fragrances among flower-pattern dresses. Children were the main attention. Watching like hawks, the mothers circled to ensure the little ones behaved. It just wouldn't do to have their brood pitch a fit and draw attention. Appearances were everything. Maud always thought of mothers in church like wildflowers along the road, pretty to look at but too hardy to ever cut down.

As per his usual routine, the good Reverend addressed the women's side first.

"Bow your heads young women and be humbled among your betters. Yours is a life of service and grace, an existence behind and below. Children and the home are your domain. Hide your body, for it is shameful. Be kind and thankful for what is provided. Never ask to receive more, for you are given all that is necessary. Anything more is nothing but vanity."

The message was clear and constant. Be humble and find happiness in your kitchen, with your wash basin, working the laundry line. Sit and tend to the sewing, the mending, and the men. Everything rested on the tireless backs of women.

Maud gazed around the men's section, searching for her father. She found him quickly enough at his usual spot in his pew. His gentle eyes stared forward and focused on the preacher. His mop of dark auburn hair, so like her own, had already broken free of the pomade.

Maud tried to get his attention, tried to share a smile.

Instead, the attention she captured was that of her Uncle Vern. He was crammed between her father and some other men. The space was tight since he wasn't a regular. People had to make room for him without giving up their rightful place in the pew.

Maud's uncle met her gaze, startling her a bit. His eyes bore into hers, his smile turning into a leer—an unclean look. She looked away and focused on the preacher.

During one of the mid-sermon prayers, Maud tried once more to work on her drawing. This time, her mother pinched her hard on the thigh. It took most of Maud's restraint not to call out in pain. That wouldn't do; it would only call attention to her misdeeds. Her mother was already furious.

Maud rubbed her thigh, now hot and swollen. Best to treat it like a mosquito bite that itched against her cotton dress. She composed herself, shut her bible quietly, and replaced the pencil behind her ear.

She was quite sure she was in for a beating when she got home, but it was useless to worry about that now. Instead, she took to gazing out one of the only windows in the church. There, the sun shone against a pure, blue sky. Pale wisps of clouds smeared against the blue like the hairs of a white horse's tail. The tiniest chirping of a bird tickled the air—a piano's song. If this church was to be her coffin, at least she got a window. That's more than a corpse got.

Being cooped up inside church was bad, but Sunday evenings were even worse, especially if, as happened today, she was caught drawing in her bible. That's when the manners her mother reserved for other people melted away, and she became a storm unto herself, building quietly into a thunderhead of malice.

"Had someone seen you," her mother said, raging in Maud's face. "Just think of the talk! Imagine how that'd look. We didn't raise you to be a heathen in our own home."

"Yes, Mama."

"Time and time again, I told you to pay attention. Your doodling ain't right in the house of the Lord. You know that!"

"Yes, Mama."

Mrs. Stevens paced the small kitchen with a proper head of steam. It seemed the more she moved, the more the air sparked with the taste of her ire. Her worn shoes *knock-knock-knocked* against the wood of the floorboards as though she were a clock ticking down the seconds. Even the men stuck to the corners of the room. There was no use wondering what awaited Maud at the end of the knocking. She knew it would be violence.

"What do you have to say for yourself?"

"I'm sorry, Mama."

Maud's words were always uttered with the same defeated tone. A year before, Maud tested the waters with insubordination. She defended herself and tried to explain why her drawings were important. They weren't against God; they were because of him. But in the end, it didn't matter. Her mother never backed down once she got going. An object of momentum, she was the wind, and all Maud could do was recoil from her wrath.

"Go outside and cut yourself a switch," her mother said.

Maud grabbed a knife and walked to the hickory tree behind the house. Choosing a switch always presented a dilemma. A small, thin branch stung more. Sometimes the thin ones even cut into her flesh and made her bleed. Also, her mother often saw the thin switches as a challenge and whipped her even longer. Selecting a thicker one meant more bruises. Maud chose one in the middle, opting to take her chances by splitting the difference.

The switch came off cleanly, meaning the knife was sharpened recently. For a moment, longer than could be ignored, Maud looked down at the blade. A sudden urge to press its edge into the flesh of her arm overwhelmed her. It didn't make sense, for she was certainly about to be whipped until bloody, but the idea set off a twinge of power that could not be denied.

Maud took the tip of the knife and pressed it against the fleshy part of her forearm. The next step was up to her. She could force the blade down and feel the pain of it, all her torment leaking along with her blood, or she could remove the knife and leave herself in intact. The most intoxicating part of the situation was the choice. Her choice. In a world where she merely reacted like a stalk of wheat in the breeze, she had power here… in this choice.

"Maud Stevens, you hurry up, or it'll be twice as bad for you!"

She snapped out of her fantasy and hurried back to the house. Once inside, her mother took possession of the switch and promptly handed it to her husband.

"Sarah, I don't know if we need to…" her father began.

"It's a father's duty to discipline his daughter," her mother said. "It was the way with my father, and it will be the way here. Don't be a coward, David."

"What did she do really?" he asked, crossing his arms over his chest. It was rare to see him take a stand, especially against Maud's mother.

"She was disrespectful in church. I told you," her mother said in a low growl. Something about the standoff was turning her practically feral.

"I'm not going to beat her over a drawing."

"Fine. If you are going to be a coward, I'll just have Vern do it," she said.

Maud's father looked over Vern with an unreadable face. Vern allowed the smallest of grins to tug at the corners of his lips. Maud shivered all over with the thought of her uncle doling out the punishment.

Her father blew out a long sigh and motioned for his wife to hand him the switch. Maud raised her skirt to present the back of her legs. At least it was Daddy this time, she thought. He always tried to make it hurt less, and it was always over quicker. Little mercies made life bearable.

At dinner, they all sat in silence. Maud's legs were so tender that she perched at the edge of the chair. It made her back ache to sit so tall, but it was better than the pressure of the seat against her raw flesh. Maud sat across the table from her mother, which allowed the furious woman to watch her every move.

Her uncle's hand roamed under the table when he sat next to her. It slithered just below the surface like an eel, never showing itself—at least not until Maud felt it brush her leg. When his hand touched her thigh, it sent shivers through her body.

Though his groping hand landed over Maud's dress, the fabric was thin, and it felt like he was caressing bare skin. Revulsion engulfed her, and she had to try hard not to spit up her chicken. She snapped her knees together, knocking the table leg and jostling the dinner plates.

"Maud Stevens, what is the matter with you?" asked her mother.

"He's touching me. Uncle Vern is touching me again," Maud said. Using her eyes, she pleaded with her mother to believe her this time. Her father scowled at his brother-in-law from across the table.

"Vern? What is this? You touching my daughter?"

"Of course not, David," her uncle said with a relatively good impression of surprise. "I think little Maudie here is just looking for attention. You know how she gets."

"She's always looking for attention," her mother said.

Her father turned his gaze toward Maud. She hoped he might believe her this time. Her mother didn't—and never would, but maybe this time, her father would rise to the occasion and stand up to the two of them. He could protect her if he only tried.

"You ought not tell stories," he said softly and turned his face back to the food in front of him.

Maud exhaled. The fruit of hope in her belly died on the vine. When her uncle's hand returned to her leg, he pried her knees apart and ran his fingers up and down her thigh. He grinned and acted as though nothing was happening. For all the world, the scene above the table appeared innocent and normal.

She was a wheat stalk in the wind, merely bending this way or that. Then, she remembered the incident outside. The power of holding that knife over her arm. The surge of adrenaline from suddenly having a choice. Even if the rest of her life was out of her hands, Maud's body could still belong to her.

No, she thought. Not this time, you son-of-a-bitch.

The bit of pencil was still behind her ear, and she had sharpened it earlier to a fine point. Maud ran her hand through her hair in that innocent way she did in church. A maneuver effortless because she had performed it a thousand times. She retrieved the pencil without anyone noticing. The comforting scent of wood and graphite passed her nose, somehow giving her more strength.

Vern had reached the area just above the inside of her knee when she stabbed the pencil into his hand. She hit the soft patch of skin in between his knuckles and felt the pencil dig into his flesh and tendons. Her uncle jumped and yelped at the same, bumping the table and nearly knocking over the glasses. The bastard yanked away his hand, and Maud glared at him with triumphant eyes. Her uncle clutched his hand, looking surprised.

"What on earth just happened?" Maud's father asked.

"I... uh..."

Maud stared down her uncle. Go on, she thought. Tell them what happened. Tell them I stabbed you. Tell them where your hand was just now.

"I... had... a pain in my arm," he said. "Damn change in weather always makes my joints hurt. Must be a storm brewing on the horizon."

A storm was brewing, all right, and it would change everything.

***

It was a brisk autumn day when her father announced that the family was in for a treat. The dime museum in town had a special visiting speaker, and they would see the attraction. None of them knew who the speaker would be, but Maud yearned for any break in the monotony of farm life.

Gusts of wind blew their best dresses and hats as their mule pressed forward down the old roads toward town. Each blow brought with it a fine dirt that embedded in their clothes and crunched beneath their teeth. It left Maud itchy all over.

Once they reached town, they found it bustling with people. Normally a sleepy place, the streets now teemed with families. Children ran along the boarded walkways and dusty alleys. Women smiled and chatted with one another. Husbands played at being benevolent kings as they bought peppermint candy for their families who rarely saw such luxuries.

A good crowd swarmed the sleepy dime museum, wanting to buy tickets in advance. Her father returned to them saying the first show at 2:00 was already sold out, but he managed to procure them tickets for the 3:00 show.

Maud couldn't help but wonder who could possibly entice the attention of everyone in the county. It seemed just about everyone they knew was there, eager to witness the spectacle, yet without any knowledge of the main attraction.

After eating their sack lunches, her parents allowed her to go visit with some of the other young ladies she knew from church and school. Sarah Guthrie and Marcy Bennett were her first choices. Girls could be so flighty and easily occupied with trivial things. Sarah and Marcy were guilty of that in spades. Still, they were fun to talk to, so she went to stand by them.

"Can you believe all these people?" Maud asked as she approached her friends with a wide grin. They reciprocated with eager eyes and excited conversation. The girls smelled of rose water and peppermint candy.

"It's amazing," said Sarah. "I don't think I've ever seen so many folks."

"I bet we could flirt with the Jameson boys and get lost in the crowd. Right out in the open. No one would be the wiser," said Marcy.

Maud rolled her eyes. Marcy was the boy-crazed one of the trio and relentlessly prattled on about them during school. She had been the first to get her breasts to show beneath the baggy aprons all farmers' girls wore, which was even more noteworthy because cloth for new clothes was an expense, so many girls wore dresses a few sizes too big for them. Maud had to admit that she and Sarah were a tad jealous. Maud's own breasts were so small; her chest was still unrecognizable from a boy's.

"What time did your pappy get tickets for?" asked Sarah.

"Three. Yours?" replied Maud.

"Both of us have to wait until the four o'clock one. What do you reckon the show will be about? Must be something big."

"I heard it was one of them freaks you see at the circus," said Marcy. "The lobster boy or wild man or something."

"Really? A boy raised by lobsters?" asked Sarah with wide eyes.

"As I live and breathe. One of the Clark boys said he saw one at *The Great Barlow Show* outside Wichita last summer. Said the boy was red all over and had claws for hands and everything."

"A boy couldn't be raised by lobsters," Maud said. "How would he even breathe if he lived underwater?"

Marcy rolled her eyes. "All's I'm saying is when them Clark boys came back it was all they could talk about."

Wichita was a long trek for them, and only the richest of families could afford it. The Clark family owned more land than any of them, so the children were afforded things like trips to the big city. The rest of the families in their town were fed and clothed, but not much else.

"I heard that today it's going to be the world's tallest man," said Sarah. "I heard he's nine feet tall and has to bow to enter any room."

"Who told you that?" asked Marcy.

"Mr. Whitner over at the candy store."

"Mr. Whitner will tell any bit of story to get you to stay longer and buy more candy. The old coot is crazier than a Junebug," Maud said.

"What do you think it is, Maudie?" asked Sarah.

Maud mulled it over, trying to come up with something outrageous to add to the giddy conversation. Maybe she could invent a person they hadn't heard of. When pressed to conjure something on the spot, nothing of worth came to mind, so she went with the truth.

"I honestly have no idea what it could be, but I can't wait to find out."

When three o'clock came, Maud stood in the long line outside the dime museum's doors. As the two o'clock show patrons filed out, she searched their eyes for some hint as to what they saw. Shock seemed to be the universal emotion. All were wide-eyed and whispering to one another as if they had witnessed some great thing. For the life of her, Maud couldn't make out any of their words.

When the crowd poured into the museum, they were greeted by a curator who boasted about curiosities too spectacular to believe, yet most of the offerings were taxidermy at its weakest.

The onlookers passed the amazing chicken who had been sucked into a milk jug during a tornado. Maud noticed one of its glass eyes was now sitting at the bottom of the jug, leaving it a pathetic one-eyed wonder.

They walked around the case that claimed to house the femur bone of a genuine Egyptian mummy. Of course, any farmhand could tell a worn steer bone when they saw it.

Not even her mother stopped to gaze upon the incredible Fiji mermaid sitting in its cradle behind glass, even though it had once been her favorite. Maud could remember when it first arrived at their town's museum. She had been about seven, and her mother treated her to a trip to see it. Maud remembered standing next to her mother, staring wide-eyed at the feat of taxidermy. Back then, it didn't seem fake. It was a genuine relic of the magical. They gazed in wonder together.

The Fiji mermaid remained the museum's prized possession and most prominent attraction, but it aged poorly. Any fool could see it was a fabricated monkey skeleton sewn onto the dried tail of a fish. After years of wear, the threading was visible to anyone who chose to take a close look. In a way, it resembled Maud's relationship with her mother. What had once been believable was now tattered and worn. A dried husk that lost its façade one scale at a time.

One by one, they all filed into the back-exhibit hall and took their places among the wooden benches. Maud sat in between her mother and father, starring up at an empty stage. The hall could accommodate around two dozen people, but more than thirty folks filled the room. People stood in the aisles and pressed their backs along the wall.

For a brief moment, Maud was reminded of the confining, coffin-like feeling of their church. The room was musty and enclosed by wood. People squished together like sardines. Everyone waited in order to fixate on one spectacle, but this was different somehow. The air was electric with anticipation. By the time the proprietor of the museum, Mr. Calhoun, dimmed the lights to signal the show was about to begin, the room had warmed with breath and perspiration. The gas lights along the bottom of the stage illuminated a small half-circle before them. This left the rest of the room in near darkness. Everyone shifted in anticipation for the spectacle on the other side of the flowing curtain.

The sound of boots knocking on wood signaled that the speaker was approaching the stage. Was he gruesome? Horribly disfigured maybe? Was he a giant among men? Everyone held their breath as the curtain rustled. Maud's gasp caught in her throat as the most amazing person stood before the crowd. It was perhaps the most unexpected sight she had ever seen, and she couldn't help but gawk wide-eyed with everyone else.

The speaker was a tattooed woman.

"Hello and thank you for coming today. I'm so pleased you all came to hear me. My name is Olive Oatman, and this is my story."

Olive Oatman was dressed finer than anyone Maud had ever seen. She wore a corseted dress that flared out beautifully. Fine silk and embroidered accents gently brushed the scratchy wood of the stage. The top part of her smooth, dark hair was pulled up, leaving the rest to cascade down her shoulders in fine curls.

What really set her apart though was not the finery she dressed herself in nor the sleekness of her hair. It was the tattoo on her face. Five lines running from her lower lip to the bottom of her chin. Triangles jutted out from the outer lines. Black tattoos permanently drawn to follow the contours of her chin.

"Savage," whispered her mother.

A few others echoed her sentiment. An older woman in the back gasped. Maud could hear a man near the door grunt and stomp out of the exhibit hall. Olive Oatman smiled broadly and looked around at the room before her.

"I was but fourteen when my family was attacked in 1851 by a war party of Yavapai Indians. My sister was only nine. Nothing but children. The war party killed our family and took us captive as slaves."

Olive paused, allowing the story to sink into the minds around her. With only a few sentences, she had turned herself from a sinner to a victim. Maud couldn't help but look over at her parents. Both of them, even her mother, were enraptured. Everyone sat silent and waited to hear more.

"The Yavapai feared us for our white diseases and eventually sold us to a band of Mojave. This, my friends, was a great fortune for us. The Mojave Indians were kind to me, even after my sister died of a fever, and they made me one of their own."

With a flourish, she gestured to the markings on her chin. "You good, Christian folks might think the Mojave forced this tattoo on me. That they held me down and made me harm myself in order to forever mark me as one of them. Perhaps to keep me away from white society forever. But I tell you this today, they did not."

Her mother gasped and brought a worn handkerchief to her mouth. The sentiment echoed among the women in the room, yet no one dared look away. The air around them grew thick with heavy breathing.

"The Mojave were my family, and a tattoo such as this is given only with the permission of the person being tattooed. It is a symbol that you belong and to help your spirit reach the holy land of the ancestors after you die. The land of ancestors is their version of heaven. I chose this when I was sixteen, and I wear it proudly."

Maud had never thought about any other heaven than the one she was taught. The tattooed woman had a hook in Maud, and it appeared Ms. Oatman knew her audience well enough to let it net itself before she continued.

"After five years with the Mojave, I was given to a group of government scouts who found me, a white woman, among the tribe. If the tribe were to be granted safe passage to a reservation, I had to be given back to the whites. I didn't want to go, but I had to for my Mojave family."

Whispers filled the hall but never raised loud enough to disturb the storyteller. "Monstrous," said someone behind Maud.

"How sad," said another.

"What an ordeal. That poor girl."

"Who would wish to stay with savages?"

"Brave. How brave."

"Savage as an Injun, I bet."

However, no matter what their thoughts, it seemed everyone wanted to hear the rest of Olive Oatman's story. She spoke of the kindness of the Mojave and integrating herself back into white society. Maud dared to cast her eyes around the hall again. Every person was listening like children at story time. A beautifully savage woman stood before a crowd of farmers, and they clung to her every word.

It was her tattoo, Maud decided. The mark set her apart from the crowd and made her untouchable. Part savage, part white. A woman to be admired from a distance. Maud gazed at Olive Oatman and envied the power she wielded. Freedom. Respect. Independence. This woman would never end up wasting away in a pew, rotting inside under a curtain of polite manners and talcum powder.

Maud spent a good part of the ride home in a state of silent awe. Floating just above the dirt, she glided along with a tide of fanciful speculations. Unfortunately, her opinion wasn't shared by everyone in her family.

"A waste of money," her mother said. "Just a waste. If I wanted to see a savage, I'd go west into the wild."

"Come now, Sarah. It was an interesting sight to be sure. Besides, if you went into the wild, they'd probably scalp you," her father said with a smile on his face.

Maud saw a little light in his eyes that rarely showed itself. It meant he enjoyed himself enough to venture a joke. Maud smiled along with him and tested out a laugh. It fell on deaf ears. Her mother didn't seem to think any of it was particularly amusing.

"Scalp me, would they? Think that's funny?"

"No... I just... it was meant to be a joke," her father said.

"Don't tell jokes, David. You're terrible at them."

Her father reached into a crumbled paper bag and piece of candy wrapped in wax paper. "How about a peach taffy? I got them because they're your favorite."

"I haven't eaten those in years. How frivolous. You're just teaching Maud bad habits."

That sweet light disappeared again, and they spent the rest of the ride in silence.

Weeks after Olive Oatman's visit to their sleepy part of the world, people still gossiped about the experience. Children played at being kidnapped by savage Indians. Some drew designs on their bodies in mud.

Maud became popular during that time. Her proclivity for art made her a sought-after commodity in the post-Olive Oatman era. Normally, her mother would beat her senseless for pretending to tattoo people, but the whole of society thought it great fun.

"Come now, Sarah. It's all harmless," said their elderly preacher as he approached Maud's mother. She was chastising Maud while a gaggle of children twirled around on their toes. The preacher moved between them with a grin. "I distinctly remember you when you were a lass drawing little bugs and flowers on every bit of paper you could get your hands on."

Maud gaped up at her mother who was now blushing under the scrutiny of the nearest parishioners. It was an odd sight. For the briefest of moments, her mother looked embarrassed. Her cheeks were rosy with a youthful glow. Maud caught a rare glimpse into who her mother used to be. Perhaps, it was who she'd wanted to be.

It didn't last, of course. When her mother locked eyes on Maud, the hardness returned. She snapped back to the angry individual she was and stormed away from the gathering crowd. Maud briefly thought about running after her, but the group of children pulled at her, begging for attention.

"Please, Maudie. Draw me one too!"

They lined up while Maud mixed clay and water. She drew flowers and birds and faces on their arms with a stick, delighting the masses. The stain the mud left never lasted long, rubbing off within a washing or two, but it was still a good bit of fun. Soon, even children her own age stood in line, vying for her attention. One in particular stood out among the rest.

"I'm next, Maud. Can you draw me a bird?"

When Maud looked up, she spotted the dusty, handsome face of James Clark. He was sixteen and a nice boy. He had been one of the few to go to a circus, making him quite the catch by her friends' standards.

"You want a tattoo?" Maud asked.

"You gave my little brother one. Why not me?" he said with a grin.

"What sort of bird?"

"Whatever one you want," he said.

She smiled back, a little quiver in her stomach. He didn't stop staring at her the entire time she drew on his arm. It made her excited and a little uncomfortable. When he looked at her that sweet way, it was nice. Still, wispy shadows of her uncle danced in the back of her mind.

***

Rumors of another circus circulated around the town the next summer, passing from farm to farm. This time, it wasn't all the way in Wichita. Posters went up on every storefront, school, and church door. *The Great Barlow Show* would be stopping in Emporia for two whole days. Emporia wasn't far away from their sleepy, little Kansas town. Maybe six miles due east, give or take.

Maud's pleaded with her parents to go, but they couldn't possibly leave the farm for something so frivolous. The crops had only been fair the past few years, and her father had taken on an extra plot of acreage. He had even hired on her uncle to come up from Oklahoma to help manage the farm full time. Much to Maud's dismay, that meant Uncle Vern would no longer be a visitor. He would live with them in a room next to hers.

There was nothing more terrifying than the hard steps of a drunk man in the hallway. Those inconstant stumbles that never seemed to find a proper rhythm. More often than not, those footfalls stopped outside her door. The dark shadow of her uncle first appeared as a column of blackness in the hallway. Maud could see his shadow in the space under the door. Then, he would wrestle with the doorknob until forced his way into her room. No pencil, no matter how sharp, could protect her.

When he would come, she'd resist. Squirming under her quilt, pushing him away, she'd threaten to scream. One scream and he'd be sorry.

"Come on, Maudie. You know they won't believe you. Besides, we don't do what a husband and wife do. That's special. That's only if we were married. This is just fooling around."

"I don't want to fool around. Leave me alone."

"I saw you with that boy. That Clark boy. He looks sweet on you, but he won't want you. Not when he finds out. Because you're a whore. You're a whore for fooling around with me."

The night she decided to leave wasn't particularly special. It had been a long, tiring day, but so were so many others. Nothing noteworthy happened as she readied herself for bed. However, when she heard the footsteps outside her room, something seized inside her breast. It was a new kind of agony, born out of terror, and she was afraid it might kill her.

Maud silently leapt out of bed and padded over to her desk in the corner. She retrieved her high-backed chair and brought it straight to the demon's door. As quietly as she could manage, she braced the back of the chair underneath the doorknob.

Her uncle stumbled on the other side of the door. The shuffling reawakened a tremor in her body that wouldn't cease. Suddenly, her breath caught, and she couldn't see parts of her room any longer. Her vision tunneled as blackness closed in around her. A sharp, persistent pain gripped her chest, and she fell to her knees on the floor. Maud had to clasp her hand over her mouth in order to stifle a scream that wouldn't stop. She wondered if she was dying.

"Maudie, open up," he whispered.

Her uncle shoved against the door, but only enough to test it. After a number of fruitless attempts, he gave up. Maud could hear him grunting with frustration on the other side, and a little part of her trembled to think of what recourse might be in store for her later.

Perhaps he would do worse. He might go farther than he dared before, just because she fought back. What if he meant to do with her what married people do? She didn't know what that meant, but the thought of it wracked her body with convulsions all over again.

She collapsed on her bed and held a pillow over her face. She screamed into it for what seemed like an eternity. Maud sobbed, holding herself together by sheer will alone.

Her body was still sore from whatever attack she'd suffered. It had felt like dying, and maybe that's what it was. A small death to warn her against an impending one. Either way, it cemented her decision.

She won a few battles, but there would be no winning this war. No way to end the torture. Maud had no choice but to run. She couldn't fight them all, and if she stayed, she would surely die, one way or another. Before leaving, she took a few coins from her mother's savings jar.

It was in the early hours of the morning that Maud snuck away from her house. There was no sun yet. The light was only strong enough to barely illuminate her path through the wheat. It was a long walk to the Clark family home, but she made it there just as the family was finishing breakfast.

James Clark was sweet enough on her to let her ride along with his family to Emporia to see the sights. No one asked if her parents consented to the trip. They assumed Maud would never do anything without their permission. The Clarks didn't even need to pay her way; she used her mother's savings coins.

Once she saw the lights and banners of the circus tents, Maud lit up like a fire at Christmas. This world was so vibrant and alive, she could barely stand still. She spun in place like a top, not knowing where to look next. Drawing in a huge breath, she could detect a myriad of different types of food she couldn't possibly name. In her world of bread and roots, this was pure decadence.

Color, oh such colors all around her. Never had she seen costumes like the ones the performers wore. They glittered with the sunlight. Every turn provided a new barrage of sparkles, reflecting starlight in every direction. They looked like beautiful gems from some far-off land. Crystals in a crown.

The Clark family led her around, making sure not to lose her. James was especially keen on sticking by her side. He was a kind boy, trying to steal flirty glances. He offered her some of his blue cotton candy. Maud smiled at him, all the while watching for an opportunity to steal away. As a silent atonement for her plan, she tried not to eat too much of his cotton candy no matter how much she liked it.

A niggling part of her felt wicked. Most girls would have been overjoyed by James's attention. She should feel that way, but there was nothing in her heart for him. He was a handsome boy, but the Maud he wanted went to church and bent to the will of men. The Maud he desired cowered at home in her room, waiting for the sun to rise so she might begin her chores. That wasn't her. Not anymore.

They approached a tent with posters along it's fabric walls. Freaks of nature and strange people doing amazing feats of strength were pictured. Everything was painted with a heavy hand and in a rainbow of colors. A man stood out front calling to the passing masses.

"Come one, come all! The show is about to begin. Just a penny to see the most horrific of sights. An abomination of nature. The marriage of land and sea produced the most unholy child the world has ever known. Line up folks and see it for yourselves. The Lobster Boy of Poseidon's Deep!"

"Oh, I've seen this one," said James Clark. "It's amazing, Maudie. You gotta see it. He's just disgusting."

Though a part of her really wanted to go in and see the spectacle with the Clark family, her practical side saw this as an opportunity. "You go on in. I'll be there in a minute," Maud said.

"Why? Where you gotta go?"

"The lady's necessary," she said, pointing to a sign for the toilettes.

"Oh okay," he said. "We'll wait for you inside. I'll save you a seat."

He disappeared into the tent. Maud swallowed down her guilt and took off in the opposite direction of the toilettes to where the Clark's wagon was parked. She retrieved her bag and hurried back into the circus proper.

There was no sign posted about enlisting with *The Great Barlow Show*, but she thought someone must be the gatekeeper. One of the people working the attractions had to know a person she could speak with about employment.

Rounding a corner, she nearly ran into a woman in a sparkly, green costume with a giant snake wrapped around her body. Her raven hair was pulled up and wrapped into a green turban with an emerald pendant dangling down her forehead. Thick, dark eyeliner rimmed her eyes, so the yellow of them pierced into the gaze of anyone who dared look upon her. Much to Maud's surprise, the snake was alive and slithering along the woman's slender arm. It came so close to

Maud, she jumped. It reacted with a flick of its tongue.

"There there, darlin'. Ole Morty here ain't gonna hurt ya," said the snake charmer.

Maud had expected the sultry voice of a Turkish dancer or perhaps something else with an accent from far away. This woman sounded as if she were from Georgia or perhaps Alabama. Her voice was smooth like molasses. Still, she was a sight to behold, and Maud petted her own hair quickly and straightened her frock. She wiped her hand across her face, feeling self-conscious. The woman smiled and watched her.

"Name's Dora, honey. What yours?"

"Maud. Maud Stevens."

"Well, Maud Stevens, don't you be afraid of Morty now. He's much like any other fella out there, I reckon. The tongue gets to flickin' when a pretty girl comes around."

Maud smiled and blushed, despite herself.

"You ever come to a circus before?" asked Dora.

"No, ma'am."

"How do you find it?"

Maud took a moment to think about an answer. This wasn't just any question, even if it sounded like it was. There were times people asked you a question without any want to know the truth. Then, there were moments when someone looked into your eyes and really asked you a thing. They waited with bated breath, truly wanting to hear what you had to say. Those moments, when they happened, had to be answered honestly.

"I think it's the most wonderful place in the whole world."

Dora broke out a smile that seemed too cunning for her age. Maud pegged her in her twenties, but the guile this woman threw about was uncanny.

"You lookin' for work, darlin'?"

Maud's jaw fell involuntarily. "How did you know?"

"Ain't nobody come to the circus with a rucksack that big who don't want some work."

Maud dropped her bag. She nervously started fumbling over her words. "I'm a good worker, and I don't need much. I'm real strong for my size, and I'll do just about anything needs doing. Just please... please take me away from here."

Dora smiled and raised one delicate hand. Morty slithered back to her torso and coiled around her body from her waist to her shoulders.

"Hold on, honey. Whoa now. It just so happens we lost a couple of girls to the *Campbell Brothers Circus* right as season started. I think you're just about their size, and I bet we could find quite a beauty under all that dust. You know anything about the trapeze?"

"Oh no, ma'am." Maud blushed again as Dora laced her one unoccupied arm around her, leading her behind the façade of posters and tents. Maud's arm brushed against the snake's body, making her jump a little. She had expected it to feel slimy, but it was cool and ribbed. Almost like the skin was made of little pebbles all lined up to make a pattern.

"Dora, honey. Call me Dora. And it don't matter really. I didn't know much about snakes until I joined up either. A pretty face gets you in, child. Learnin' a trade happens later. Come now, I'll introduce you to Mr. Barlow himself. You'll see soon. We are all family here."

Behind the scenes, another world unfolded itself for Maud. Clowns caked white makeup on one another, rough men hammered stakes in the ground, and handlers adjusted crowns of feathers on beautiful horses. Everything was color and flash. It smelled like sweat and spices. Maud felt as though she walked into a page from a book. This couldn't be real.

When they turned another corner, Dora motioned a greeting in the direction of a man sitting on a bench. He was scantily clad in little more than a loin cloth. Maud's first inclination was to avert her eyes, except she couldn't. She just couldn't.

He wasn't naked, exactly. The man was so handsome, like he could be famous. No one she had ever met looked like that. His entire body, from his ankles to his head, was covered in tattoos. That alone should have frightened her. Maud should have turned tail back to the Clark family, but she did not move. He smiled at Maud as friendly as could be, and she blushed. She fixated her eyes on a rose tattoo on his calf.

As Dora guided her inside the world of the circus, a thought crawled beneath her skin and buried itself like a tick. There was a deep need to belong here in a world of freedom and color. Maud could not deny the fit.

When she left home, her heart ached from the uncertainty of her decision. She could always turn back and find the Clark family to take her home. It had been reversible, but now? Now was different. She was different. Maud Stevens went behind the curtain and never came out again.

Part Two

1894

Maud's back hit the ground with a jarring thud. Dust and small pieces of hay flew up around her. Walter slammed his cane on the floor of the boxcar with a *knock knock knock*. Every time he did it, the sound reverberated in the open space and made Maud's back vibrate.

"No. No. No! What have I been telling you? Your hips, girl. Your hips. They have to be square above your shoulders!"

When she pulled herself up to her feet, he was pacing. Walter was a small, squat man with the build of someone who was once lean and fit. In his heyday, Maud guessed he had been quite the performer. Now, he was a small, angry man with sagging skin that rippled under his arms when he beat his cane against the floor, which was visible because, despite his declining physique, he still refused to wear shirts with proper sleeves.

"I'm sorry, Walter. I thought they were," Maud said.

"Well, they were for a second… and then… they weren't!" called a voice from behind Maud.

Petty Parks, Walter's wife, lounged on her settee holding a drink. The chair had seen better days. Though the frame appeared to be sturdy, the upholstery was worn and frayed at the corners. Maud guessed it was once a maroon color with a filigree pattern of gold, but now, it looked like blended shades of rust.

Walter and Petty's boxcar was an odd sight. The couple shared a stock car with the trick horses. One half was theirs to call home, and the other was nothing more than bare boards covered in hay. Old tapestries, carpets, trunks, and ancient furniture adorned their living space. All of it was bolted down so it wouldn't move around in transit. Only a series of rough ropes separated them from the pony manure on the other side.

Petty, short for Petunia, stretched out on the old settee as though she were a woman from a painting. Rumor was she had once been a dancer and quite beautiful. Her face was caked nearly white with make-up and the eyeliner she wore ran black around her eyes. What was left of her hair was pulled into a turban on her head. She was shadow of what she once was, much like everything else in their corner of the boxcar.

"You're not helping, Petty," said Walter.

He glared at her. She was drunk again, and he afforded her very little patience when she was like that.

"Oh, Maudie knows I'm just kidding with her," said Petty. She turned to Maud with a wobbly smile. "You're getting better, child. Truly. It's all in your belly. Keep that part tight. That's the key."

"Yes, ma'am."

"Don't you just love it when she calls me ma'am?" Petty said to Walter. "It's so respectful. You should take a page." She rose her glass as though toasting him and threw back what was left. Walter glared at her for a second before turning back to Maud.

"My wife may be irritating, but she's right. It's all in the muscles right here," he said, reaching out with a knobbed finger and touching Maud's abdomen. She recoiled from his hand. Walter never meant her harm, and she knew that in her head. Her guts, however, had other ideas. It was like having your underbelly grazed without warning. Walter pulled away his hand and softened his tone into a gentle rumble.

"That's how you balance. Once you get that strong, you can do just about anything upside down. You can do this, Maudie."

"Don't tell her that, or she'll try to be an attraction at the cooch tent! Come see upside down Maudie!" Petty said. She cackled at her own joke. Walter glared at her again. The anger radiated from him in waves.

"Don't pay attention to a drunk's blather. Listen Maud, you're good on the floor, and you're pretty. I hear you've also been helping with painting banners and the like. That'll get you far for a bit but make no mistake. You have to master the standing up contortions to make any real money. Pretty fades."

"Yes, sir. Thank you for helping me, Walter," Maud said.

"It's all I'm good for anymore," he said with a bit of grey behind his eyes. Maud wondered if they used to sparkle. Back in his day he must have been a sight to behold. Walter shook his head and continued. "Mr. Robins only keeps me around because I train pretty girls like you, so you better practice. You hear me?"

"I hear you, sir."

His face tightened, and he cracked the butt of the cane on the floor once again. Maud flinched a little at the sound, remembering her last tumble to the ground.

"Good. Try this. When you get to rolling again, try doing a handstand and holding it. Not when the train first starts going. That will just knock you around. Wait until the train gets going on a steady pace. It will help you fight for your balance and build up those core muscles."

"And if you fall, Maudie, just tuck and roll," Petty said. "That's what I used to do. If you roll into a somersault and pop up with your hands in the air and a smile on your face, no one will be the wiser that you screwed up. Make it all part of the show. Everyone loves a good show."

When Maud left the boxcar, Petty's head was lolling back against the headrest of her settee. This was the time when Petty usually passed out, and Maud knew not to stick around. Walter would be embarrassed, and his hot temper often traveled with his embarrassment. Still, Maud lingered near enough to watch the two of them. Curiosity was a great motivator.

Walter lifted his wife from the settee with the fluid motion like it was second nature. Even though his legs had seen better days, Walter's upper body was as strong as a man double his size. It was odd to see a man with a cane lift a grown woman with relative ease, but Petty was light. Years of muscle atrophy and hard liquor made the woman look about hundred pounds soaking wet.

You wouldn't know it when she was sitting, but Petty was a good deal taller than her husband. If she had been able to stand, she would have a few inches on him. Walter managed just fine as he positioned her on their bed.

Petty's legs dragged lifelessly underneath her. Everyone said an accident injured her spine, rendering the bottom half of her body lifeless. No one would tell Maud what exactly had happened—only that it ended her career.

Maud looked on as Walter lifted his wife's legs, one by one, onto the bed. Maybe it was her imagination, but when he handled each one, they looked like they were made of gelatin. Flappy pudding around bone and encased in skin.

A small convulsion ran down her backbone. She turned from the spectacle and raced from the scene. That familiar urge to run hit her, fueling her legs to pump faster. As long as her legs moved, she was alive. As long as she moved, she had choices. She would never be Petty, not as long as she kept running. Maud didn't stop until she made it to her own boxcar. The train would be setting out soon, and she had to practice.

"Okay, okay. Let me go," Maud said.

"You sure, honey?" Dora asked.

Maud was upside down in the car she shared with five other girls. Three of them encircled her with their hands placed firmly around her body. The train hit a smooth patch of track, so it was a good time to have a go at this.

"I'm sure. Just stay nearby, okay? I don't want to kick anyone."

On cue, six hands slowly released her to stand alone. Maud went over the checklist in her mind even though the blood rushing to her brain made it harder to think. Keep your belly tight. Shallow breaths. As long as you have balance, you can do anything. To her delight, she was holding just fine as the train coasted through the countryside.

The train hit a bump, probably a branch or something else on the track, and it jostled their car. Maud fell to one side. She kept her belly tight, and Dora caught her before she hit the floor. Another set of hands grabbed her shoulders. The three women and Maud laughed hysterically as they righted her body and helped her to her feet.

"Well, at least I didn't hit my head this time," Maud said. She pressed her palms to her eyes. Her face was hot, flushed with all the blood that pooled there.

"You should have us spot you all the time," said Aponi.

"Then who would ride the ponies?" Gretchen asked. "I sure as hell am not going to. Riding the men is exercise enough!"

Everyone chuckled, even Dora who hadn't laughed at much since she and Maud joined up with the *Robins Brothers Circus* earlier that year. When Maud pressed, Dora couldn't seem to articulate why she felt so uneasy, just that she smelled something off about the outfit.

Maud felt none of Dora's convictions. It seemed no better or worse than the last circus they traveled with. The pay was a bit better, but they had to share the car with more girls. Some of their friends from *The Great Barlow Show* had made the move with them. The *Robins Brothers Circus* was covering a larger swath of territory, and there was an allure to seeing new places. It was always good to get a fresh start. Maud was learning that most circus folk were made of the same stuff. Though they came from different places, different religions, and different races, the circus made family of them all. When you were a citizen of dozens of cities, home was where your family was. Most circus folk called the train home, so family they all became.

That was the way of things. You traveled the countryside from May until November, making sure your last months were in the south where it was still warm. In the winter, everyone hibernated in various places, either with family or in towns with plenty of off-season work.

Dora and Maud had stuck together like glue since they met, preferring to winter in the southwest. They shared apartments, living off savings and wages from odd jobs. When the coldest months were over, they joined with whatever outfit made the best sense at the time. Who could pay the most? Who went to the places they preferred? Where were your closest friends going?

In their little boxcar, the six women hailed from all over. Maud came from Kansas, Dora from Mississippi, Gretchen was born in Missouri, Margot joined up with the circus in Wyoming, and Jan, the Mormon of the group, was from Utah. Only Aponi kept her origins to herself. She was an Indian of a tribe she wouldn't name. Maud often wondered if she kept it secret out of fear she'd be sent back to her people somewhere terrible, like a reservation.

Of the six roommates, three of them were prostitutes working the cooch tent at night. While Dora performed her exotic animal show, and Aponi did her stunt riding for the big top, the ladies of the cooch tent had their own schedule.

They lounged around, sleeping in corners of the circus not reserved for rubes and the masses. It was best to hide themselves from polite society until the sun went down. Once that happened, the powder went on their faces along with the lights of the cooch tent.

It was the only unmarked tent in the circus, but somehow, every interested man knew where it was. Callers shouted the main attractions to the women and children, but they whispered the virtues of the sign-less tent to the bachelors. Like moths to a flame, the men flocked to where the girls were. Breathing the air, which was heavy with booze, the men marveled at strip shows and lined up to pay their money for private audiences.

"Maud, you know, all that looks very hard on the body," said Margot laying on her bed.

Margot had milky skin and slender thighs that showed under her revealing nightgown. Had Maud not seen those legs a million times, she might have blushed. One thing for sure, the Maud Stevens before *The Great Barlow Show* would have turned away and choked on her own embarrassment. Today, however, Margot's bare thigh were nothing more than set dressing in the play of her life.

"It isn't easy," Maud said.

"There's always room in our tent," said Margot.

"Talk about bein' hard on the body," Dora said.

They were all seized with a laughing fit. Maud had a hard time catching her breath from standing upside down for so long, so she bent over and gasped for air. The corners of her mouth were sore when she caught her breath again, and she clutched her belly. Waggish merriment in cramped quarters always seemed a funnier sort than anywhere else.

"Seriously, Maudie, you might wanna think about coming over to this life. Maybe contortion work ain't for you," said Jan. "I would have never thought I would cotton to it, being the way I was raised, but it can actually be a lot of fun. Plus, the smitten ones get you presents.

31

Then, you never have to see them again. One fella in Kansas City bought me a silver-plated hand mirror. No fooling."

"Oh, Jan. Either you're full of it or he is," said Margot.

"Why do you say that?"

"Because silver tarnishes. That mirror you go prancing around with is just as shiny as the day he gave it to you."

"I polish it every day," Jan said as she crossed her arms in a huff.

"Sure, you do."

"Maud honey, we ain't here to say it's glamorous," said Gretchen. "The truth is not everyone is cut out for it. The tent can hollow you out if you aren't of the right mindset. We're just saying it looks like you're libel to hurt yourself doing what you're doing. Just look at poor Petty Parks."

"Petty Parks is ancient," Dora said.

"She ain't *that* ancient. She just looks it," said Jan.

"Come on girls, leave Maud alone," said Aponi. "It takes time to learn a skill like that. I fell off plenty of times before I got good at riding. Don't listen to those three hens. You did real good that time. If the train had not bounced, who knows how long you would have stood on your own."

"Well, these hens need to sleep," said Margot motioning for everyone to make their way to their bunks. "You turkeys need your sleep, too. I'm about to turn off the lamps so get yourselves settled.

The six women moved about the car clucking and making *gobble gobble* noises at one another. A few pretended to scratch at the floor like a chicken after a worm. Jan squawked loudly and jumped from her bed, producing a silver mirror from underneath her like an egg she had just laid.

"That's enough. Lights out!" Margot shouted in a fake angry tone.

Maud crawled up to her bunk above Dora's. It was a familiar motion, so it didn't matter she couldn't see much of anything. When she plopped down on the stiff mattress, the smell of broken hay and warm cotton rose up to meet her.

After Maud settled herself in among the blankets and pillows, Dora whispered up to through the gap in the bunks. "Don't forget to tie yourself in, honey."

"I won't," Maud said.

It was a mistake you only made once. The youngest got a top bunk since the lower bunks were much preferred. A big reason for this was the fact that trains occasionally made powerful stops and starts. One jolt during a deep sleep could send an unfortunate soul crashing out of her bed and down to the floor below.

This had already happened to Maud, giving her the worst kind of headache for two days. After that fiasco, she tied a long scarf around her body and to the bunk's post. It was her safety tether—one she'd never forget again.

"Dora?" Maud whispered. "I'm getting the hang of this, right? I can do this. I can be a contortionist. At least, for a little while. I don't want to work the cooch tent."

The thought of those men staring at her, leering the way her uncle used to, sent chills through her limbs. No, she'd rather die first. Even if Jan and Gretchen and Margot didn't mind it, Maud knew she would. She'd mind it too much, and it would empty her out like Gretchen said.

"Don't you worry, toots. No one's gonna make you do anythin' you don't wanna do. I won't have it. We are all friends here. Now, hush for the night. We got us a big day tomorrow."

"Dora, I'm getting better," Maud said.

"You sure are, sugar."

They drifted to sleep easily as the train floated over the tracks toward Harrisburg. Sweet dreams of spun cotton candy, morning biscuits with coffee, and the whinnying of horses lulled Maud into the deep, dreamless sleep. No muscles rested more completely than ones over-used and taxed from exertion. Even if her tether had come untied, and the train had stopped suddenly, the fall itself wouldn't have been able to wake her.

***

The next day began promisingly enough. The circus opened its doors to a clear sky and a light breeze. An early taste of autumn flavored the wind. Maud chewed on it a little when she inhaled. Mornings like this made her want to add a little extra sugar to her coffee so she might savor it better. She normally drank it black out of necessity, but it didn't seem fitting when the world felt so lovely.

Though she couldn't hold a stage all to herself, Maud still earned her keep by manning a carpeted platform outside the freak tent. Her job was to assist the caller who rounded up onlookers and convinced them to pay their pennies to see the spectacles inside.

Despite her struggle with handstands, Maud drew a good crowd with her sitting routine. She wore a leotard with a blue, watery print. It was so snug the girls back home in their farm dresses would have fainted to see her in it. The trick to bringing in the rubes was a cunning mixture of beauty and manipulation. At their basic level, Maud's poses were not that complex. They only appeared elaborate when she turned her head a crooked way or waved hands that should have been pinned under her weight. Small touches could make her appear otherworldly.

Lunging on the floor while tucking one leg up underneath her was a good start. If she lifted the leg and bent her head back to meet it, she got a few people to stop and watch. Standing up tall and raising one leg behind her like a ballerina was one thing but pulling that leg up over her head was a different kind of draw.

A winning smile and noisy caller didn't hurt either. People were far more likely to be impressed if someone loud told them they ought to be.

"Hey, Rube!" shouted the barker next to her. "Come see the show. Only a penny to view the obscene!"

Maud was folded on the platform and waving to a gaggle of children with both her feet tucked behind her head. Her face faltered when she saw Walter stomping after Mr. Robins. The two men were heading straight for her.

Walter's cane dug into the ground with every step. Little divots followed the footprints in the dirt. Their appearance ushered in an agitated sensation. Even the freak show caller ceased his chanting when they approached.

"You girl," said Mr. Robins pointing at Maud.

"Her name is Maud," said Walter. He crossed his arms over his chest and snorted like an angry mule.

"Yes, my apologies. Maud, my dear, won't you come down from there? I'd like a word."

She looked to the caller, who just shrugged. Whenever she tried to make eye contact with Walter, he merely tapped his toe and stewed. His gaze was fixed to the ground. Something was off, but what choice did she have? Mr. Robins was her boss too. Maud stepped down and crossed the distance to the men. Mr. Robins laid a gentle hand on her back and escorted her away from the freak tent.

"My dear Maud, we are having a little argument here, Walter and me. We are hoping you might settle it for us."

"This ain't no little argument. I am owed payment, and you haven't paid me. That's the end of the argument. There's no reason to loop Maud in on this," said Walter.

"Ah, but I think there is, Mr. Parks. Please, let's step inside the menagerie. The back yard is free of people right now." Mr. Robins led Maud and Walter past the crowds and through a tent flap in the back of the menagerie. The back yard was where the animals were kept. Those fit for humans to see and touch were in the front part of the tent. The gentle creatures who could be trusted spent their days out in the open for the public to view. Mr. Robins escorted Maud and Walter into the room of manure, fresh hay, and carnivores. Two scarred lionesses paced in their respective cages, and a tiger chuffed from his holding cell in the corner.

Maud tried to get Walter's attention, but his avoidance of her gaze seemed purposeful, and it worried her. Only when Mr. Robins stood her in the middle of the room and backed away did Walter finally meet her eyes. He looked solemn and a little embarrassed. For himself or for her, she couldn't tell. Either way, it made her tense all over.

"Thank you for your patience, Maud. Now please. Won't you settle this argument? Perform a handstand," Mr. Robins said.

"What?" Maud asked.

"Can you perform a handstand?"

"Well, sort of. I am getting better at holding it, but Mr. Parks has been helping me with that," she said, feeling as though she were having to defend herself from an enemy she didn't realize she had. "Haven't tried touching my feet to my head yet until I'm good at holding it."

"So, you can do one? A handstand?"

"That's not the goddamned point. I tried to tell you this earlier," said Walter. His face turned redder the longer he spoke. Maud had never seen him so flustered. Even when Walter was angry, he was still solid. This version of Walter seemed shivery and weak.

"I believe it is. Go on, Maud dear. Do a handstand."

She couldn't tell what Mr. Robins was trying to prove or what Walter wanted her to do. Every time she searched for Walter's eyes, he wouldn't give them to her. Was this some kind of test? Surely Mr. Robins wouldn't kick her out of the circus for failing at a handstand, she thought. Regardless, if Walter was going to bat for her, she had to prove herself. Maud decided to give it a go and hope for the best.

She posed with her hands up in the air with her arms straight and strong. Lifting one foot in front of her, Maud leaned forward and placed her hands on the ground. With one foot to the ground, she propelled both legs over her head. Normally, this was where she fell. She would kick too hard and the momentum would send her flying over herself, but Maud tensed her gut and kept herself upright. Shallow breaths, she reminded herself.

No one said anything. She wasn't totally sure what this was proving or disproving, and most importantly, she didn't know how long she had to hold this pose. The room was silent except for the grunting of the lionesses nearby. Maud could hear them breathing hard and bumping into the bars.

"That's good enough, Maud dear. You may come down," said Mr. Robins.

When she bent her knees to bring her legs down, her balance gave way, and she began to fall backwards. Petty's words shot into her brain, and she used the fall to tuck and roll into a somersault. She sprang up as though it were part of the performance. Maud's arms shot up triumphantly, and she flashed a winning smile.

"Very nice," said Mr. Robins with a smile of his own. "That was a lovely demonstration."

She looked over to Walter, hoping for the same encouragement. His fury was gone, but it wasn't replaced with the relief she expected. He appeared weary and defeated.

"There you go, Mr. Parks. This is why your services are no longer required," said Mr. Robins.

"Who do you think trained her to do that? Me, that's who. You owe me money, Robins."

"And you will be paid your contract rate to date, but nothing more."

"That's not what my contract says. It says I'm employed until end of show. Maud can do a handstand, but who's gonna teach her the rest? Who's gonna show her how to walk that way? How's she going to know to bend her legs around that don't look natural? People don't come to look at a pretty girl doing a handstand. They want a real show. You hired me to teach her and the other girls that," said Walter.

"And you've done a great job. The other girls you speak of have mastered their various acts, and our Maud here has almost done the same. From what you tell me, she's a resourceful young lady, and I'm sure she can figure out the rest without your tutelage."

"She ain't ready. Put her out there now, and she's likely to get hurt," Walter said.

"My mind is made up," Mr. Robins countered.

As her head bounced from one man to the other, a clearer picture began to form: This wasn't an argument as to whether Maud could stay with the circus; they were arguing about whether or not Walter could stay. She had done her best to present a solid handstand for the big boss man to save her neck. Now, it looked like she might have hurt Walter in the process. That knowledge made her stomach quiver.

"End of show, that's what you promised me," said Walter, sticking his finger in Mr. Robins's face.

"I did promise that. You are correct. What I didn't promise was accommodations for your wife. She contributes nothing to the show whatsoever and consumes my resources. I've tolerated it since you were helping with the girls, but now your services are no longer required."

"She doesn't take up any resources. We share the same car as I would if I were alone, and she eats less than a bird."

"True but she drinks more than two roustabouts. The decision is made, sir. Good day." Mr. Robins turned on his heel and walked away. Walter seethed. Maud hadn't thought his face could get any redder, but she was wrong; his ears looked as though they might ignite.

"Oh Walter," she said with trembling fingers over her mouth. "I'm so sorry. I didn't know that's what you were arguing about. I should've fallen. Had I known I would have let myself hit the ground."

Walter shot a hand to stop her as she tried to move closer to him. His body shook but not like he was going to hit her. His fury wasn't for her, but he was too volatile to touch.

"Not your fault, Maudie. Just go back to working the freak tent. I'm going to get that bastard. I'm gonna tell everyone I can find what he's done. I'm gonna put up a big, damn fight. And if he thinks he can get rid of me and Petty, he's got another thing coming."

Walter stormed off into the oddly pleasant day.

***

Scranton was by no means a major metropolitan area, but it did boast a reasonable turnout for the first performance. Maud spent her day as she always did—doing her minor contortions in front of the side act tents. Her youthful body and sparkly costumes brought the young and old alike, and the money man seemed pleased at the hourly take.

When it was time for lunch, she wandered around the fairground, looking for Walter. The train had made several stops along the way to Scranton to water the animals. Each time, Maud made her way to Walter and Petty's boxcar to see him. Each time, he wasn't there. She made her way back there again, hoping this time would be different.

"You can stop trying, child. He ain't comin' back for me," Petty said as Maud entered the car. Her words were slurred and barely understandable.

"Of course, he will," Maud said.

Petty rolled her eyes. It was such a dramatic move that her head followed suit and fell onto her pillow. It took a hard few seconds before Petty pried her eyelids back open as though they were glued together with molasses.

"He's been gone off and on since his little meeting with Mr. Robins. Something about a strike."

"What's a strike?" Maud asked but got no reply.

She moved closer to the half-unconscious woman. A deep smell of booze and cigarettes wafted up from her. It was enough to overpower the persistent smell of pony manure from the livestock side of the car. The way Petty slurred and her lack of focus seemed like more than just drunkenness. Had she been taking Laudanum?

Maud thought she smelled the tang of urine as well but didn't know what that meant. Petty was unable to walk, so someone had to take care of her necessities. That had to be Walter. How long had he been gone? She couldn't just leave Petty resting in her own filth, could she?

"Petty, do you need to... use the... uh..." Maud stuttered. She had no frame of reference here. How did one do this when they legs were useless. "Do you need to relieve yourself?"

One lolling eye opened, took Maud in, and shut again. "Already have, dear."

Maud bit her lip and scratched her arm nervously. She shifted her weight from foot to foot, not knowing what to do. Petty's breathing became heavy, and the slightest snore arose from her mouth. Maud couldn't just leave her that way, lying in her own mess, but she didn't know what to do. Who knew when Walter would be back?

Maud looked around the boxcar for something to help her. She spotted a large trunk bolted to the floor. When she opened it, she found nightgowns, day dresses, and a thick stack of cotton towels. The towels would do. They would have to.

She raced over to the boxcar door and shut it with a loud thump. Maud threw the bolt that latched the door. The car would get stuffy, but they would have privacy. Luckily, the ponies were out working the circus, providing rides to the kiddies. They were alone. She could give the affair as much dignity as she was able.

None of the ruckus woke poor Petty, who continued to snore on the settee. Maud stood in front of Petty and bit her lip again, harder this time. She tasted coppery blood before she stopped. This wouldn't be easy. Maud had never changed someone before, not even a baby.

She pulled the feather-light sheet from Petty's lap and bunched her thin dress above her thighs. Sure enough, there were several towels folded over the old woman's nethers soaked with yellow urine. The acrid scent of it amplified as Maud peeled the towels away from Petty. Maud flinched when faced with the lack of undergarments. Unlike her young, boxcar roommates, Petty's body lacked humanly color. Her paralysis left very little room for muscle or elasticity. Everything was lifeless, sagging into itself, and Maud struggled to hold Petty's legs in place while she reached for the clean towels.

Luckily, Petty's dress had not been soiled, so Maud didn't have to remove it. She deftly pressed the clean cotton in between the old woman's legs and folded the end up around her pubic bone. When the deed was done, Maud replaced Petty's legs on the settee and put her dress and sheet back in place.

Maud breathed a sigh of relief. The deed was done.

A loud knock on the boxcar door startled her. It was sudden and reverberated angrily throughout the car. "Who's in there? Let me in, now!"

Maud gathered the soiled towels from the floor, careful not to touch the urine with her bare hands. She quickly opened the door to find Walter on the other side. His surly demeanor only deflated by a few degrees when he recognized the intruder to be her.

"What in blue blazes are you doing in here?" Walter said with a snort.

His eyes cast downward to the towels in her hands and then over to Petty asleep on her settee. Maud shivered as she watched him put together the scene before him. A mixture of embarrassment, fear, and anger warred in his eyes.

"She… she was… I came looking for you, and she was… dirty."

In a smooth, quick movement, Walter snatched the soiled towels from her grasp. Unlike Maud, he didn't seem to care about touching the mess. Maud jolted and cast her eyes downward. For some reason, this felt like she'd been caught doing something wrong. Shame colored her cheeks a deep crimson.

"You need to get," Walter said sharply. "Collect your girlfriends and leave this outfit. I aim to finish getting my strike together. Best if you high-tail it before it begins."

"But Walter, what's a strike?" Maud asked.

"You can't be *that* naïve," Walter said. When Maud returned his stare with innocent curiosity, he blew out an exacerbated sigh. "Go ask your girl, Dora. She ought'a know. Now, get!"

He pulled himself with much effort into the boxcar, and slammed the door shut between them. Maud was left standing outside without a clue as to what to do. She decided to take Walter's advice and go find Dora. Whatever a strike was, it didn't sound good. Dora was always good at explaining these things to her.

Maud headed for the cookhouse. Surely, Dora would be there. It was late into the midday mealtime, and Dora and the girls always ate later than most. Before Maud could enter the cookhouse tent, three bodies intercepted her. Two of them she recognized. They were aerialists from the night show—a man and wife team—part of *The Great Bernini's Flying Family*. The other was Mr. Robins himself.

"This is the one I was talking about. She's been training with Walter," Mr. Robins said while stopping Maud with one hand.

"Oh Lord, what is she wearing?" the wife asked with a look of disgust on her face.

Maud was so surprised by the sudden interruption she gawked like she was missing the reasoning part of her mind. Try as she might, she couldn't get her voice to make the proper words. Slowly, Maud's senses returned, and she took in her appearance.

Her sparkly leotard still clung tightly to her body. In her haste to find Walter, Maud neglected to change. She did, however, pull on a pair of small men's trousers over her waist and pulled it taut with a bit of cord. It definitely made for an unusual costume. Compared to bloomers and a dress, the trousers were so comfortable she'd forgotten to change. Maud bit her still-sore lip and folded her arms over her chest. She suddenly wished she could shrink to the size of a toad.

"How she's dressed now doesn't matter," Mr. Robins said placing a warm hand on Maud's shoulder. He turned to the woman aerialist. "What matters is she's young, springy, and can fit into your sister's costume."

"I don't know, Bob. What can she do?" the husband asked.

"She can twist in lots of ways. She can stand on her head. Such coordination this girl has. I'm sure you can use her with the trapeze."

"What? I can't do…" Maud began, her mouth finally catching up to the conversation only to be interrupted.

"Of course, you can, my dear. You worked under the great Walter Parks! See John and Linette, I told you. I can't do anything about your sister and brother-in-law running off, but I can deliver you a replacement for now." Mr. Robins spoke with a smooth, silky tone. Even Maud half-believed him when he was done.

Linette Bernini appraised Maud with a hard glare that made her squirm in place. The aerialist was on the gentler side of forty, and a youthful-looking woman at that, but her scrutiny was one that Maud knew well enough. Maud was only seventeen, and her body showed off her youth. Smooth skin, rosy cheeks, taut belly. These were the trappings the older circus women envied. They glared at Maud when they thought she wasn't looking, longing for the old days when they were so beautiful and lithe. Maud wondered if she too would feel that way when she got older.

"I suppose we can use her," Linette said after her inspection.

"Good!" Mr. Robins exclaimed. "She's all yours. I'll have a cook bring some biscuits to your tent so you can get to work."

"But I don't want to. I can't do trapeze," Maud muttered, but no one was listening.

She tried to look past the trio into the cookhouse. Maud longed to lock eyes with one of her friends, especially Dora. Dora could get her out of this mess. Alas, she couldn't find their faces, and the boss man turned her around and handed her off to John and Linette. They hurried Maud away before she could protest any further.

***

The costume Linette stuffed Maud into was ill-fitting and extremely itchy. The woman who normally wore it was taller and lankier than Maud, and the costume showed just that. Dora would have been a better match. The leggings ran long enough to encapsulate Maud's feet, and the bodice pinched at her hips. It didn't help that Linette was frustrated and cursing the whole time.

"Damn it! This won't work," Linette said after trying to fasten the lowest point of the bodice. No matter how hard she tried, and no matter how much Maud sucked in her breath, they just couldn't secure that bottom loop. "And those leggings! You look like a child trying on your mother's costumes!"

Maud sucked in a rush of air at that. A deep pit yawned open in her gut and made her quiver all over. Her mother. She hadn't seen her mother in a year.

Linette must have seen the change because for the first time all afternoon, she softened toward Maud. Her words came out gentler,

"I'm sorry for yelling. It's not your fault. Your mother is probably working somewhere here, and I'm keeping you from her."

"No, she's not," Maud said quietly.

"Oh? But you're so young," Linette said.

"Let's cut it."

"What?" Linette said, taken aback by Maud's sudden rudeness. "I mean, I didn't intend to upset you, Maud. I have been a bit sharp, I know."

"No. Cut it. Cut the leggings at my ankle," Maud said marking a line with her finger. She wanted to get the focus off her mother as quickly as possible. "You can cut the fabric here and pin some fringe to the bottom. Or you can fold it under and hide the seam on my leg with tassels."

"Oh. Yes, that could work. I can put a skirt around your waist to cover the bottom of the bodice," Linette said with a nod. "Look, I'm sorry you got roped into this. Our partners ran off to join in with that stupid strike. Mr. Robins offered us double our daily take if we'd perform tonight."

"The strike? It's tonight? What is it?" Maud asked.

"It's silly. Thing will never get off the ground. Most don't. I heard Walter Parks got some of the clowns worked up about contracts and back pay. Those clowns are a rough lot. Don't let the makeup fool you."

"But what are they going to do?"

"They are planning to strike at tonight's performance. It means the dancers won't dance, the animal trainers won't let their beasts perform, and the money men won't give refunds. Mr. Robins will have a madhouse of angry rubes wanting their money back, and they won't get it until the boss man agrees to their demands. Basically, they're trying to force Mr. Robins to pay more money."

"That's horrible! We shouldn't be there. It sounds dangerous," Maud said as a cold sweat covered her body.

"Take it from me, girl. Nothing is gonna happen. I've seen a dozen of these strikes, and not a one has done what they claimed. Not one. Mostly, you get a few inconvenienced rubes. What are they gonna do? Go to another circus in their town? The whole thing is harmless. You'll see, nothing but smoke. It's good for us to perform. Mr. Robbins appreciates our loyalty and pays us extra."

Maud nodded and held still while Linette finished pinning her leggings and fastening a sapphire-colored skirt around her waist. To hear Linette talk about a strike, it sounded like little more than a few workers holding an organized tantrum. But Maud remembered Walter's face when he told her stay away. It felt serious to him.

"Don't squirm, child. I don't want to stab you," Linette said around the pins in her mouth.

"Sorry."

"If I do this well enough, nobody will be the wiser. Well, as long as they don't look at you too close."

"What exactly am I going to be doing?"

"Nothing big," Linette said while putting another pin in the cuff of the leggings. Between the aqua costume, the blue skirt, and the teal tassels, Maud was feeling like some sort of water fairy. An itchy water fairy. "Just stand on the platform with us and smile. Act surprised when we do flips."

"I have to be all the way at the top?" Maud asked, feeling her skin break out in a cold sweat. The trapeze platform was easily thirty feet off the ground. "Oh Linette, I don't think I can do this."

"Don't get clammy, child. If you start sweating in this thing, it will be hell to get you out of it," Linette scolded. She fluffed some fringe out and away from leggings and stood to inspect her work. "Not bad. This will do."

"But I can't swing on a trapeze. I haven't practiced."

"Shush. You aren't going to swing. We will. John and me alone don't command a lot of oooh and ahhh. We need a third to round us out. Not much of a "family" if it's just us. Just make big faces and react to how great we are. Stand up there and smile. Wave. You can do that. Even a monkey could do that. What do you say?"

"I… I don't know."

"Mr. Robins will double your pay," Linette said with a smile.

Maud gazed into the nearest mirror and took in her reflection. Linette was right. If you didn't inspect the costume too closely, she did look the part. Double her pay could go a long way in the winter months. Maud nodded her head resolutely.

"Alight. Show me what to do."

***

The evening show time came with dusk, and what was left of *The Great Bernini Flying Family* waited anxiously behind the curtain for their signal. Maud never worked the evening shows. The daytime was meant for the freaks and the dancers. Smaller, intimate wonders that drew in the individuals and gave them special memories to take home. Evening shows at the big top were different. The clowns, the animal acts, the aerialists, and the larger-than-life performances took up all the air in the tent. A grand finale of wonders after a day of curiosities.

She didn't know what to expect for her big top debut, but there was no doubt something was wrong. The acts moved too fast. The music was only half as loud as normal. A general listlessness took over all the performers waiting in the wings. Even John and Linette were twitchy.

"They skipped the pony parade's song," Linette whispered to John and Maud. "I didn't hear the overture for the clowns either."

"Did the clowns even show up?" John asked. He wore the same worried face his wife did. "I haven't seen them in the back yard since breakfast."

The words bubbled up in Maud's trembling lips before she meant for them to. "Is it the strike?"

Linette and John gaped at her, but neither disputed her question. The truth was they were worried too. That much Maud could read on their faces. The tense set of their lips and the quivery darting of their eyes. Maud searched for other performers in the back yard, keen on reading their faces. It was grossly apparent that at least half of them were missing. Perhaps more.

"Maybe we shouldn't go on, John," Linette said. "Maybe this is bigger than we thought."

The music for the trick riders ended as the horses raced through the tent's curtain and into the back yard. Maud's gut dropped when she saw only one trick rider commanding several horses when there was supposed to be three. That one rider one was Aponi. She dismounted from her horse and ran to Maud with eyes wild with worry.

"It is not good, Maudie. Do not go out there," she said grabbing Maud's hands. "The strike has taken most everyone out of the show. The rubes are agitated because the show is only part of what was promised. Men are surrounding the exits, keeping people from leaving. Things are bad. You need to go."

Maud turned to grab John and Linette. Together, they could all escape through the back-yard exit. Suddenly, Mr. Robins moved in front of her. His body was all she could see. The stench of cigar smoke and his salty sweat filled her nose.

"You can't go, my girl. None of you can," Mr. Robins said darkly. He moved his gaze around, taking in all the performers in the area. "You want to keep your jobs? You want to keep this audience from turning into a mob? You will go out there, and you will entertain them! You will give them a show to enjoy or else."

"But sir, it's dangerous. If we just give them a refund or let them exit through here…" started Linette, but she was cut off by the booming voice of Mr. Robins.

"Go out there and entertain these sheep so they don't panic and trample this goddamn tent to the ground!"

Just then, the band began to play the introduction music for *The Great Bernini Flying Family*. John and Linette jumped in their skin but quickly made their way to their entrance point. Maud was frozen in place, still trembling. Mr. Robins locked onto her wrist and dragged her after the two Bernini's.

"Maudie!" Aponi said as she ran after her.

"It's okay. I'm okay," Maud said over her shoulder as the boss man shuffled her along. "Get Dora. She'll know what to do."

With a blink and push, Maud was standing in the spotlight next her two fabricated, flying family members. When one lives as an entertainer for any amount of time, certain things become muscle memory. Never lock your knees when you land. Never show an ounce of pain to the rubes. Always *always* smile when the light hits your face.

Maud stood in the spotlight as terrified as she'd ever been, but she smiled like the performer she was. That face became her mask. It was a filter by which she could process the world around her. One glance out into the audience told her a complete story.

Only about half of the rubes were in their seats. Most of the others were congregating around the three exits to the big top. At each exit stood several of the outfit's biggest roustabouts. They stood unmoving, like statues, while men argued and raged in their faces. Children clung to their mothers in the chairs. Of the people still seated, only a few looked at *The Great Bernini Flying Family*.

The agitation in the crowd was palpable, and it was getting worse. The air was thick and electric. She hated to admit Mr. Robins was right, but he was. If they couldn't calm the crowd, things could get violent. To make matters worse, the clowns appeared at the doors.

With their makeup only halfway applied, they looked more like ghouls than anything else.

"We want our money back!"

"This is a sham circus!"

"Take all your complaints to Mr. Robins. If he'd paid us like promised, we wouldn't be here in this mess," shouted one of the clowns.

"Let us out!"

"Not until he pays us what's due!" yelled a roustabout.

The band played a flourish, and The Great Bernini Flying Family posed again, but no one was watching. A din of angry shouting and pushing swelled louder and louder around the exits. It infected those in the tent like a virus spreading its disease of discontent with invisible fingers.

"This is not worth any amount of money," Linette said. The fairer Bernini lowered her theatrical arms and ran to the entrance of the back yard. Without a word, John raced after her, leaving Maud alone in front of the aerialist stage.

Maud peered behind her to see the two ladders that led to the top platform. Her stomach rolled just thinking about climbing it alone. However, she did spot an aerial hoop on the floor leaning against one of the ladders. Though it was limp, it was still tethered with wires to the trapeze apparatus.

Everything in her rational mind told her to run away. She could easily cut back through the back yard and out to freedom the way Linette and John had. But she couldn't stop looking at the children. Little tykes, thinking they were going to see a wonder, were now trapped in a terrifying place. Most huddled with their mothers near the front of the stage to avoid the fighting at the back exits.

Though her smile was still pasted firmly on her face with the high gloss of a mask, inside Maud's heart was trembling. She locked eyes with a young mother holding a baby who couldn't be yet a year old.

The mother was Maud's age; perhaps a little older. Seeing that helpless fear reflected back at her, Maud made a decision.

She spun around like a dancer and nodded to the band to take up their instruments again. Though they were bewildered, the rag tag musicians obliged. They played a few invigorating beats and got the attention of the crowd. Even the most hot-headed in the back turned.

Maud danced over to the aerial hoop and took it in hand. The metal was cold under her clammy hand, but it felt heavy and certain in its weight. She took comfort in that as she locked eyes with one of the men behind the curtain of the stage. Maud made the universal sign for "up" with her thumb, and the young man sprung into action. He moved with the speed of someone grateful to have a task.

When the hoop shot up, it was jarring, but Maud managed to position her rump, so its ascension looked planned and theatrical. Inside, she felt as though she might vomit at any moment. Yet that winning mask never faltered. It couldn't. She was finally calming the crowd down.

Maud knew full well she would be no good with the trapeze bars. All that swinging back in forth; she'd have to train for weeks to get the hang of it without killing herself. Not to mention, it was only interesting with another person, and *The Great Bernini Flying Family* had left her all alone. She had watched the aerialists using the hoops with interest in the past. There was no swinging. It was more like contortions in the air, and she could do that. At least, she hoped she could.

Once she reached the show height of the stage, Maud sat stunned for a hard second. Someone had gathered their wits enough to man the spotlight, and it was pointed directly at her, blinding her to the audience below. The yelling had turned into shuffles and murmurs. Everything stalled while the band did a drumroll for her first trick.

With a dramatic switch of movement, Maud straddled the hoop

and shot her legs away from each other. She bent them at the knees to give the look a dramatic effect. She grabbed the upper part of the hoop with both hands and held on for dear life as the tossed her head back. The building drumroll popped on cue and went silent for the onlookers to feast their eyes. Though she was blinded by the spotlight, she could hear some clapping.

The drumroll built again, as Maud prepared for another contortion pose. This time, she brought her legs together. She pointed her left foot to the ground and the other bent hard at the knee to wrap around the hoop. Backbends were easy, but backbends in the air were a new one on her. Maud forced her body to bend backwards by walking her hands down the hoop, so her head pressed near to her foot. At the drumroll pop, Maud turned to face the invisible audience and smiled. More applause than before.

She continued this way through several more poses. Each one, she got bolder and bolder. Maud tested hanging one leg out and leaning into to a bend that made her whole torso jut forward. Once, she laid on her back with the hoop supporting her spine. Maud curled into a half moon inside, balancing her feet against the top of the hoop and throwing her hands out.

The applause came easier now. There was no more angry fighting and shuffling of terrified feet. Maud had, at least for the moment, distracted the mob away from violence. She felt the confidence swell as she attempted the most dangerous pose she could imagine pulling off.

Maud spun around inside the hoop and held onto the part near her rump. Slowly, she eased hoop's position under lower back. Her legs shot out into open air before she let them fall down. She made a gentle arc with her body, so the hoop supported her weight under her lower back. Her hands clung fast to the bottom part of the hoop to keep her still.

There was hush around the tent. Everyone, even the band members, were quiet and watching her every move. Maud might have felt honored if she wasn't so terrified. How did she get here? How was it possible a dusty farm girl from Kansas could balance on an aerialist hoop in front of an adoring crowd?

"It's not who you used to be," Maud whispered under her breath. "It's who you *can* be."

Maud's hands creaked under the strain of her grip. Sweat beaded between her knees and along her neckline. Somehow, she found the core strength she needed to slowly raise her legs to the top point of the hoop. She pressed legs together tightly, pointing her toes straight to the moon. She hadn't noticed the building crescendo of the drumroll until that moment.

It was imperative that she kept her back arched. Without that bend, there would be nothing supporting her for this next part. Maud took a deep breath and released her hands from the hoop. She slowly unfurled her torso, head, and shoulder downward. When the drumroll finally popped, Maud flicked her arms out dramatically and smiled. For a singular, dizzying moment, Maud floated above the world. The audience roared to life, applauding her.

It wasn't until Maud looked down that the realization hit. She was upside down. All the blood was rushing to her head, and she didn't know how on earth she was going to get out of this. Luckily, the band had read her pose as a final trick and ceased their dramatic music. They started playing a fun, bouncy tune with which to end the show.

Maud reached up and gripped the bottom of the hoop once more. There was a calming reassurance in that. The thing was she didn't know how to right herself gracefully. Holding her legs on high for that long had taxed her muscles. Everything quivered from overexertion. After running several scenarios through her head, she quickly decided on a plan.

While holding onto the hoop, Maud would bend her knees and run her legs through the hoop. Once there, she'd tuck and roll the legs through, hanging onto the hoop with her arms. From there, she could pose as they lowered her to the floor she missed so much.

At first, her plan worked perfectly. Maud managed to tuck her knees and roll her legs through the hoop. The problem was her stomach muscles were exhausted and couldn't control the pace of the weight redistribution. For all her practice in the train car, her body couldn't account for this. Her knees dropped through the hoop and toward to ground dragging the bulk of her weight with it.

Maud panicked but tried with everything she had to grip the hoop and catch herself. The deathblow to her performance came in the form of sweaty palms. No matter how hard she tried, she couldn't hold on, and Maud Stevens tumbled to the floor.

The fall felt slow and fast at the same time. Time decelerated while she reached to the sky, trying to grab the support of the hoop again. It was almost as if someone wanted her to see every aspect of her failure before she plunged to her death. Or maybe it was her mind trying to process her loss and taking its sweet time getting there.

As soon as her fingers were beyond saving, the world sped up to a too fast to comprehend. One second, she was reaching to the sky, and the next, the world whooshed by her with the gasp of the audience. The hoop above her went from a symbol of stability to something so small and far away, it could just as easily be ring on a lady's finger.

The impact was not as expected. There was, in fact, a safety net, but it wasn't pulled as taught as it should. While coarse rope cushioned the bulk of her fall, Maud felt her head smack against the packed earthen floor. It left her dizzy. The jarring hit made her brain shimmy inside her skull. When she opened her eyes, everything was too bright. The smell of packed hay and crushed peanuts felt overpowering, and the exclamations of the crowd made her wish for temporary deafness.

Two strong men lifted her from the net and sat her up. She recognized them as roustabouts by their odor of grease and tobacco before she ever saw their faces.

"Ah jeez, are you okay, miss?" said the one to her left.

"Why didn't you pull the net tighter?" hissed the one on the right.

"I was watchin' the crowd. Making sure they wasn't gonna rush us."

"You're an idiot. She fixed the crowd. You saw it."

"Shut up, the both of you!" The voice was all too familiar, and Maud opened her eyes to take in Dora. She was dressed in her plain, calico dress instead of her costume. Her appearance must have thrown off the men holding Maud because she had to reassert herself. "Do I look like a rube to you. Shall I get my snake to remind you who I am?"

"No, no, Miss Dora," they muttered together.

"Hey toots, you okay? Let me see your eyes," Dora said moving in closer. She cradled Maud's chin in her palms and took in her face. Maud tried to stay focused, but her eyes kept wanting to blur and close.

"I'm okay," Maud got out in a raspy voice.

"The hell you are," Dora said while feeling Maud's forehead. "What ev'a possessed you to do somethin' like that, Maud Stevens? You could've ended up with somethin' much worse than a smack on the head."

"I had... I had to," Maud stuttered. Words were becoming harder and harder to form.

"Is she here? Is she okay?" Another voice came from behind Dora. Maud saw Walter limp into her view, though it was hard to track him. She focused on the sound of his cane pounding against the ground. All she wanted to do was fall asleep. "Oh, Maudie. Are you alright? Maudie? I told you to stay away. The strike..."

"The strike that you started," Dora interrupted. There was more than a little bite in her words. "You are the reason for this mess. You are the reason our Maudie did somethin' so foolhardy. All because Mr. Robins ain't fair. You could've gotten these people hurt or killed."

If Maud could process laughter, she might have just then. Dora was only a handful of years older than Maud, yet she spoke to a man of Walter's advancing age as though he were a child. Walter, in kind, bowed his head and acted appropriately scolded.

"I know. This is my doing. It wasn't my intention though. I never wanted to get anyone hurt. Mr. Robins owes so many of us back pay, things got out of hand," Walter said.

"I knew I had a bad feelin' about this outfit. I just knew it," Dora said before looking over her shoulder. A harried older man with a doctor's bag was heading straight for them. Beyond him, Maud snagged a glance at the audience filing out of the big top, calmly and unimpeded. "Here, toots, look alive. A doctor is here for you."

Maud barely focused on the doctor as he checked her forehead and ears. He raised her head toward a light and pried her eyelids open. Somewhere in the shuffle, the roustabouts had handed her over to Dora and Walter. When the doctor was through with his examination, she slumped back into the net in between the them. Dora's smell of light perfume and talcum powder was preferable to grease.

"I believe she has a concussion. We need to get her to the hospital. We need her family to come with us. Where are her parents?"

"Mama? Daddy?" Maud said deliriously. The names didn't make sense in this place. They weren't here, were they? She couldn't think straight.

There was a long pause, as though no one had the correct words. Dora knew everything about Maud, including her parents. Walter didn't know, but surely, he'd seen enough runaways like Maud to piece together the story. It wasn't an original tale by any means.

"Listen, I need to know where her family is to notify them. She's too young to be out on her own. Where are her parents?" the doctor asked.

Suddenly, the real notion of her mother and father finding her here hit Maud. How might this look? What would they say? What manner of beating would be her punishment for running away like this?

The thought of the kindly doctor sending a telegraph to her sleepy town, informing her parents of what their Maud was up to, sent a cold shiver down her bones. She had escaped, thinking there was no going back, but they could collect her if she was half-addled in a hospital. Maud grabbed Dora's hand and squeezed it, shaking her head ever so slightly so only Dora might notice it.

Dora turned and flashed her winning smile at the doctor. "I'm her sister," she said.

The doctor looked her over skeptically. Other than their fairer complexion, Maud and Dora didn't resemble each other at all. She was all sinew and height, while Maud was shorter with a round rump. Even their accents were drastically different.

"What? We had different mothers. Don't judge our father's roaming eye," Dora said with a bucketful of southern charm in her voice.

"I'll ask again. Where are her parents?"

"I'm her father," Walter said suddenly. All eyes moved to him. He seemed unsure in his footing, but he leaned on his cane for support and stood taller against the doctor's questioning eye. "She's my little girl. Both... both of them is my girls. Maudie's mama passed, so it's just me. Let's get her to that hospital."

***

Something celestial begged Maud to pry her eyes open. A new day was just barely waking. The first aurora of sunlight filtered into the boxcar in indigo and green. Morning dew made the air smell freshly wet. A brand-new day with the circus. But wait, that wasn't right. The feeling of the room was not at all correct for her boxcar. Not nearly.

Maud awoke fully and sat upright in a bed. The movement was too fast, and she slumped back into a fluffed pillow with the pain of it. A few glances around told her she was in a small, hospital room. It felt unnaturally cool inside and very alien. Tope paper on the walls and thin sheets printed with blue and yellow dots. Everything washed out compared to her colorful world. The room made her feel exposed like someone peaking underneath her mask.

A low rumble came from a pile of clothes near her. It was a constant sound, making the pile of linens rise and fall. Maud thought briefly she was watching a very small, concentrated tide. The thought was ludicrous, and picturing it made her head hurt even more. Finally, her addled mind realized the sound was a man snoring. Why were her thoughts so sluggish?

"Walter?" Maud asked.

The pile ceased snoring, and a very disheveled Walter arose from the laundry. His hair was a mess, and his eyes were red rimmed with sleep. At first, Maud wondered if he had been drinking, but she didn't smell liquor on his breath, and when he looked at her, his eyes were sharply focused.

"Maudie, you're okay. Thank goodness," Walter said with genuine affection. He stood and took her hand. Maud warmed under his kindness. It was a rare sight after all.

"Oh, she's up!" Dora said, opening the door and bringing in some coffee in little white cups. She joined Walter at Maud's bedside. "Hey, toots. How are you feeling?"

"Like I fell from a trapeze," Maud said with a giggle. It hurt to laugh, and she rubbed her head to steady her vision. If she moved too fast, the world wobbled.

"Good to hear," Dora said. "Just so ya know, there's some folks calling you a saint for stoppin' that mob. Nobody got hurt thanks to you. Well… except you, that is. They are callin' you *Marvelous Maud*. If that don't beat all. My little Maudie."

Suddenly, Maud tensed all over and tried to sit up straight. Everything was so groggy, like moving through tar, but thinking about the circus brought her to attention.

"The train! Did it leave us?" Maud asked. Panic rolled down up and down her spine.

"Hey, toots. Let's calm now. Here, let go of that railin' and hold my hand instead. There you go," Dora crooned. "Doctor says you have a concussion. No sudden movements."

"But the train…"

"The train ain't going nowhere, Maudie," Walter said next to her. The next words died on her lips as she looked to him for an answer. "The circus is done. Mr. Robins mucked it up bigger than we thought. He had debts all over. All the hubbub about the strike and the girl who saved the show brought out the creditors from the woodwork. It's done."

"But, what does that mean?" Maud asked turning from Walter to Dora. "I can't go home, Dora. I just can't go back. You… you know what they'll do to me!"

Tears came unbidden and hot. It wasn't the gentle build up she was used to. That was something one could plan. Once the pressure made itself known, Maud could reach for a handkerchief or excuse herself to cry in peace. This came in a burst. It was a wracking, terrified explosion of fear and crying so violent it sent shock of pain through her brain.

"No one is going to take you, Maudie," Walter said, seemingly unphased by Maud's outburst. He reached one knobby, rough hand out and took hers. With a little squeeze he said, "I won't let you go back, and neither will Dora. This is all my fault, Maudie, and I'll be damned if I let you pay for it."

59

"But what about money? We are stranded," Maud said.

"Not for long, toots. *Ringling Brothers* is in Philadelphia. That's a big outfit, and they ain't lookin' to get smaller. Word is they've got a train headin' this way. *Welsh Brothers Circus* and P.T. Barnum too, I hear. Several outfits heading to collect on Mr. Robins stupid ways. Gonna buy up every bit of this circus they can. Give us all jobs."

Maud sighed with deep relief. It wasn't the end. She wouldn't have to return to Kansas. Just those notions alone helped to ease the pain rolling itself over in her brain. She turned to Walter. "Ain't that grand, Walter. You and Petty can come with us. No more nailing furniture down in a pony car."

Walter's face turned dark suddenly, and he turned his gaze downward to his shoes. Something inside Maud dropped like she was falling all over again.

"Nothing happened to Petty, did it?"

"No no. It's just... they ain't gonna take us, Maudie. I'm a washed-up old trainer, and Petty can't even hold her water no more."

That last comment hurt Maud in her gut. It made her insides turn, and she clenched her knees together as though she might wet herself at any moment. Dora saw her unease and patted Maud's shoulder.

"No need to worry, toots. There's no way they ain't gonna take you! You are all anyone can talk about. '*Marvelous Maud*, the savior of the circus'. We just gotta work on your dismount, sugar," Dora said with a teasing glee.

Maud couldn't take her eyes off of Walter. "But Walter..."

"No need to worry. You go be famous while you can," Walter said, and the deep sorrow in his words broke Maud down to her core.

"No! No, you're coming with me," Maud said. Dora and Walter jumped at her sudden determination. "I hear Ringling's a family circus, yes?"

"Yes," Walter said with a question in his voice.

Maud turned back to Dora, "And you're sure they will want *Marvelous Maud?*"

"My guess is we can get all sorts of offers after this," Dora said with a smile. She gave a little wink as though she knew where her faux sister was going with this.

"Then, I'll insist Ringling takes my family with me," Maud said with a decisive nod. "It's unseemly to have an underage girl performing without her father."

"Maudie, I don't understand," Walter said.

Maud leaned in closer to Walter even though the movement made the space behind her eyes hurt. She squeezed his hand hard and placed a light kiss on his stubbled cheek.

"I'm not going anywhere, not to another circus, without you, Daddy."

Part Three

1904

The World's Fair was in the city of St. Louis, Missouri. The fancy folks called it the Louisiana Purchase Exposition, but regular people knew it as the biggest circus ever. All of Maud's friends were there performing in the booths and trafficking among the throngs of people. Almost eleven years had passed since she first left the farm in Kansas, and not one second had been spent with regret.

Circus folk were a close bunch, as prone to gossip as any other, and everyone knew the World's Fair was the prime spot to scout out the next outfit to tour with during the upcoming summer. Not to mention, one could make a small fortune with all the people it drew.

Maud had procured a space next to Dora. Now that Maud was twenty-seven, they were roughly the same size and could exchange costumes with one another to appear fresh each day. People got tired of looking at the same snake woman in green, so perhaps the next day, she'd be the bird lady in red.

Though Dora thought the world of her new parrots, Maud hated them. She and Dora shared a wagon in the campground, and the damn birds trilled with every rustle in the night. She had half a mind to feed the terrible things to Maxine, Dora's latest boa constrictor. However, working The World's Fair was far easier with someone to watch your back, so Maud tolerated the squawking birds. Besides, the world wouldn't feel right without her Dora.

While Dora the Charmer undulated on a carpet a few feet away, Maud perched herself on a stage made of a wood plank placed over some milk crates. A bit of an old, purple curtain draped over the structure giving it the mask of professionalism. She wore a pink, silk ensemble with little sparkles that ran in darts to accentuate her waist and harem pants. The costume was slinky and fit as close to second skin as possible. Maud had long ago ceased caring about the trappings of modesty.

Laying on her stomach, Maud lifted her right leg and left hand, twirling it at the wrist for a dramatic flair. She caught her leg just above her head in a quick motion that halted the nearby looky-loos. Then, she did the same maneuver with the left leg. That got the attention of a few more.

Gently, Maud rocked back and forth like a rocking chair on her underside. One little boy in the crowd giggled. She could feel the crowd turn toward her, all waiting for the next trick. She stiffened on the upswing and let go of her feet. She rocked forward into a handstand, extending her legs high above her head.

More people gathered around. Their combined breath filled the air with the thrumming cadence of the living.

The tentative steps of a small person approached her stage. Maud popped her head up and scared a boy with a quarter in his hand. He held the coin precariously above the ornate metal basin in front of her. She had painted it with gold paint to give it an exotic quality. If this were her longer show, she'd astound the people with a tall tale of visiting the orient and dazzling emperors with her contortions. The bowl was a gift from the Emperor of something or another.

She didn't have time for the long version today, so this had to be less talk and more show. When she caught the child's eyes, she only goaded him a tad bit.

"Not just yet, dear boy," she said.

The boy stared wide-eyed at her, not knowing what to do. His cherubic cheeks flushed pink in little apple spots.

"Wait until after my big finale. You won't want to miss it!"

Slowly, like two snakes falling from a branch, Maud lowered her legs so that her feet touched the top of her head. The boy's eyes grew even wider, and she smiled at him. People hushed as she drew their attention to her interaction with the boy.

There was nothing better than this. Picking out one lucky kid and playing with him. It humanized her somehow, and the kid would have a memory for the rest of his life. For years, he'd talk of the day the contortionist picked him out of the crowd—the day he was special.

As her toes touched her head, she stuck out her tongue and pulled a silly face. The boy laughed, and the sound reverberated throughout the crowd. It was hard to judge how many people were watching her with the echo in the hall.

"You reckon this is as far as I can go?"

The boy nodded his small head of blond hair. Maud suddenly looked shocked and a little hurt. She pouted her lower lip. "You really think so? No farther?"

With a tilt of her torso, she lowered her legs farther. The boy's eyes flashed with shock as her feet went past her head and locked under her armpits. Gasps and murmurs resonated all around. She had them now.

"Pay attention, kiddo. Here comes my big finale."

In one swift motion, Maud pulled up her legs and catapulted herself into a standing position. Her arms raised high above her head, and a huge smile flashed across her face. The whole view went dark as the blood rushed back to the appropriate places. She smiled all the same, eyes wide and bright. Maud knew the world would come back in a few seconds.

A clear image appeared in front of her as the blackness of her vision fizzled away. It was like a dark fog lifting, allowing her to see land through the mist. With a good view of the crowd, she reckoned she had roped around seventy-five people. A good pull. She made sure to immediately spot the little fella in front still holding his coin. He seemed frozen in time. Maud lowered her arms and nodded to him.

"Now you can drop your coin, son," she said with a wink.

He did, and everyone laughed. A grateful couple hurried him away, but thankfully, his wasn't the last coin in her tip basin. While a lot of the back crowd dispersed, a good bit of the fore crowd lined up to add to his quarter.

Maud smiled at everyone, thanking each one for their generosity. A few younger men made eyes at her, but none dared to take it to an actual conversation. Flirting with the strange was one thing, but the reality of talking to it was for someone made of stronger stuff.

When the crowd finally left her makeshift stage, the only one left watching was an amused Dora. She leaned against the nearby wall. Maxine was coiled in her crate, and Dora was smoking a cigarette. Maud jumped down from her stage and pressed one hand against her back. Before Dora could say anything, Maud grabbed the cigarette from her mouth. After a long drag, Maud used the wall to twist her body and pop her spine in three places. She groaned with relief, and Dora winced at her.

"You decided to take a break?" asked Maud.

Dora snatched the cigarette back, leaving Maud to let out her smoke in a giggle.

"I know better than to work while you are doin' one of your stunts. You should've paid that kid for all the rubes he helped you draw in."

Maud grabbed the cigarette again. Dora elbowed her playfully in the ribs.

"No. He got a memory out of it. Worth the money if you ask me."

"Just wait until he's old enough," Dora said. "That memory'll serve him in a totally different way."

Maud slapped her friend on the arm, and the two laughed. Maud turned her neck this way and that, eliciting more cracking sounds. Dora cringed and handed her the cigarette back.

"Please tell me why you keep doin' this act again? I told you I'd share my animals with you."

"I don't much care for birds. I just like painting them." Maud took another long pull and let all the smoke float gently up her face, stalling in and around her hair.

"What about snakes?" asked Dora.

"Maxine's just fine, but she's a terrible model."

They laughed a little, passing the cigarette. Several groups of families walked by, eyeing the women from a distance. Had Maud and Dora been properly dressed, they might have been in for some hard scowls. Single women having a smoke in public? It was a scandal in proper society, but as single circus women, no one much cared. Their glittery costumes were shields to everyone.

"I don't recall you ever craklin' and poppin' this much after the trapeze. You ever think about trying that again? You're gonna wear your body out."

"Maybe, but I don't want to go back to the trapeze."

"Why not?"

"Because… at least this way, I don't rely on anyone to catch me. I get to catch myself."

"Fair enough, toots."

Maud grabbed the cigarette from Dora and held it loosely in between her lips. She dug around in a bag behind their stages for a moment before producing an envelope. On it, Maud's perfect handwriting scrawled a familiar address. She handed the letter to Dora who took it with a scowl.

"Do you mind?" asked Maud after taking a long drag.

"Not again, toots. Really?" Dora stole back what was left of the cigarette.

"Come on. Your fella gets the stamps free. Please? You did the other ones for me."

"I did. I did. But honey, I'm tellin' you. They ain't never gonna write back. Some folks are just incapable of changin'. From what you've told me about your folks, they ain't worth writing to anyway. I only tell you this because you're my friend, and I love you."

"I know. I know you do. But I still love them, so I gotta try."

Dora pulled Maud in for a close hug. Maud leaned into it longer than usual. Holding the letters in her hand always made her feel a tad raw inside. When Dora stepped away, a wide grin pulled itself across her face. She locked eyes on something in the distance and her eyes lit up. Maud whipped around to see what was so wonderful.

There, leaning on a worn cane, stood Walter. He was all alone. A spectator in the crowd who somehow knew that if he waited long enough, and he would be noticed. Most people would have interrupted the women, but not Walter Parks. He merely waited for them catch on.

Age had softened the once grizzled man. Well, age and perhaps the acceptance of the kindness of others. After the strike, he had been humbled, devoting all his power to caring for Petty, Maud and Dora. Maud hadn't heard the hard *knock knock knock* of his cane in some time, but her respect for him stayed intact.

Walter still wore the shirts without sleeves. His upper body had lost much of his muscle tone, leaving loose skin to drape around his armpits and along the seam of his elbow. But his face appeared more youthful somehow since Maud had last seen him. He'd grown his soft grey hair longer, slicking the front just enough to tuck it behind his ears. Though he still leaned heavily on his cane, it didn't appear to pain him the way it used to.

With a gentle smile, Walter steadied his stance. He opened his arms out wide for an embrace. The gesture was for both women, but his eyes were mainly for Maud.

"Forget the letters, toots. Your *real* daddy just arrived," Dora said with her silky drawl.

***

Dora wasn't calling it quits for the night, but Maud sure was. There was a dull throbbing in her lower back and a catch in her shoulder that needed some rest. The fairgrounds were the perfect place to walk it out, and after she changed into some normal clothes, she set off to explore the offerings.

Walter awaited her return patiently. He even rolled up her carpet for her and stowed it off the side. Maud found him sitting on her stage, quietly watching Dora perform. The faintest smile betrayed his pride as though he were watching a prized pupil. When Walter noticed her return, he pulled himself up with effort, relying heavily on his cane.

"Shall we," Walter said with a smile. He offered his arm to Maud, and she looped her hand around his crooked elbow.

The fair was a tremendous place.

When she and Dora arrived, they were still setting up things, so the scope of the fair wasn't clear. The first week or two brought with it the hustle and bustle of assigning places, figuring percentages, and all the other nonsense that bureaucracy loves so much. Now, as the afternoon sun slapped her face, Maud found herself in this city of carnival for the first time. The building where she performed, which was a massive exhibit hall, was filled with individual circus performers. To them, it was an enormous place, but it was nothing compared to the rest of the fair.

All the fair's splendor sprawled out before her practically teeming with people. Every manner of food filled the air with delicious aromas as the raucous crowd laughed and bantered. She could hear children squeal and men calling out their wares. Women giggled and yelled after their rowdy brood. The whole place hummed with life and merriment.

Not even the air was off limits. Gargantuan dirigibles floated just above the dome of the main building, tethered to some unseen handlers below. Banners and flags snapped in the wind. And the Ferris wheel, oh the Ferris wheel. That great feat of machinery turned and sparkled against the sunlight, allowing each passenger to sit among the heavens.

"Mama and Daddy. If you could only see me now," Maud said to herself. The memory of them hit her gut harder than she expected, and she had to shake her head to rid herself of it.

"What was that, Maudie?" Walter asked.

"Oh nothing. It's just such a marvel."

Maud didn't want to think about the number of letters she'd sent to her parents. It had to be thirty at least, and not one was answered. But she didn't want to think about that now. Today was a day of wonders, and the past was unchangeable.

They decided to start with Art Hill, a rise in the grounds where *The Palace of Fine Art* stood. Maud had always been quite fond of painting her flowers and birds, but she longed to do more once the shackles had been released. Maud went so far as to help the circus drawing posters. She would create portraits of other performers with salacious words all around them.

While the works on display in the palace were lovely, Maud and Walter bored quickly. She ended up following a caller into what he dubbed "a recreation of the Roman Baths of Caracalla."

She didn't know a thing about Roman Baths, but if they were half as beautiful as this, she reckoned living in Roman times wouldn't have been a bad thing. Grandiose rooms opened around her with ornate columns. There were statues of nude women and cherubic children. Nothing scandalous about them. Just beautiful. Maud drank them in and tried to commit them to memory.

Maud sauntered up to one statue of a young woman holding a long, feathered quill. Walter got sidetracked—talking to a someone out of Maud's hearing. The statue was positioned against a corner of the entrance, billowy sculpted fabric covering the tender parts. At first glance, there was nothing overly remarkable about her, yet Maud was drawn to her more than most. Perhaps her round face and curvy physique, so much like her own now. Over the years, she had blossomed into a strong, womanly form.

One perfect arm peaked through the folds of the statue's dress, allowing a delicate hand to rest on her thigh. That arm. Maud was fixated on it.

The world around her tunneled and morphed into something else. She was in Kansas again, standing next to the switch tree with a knife. One stab and the pain could leak out of her. The statue's arm became her arm. Flesh and stone. Though she had no knife on her person, she did have a cigarette. A sudden urge overwhelmed her to strike out.

"Nothing should be so pretty," Maud said aloud without thinking.

She reached out and pressed the butt of her cigarette on the statue's perfect arm. It didn't hit her until she pulled back and saw the smudged ash she left on the white statue. A scar on something that couldn't be scarred.

"Maudie, what are you doing?" Walter said, suddenly at her side. He quickly brushed the ash away with his hand.

"Oh, God. I don't know!" Maud said. She recoiled in horror at what she'd done. Walter took her by the hand, and they hurried away from the gallery of pretty things.

Everywhere there were wonders, and she decided to lose herself in them. One area held *An Exhibition of Savages*. Indians stood among the callers in their various primitive garb. The Apache people she recognized, but there were other people from Guam, Puerto Rico, Alaska and The Philippines. One tribe called the Igorette sat on baby elephants with fancy head dresses. A small dark man dubbed "The Congolese Pygmy" stood on a milk crate smiling a toothy grin for all to see.

Maud couldn't help but frown. She searched the faces of the Indians, looking for some semblance of unhappiness at their current plight. Most were stoic and gave nothing away. The pygmy just smiled at everyone, and she wondered if he knew he was a novelty. Was this all a game to him? Perhaps he thought this was a beautiful parade of people while not knowing he was the show? Was he just happy to have some money and food?

Sure, Maud made her living as a spectacle in the circus, but she chose it. She knew why people threw her coins and decided it was a life for her. However, some of the people she had seen in circus and fairs were not there by choice. They were desperate or just didn't know any better than what was offered.

Maud left *An Exhibition of Savages* with a foul taste in her mouth. She and Walter said nothing to one another. Judging by his countenance, he wasn't a fan either.

The *Creation Exhibit* helped to wash it away—that, and a new fizzy soda called Dr. Pepper, which she picked up from a vendor on the way. Walter and Maud laughed when the bubbles kissed their noses. It was sweet and overpowering.

"For a snake oil tonic, I'd say it's pretty good," Walter said after licking his lips.

"I don't think it's snake oil. They didn't say it cured anything. Just that it's fun to drink."

"Well, I don't care what it cures or doesn't cure. I'm gonna get me another one when we head back."

The entrance to the *Creation Exhibit* featured a lavish arc held aloft by an angel that had wings spread so far across that any patron had to walk under them to enter. It was so massive you could stand twenty people upright on each shoulder and still not touch the angel's arm. Maud was enthralled and felt compelled to take a close look at one of the stone feathers in its wing.

How could they have made this? In the short amount of time it took to plan and erect the fair, who could've possibly carved such a thing out of stone?

When her hand brushed the feather, the feeling wasn't cold and smooth as stone might be. It was warmer and rough. Maud looked closer and saw it was solid but fibrous in nature. She couldn't help but giggle.

"It's staff," she said giddily.

"Well, I'll be," Walter said, feeling it for himself. He thumped a fat finger against it.

A mixture of Plaster of Paris and hemp fibers, staff was used by circus folks all the time to make quick sculptures. It was a fast and versatile. They often painted the sculptures gold or silver and pawned them off to rubes as treasures from antiquity.

Maud did it all the time to suit whatever extravagant story she was trying to sell. While this one was a tremendously well-done arc, it was still just as fake as her little makeshift, milk crate stage back in the hall. All superficial for the show.

The Ferris wheel had been on her list to see, but Walter was tired. They chose a bench seat with a view of the wheel and sipped their second helping of Dr. Pepper.

"I'm so happy to see you here. We haven't heard from you since..."

Maud caught herself before she said Petty's name. It felt a bit too raw to discuss in a place with so much life.

"It's alright you can say it. After Petty passed," Walter finished it for her. He took a deep breath in, and when he let it out, he reached for Maud's hand. It was still just as rough and warm as she remembered. Walter kept his eyes on the Ferris Wheel.

"Dora and I wanted to come to the funeral, but we didn't get your letter in time," she said.

"Wasn't your fault. I didn't tell anyone about the service. Just a few people who were nearby."

"Where did you go after? We couldn't find you. No one in the circuits could say where you went," Maud said, trying to keep the hurt from her voice.

Walter had, in fact, disappeared from their little world. If nothing else, the gossip mills were good for finding people. Circus folk were more connected than the telegraph lines, but Walter had fallen through the cracks. No one had heard from him. No one knew where he was. Maud had worried he went the way of his wife, and no one knew to tell her.

"I retired... properly. I actually live here now. I know a few fellas who helped set me up with a room in a boarding house that caters to a lot of wintering circus folk. I make a little money on the side teaching kids to dance and tumble."

"Ha! I bet none of them fell as much as I did," Maud said with a guffaw.

"You... might have them beat," he said.

Maud squeezed his hand, trying to catch his gaze, but Walter stayed focused on the wheel. The slightest of moisture pooling in his eyes. "How did you know I'd be here?"

"Oh well... that's easy," he said. Finally, he turned his head and looked deeply into her eyes. "You're *Marvelous Maud*. Where else would you be?"

A small tear ran down his cheek, and Maud wiped it away. She didn't know what to do with this version of Walter. So tender and raw. She scooted closer on the bench, laying her head on his shoulder. He wrapped his arm around her, and she chastised herself for not being there when Petty died. She'd regret it forever.

They didn't say anything for a long while. Maud was eternally grateful he didn't ask her about the incident with the statue. It was embarrassing, and she wouldn't know how to explain it. She returned the favor by not questioning why he didn't reach out after Petty died. Best to enjoy what they had in that moment.

Despite the roar of noise around their bench, a comfortable silence embraced the two of them. In their own little world, they sat watching the Ferris Wheel and observing the people running by. It wasn't until the afternoon sun cast long shadows across the ground that Maud pulled away.

"I'm going to head back. Do you wanna come?" she asked.

Walter shook his head. "No. I think I'm gonna sit her a while. It's just too pretty. I'll see you later." Maud started to protest, but he rose a hand to silence her. "Don't worry. I'll be fine. Just want to take it all in while I still can."

"But Walter?"

"I'm old, Maudie. Losing Petty showed me how old. I don't know how long I have, but what I can do is sit here and watch this here sunset. You gave me a great afternoon. Go now and see to Dora. I'll find you girls later."

***

Maud entered her exhibit hall on a cloud of fatigue in the dimming twilight. She passed a few performers she recognized. A fellow contortionist and a strong man she had travelled with smiled as she waved. Gail, the bearded lady, called after her about going out that night, but she politely declined. Her feet were so swollen from the walk.

Overall, the exhibit hall was emptying of patrons, and her friends were packing up for the day. Surely there would be parties that evening in the campgrounds, but Maud wasn't sure she'd have the energy to be social. The dull ache in her back had turned in to a swollen throbbing in her feet. All she wished to do was sit and relax.

She rounded a corner, and she saw someone she hadn't noticed before. He was handsome, if you didn't mind a big nose, and he had a prettily waxed mustache. His dark hair curled just a tad on the edges in an attractive way. He sat in one of two chairs behind a table covered with papers of tattoo images. Though he wore a fine shirt and vest, the sleeves were rolled up above his elbows, showing a picture gallery of tattoos along his arms.

Maud was intrigued, and by the time she realized she was staring, his gaze had become fixed on her as well. Had she been younger, she might have blushed.

"The pictures are much prettier when viewed up close," the man called.

With just a crook of a smile, Maud approached his table.

"August Wagner," said the man while offering his hand. "Everyone calls me Gus."

"Maud Stevens," she replied, shaking it.

"*Marvelous Maud.*"

"You... saw my act?"

"Yes, ma'am. Well, to be fair, I saw your poster first. Very well drawn I must say." When he spoke, his voice had the cadence of a circus man. All charm and bluster. Gus's voice was mellifluous, like honey on the ears. It was never a good idea to trust any words that came out someone who sounded so sweet. But in his eyes, she saw something else. Sincerity maybe? "You do that poster yourself, Maud Stevens?"

"I did."

"It's impressive."

Maud was afraid she might blush after all and changed the subject. "My poster's not half as impressive as your tattoos here."

Gus Wagner sat back against his chair and smiled. His eyes lit a little, obviously understanding her conversational maneuver. It was a dance, this flirtation, made all the more interesting given that they came from the same world. Charming a rube was one thing, but one of their own? That was another matter.

"Well, madam, I have been trained by the best. Alfred South himself. I met him in my sea going years. Hell of a man, that Alfred. He even tattooed the great Queen Victoria of England."

"Is that so?" Maud crossed her arms over her chest with a skeptical smile that matched her eyebrow.

"Ah, you've been working the circuit too long, madam. Can't you tell the truth from exaggeration?"

"Normally, but I'm not so sure with you," she said.

"I assure you it's true. It was all the rage among English high society to get a tattoo somewhere discreet and then reveal your daring nature at parties." Gus mimicked a shocked face.

"If that's so, what tattoo did Queen Victoria get?"

"A Bengal tiger fighting a python."

Maud couldn't hold it in. A loud laugh burst from within her so violently she almost spit on the handsome Gus Wagner. His eyes lit up further as he chuckled along. For the life of her, Maud truly couldn't tell if this was a lie or not, but she didn't really care. The fellow was entertaining, if nothing else.

"How much would you charge for a tattoo?" she asked.

"For you or the Queen of England?"

"Well, I don't know the queen personally, so for me," she said. "Not a thing."

Maud's look turned sour, and she raised a skeptical brow. "I don't deal in that sort of trade if that's what you're getting at," she said.

Gus looked appropriately surprised. "No. I didn't mean that."

"Then what did you mean?"

"I was hoping you might go on a date with me," he said.

He sounded rather sincere, but Maud was wary. When her gaze turned into a scowl again, he added to his statement.

"Nothing attached. I would just like to take you out on a date. Food, conversation, and the like. Nothing more."

She softened a little and looked at the papers in front of her with all the lovely drawings. It would take her years of training to ever be able to draw pictures half that pretty.

"You want to trade a date with me for a tattoo?" Maud asked.

"Yes, please."

"Wouldn't I be costing you real customers?"

Gus grinned, his previous charm returning. He reached under the desk and plopped a wooden lock box on the table. When he opened it, it was just enough for her to peek inside. The lockbox was nearly full of coins. A small fortune's worth.

"Already tattooed two hundred and sixty-three people at this fair alone. I expect to hit fifteen hundred by the time it's all said and done. Besides, I am about to pack up for the day. You'd be my last one."

She thought about this proposal. It had been a long time since she'd had a proper date, and Gus was a handsome fellow. Her finger traced a line along the papers before her, allowing wisps of fantasies to dance in her mind. An old longing stirred in her gut, reminding her it was there.

"I tell you what. I will give you a date, if you give me a tattoo and a lesson."

"A lesson? You want to learn to tattoo?" Gus asked.

"You said you saw my poster, and I had talent, didn't you? Was that just a flirt?" she asked.

"No. No, not at all."

"Then I would make a great apprentice. Don't you think?"

"Well... yes."

"Then that's the deal. A tattoo—and a lesson—for a date," Maud said resolutely.

His smile widened, hidden only slightly beneath his mustache. Gus crossed his arms and chewed on his lip. Maud wondered if his brain was puzzling out how to answer without losing the flirtation. At last, he stood and gestured grandly to the empty chair next to him. "Madam Apprentice, it would be my honor."

She uncrossed her arms and relaxed her shoulders a tad. Her feet groaned in protest as she walked around the table, but soon she found the chair, and sweet relief returned to her soul.

***

Gus and Maud walked side by side through the fair grounds. Even though the exhibition halls were closed, the grounds were lit and still buzzing with people. The May evening breeze was serene, and the night hummed with lovers' mutterings.

Her arm was a little sore, but she was proud of her new work of art. The only regret was that Gus refused to let her show it off immediately. He insisted on bandaging it to keep it clean. Underneath her wrapping was an eagle atop an American flag. Her full name was stenciled above it.

"You know, most people get the names of their sweethearts on their arm," Gus said with a gentle smirk.

"I don't have a sweetheart," she replied.

"Never had one?"

"Well, aren't you nosey?"

"My apologies, Madam Apprentice. I meant to ask if you had a sweetheart at the present time."

"If I did, I wouldn't have agreed to your proposal. That would be dishonest," she said in a flat tone.

"Fair enough."

They walked along and talked amicably. Gus had a quick wit and a kind nature. He seemed amused by Maud's wry banter, a staple of any conversation when traveling with circus folk. Her distaste for girlish laughter typically intimidated normal men, but Gus appeared to find it charming. Every skeptical crook of her eyebrow elicited nothing but an admiring smile from the gentle man.

He was true to his word. Not once did he allude to any sordid obligations. They merely strolled as young couples might among the crowd. He was so jovial it was infectious—even to the passersby. Young men and women nodded to him in a friendly manner. Those who recognized *Marvelous Maud* smiled politely, but many shied away from the man covered in pictures.

"Does it bother you?" Maud asked. "The way people look at you, I mean."

"Don't they look at all of us that way?"

"Yes, but I can hide it. I can put on a decent dress and act like a proper woman, and no one is the wiser. But you, you can't hide this. It's forever visible."

"I don't mind. To me, it weeds out the people I don't want to know. When everyone stays at a distance, you know the ones who move in closer are your friends."

The tinkling of bells caught their attention. When they turned, they saw a woman dressed in veils and bangles. She balanced a thatched basket of roses on her head. Gus purchased a red one and presented it to Maud with a theatrical bow.

Her first reaction was to turn it down because of how ridiculously corny it was. However, the sweet smile he offered with the flower melted her from the inside out. She accepted the rose and tucked it into the loose knot in her hair. They held hands and disappeared among the throngs of happy couples.

A grinning Texan ran a stand that introduced a new food he called a hamburger. It was served with French-style fried potatoes. He boasted it as 'the best damn food you ever tasted.' While Maud wasn't the biggest fan of ham, Gus insisted they give it a try.

"When will you ever again get to taste such a thing?" he asked.

Much to her surprise, the meat wasn't ham at all. It was a delicious patty of beef. The buttery bread that held it was just heaven in her mouth. The fried potatoes were warm, leaving grease and salt on her fingers. She loved it, and Gus insisted on ordering another helping. The two practically rolled themselves onward they were so stuffed.

After a while, they found another anomaly. A vendor selling ice cream held in an edible, waffle-style cone. Again, Gus insisted they give the treat a try. When Maud complained she was already too full, Gus presented her with some facts about his seemingly unusual anatomy.

"Well, you just aren't using all your stomachs."

"All my stomachs? What are you on about now?" she asked incredulously.

"I have four stomachs. One's for regular food, one's for drinks, one's for whiskey, and one's for sweets. I haven't filled up my sweets stomach today, so we have to eat the ice cream. It's practically growling."

"I think you might have a fifth stomach that's full of shit."

Gus barked with laughter. "Now now. No need to be jealous of my many stomachs. You may only have two or three, but that's nothing to be ashamed of. We are all equal in the eyes of the Lord." Somehow, among all the flirting and banter, Gus convinced his date to order an ice cream in a new waffle cone.

It wasn't until they reached the Ferris wheel that her heart began to race. The *thrum thrum thrum* of her pulse beat in her brain. She had been wanting to try it since she first saw the wheel glistening in the sun that afternoon, but the reality of it began to frighten her. After all, it was horribly tall. Much higher than any platform or trapeze she had ever climbed. The mechanics of it creaked and rocked in the evening breeze. Somewhere in the air, she smelled oil with just a tinge of rust. Inside her gut, there was the familiar twinge of falling out of control. She swallowed it down where it threatened to bubble up again.

"Come on, Maud. You aren't going to back out on me now, are you? I've been wanting to take a ride all week. I'll just look foolish doing it alone. Everyone will think I'm pathetic."

That face, that warm inviting face, was hard to resist. Gus reached out his hand, she took it, and they stepped into the little carriage together. As it turned, letting on more and more people, Maud and Gus took in the nighttime sky. Once they reached the very top, it felt like they were so high, they could reach out and touch the stars. Whatever fear that threatened her mind earlier, seemed to bid a hasty retreat as they floated among the heavens. They breathed in the air of angels. The whole thing was wonderful.

"If you don't mind me asking, how long have you been in this line of work?" he asked her after a good bit of silence floating in the night's sky.

"Well, Mr. Wagner. That is a very gentlemanly way of inquiring about my age."

He laughed. It was a nice sound, like the gentle cadence of a purring cat. "No offense intended."

"None taken." Maud felt a touch of heat in her cheeks. She wasn't an old maid by any standards, but neither was she a teenager. Being with this man made her feel young, and the feeling was embarrassing on so many levels.

"Well then?" he asked.

Maud took a deep breath to cool her face. "I left home when I was about sixteen, and I've been doing this ever since."

"Contortionist at birth? Must have been hell on your mother," he said with a chuckle.

"Not hardly. Learned mostly on the road. I started with contortions. Then, I was an aerialist for a time. When my body got fuller, I went back contortions. It's less taxing."

"What you do now is less taxing on your body?" he asked with a confused look in his eyes that bordered on cute.

Maud twisted in her seat, using the railing to stretch her upper body this way and that. The act elicited a barrage of pops and cracks from her spine. Gus startled.

"Well, it is in a way. Sometimes, it's just terrible on my back, but I like working alone. Independence and all that. It's nice not relying on how sturdy the ropes are. Ropes can break, partners hands get slippery. Nets drop you. This way, if I fall, it's my own damn fault."

"I see."

"What about you?" Maud asked.

"Me? Well, being a sailor was a job, but once I got into tattooing, I realized the difference between a job and a passion. This way I still get to travel but without the hard labor of a sailor. Drawing pictures on pretty girls is far better, I would say. I love what I do. Besides, I was just awful at tying knots. The fellas picked at me about it relentlessly."

They laughed together. Maud lifted part of the bandage and looked down at her new tattoo. It was such a pretty drawing. Her skin was red and raw around the ink and just beginning to feel sore.

"It didn't hurt as much as I thought it would," she said.

"That's the hook of it. Everyone thinks it hurts terribly until they do it. The first one gets you, and before you know it, you're asking for another and another."

"I see you fell prey to your own hook," she said, gesturing to his arm.

"Yes. It becomes an addiction I suppose, but what a pretty addiction. May I ask why you never got one before? You've been touring the circuits. Surely there were artists along the way who would be happy to make you their canvas."

"I admit, you are not the first tattooed man I've met."

Maud smiled cautiously. She wasn't even sure why she said that. Her flirting had gotten away with her.

"The plot thickens. Yet, I am the one you asked for a tattoo. Why is that?" he asked.

"I never came across a tattooist like you. There are all kinds of stories. People working in grubby areas, giving folks diseases. And that one lady down in Texas who started removing them with acid. Besides, I figured if I could draw better than them with no training at all, then they weren't fit to draw on me."

"But I am?" he asked drawing nearer to her.

"Your tattoos are so pretty," she said leaning in.

"I was thinking the same thing, but not about my tattoos."

***

Every day they worked their exhibition hall, and every day Gus left a red rose somewhere around her stage. It became a game of sorts. Finding where he'd left the flower quickly turned into her favorite part of the day. Maud hadn't given into girly impulses in years, yet she woke every morning excited to search for her daily token of his affection. She found herself falling into a juvenile type of limerence that she couldn't fight.

Sometimes the rose was in an obvious place. Tucked in the basin she used for tips or laying out in the open on her carpeted stage. Other times, she really had to go looking for it. Once, it was so well hidden, Maud was certain he forgot. After all, how could one man keep this up every morning?

It was Dora who found that flower and signaled Maud as to its whereabouts. When she followed Dora's gaze to Maxine's crate, she discovered a perfect red rose sticking out from the coils of the snake's body. It was as if the writhing creature had been instructed to create the perfect vase for her flower.

Dora rolled her eyes as Maud beamed. Giddiness hadn't been in her repertoire in a good long while, but she was truly beginning to feel its affects.

The dates continued and so did the lessons, but one was no longer payment for another. They became mutually satisfying things. Maud had always been a guarded woman when dealing with men. In her opinion, they were a lot of bother, but with Gus? Well, it was different.

Every lesson Gus taught her was done with the utmost tenderness. When she made a mistake, he would smile and tell her a story about a time he made the very same mistake on a very angry sailor or an indignant Duchess. They would laugh, and she felt better about trying again. When they hit the town, it was fun with no pretense. Nothing expected, nothing pushed.

As time passed, Gus dared to move the tattoos to more delicate areas. Maud permitted it but only in the privacy of the wagon she shared with Dora. Sometimes Dora stuck around as a casual chaperone. She'd peer over Gus's shoulder and remark on whatever he was drawing.

"Why so many birds? You know Maudie hates birds," Dora said.

He stopped what he was doing and looked Maud astonished. She had never told him she didn't like birds, and she refrained from scolding Dora's parrots when he was around.

"You don't like them?"

"Well, I like *your* birds," Maud said.

It wasn't a lie. Gus tattooed two lovely sparrows along her neck one day when she told him to tattoo whatever he wanted. She liked the way they looked so much she didn't correct him later. Currently, he was working on a larger bird positioned just under the butterfly on her right arm.

"Sure," Dora said with an eyeroll. "You like *his* birds."

Maud threw a pillow at her friend. Dora pulled a screwed face and fled the wagon with a wink.

The art was intoxicating as was the addiction inside the tattoos. Each time the pain dulled, and each time the wanting for another one grew. By the time the fair ended in December, Maud had half a dozen more tattoos on her arms and shoulders. Birds and flowers and butterflies. There was even a dragon on her right forearm. She had become a canvas for Gus's art. He now tattooed whatever he liked on her, and she didn't mind it at all, loving every new image he made just for her. The two of them became a couple of picture galleries.

The lions were a different story. One evening, when a cool breeze invigorated the fairgrounds, Gus asked if he could tattoo Maud's chest piece in the privacy of the wagon. It would be a long sitting and one where she'd have to disrobe more than before. This wasn't an exposed leg or a peekaboo shoulder. This was her chest.

Maud found herself alone in her wagon, holding a swath of fabric low over her bosom. Below her waist, she was fully dressed. She twitched here and there trying to position herself on the cushions in a comfortable way that didn't bunch her bloomers. Her fingers trembled while she synched the cloth under her arms. A roll of sweat ran down from her armpit. She gathered the fabric in her hands so it wouldn't stain and embarrass her completely.

Why was she so nervous? Hadn't Gus seen her similarly undressed? No, this was different, she told herself. This was closer.

Gus cleaned his tools and approached with the drawing utensils. "The chest piece is the most important tattoo you can have. It's the one that tells the world who you are. I can draw birds and flowers all over your body, but this part," he said while grazing his finger over her sternum, "is what makes you unique. Your centerpiece."

Gooseflesh sprouted all over Maud's skin at his touch. He noticed and pulled his hand away. She could feel her face flush red. It was stupid. She wasn't a little girl anymore. She was a woman. It wasn't the first time a man touched her, but this was something else. Gus had hardly been her first date in her life, but this was... pure intimacy. When his fingers brushed her chest, it felt exhilarating and terrifying all at the same time.

"I'm sorry," he said. "We don't have to..."

"I'm not sleeping with you if that's what you're thinking, Gus Wagner," Maud said in a joking tone. She meant it to lighten the mood, and Gus smiled in response.

"Here. How about I show you mine?"

He removed his shirt. She'd seen his bare skin many times. It was part of his business, after all. Occasionally, Gus would stand in front of his tattoo table shirtless to display his wares. In the seclusion of her little wagon, it made her breath catch. Dora's parrots whistled, and she smacked the cage to shut them up.

"This was my choice," Gus said while gesturing to the piece on his chest. It was a lovely tattoo of two American flags framing a world with an eagle and serpents in the middle. Below it, on his abdomen, was a lighthouse with a boat. "I'm a patriot and a sailor, so I chose this."

"I'm a patriot," Maud said gesturing to eagle and flag Gus tattooed on their first date.

"Yes, but that isn't all of you. I'm thinking lions."

"Lions? Why lions?"

"They are wild and brave. I think two of them, and a woman... you!" Gus said with a renewed excitement. "*Marvelous Maud* astride a lion. In the middle of a jungle with trees and danger, but you aren't worried. You can tame lions."

"That sounds like a lot to put on my chest."

"What? You doubt me?" Gus asked with mock hurt in his voice.

"No, but..." Maud said stalling. She looked all over the room, trying to find something to talk about. It wasn't until she looked down to see the tattoos on his bare feet that she found what she needed.

"Why on earth do you have a pig and a rooster on your feet!" she exclaimed with a burst of laughter.

"Oh, ha! Are you laughing at me, Maud Stevens? I'll have you know this is for good luck," Gus retorted.

"I've been around pigs and chickens. How are they good luck?"

"Another sailor thing. We bring pigs and chickens on board because if our boat sinks, they are the animals who float. If you have them on your feet, it means you won't sink."

Maud barked with laughter again.

"Well, you don't have to worry about sinking, Maudie. No chickens for you. How about those lions?" Gus asked.

Maud stopped her laughing suddenly, drawing inside herself. "Are you sure?"

"Trust me," Gus said. He placed his hand over hers and lowered his voice. "Nothing you don't want. Nothing that makes you uncomfortable. I promise."

Maud swallowed a hard lump in her throat but agreed. At first, his touch felt like it had before. Uncomfortable in its intensity. As they went along, Gus made his usual witty conversation and silly jokes. She finally found a relaxed position among the cushions and settled in.

He warned her about the pain of a chest piece. It was fiery compared to the tattoos on the fleshier parts of her body. The nerves were raw and close to her skin and bone. She was glad for it in a way. The intense feelings she felt for him had transformed from confusing to longing, and the pain helped to douse all of it into a dull ache.

When Gus finished, he raised the hand mirror so Maud could see his creation. The lines were still raw and angry from the work, but there was no denying the beauty of what he'd done. Maud felt herself tear up as she took their mirror in her own hands.

There were her lions, elegantly sitting between two trees. A gentile woman sat astride the one in front. All of them unaware and unworried about the serpent and the trickster monkey nearby. The trees with the jungle creatures weren't the main attraction though. The lions were. The lions and the woman. Serenity and strength. It was perfection.

"No crying, my dear. Not until I give you this," Gus said.

He rummaged through his pack and brought out a small, blue box. With a hurried flourish, he opened it, presenting her with a gold ring perched in a bed of cotton. Maud was so surprised she dropped the mirror. Luckily, it fell on a pillow without breaking.

"What is this?" Maud asked. Her voice sounded shrill to her ears.

"Maud Stevens," Gus began. He held the ring out to her and bent to his knees. "You are the most beautiful, talented woman I know. I've tattooed fifteen hundred people at this fair, and none of them held a candle to you. I want a partner in this world, and I couldn't find a better one than the woman right in front of me. Will you marry me?"

"Oh, Gus," Maud said with tears running down her cheeks. She took the ring, nearly dropping the fabric covering her breasts in her flustered state. "Of course, I will."

**

Maud straightened her dress nervously as Dora adjusted the roses in her hair. The women could hear music from the other side of the door in the small church chapel. It wasn't a large band. Mainly, it consisted of a gathering of circus folk playing wind and brass instruments. The pastor had kindly lent the use of his organ for the affair as well.

"Stop your fidgeting, Maud Stevens. I can't fix you otherwise," Dora said.

"Maud Wagner. I'm Maud Wagner now." Even though she said the words, there was a bubbling in her gut. It made her tug at the lapelled collar of her dress. Dora swatted away her hand.

"Not until the *I do's*, toots. Besides, if you don't stop scowling, he won't say yes."

Dora grinned, but Maud didn't take the bait. She knew her friend was trying to get her to laugh and shake away her worries, but the whole affair was overwhelming. The church was nothing like the stifling religious affairs of her youth. The high ceilings and colorful windows didn't resemble a coffin in the least, and the clergy were considerably gentler. The kindly priest accepted them warmly. He didn't bat an eye when the tattooed couple asked to marry in their small chapel, despite their mixed religious backgrounds.

The idea of walking down the aisle and professing her love for Gus didn't make her quiver. After all, what was another performance in front of an audience? So why was she so nervous?

"Ain't you happy, toots? Do I need to whisk you away out the back? I thought you loved Gus."

"I do. It's not that."

"Did he hurt you recently? Because I swear, as I live and breathe, I'll make Maxine's crate his pillow."

"No," Maud said. She placed her hand up to Dora's mouth to quiet her friend. Dora's voice raised a few octaves when she got a decent head of steam.

"Then spill, sugar," Dora said in a softer tone.

"I just... I just never thought I'd be here. I didn't think I'd be married. I mean, the things that happened... I assumed this wouldn't be a thing that happened for me." Maud began to shake all over, and Dora wrapped her arms around her friend. She pressed the quivering bride against her beaded bosom, and Maud held her in return. Neither woman let go until the last tremble ceased.

"Maudie, it don't matter what happened at the farm or what happened until now. You deserve this. I'm right here, toots."

Maud nodded and took a deep breath. Dora tucked a stray curl under the rose in her hair.

"Now, you smile, honey. Today is a grand day."

"It certainly is," said a gruff voice behind them.

Maud and Dora turned to see Walter wearing a worn suit behind them. It was an old fashion but still respectable. His hair was combed, and his shoes shined with fresh polish. Maud had only seen him in sleeves when the weather got too cold. Looking at Walter now in the golden light of the church, dressed in his best, made her heart swell. She crossed the room and hugged him.

"Dora said you might need someone to walk you down the aisle," he said.

"I... I do."

"Not yet, Maudie. That's for the groom." Walter said as he wrapped an arm around hers. "Let's go make this official."

When they opened the door to the chapel, a motley gathering awaited them. Contortionists, tattooists, trapeze dancers, clowns and freaks. They all bore witness to vows. All looked to Maud, smiling and gasping with delight. But not Maud; she only had eyes for Gus. When she saw him waiting for her at the altar, her smile came truly and effortlessly. No need for a show. Not here. Not today.

***

Since circus season was only in the warm months, most of their friends pressed on to their respective winter homes. However, Maud and Gus stayed in St. Louis for an extended honeymoon. Gus purchased a small storefront with a modest apartment above it. After the windfall of the World's Fair, he had the money to pay cash for the home.

Gus used the storefront to open his own parlor where he tattooed the brave and the curious alike. All the while apprenticing his lovely wife in the art of hand-poked tattoos. The new-fangled tattoo machine, while providing a faster result, was seen by Gus as a gimmick. A quick and lazy way to make art on someone's skin.

"Why pay for a tattoo by a real artist if they let the machine do all the work? Where's the art in the gears?" he said to say to anyone who would listen.

Gus took chopsticks and whittled a smooth groove in them that nestled perfectly in the crook of his hand. With silk thread, he would attach fine, British sewing needles that he cleaned with alcohol. A single needle made the perfect instrument to start out a tattoo with gentle, nondescript lines. Some tools were fitted with several needles bunched together to allow quick coverage when shading. Others had a thicker needle which was used to make hard, dark lines and give a picture a bolder feeling.

Maud quickly took his technique as her own. She learned how to stencil a drawing on skin with graphite or small bits of charcoal. The flash designs they provided for their customers became second nature to her. Flash was what they called the stock images. Designs that were popular and ready-at-hand. Birds, skulls, and pretty ladies. It wasn't long before she could tattoo them without drawing it out beforehand. The tangy odor of India ink as it hit the open air became so familiar to her it caused her right hand to itch for a needle. The smooth grooves of the chopsticks melded into her body like a second skin.

The beautiful euphoria of creating art washed over Maud again and again. Contortions had paid the bills, but this? This was her calling. These drawings never withered in between dark pages, unable to be viewed by everyone else. They walked among the world, telling tales for all to see.

In 1907, two noteworthy things happened. *The American Society for Keeping Woman in Her Proper Sphere* formed as an organization to promote family values and Maud Wagner officially began her professional career as a tattoo artist. No longer an apprentice, Gus boasted that his wife was the first woman tattooist in the United States of America.

Sparrows, anchors, pretty girls, patriotic flags, scenes from the bible. Maud conquered them all. Dozens came through their doors looking for the pretty pictures. Ladies began asking for Mrs. Wagner to tattoo their birds and butterflies. Even some men requested her.

By the time Maud gave birth to their daughter, Lotteva, in 1910, she was covered nearly head to toe with Gus's art. Her favorite was a scene was still the two lions on her chest. It was normally the first thing people noticed when meeting her, and she was glad of it.

Their daughter pushed forth into this life with a wail no one could deny and a gaze that locked on a person without hesitation. A healthy baby girl, pristinely flawless compared to her tattooed parents. She was gorgeous, and Maud felt a great relief when she heard the child's wails. Lotteva was strong, willful, and began living her life out loud from second one.

Life was blissful and quiet for a time. However, there was no doubting the circus blood in the Wagner family veins. For a people used to the nomadic lifestyle, sitting still started to become stifling. Moving along down the road was home.

Also, Maud missed her friends. Dora and a few others had visited now and then when they were passing through, but it wasn't the same. Their real home was the road, and their family was made up of the nomads of the circus.

The next May found the Wagner family, with tiny Lotteva in tow, moving out with a circus. Charlie Grimm had become a dear friend of the family while they lived in St. Louis. The man was an accomplished tattooist himself, and he offered to rent the apartment and tattoo parlor from Gus while they were away.

With the added income of a tenant, Maud and Gus bought new canvas tents and a new wardrobe. The posters advertising "Gus Wagner, the Tattooed Man" and "Gus Wagner, Original Globetrotter" were scrapped. New posters were painted with pictures of a tattooed man and woman reading things like "Wagner Tattooists Extraordinaire" and "Wagner and Stevens, Original Globetrotters."

In the posters, the man and wife were equally spaced and holding hands. A beautiful little rose perched in the woman's hair. Tattoos became a family affair, so Maud and Gus took their family business on the road.

Part Four

1917

Maud bent over herself and away from her customer. She was unable to contain the laughter any longer. From the floor nearby, Lotteva looked up from the picture she was painting of a pony she'd seen earlier that day. The child looked from her mother to the woman in her mother's chair, confused by the joke. Both ladies were laughing raucously, so Lotteva giggled along, even though she was only seven and didn't really understand the source of the merriment.

The woman in Maud's customer chair happened to be Trixie Delmont, or Tricky Trixie as the posters labelled her. She was a burlesque dancer with the *Jones and Adams Circus*. A buxom woman with a plump bottom, Trixie was rounding the other end of forty, and the strain of dancing and thick makeup had taken a toll on her features. If she ever washed the cake off her face, someone might have seen the grooves and cracks.

"So, I told him if he were to show that thing in the cookhouse, old Betty would mistake it for a mushroom and toss it in a stew!"

Maud had to put down her tattoo stick for that one. There was no way to hold anything steady while Trixie was on one of her rants. Very few people could make Maud lose herself in laughter, but Trixie Delmont could. Both women gave a sideways glance at little Lotteva to see if the raunchiness of the joke had sunk in. The girl was completely unaware and already back to drawing her pony.

"Ah, to be young and ignorant to the ways of the world again," Trixie said.

"No thank you," Maud said.

She went back to work on the flock of sparrows she was tattooing on her customer's shoulder. Trixie steadied herself.

Maud sat in her chair with her legs hips-width apart. Birthing Lotteva had made things stretch and spread. While she could have done without the extra jiggle around her belly, she didn't mind the rest. There was something stabilizing in her hips, like they had their own memories now and knew how to best carry her. Her whole body had the knowledge of a mother. Even though Maud would have loved to have the face of a twenty-year-old beauty, she never wanted to be such a trying age again. Forty wasn't that old, but she could definitely see her younger face disappearing in the mirror.

"Oh, come now. I bet there just a little part of you that longs to be a naïve little girl once more, unknowing of the way of things."

Maud's face reverted back into a serious expression. For an instant, her dark eyes were somewhere else, somewhere among a sea of golden wheat. She pulled herself back and shook her head.

"No, not at all. Best to know the world the way it is. Those who don't know what things are like tend to get preyed on," she said.

"And what about her?" Trixie gestured toward Lotteva who was ignoring them.

"She is still young, but growing up here? I think she'll figure out the game of things on her own. Much smarter than me, that one."

"You ain't worried?"

"She's got me and her daddy here to protect her. Besides, we know just about everyone from here to Kentucky working the shows. We all watch out for each other."

"That is a truth. I tell you, Maud, I am so thankful you are helping me with this. The burlesque thing, it's just not cutting it anymore. I love having me a good time, but I'm getting too old for this."

"Frank hadn't got something for you elsewhere? I don't mind a bit, decorating you. You know you're my favorite customer. No one makes me laugh harder, but I never figured you for a tattooed woman until you came to me."

Trixie sighed in that way she did that always ended with a smile. That woman could grin like she knew twenty secrets no one else in the world knew, and she might just tell you one for a price. It was no wonder so many people liked her. If Tricky Trixie deemed you worthy of her affection, the sun shone on both sides of your face.

"Frank told me Hank had work for me, but Hank only wants me for the night shift at the cooch tent."

They lowered their voices and looked over at Lotteva again, making sure she wasn't listening. Lotteva had her back turned to them, completely engrossed in a new drawing of a lion. The pony drawing was off to the side, having been dubbed finished by the artist.

"I wouldn't think less of you if you did it," Maud said in a hushed voice. "I tattoo a bunch of those girls. Most aren't ashamed at all. No one here would judge you."

"I would."

Maud raised her now notoriously skeptical eyebrow.

"Now now, Maud Wagner. You put that thing down, you here. I know there's some folks who don't draw a line between the dancing I do and what the night shift coochie girls do. But it's different. When I'm on stage... I own those folks watching me. They belong to me."

Trixie mimed holding something in the cup of her hand. She gazed down at her invisible audience like she might eat them.

"All of them belong to me during a performance. I use their attention to make me feel alive. If I were to start at the other business... well, they'd start owning me. Pieces of me anyway. I've seen those girls after a time of working the night shift. Their light dims, and even though they may talk a good talk, eventually all of them empty."

Maud recalled the first time she saw Trixie perform. She was good, really good. Trixie could hold a crowd in her hands the way she said. Not just the men watched. Women also came to the show and gazed in wonderment at Tricky Trixie and her voluptuous dancing.

"Well, I don't blame you a bit... obviously. I feel bad for the night shift girls," Maud said.

"Did you know Hank collects thirty percent of their take?"

"Really? Is that on top of the fifteen percent the house takes these days?"

"Yes ma'am. Those girls barely get half of what they earn. I heard in some shows, it's even less than that."

"Hardly seems worth it," Maud said.

"I suppose if you got nothing else..." Trixie said as she trailed off.

"I don't know. Seems to me, I'd find something else," Maud said.

Trixie's all-knowing smile returned. "Well, of course you would, Maud Wagner. You're about the most bull-headed woman I know, and I've known a few, mind you."

"Well, Dora taught me a good bit of that from the start," Maud said.

"Mama, what's bull-headed mean?" Lotteva asked from her spot on the floor.

"Not what you think, baby. Just means Mama's stubborn," Maud said.

"Oh, okay." Lotteva, visibly deflated, went back to her drawing. Trixie gave Maud a questioning look.

"Oh, she perks up with anything to do with animals. Her daddy's influence, I'm telling you. That, and Dora doesn't help none either. She encourages the girl's love of animals too much. The other day, Lotteva brought home a skunk she found."

They laughed again and Maud went back to work on the sparrows on Trixie's shoulders. It was such a popular thing to ask for, and Maud had her own particular flare when drawing them. She added the tiniest flip at the edge of the tail and the tip of the wings. Funny how a small accent made such a difference. If the circus stayed in one part any amount of time, you could put a dollar on Maud getting a crowd of customers asking after the lady who did the pretty birds.

"You ever think of settling down, Trixie? I'd bet there's scores of men who would make an honest woman out of you," Maud said with a smirk.

Trixie started to guffaw. "An honest woman out of me? Ha! They'd have their work cut out for them. No darling. I heard the Cole Brothers are looking for a tattooed lady, so when you finish with me, I plan to apply for the job."

"No settling down for Tricky Trixie?"

"Honey, I've had way too much fun in this life to ever think of quitting it for good. The parties, the traveling, the champagne. I won't be done with it, not ever. Therefore, my good lady, tattoo me with birds and butterflies because, honey, I want to fly until I die."

For a second, Maud admired her work on Trixie's bare skin. In a way, Trixie was her first real masterpiece. A woman solely decorated by Maud Wagner. A pair of gorgeous butterflies perched prettily over Trixie's round breasts. A great eagle among the clouds took up most of her upper back. Maud had worked hard on the group of cherubic angels on her left arm, and now she was decorating Trixie's right arm with a flock of sparrows.

"I'm going to miss you," Maud said, suddenly serious.

Trixie's smile faltered, but only for a second. "Honey, I'm going to miss you too. But I can't imagine we won't day-and-date again. You know how it is in season. The different shows are always running into one another. I'll be seeing you."

98

Maud and Trixie sat for a while in amiable silence. This life could be wonderful, with adventure around every turn, but friends came and went with the seasons. Sometimes they moved to other shows, and sometimes they just disappeared. The Wagner's themselves rarely stuck with one circus more than a season or two. It was all about who was willing to give them the best rate or the better train car. Often, it was who was going to a new territory Gus and Maud hadn't seen yet.

The one constant was Dora. The years spent in St. Louis with the tattoo store front were happy ones, but they lacked the sisterly love that Dora brought. After the Wagner's returned to circus life, Dora attached herself to them like family. The exotic dancer joined with whatever circus outfit Maud did. Not only because of her love for Maud, but her love of her goddaughter. Without children of her own, Dora reserved all her motherly attention for Lotteva.

Maud would miss Trixie, but she always had Gus, Lotteva and Dora. They called all of the circus members family, but those three were steadfast.

"Have you seen the new May girl?"

Trixie's question snapped Maud from her reverie and brought her back to the here and now. First of May people were new folks. Circus season started up in May, and when it was your first time doing a tour, you were dubbed a May girl or May boy.

"No. Why?"

"She's real pretty. Best keep her away from Gus."

Maud waved her hand dismissively at her friend. "Oh Trixie, I'm not afraid about that." Then, she lightly touched the red rose bud tucked under the loose bun in her hair.

"I know I know. The thing of it is… I'm worried about her. "Trixie's tone was suddenly low and serious.

Maud put down her needle to lean in. "What do you mean?"

"She's working the menagerie," Trixie said. Her normally jovial demeanor seemed to evaporate. Seeing Trixie Delmont look worried was an anomaly, and Maud shrank inside herself a touch.

"What? Why?" Maud asked.

"She can't do nothing else. She's real pretty, small thing too, but she's got about as much grace as a one-legged hen. At first, they put her in the trapeze, but she fell right off the first day. Nearly broke her damn neck."

Maud flinched instinctively and shook her head to rid her brain of old thoughts. "What about serving up food or taking tickets?"

"She's painfully shy," Trixie said. "Stutters and everything. Ricky about smacked the poor thing after an hour of trying to train her. Ended up sticking her in the menagerie for lack of knowing what to do with her. I think she's shoveling manure and cleaning cages."

"She got any family to go back to?"

"I don't think so. When I tried to talk to her, she said something about them dying. I don't know how true it was. She barely would look at me, so I didn't want to ask anything else," Trixie said. Her voice was getting quieter with every word. It was as if the more they gossiped, the more likely it was they'd be heard.

"I guess the animals won't mind her shyness. How is she doing there?" asked Maud.

She took her needle and began to finish up her sparrows. Trixie was one of the rare customers who never flinched a bit under the needle. The pain just didn't seem to register.

"Peter thinks she's getting circus headaches. You know...from the smell of paint and manure. I think Peter and the others don't get them because they plum can't smell anymore. Poor stammering thing must be miserable."

"Must be. I haven't seen her yet. At least, I don't think I have."

"You'd know if you had. She's pretty but a little ghost of a girl. Couldn't be more than seventeen. I overheard old Hank talking to

Ricky about her though."

Trixie leaned into Maud again as close as conspirators. Their faces were only a breath away from each other. Luckily, Maud had already finished the tattoo and wiped it clean. Trixie kept her voice low so Lotteva couldn't overhear.

"Hank has designs on her for the cooch tent. Night shift only, since she can't dance."

"He does?"

"She can't do much else. I don't think she can read or write either," Trixie said. "What's he supposed to do? Give her roustabout work? Driving stakes with the fellas?"

"Yeah, but if she's as timid as you say," Maud began with a feeling of rising anxiety in her gut. "That could just empty her out inside."

"I know. I feel for her."

"Maybe she'll get used to the smell of the menagerie," Maud said.

"Maybe. I hope so," Trixie said. There was a swell of worry and sincerity in her voice.

"They can't *make* her work the cooch tent. Right?" Maud asked.

"No, I don't think they would. But if there's nothing else for her, she might choose it."

Trixie no longer wore her trademark smile, and Maud stared at her brown eyes. They were serious with thought. For a second, Maud was transported back to the World's Fair where she met Gus. There was that exhibit, the savages of the world one. The look on their faces still haunted her from time to time. It's one thing for someone to seek out this life; it was another to have no other choice.

By the time Gus stuck his head in the tent, Maud was wrapping some linen around the bandage on Trixie's arm. The smell of soap and alcohol wafted in the air. He beamed at the ladies, and Lotteva immediately jumped to her feet and ran to his side. Gus lifted her and hugged her, laying kisses all over her cheek.

"Ah, am I too late?" Gus asked, as he put down Lotteva.

"Yes, you are," Maud said. "Try being punctual next time."

"Oh, come on. I figured I'd have a few minutes since there'd be ample gossip involved. Let me see. You haven't even finished wrapping her yet."

With a smirk, Maud lifted the linen and the bandage to display the three beautiful sparrows now adorning Trixie's arm. Gus beamed while looking at them.

"She's better at these birds than you are, you know," Trixie said.

"Oh, trust me, I know," Gus said.

"Because I tell him every day," Maud said while rewrapping the bandage. The mood in the tent was lightening, and everyone was thankful for it.

Trixie playfully reached for Maud's hand and pulled it toward her. She rotated her hand to reveal a small blank spot near Maud's wrist. It was one of the only unmarked spaces on Maud's body. Trixie gave a teasing smirk and said, "Oh my, Gus Wagner, you missed a spot."

Gus chuckled. "That is intentional, my lady. I have plans."

"What plans?" Trixie asked.

"A rose. It's going to be the most beautiful rose you've ever seen," Gus said. "I just haven't found the perfect specimen to draw yet."

Maud rolled her eyes. "He never will. He keeps talking about making me this perfect rose, and it never happens. I think he just never wants to be done drawing on me."

They all laughed, but it didn't last long. The cries of a little girl interrupted the moment. "Daddy, can we go now? You promised a tour. You promised!" Lotteva pleaded with her father and danced around his legs.

"I did, didn't I?"

"And to see the lion. You said there was a lion. I've never seen a lion before."

"You stay away from that lion," Trixie said as she threw a garish shawl around her shoulders. "I saw him gobble up a boy twice your size yesterday, and that was just for breakfast."

"That's not true, Miss Trixie." Lotteva rolled her eyes, then, leaned into her father with a loud whisper that only a child could think was inaudible. "It isn't true, is it Daddy?"

The three adults erupted with laughter, and after a few bewildering moments looking from one person to another, Lotteva started laughing too. Maud fussed over Trixie, reminding her to leave on the bandage as long as she could.

"When it comes off, make sure you keep the tattoo clean and out of the sun."

"For heaven's sake, Maud Wagner. This isn't my first time. I know the speech. Now, we promised this little one a full tour with a lion, so let's commence to keeping that promise."

***

The East Texas afternoon light illuminated their faces as they stepped into the thoroughfare of the *Jones and Adams Circus*. Warm, sweet air turned their cheeks pink in seconds. A barrage of sights and smells engulfed the group as they strode proudly out among their fellow performers and starry-eyed customers. Gus had lifted Lotteva on top of his shoulders so as to give her the best possible view of their latest traveling home. There was no time in a circus's life that was finer than the first days of May.

Performers moved about the crowd, jovial and refreshed after a quiet winter. Most of them recognized Maud and Gus and waved at their party in greeting. Those who didn't know them personally, recognized their posters and saluted them all the same. Lotteva gazed around at the spectacle, gleefully taking in the sights. Maud beamed at her daughter, remembering the first time she herself saw a circus. So much magic. The world was never more beautiful than through the eyes of the young.

On one stage, a group of onlookers marveled at the bearded woman. For a penny, you could gain admission to hear her sing in operatic falsetto. The adjacent tent boasted a strong man who could bend steel and lift five women on a platform at once.

Another stage held an incredibly tall man standing next to tiny woman. Martin and Isadora were an odd pair. He stood at six foot ten inches. She was only three foot five. Martin lifted Isadora high with one hand, and they waved to Maud's party as they moseyed by.

A man walked on stilts covered in striped pants among the throngs of people. He wore a matching top hat and the white paste makeup. An entourage of clowns followed in his wake. They danced about his long limbs, squeezing bulbs that squirted water from fake flowers. Several pretended to box one another.

When the man on the stilts spotted Lotteva on her father's shoulders, he bowed down to her, removing his hat in a gesture of reverence and said, "My dear queen! Don't you people know who this is, my people? Why it's Queen Lotteva, the empress of the fair!"

Everyone turned to Lotteva, and she beamed, her mouth opening wide with an infectious smile. She had been self-conscious about a tooth she was missing in the front but in that moment, she hadn't a care in the world.

Everything was colorful. Everything smelled familiar and tasty. The air hung heavy with the scent of sugar and bread. It was no wonder some people suffered from circus headaches. A person couldn't turn in any direction without seeing some colorful poster or performer vying for their attention. Nowhere were they safe from the sights and smells of fun.

They found Dora in front of the petting tent with a white and black monkey clinging to her shoulder. These were the animals for the tykes. Small, tame and accustomed to being stroked by grubby little hands. She fed the monkey an apple. Children giggled as he ate it in veracious, little bites.

Gus put down Lotteva, and the little girl ran to her Auntie Dora with a wide grin and excited eyes. Dora handed her a slice of apple. The other children gasped in wonder as the monkey leapt from Dora's shoulder to Lotteva's.

"Hello, Jake," Lotteva said in her best show voice.

She rewarded the monkey with the apple slice and basked in the attention of the other children. They were so eager to learn her magic with the creature. One of the children asked if she was a witch. Lotteva held out her arms so Jake could climb on them.

"I'm no witch," Lotteva said laughing. "I'm the queen."

Maud beamed at her daughter as she hugged Dora.

"She's already got the gift," Dora said.

"Yes, yes. I foresee a barrage of creatures in my future. I'm sure you already heard about the skunk," Maud said.

Everyone laughed, and Dora lit a cigarette. "Could be worse, ya know," she said.

"How?"

"She could love men."

"That *is* worse," Gus said, laughing.

Maud went to snatch a puff of Dora's cigarette, but Dora smacked away her hand. They jostled one another like little girls.

"I thought you quit," Dora said.

"I thought you were going to get your nose snipped."

"What does that mean exactly?" Dora asked.

"You know? Because you keep sticking it in other people's business," Maud said.

She grabbed the cigarette and took a long puff before Dora jabbed a finger in her ribs to make her let it go. The smoke puffed out in bursts from her laughter.

"The two of you are like quarreling sisters no matter how old you get," Trixie said.

"I keep telling Dora she ought to have a girl of her own so Lotteva can have a sister. Lord knows I'm not going to do it again. My body has been through enough hell. Hey, where is Lotteva?"

Collectively, everyone stopped talking to listen for the voices of children. Jake, being the clever monkey that he was, leapt onto Dora's arm screeching in alarm. It sent everyone into a panic. The group had lost sight of the little girl. It was only a second or two, but in their merriment, their attention turned away from her.

Maud reeled around, expecting to see her daughter. Instead, she saw just a bare patch of grass and hay. There was no Lotteva and no children. Suddenly desperate, she spun in place looking for her among the sea of legs and arms and bodies that made up the crowd. No one looked at all familiar.

"Lotteva?"

Gus glanced around with alarm. Trixie quickly ducked her head inside the tent, and Dora wrangled some children playing nearby. A few of them had been the ones watching Lotteva and the monkey.

"Hey, kids. Where's the girl? The one with the monkey?" Dora asked, startling the group.

"The little witch girl?" asked one of the boys.

"Yes, her. Did you see where she went?"

Two of them pointed one direction while the others pointed in the opposite. When Gus and Maud approached, the children's eyes bugged. The tattooed duo must have seemed terrifying because the lot backed away. One little girl took a look at Maud's lions and fled. The rest of the kids followed shortly afterward.

Terror infested the small party of carnival folks. Waves and waves of shock. Tremor on top of tremor. Maud felt as if her heart had dropped into her pelvis. She could barely breathe beneath her collapsed chest. The world around her spun. For a moment, she wondered if she was having a seizure. Was this what she felt all those years ago hiding behind her bedroom door in Kansas? Was this another small death? Was her next moment going to be on the ground, helpless to find her daughter?

One breath and then another. Each inhale was a pearl she strung on a thread. After putting enough of them together, her mind returned well enough to panic properly. She had been so happy only moments ago. Mere seconds before, her daughter was there laughing, happily the center of attention.

Trixie emerged from the animal tent with a terrible look of fear. Her words fell out of numb lips. "She's not there."

"Here, take this," Dora said, handing the monkey to Trixie. "Put him in his cage. I'm goin' find Frank and get the word out to look for Lotteva." Dora turned to Maud who was beginning to hyperventilate again. She couldn't get in enough air. Dora grabbed Maud by her shoulders and shook her. "Maudie. Hey toots. You two go look for your girl. She's here, and we'll find her. Go now."

Gus took his wife's arm and cradled her as they moved along. There, searching among the throngs of people, Maud finally managed to take in some wind. Not a lot, but enough. One pearl at a time. Each little inhale strung together helped her breathe. Looking for her daughter meant having something to do. It meant she wasn't helpless, but she had to breathe.

"She couldn't have gotten far," Gus said.

Maud heard the fear in his voice. That more than anything frightened her. There was a thick layer of serious calm, but underneath, the terror rattled his usually jovial tone. When Gus Wagner's façade moved, so did the world's.

Maud's eyes scanned the crowd of men, women, and children. A tide of faces, and none of them Lotteva. She tried to remember what dress Lotteva was wearing. A blue one, she thought. It was the blue dress with the white striping, or was it the other way around?

Once, Gus thought he found their daughter standing in front of a caramel apple cart. Lotteva loved caramel apples. He let go of Maud's shoulder to closer, but when he turned the girl around, the wrong face looked up at them. Maud started to think maybe Lotteva had worn pink that day. Oh God, why couldn't she remember?

She felt the hot pressure of tears forcing their way to the surface. The world spun and mocked her. Maud heard the words again. The ones she knew from her childhood. They surfaced from time to time when she was afraid. Words that judged her, that threatened her. Words that she ran away from so long ago.

Bow your head young woman and be humbled among your betters. Yours is a life of service and grace, an existence behind and below. Never ask to receive more for if you do, all shall be taken from you.

All shall be taken. Your daughter shall be taken because you wanted more.

Suddenly, she was a girl in church again, her mother looming over her with a suspicious glare. Such a small woman—who could look so impossibly big. Her mother glared down at her and slapped a hand across her face.

Gus squeezed Maud's hand, as he noticed his wife begin to melt away underneath her tears. "We'll find her, my love. We will. Just have to think. Where might she go?"

Maud shook her head vigorously, snapping back to the fore. How could he be calm? Their daughter was gone. Gone! There was no time to think, no time to stop. They had to keep moving.

Tent after tent was invaded. Each one without the tinkling of Lotteva's laughter. Every one devoid of her bubbly presence. Word spread fast among the circus folk, and they were frantically running here and there. People regularly checked in with Maud and Gus as to where they'd looked and if anyone had found Lotteva.

The notion came so fast to her mind, it was as if it had been sent by the Lord himself. It burst into her eyes, drying her tears and silencing the wretched words from a time long ago. Her mother's presence evaporated. Everything became clear in an instant, and the answer was far more terrifying than just her missing daughter.

She knew where Lotteva went. "Gus, the lion. Oh God, she went to see the lion!"

Hand in hand, the Wagner's raced toward the menagerie. Had Maud been a normal woman, her long skirt and modest ways would have slowed them down. Being the tattooed woman of the *Jones and Adams Circus*, she wore a short dress with pantaloons down to her knees. Her blouse wrapped around her just above her breasts, leaving her shoulders and arms free.

Gus lost no time waiting on Maud to keep up. In fact, they both nearly collided with the man on stilts in their haste to get to the menagerie tent. Her heart raced. Her arms ached to hold her little girl, but at least now she had a destination. They weren't aimless. It wasn't random. She would be there. She would. Lotteva would be in that tent, and all would be right in the world.

Each breath came to her in a steady rhythm. Her heartbeat. Lotteva's heartbeat.

A brief flicker of dread entered her mind. She imagined throwing herself into the tent and finding it empty. Her gut hollowed at the thought, and she swallowed down the threat of vomit. Gus and Maud practically flew into the menagerie tent, breathless and desperate. They looked around, their eyes darting from side to side. The patrons turned to stare at the spectacle of the tattooed couple who seemed to have lost their minds.

For a horrible, terrible moment, they didn't see her. Maud fought the urge to submit to her nausea. Her eyes tracked the lines of cages painted different colors and with lavish lettering. There was a panther pacing back and forth, staring hungrily at the trio of zebras tethered together at the end of the tent. Off to the side, a camel spat in the direction of an elderly couple. A mother and father held their little boy back from the bear's cage, even though he desperately wanted a closer look.

Then, Maud saw her. Lotteva, in her blue dress, stood only a foot away from the lion's cage. The beast paced back and forth, sizing up the little girl. Danger hung dense in the air. This ordeal wasn't over.

"Lotteva!"

Lotteva turned, and when she saw her parents, she waved. She didn't seem to have a clue that anything was amiss, nor that she was at the center of their fear. To her, this was just another day in her unusual life. She was getting to meet a lion. Lotteva beamed brightly.

But Maud's panic didn't lessen. She knew animals well enough and she knew their agitation. The lion was new to the circus, unaccustomed to children and noise. He was looking at Lotteva the way a barn cat looked at a mouse or a bird. Though the size might be different, the intent was perfectly clear. The lion's eyes widened and filled with black. His ears pressed against his head. He was going to strike.

"No!"

There was no time. Not enough time to get to her. Big cats were fast, too fast.

Everything slowed. The air itself felt like breathing molasses. Maud broke away from Gus and ran for her daughter. She begged her with outstretched arms to move away from the cage. Everything in her willed her daughter to take just a few steps back. Poor Lotteva, she didn't understand.

Maud saw the paw. She could see the claws glint in the tiniest bit of light that filtered in through the canvas of the menagerie tent. It was moving too fast. He would get to her before she could. If only Lotteva would move.

In a blind second, it was over.

The huge cat scrambled and thrashed about, clawing at nothing but air and roaring with a terrible ferocity. Several families left the menagerie in a hurry, and the rest merely gawked at the spectacle. At first, Maud didn't understand what had happened. Her daughter was there a second ago. The lion had her dead to rights.

One hard blink later, Maud's brain caught up.

Lotteva was alive. She was standing off to the side, panting hard and looking frightened. A small woman, barely of age to be called a woman, stood behind her. Her arms wrapped around the little girl. The woman gaped at Maud with grey eyes that took up too much of her face.

She had grabbed Lotteva and yanked her to safety just before the lion attacked. Maud didn't waste another second. She raced to them. She fell to her knees and hugged her daughter so tightly, Lotteva cried out in pain.

"Mama, I can't breathe!"

"I don't care!"

"Mama, let go!" Lotteva screamed as she tried to squirm away.

She didn't mean for it to happen—it just did. The fear, the frustration erupted inside her, and her daughter's struggles lit the fuse. Maud pulled Lotteva from her and slapped her across the face. It was hard to tell which one of them was more surprised.

"Don't you ever do that again, young lady. You scared me half to death! You could have died. You could have been taken from me!"

Lotteva's small mouth was open, horrified at her mother. Her little hand pressed close to her cheek where a red spot was forming. Tears welled up and stuck to her eyelashes.

In that moment, Maud saw herself through Lotteva's eyes and thought about her own angry mother screaming down at her. Had she become her mother? Would she start making her daughter go out and cut her own switches?

"Oh honey. Oh honey, I'm sorry," Maud said as she reached for Lotteva and hugged her again. This time the little girl didn't struggle. "Mama's so sorry for hitting you, baby. I didn't mean it. Mama was just so scared."

Gus was there in the next second, grabbing Lotteva from Maud and squeezing her harder. "Don't you ever *ever* do that again!" he said.

Lotteva stopped crying then, hearing the fear in her father's voice. Maud stood from her crouching position, feeling cold all over from the absence of her daughter's warmth. She shook off the trembles and attempted to wipe the tears from her face as bits of hay stuck to her fingers.

The intimate scene was too raw for outsider eyes. It was wrong to gape, so the bystanders turned their attention elsewhere. Townspeople left the tent. Only the people on the outward fringes dared to intrude on the reunited family.

When Maud turned to her savior, the woman was averting her gaze. Maud didn't recognize her, and she knew just about everyone in this outfit. Trixie's description of the May girl came to mind. This one was definitely pretty and timid. A ghost of a thing working in the menagerie.

Maud walked toward the possible May girl.

"You saved my girl," Maud held the woman's gaze, not letting the shy thing turn away.

It was obviously hard for her. The emotion was so raw. When she spoke, it was in a tiny, quivering voice. "Yes, ma'am. She was too close to the lion. He's not…"

Maud cut her off with a hug. She wrapped the waifish thing in her arms and held her. Seven years of motherhood gave her the upper body strength of someone twice her size. Maud never hesitated to lift her own daughter to the stars, so her arms could squeeze like a vice.

The poor May girl stiffened under her embrace, but Maud didn't let go until her own tremors ceased. She would get her warmth back. If not from her own daughter, then from this stranger.

"Thank you. Thank you so much," Maud said as she finally let go.

"You... you're welcome, Mrs. Wagner."

This girl with the big eyes, dressed in a baggy shirt and high-waisted pants, knew Maud's name. She felt extremely guilty not knowing hers in return. Maud searched Gus' face to see if there was any recognition. He looked oblivious; he didn't know their daughter's savior, either.

"Thank you," Gus said with a shaky lower lip. "Thank you for being there and saving our girl. We looked away for a minute... and... He looked at his daughter, who was still quivering in his arms. "Lotteva, you can never do that again."

"You're welcome, Mr. Wagner. It was nothing. Anyone would've done it." She stooped her head, embarrassed. There was a small wince in her eyes. Maud had seen that look many times before. She herself used to make it when a tinge of back pain hit her during a performance. That was the look of concealed pain.

It wasn't until then that Maud noticed the manure smell of the menagerie. All her senses seemed to have stalled, frozen in time, while they hunted for their missing daughter. But now, the stench was actually quite strong. Manure mixed with the freshly painted cages that hadn't been properly aired out caused a lot of people terrible headaches.

"I won't, Daddy. I'm sorry."

"You bet you won't. Frightened everyone to death. I'll tan your hide next time, but there won't be a next time, will there?"

"No, Daddy."

Maud squeezed Lotteva's calf, wanting the feel the fleshy realness of her girl in her hand. Somehow that helped seal it. That feeling that Lotteva was in alive and safe in Gus's arms. However, she still couldn't look away from the small woman. If this was Trixie's May girl, Maud definitely couldn't let this go.

"Maud? Did you hear me?"

Gus's question snapped her back to attention. "What? I'm sorry, dear. The blood is rushing in my head."

"I said I'm going to take Lotteva back to find Dora and to call off the search party."

Maud nodded absently. "Yes, yes. Do that. They'll be worried. I'm going to stay here and make sure Miss...?"

"Bethany, ma'am, but everyone calls me Toddy."

"Toddy. I'm going to make sure Miss Toddy here is properly paid for her help."

Gus nodded and walked away with Lotteva. Maud could hear her little girl chatter fade as they left the menagerie.

"Daddy, don't be mad at the lion. It was my fault. I didn't read him right. I could tell he was awful put out by me, but I didn't move. I should have. He was just so pretty..."

Maud was left alone with Toddy. Most people had already exited the tent; the spectacle of the little girl and lion cleared most of them away, and the few who lingered scattered under Maud's insistent glare. Toddy gulped as though she were about to get a good thrashing.

"You saved my girl," Maud said.

"Yes, Mrs. Wagner."

"I owe you everything. I have some money..."

"No. I mean, no thank you. I couldn't take your money. Anyone would have..."

"Is this your first season?" Maud asked.

When Toddy failed to answer, Maud clarified her question. "Your first season with the circus."

"Oh, yes."

"The menagerie, it gives you headaches."

"How did you know?" Toddy asked, looking genuinely surprised.

Maud decided not to spout off about Trixie's gossip. It might make Toddy feel self-conscious to know people were talking about her. Maud decided to go about her answer a different way. Better to not bring idle chatter into this. That sort of thing never ended in trust.

"I can see it in your eyes," Maud said.

Toddy nodded, allowing the pain to flash in her eyes. "Yeh, it's hard, but I don't complain. Plenty of folks don't have a job at all."

"That's true," Maid said. She tried for a gentle smile to put the girl at ease enough to go on, but her body still trembled from the trauma of almost losing her daughter. Maud worried her expression was coming across as a sneer.

"I'm lucky they took me on, what with how clumsy I am. You circus folk are so graceful. I never thought in a hundred years they'd give me a job, but here I am."

Maud scanned the girl's eyes. She seemed sincere and genuinely grateful.

"There are other jobs around the circus, you know," Maud said. "Ones that don't have you smelling this sort of stuff. Those headaches of yours. I've seen them break grown men before. There are other ways to make a living in this life."

Toddy looked down. Her face flushed red from her cheeks to her forehead. Her fingers suddenly fidgeted, intertwining with one another.

"I don't want to do that sort of job. I'd rather the headaches."

There. That was what Maud was looking for. A semblance of reluctance. It sealed the theory that Hank had gotten to her already and offered her a job in the cooch tent. Hank wouldn't force the girl, but if those headaches kept up, suddenly the night shift might sound more appealing. More often than not, that's how it worked. Not forced by physicality, but by desperation and manipulation. It was a snake's way, slithering up to unsuspecting prey.

Toddy didn't want it. That was the deciding factor. Maud couldn't let this go.

"I don't mind hard work, Mrs. Wagner, but I don't want that sort of work."

Maud smiled and lifted up the girl's chin, so she looked her in the face. Toddy was almost Maud's height, and probably had a tiny bit to grow. Those grey eyes of hers were almost level with Maud's dark ones. Trixie wasn't kidding. The girl truly resembled a walking specter of a woman.

"I owe you, honey. You come visit my tent after supper. You know where we set up for tattoos?"

"Yes, ma'am."

"Good. Come and see me. I think I have a way to repay you."

***

Night came on the wings of laughter and lightning bugs. The day-shift made their way to the outlying campfires of their fellow circus workers. They tucked into hot dinners and traded stories from the day while the rubes enjoyed their evening entertainment.

The tale of Lotteva and the lion was the hottest topic on everyone's lips. It was very nearly a disaster, and the menagerie workers discussed ways to avoid such accidents in the future. Small outfits like theirs didn't always think to take into consideration all the dangerous possibilities. The big bosses procured animals anyway they could, from collapsing circuses or shady animal trappers. Only after the fact did they figure out how to house and feed the beasts.

The primary plan was to stake a rope around the cages of the carnivores so patrons couldn't get too close. Others thought separating the carnivores from their grazing food of choice was also in the cards.

The unlikely hero wasn't part of the gathering. The May girl, Toddy, had disappeared. Dozens of circus folk made their way to the menagerie to bid her thanks and pat her on the back. Gus even brought her a painting Lotteva made of Toddy and the lion. The little girl had insisted she have it. Yet, every single person found the back yard devoid of their heroine, so their gifts and praise were put on hold.

Only Maud knew where to find Toddy. After dinner with her family, Maud left her daughter tucked away in their train car. She kissed Lotteva to the point where the little girl begged her to stop.

Gus occasionally enjoyed evening drinking and joking with the other men. His own life was beset with women all day, so some male conversation was welcomed. After the events of the day, he promised to stay inside with Lotteva. He, too, didn't want to let her go.

"Where are you off to?" Gus asked Maud.

"There's a customer waiting in the tent," she replied.

Gus looked at her with skepticism. Though he could never come close to her signature dubious eyebrow, he was expressive enough. A customer this time of night was improbable, and Maud was carrying a flask of whisky on her hip.

"What are you getting yourself into?"

"Nothing to trouble yourself about. It's not a man, if that's what you were thinking. Honestly, Gus Wagner, you flirt with women all day long, and here you are interrogating me."

"I don't flirt. I only tempt ladies into the tent so you might take their money and draw pretty pictures on them," he said with his infamous waxed smile.

"That's still flirting," Maud said.

"We shall agree to be forever at odds on that one, Mrs. Wagner. Besides, I didn't think it was a man. I think it's one of your little projects. You're going to exhaust yourself taking in people the way you do."

There was no point in Maud denying the accusation. Her husband knew her too well. "I have to Gus. Sometimes, they need it. What would've happened to me if Dora hadn't…"

"I know, but when are you going to sleep? You can't wear yourself out, Maudie."

"It will be fine," she said. She decided to just share the truth. "Gus, it's Toddy. The one who saved our girl. I have to do something. I can't just…"

"Mama! Daddy! Look what I found!" Lotteva said, interrupted their moment. She held a small, orange kitten in her arms. The feline appeared to be young, but not so young it needed to suckle a mother. Lotteva cradle the kitten in her arms as though it were a baby, and the creature didn't seem to mind. "I found him outside, under the car. Can I keep him? Please."

Maud and exchanged a look of trepidation. Lotteva was becoming worse than Dora about keeping animals, and there was only so much room in their boxcar. Gus sighed and shook his head.

"Lotteva, we told you no more animals," Gus said. "Not after the skunk you brought home. It took your mother forever to get that smell out of your dress."

Lotteva stuck out her lower lip and began to pout in that pleading way only small children could pull off. The girl was working up some tears to accent her look. "Please, Daddy."

"The answer is no, Lotteva. I mean…"

"She can have it," Maud said.

Gus turned to her surprised. Maud's shoulders were so tight, they were almost to her ears. He regarded his wife as her fingernails dug into her forearms, her mouth pinched around the edges.

"You can have him, baby," Maud said.

"Thanks, Mama! I'll call him Lion!"

Lotteva ran off with the kitten, and Gus gaped at his Maud, waiting for an explanation. Afterall, it was Maud who had put her foot down about the new animal policy. It was usually Gus who softened to Lotteva's every whim.

"I hit her, Gus," Maud said sullenly. "I slapped her so hard."

It might have been a trick of the firelight on Gus's face, but Maud caught a glimpse of the terror from earlier in his eyes. She knew it smacked her over and over again every time she held Lotteva in her arms. Every time she took in her daughter's sweet fragrance, it was accompanied by the memory of how afraid they were. How they'd almost lost her.

Without another word, Gus nodded and waved her away.

"I understand. I'll keep her. Go off to your project, my dear."

***

As Maud made her way to her tattooing tent by lamp light, she found it already lit inside. When she opened the flap, she found Toddy sitting in one of her chairs. The May girl was pouring over the various pieces of paper displaying their flash . They were the generic tattoos they did the most, and it was usually the most popular. Very few people got to signify anything in particular. Sometimes, people just wanted something pretty. Already made designs cost a flat price. Maud could do them in her sleep.

Toddy looked up, seemingly pleased to see Maud.

"You've got quite the crowd out there ready to buy you a drink," Maud said as she let the flap to the tent close behind her.

She could see the girl flush red and avert her eyes.

"You don't much like the attention, do you?" Maud asked.

"It's nice. They're being nice to me. I know that."

"They are, and you deserve it."

"Anyone would've helped your little girl," Toddy said.

"Maybe," Maud said. "But it was you who did."

Toddy fiddled with her hands and returned her gaze to the ground. "Why did you want to talk to me, Mrs. Wagner? I... I told Mr. Wagner earlier I'm not looking for any money or nothing."

"I want to have a talk with you. I think I can help you in a better way than money. Can I sit and talk with you awhile?"

Those big, grey eyes gazed up at Maud with a curious expression. Toddy seemed tense, but she nodded. Maud took a seat in the chair next to her.

"How old are you, Toddy? I mean, if you don't mind me asking."

"I'm seventeen."

Seventeen. Oh Lord, thought Maud, how tender and sensitive was that age. Like a Georgia peach fallen to the ground waiting for anyone and anything to take it. No, she never again wanted to be such a delicate number.

"Did you know I was younger than you when I first joined up with a circus?" Maud asked.

"No ma'am, I didn't."

"Do you like it here? The circus, I mean."

"Yes. It's not like I thought it'd be, but I like seeing things. I never thought I'd see a bear or a camel or nothing like that. But..." Toddy paused, looking around the tent as if to find the words she wanted creeping around in the corner somewhere. She glanced at the ceiling. Maybe the lost words were there, hanging upside down like a bat.

"But the menagerie gives you terrible headaches, doesn't it?" Maud asked.

"Yes ma'am."

"Lots of people get those, you know. They still do circus work."

Watery eyes, suddenly full of emotion, met her own. "I'm not good at nothing else. I slip and stumble with the ropes, I never learned my letters and kept making mistakes at the ticket booth. Everyone kicked me out the first day except the menagerie. Nobody trusts me with the games or nothing. And I can't work the cooch tent. I just can't. Mama and Daddy would turn over in their graves if I did that. The girls are real nice and all to me, but I just can't."

"Hey now. It's okay."

Maud wrapped a steady arm around Toddy and patted her back. She hugged her as far as was possible with one so timid. Any harder, and the fragile girl might break. When the sobbing ebbed, Maud began the pitch she'd prepared.

"Toddy, listen to me. I've got an idea for you. You may be averse to it at first, but don't decide until I've said my piece, okay?"

Toddy stared with huge, swollen eyes at Maud. The girl almost looked like a frightened owl, but she managed to speak. "Okay."

"Have you ever thought about tattoos?" Maud asked.

"What? Tattoos?" One would have thought Maud had fired her pistol into the air. That's how startled the poor girl looked. Toddy even jumped a little in her seat.

"You know my friend Trixie?" Maud asked.

"Yes ma'am. Tricky Trixie," Toddy said through quivering lips. Maud reached out and took her hand.

"Exactly. Well, Trixie is getting a little long in the tooth to keep doing what she does. The dancing and all that. She pays me to cover her in tattoos, so she can keep traveling with the circus. It's a fun life, you know. You can wear anything you want. You can see the country, sometimes even the world. People will come from miles around just to see Tricky Trixie."

"I… I don't understand."

"You can be like her. You can be a tattooed lady. You can travel the world and do nothing but stand on display, and people will pay to see you. You will have independence and not owe anyone a thing. A woman unto yourself."

Maud spoke with the flourish of a saleswoman, making sure her eyes lit up with excitement. She wanted desperately for Toddy to say yes. Maud wanted to help this girl the way Dora helped her. She could save her, but Toddy had to agree.

"Mrs. Wagner, you want to tattoo me?" Toddy asked with a truckload of apprehension.

"I want to offer you a job, honey. If I tattoo your body, you won't have to work the menagerie anymore. No one will ask you to work the cooch tent. You will draw a crowd without ever having to flip, bend, or make change. Speaking first-hand, it's a wonderful life."

"I… I don't know. I mean, I couldn't afford…"

"You saved my girl. She's my main reason for living. I owe you. There's no way I'd accept payment from you."

Toddy looked unsure. She fiddled with her fingers again. "I'm not a stage person, Mrs. Wagner. I don't see how I could get up there in front of everybody the way you do."

Maud took her other hand so she could hold the girl's full attention. It was no good for Toddy to shut down and focus on anything else but the decision. Toddy's hands trembled warm and blistered in her own stained, calloused ones.

"It's an act, Toddy. All of it."

"What's an act?"

"I was plenty scared when I first started. Would you believe that?"

"No ma'am."

"At first, you pretend. All those nerves and quivery feelings, you hide them behind a smile and a sparkly costume. No one is the wiser.

It's like playing a part. You get to be someone else for a while. When the show is over, you can go back to being you. After a while though, something changes."

"What changes?" asked Toddy, visibly beguiled by the cadence of Maud's story.

"You start to become less the old you and more the new you. A new version of you that smiles in front of the crowd in your sparkly costume. More and more, the frightened part fades away, and the brave girl on the stage takes over. You change. You adapt. Eventually, you become the star all the time."

"But what's that got to do with tattoos?"

"A costume is something you take on and off. Tattoos are a costume you wear forever. The ink dresses you better and more permanently than the finest dress money can buy. It gives you a sort of freedom you won't find with anything else. People will pay to stare in wonderment at your skin but never touch you. You can wear just about anything at all because the ink is your clothing. I cover my body even less than my husband, and no one bats an eye at me."

"I don't know. I'm not a flashy girl," Toddy said.

"I know that. You, Toddy the menagerie worker, are a modest girl. But you as a tattooed girl? Well, you could be anything in the world you ever wanted. You could be brave, exotic, or mysterious. All of the above. Invent a person, and I can make you that person. You hide behind her a while, but sooner or later you get to be her."

It was tiny, but it was there, nonetheless. The minute flash in the back of Toddy's eyes. Something sparked in her. This scared teenager didn't have to stay that way. She could be anyone in the world, and that fact intrigued her.

"Will… would it hurt?"

"Not as much as you're thinking. Look at me. I had my husband draw all over me, and I'm still standing. Besides, I wouldn't do it all at once. I'd cover you by degrees as we travel. In fact, by the time season is over, you'll be a new woman."

Maud gently released the young girl's hands and raised her chin a little bit. Toddy's back straightened. Even the idea of being someone else seemed to inject her with a little more nerve.

"All right. I'll accept your offer, Mrs. Wagner."

"Good girl. Now then, do you know what you want me to draw?" Maud reached for her box of tools and ink well. Toddy gaped at her and started twitching in her seat. Her words came out in a squeak.

"We are doing this now?"

"No time like the present. It's gonna be hard for me to do this during business hours."

"But… I… um."

"Listen, I'll start with something small on the back of your shoulder. Something to give you an idea of what this will be like but in a place that is easy to cover. You know, in case you don't want to go through with the whole thing."

Toddy nodded her head and visibly forced down a lump in her throat.

"Okay then. Take off your shirt."

Toddy stood, still wearing the high-waisted boy trousers and baggy shirt from earlier. Involuntarily, she clutched at the buttons when Maud reached out to help her.

"Oh, come now. You and I, we got the same stuff. Nothing I haven't seen every time I look in the mirror, honey."

With the slightest twitch of the eye toward the tent flap, Maud noticed why she was afraid. Not about Maud necessarily, but about someone walking in on them. She smiled at the girl.

"I've got my closed sign up, and no one is going to come stumbling in here. If someone gets drunk and gets curious, well…" Maud reached under her table and dragged out what looked like an ordinary wooden toolbox. When she opened it, there among the hammers and tent stakes, was a small pistol. "Trust me, it's loaded."

Toddy's eyes grew about half the size of her whole face, but she started unbuttoning her shirt. Maud shut the toolbox and slid it back under the table. She bade the girl to sit back down in the chair. Toddy clutched her shirt in front of her to hide her small breasts from the air of the evening. It didn't matter to Maud; all she needed was access to her back.

Maud busied herself around the tent. She doused the needles in alcohol and lined them up on the table away from Toddy. Best to lay them out far from her sightline. Plenty of people got too spooked to go through with it when they saw her instruments, and this girl was easier to spook than most.

Toddy jumped like a jack rabbit in her seat when Maud wiped her shoulder with a rag. It had been covered with dirt and the salt of her daily sweat. No choice but to clean the canvas.

"It's okay. This is just a little water and alcohol to clean the spot. Don't want to poke anything dirty in your skin, okay? It'll get infected."

"Okay," she said with a quivery voice.

"Do you know what you want me to draw?"

"I tried to think of something. I really did, Mrs. Wagner. But I can't think of anything." She gestured toward the flash on the table. "Your pictures here are real nice. Maybe just pick one of those?"

"Those are for rubes. Let's make you special. There's nothing at all you can think of?"

"No, ma'am."

"You want me to choose?"

"Yes, ma'am. You'd pick better than me."

Maud contemplated what to draw. The bit of charcoal in her hand hovered just above Toddy's delicate, young skin. She wouldn't pick anything from her flash; that was certain. Trixie could pull off butterflies and birds well enough being the big personality she was. That woman was a natural with her charisma and comedic charm. But Toddy? No, Toddy would need something more. She needed a larger than life persona to hide behind.

Suddenly, it came to Maud. An idea of something the exact opposite of the skittish girl sitting before her. As soon as she thought it, headlines flashed before her eyes. Circus posters so real she could paint them herself. It was so brilliant a disguise, Maud was almost jealous she hadn't done it for herself.

She touched Toddy's shoulder gently with her left hand. Toddy's back went rigid, and she quavered all over.

"This is just my hand, love. I'm going to sketch out a drawing on you with my chalk, okay? No needles just yet."

"Okay."

Goose flesh broke out over her shoulder as Maud began to draw. As Toddy got used to the chalk, she began to relax. With a deft hand, Maud drew line after line, marking where the drawing would wind here and curve there. Little undulations that would look pretty even if they didn't connect to anything else.

She didn't tell Toddy when she was done drawing. No need to tense the girl before the scary part began. The ink pooled in the saucer her hand made between her thumb and finger. Reaching for her favorite needle, Maud dipped the end into the ink and began to draw.

"That hurts a little," Toddy said after a minute.

"That's because I'm poking you now."

Toddy flinched underneath Maud's hand. "I'm sorry!" Toddy said.

"It's all right. Just try and breathe." Maud attempted to ease the girl's pain by working fast, but Toddy clenched like a tortured soul. "It's not so bad, is it?" Maud asked.

"No. Not as much as I thought," Toddy said through gritted teeth.

Lying was obviously not a talent the girl possessed. "Be honest, child."

"It's like being stung by bees."

Maud stopped for a second and coaxed Toddy to sit up straight. With every poke, Toddy had inched away from her, slowly curling into a ball in the chair. Maud reached for her flask of whisky and handed it to Toddy who opened the cap and sniffed. Her face screwed into a disgusted look.

"Take a good, hard swallow," Maud said.

"But I don't like whisky."

"No, but your skin will thank you for it. Trust me. Go on. Straight down your throat, so you don't taste it as much. As much as you're able."

Toddy pinched her nose and swallowed what she could without retching. Maud began to tell her that pinching her nose would only make it worse but stopped herself. Sometimes, believing a thing helped you cope more than the truth. Toddy began coughing and spitting on the floor of the tattoo tent before handing back the flask to Maud.

"There we go. Now, let's try it again." This time, the needle moved in and out of Toddy's skin without the girl trembling half as much. Maud could feel her flesh warm and relax underneath her hand. Toddy's eyes still pinched together, but she wasn't jumping in her own hide.

"How are you now?" Maud asked.

"Better. My nose is numb, and the poking hurts a tad less."

"Good. This is a fleshy bit here that I'm drawing on. It hurts less than some other places. If you're used to those circus headaches, in no time you'll find that tattooing will be a breeze by comparison." She handed her flask to Toddy once again. "Here, take another swallow."

Toddy did as directed, and her shoulders slumped. Her skin softened once again, and Maud continued her work.

To her credit, Toddy didn't say a word, nor did she flinch again. The tattoo didn't take long. The design was a small one. It was meant to be easily hidden if Toddy hated it, and the whole scheme went to pot. When Maud wiped her shoulder clean, and announced she was finished, Toddy seemed surprised.

"Already? It's done?"

"Yeh, it's all done. You wanna see?"

"Y... yes."

Maud collected two of her mirrors from the drawer inside her table. One she handed to Toddy and one she held behind her. After a second of maneuvering, Toddy was able to view the beautiful dragon Maud had tattooed on her shoulder.

Its serpent-like body undulated from just above her shoulder blade, across her shoulder, and ended just above the crease where her arm met her torso. The creature swirled around itself with a tiny flick of the tail reminiscent of Maud's sparrows.

A memory resurfaced in Maud's mind. It was the moment back at the World's Fair, when she stubbed her cigarette butt out on the flawless sculpture. How horrified she was when she realized what she had done. Nothing should be so pretty. That's what she said even though she hadn't meant to.

Here Toddy stood, a young girl with perfectly beautiful skin, not terribly unlike that statue. Yet again, Maud interrupted flawlessness, but this time it wasn't the hateful smudge of cigarette ash. This time, she wove something divine into it.

Toddy's breath caught in her chest as she stared in the mirror. For a moment, Maud was afraid the girl hated it. Maud had taken extra care to make her dragon delicate and beautiful, but what if this dragon theme had gone too far? A tattoo was a permanent thing. She couldn't take it back.

Slowly, like the deliberate spreading of a raindrop on a leaf, Toddy's mouth rose into a grin. The lissome smile evolved into a deliriously happy one. Those big, grey eyes of her lit up, and she let out the breath she had been holding. Maud, too, found herself exhaling with relief.

"You like it?" Maud asked.

Toddy nodded her head very slowly, seemingly unable to tear her gaze away from the mirror. Her smile was so large now, it crinkled her eyes.

"Why... why a dragon?"

"Do you like it?"

Toddy's eyes sparkled in the lamp light of the tent. "I love it, but what made you pick that?"

"I thought of the bravest, most exotic, most beautiful thing to draw. This can be you, honey. You can be a dragon."

"I can?"

Toddy's words rang out with the same girlish wonder Lotteva used when talking about her animals. Maud placed a warm hand on Toddy's other shoulder.

"Honey, I can make you anything you want."

***

Maud worked extra hard to ease the tension after she slapped Lotteva. The last thing she wanted was for her daughter to be afraid of her. Too many children spent a lifetime like that, afraid of what would happen to them. *Not Lotteva*, she vowed. Not while Maud still breathed.

She doted on her daughter, praising every drawing she made and feeding her as much blue cotton candy as she liked. Dora warned Maud she would turn Lotteva into a terrible child. The wretched kind strangers wanted to whip on her behalf. But her daughter never turned that way, and Maud never minded being criticized for being kind.

Lotteva couldn't go anywhere without Maud fussing over her. She'd smooth her daughter's hair, pull at her dress, and kiss her round face.

It became a game of sorts. How many kisses could Maud get in before Lotteva finally surrendered. The same went for hugs. For whatever reason, physically squeezing her daughter was the only thing that eased Maud's nerves. It was a reminder that she was alive. This wasn't a dream. Her baby girl was all right.

Still, the incident with the lion hung over them both. Every time someone within earshot mentioned the lion, Lotteva would stiffen and look at her mother. It broke Maud's heart to see that glimmer of fear. One day, she hovered over Lotteva, halting her momentarily as she prepared to leave their train car.

"Hold still, love. You've got some hay bits in your hair. Have you been around the menagerie?"

"No! Oh Mama, I promise I didn't go see the lion!"

The shock of Lotteva's response floored Maud. Gus looked just as stunned.

"Honey, I didn't think you did. It's okay," Maud said, kneeling on the ground and holding open her arms for her daughter.

She was more than a little relieved when Lotteva ran to her and snuggled under her neck. Maud surrounded her in a strong embrace. There's an ache in the depths of a mother when her child needs her like that. It never goes away, and whenever it hits, no mother of value can resist the call. Maud didn't relent until her baby let go first.

Finally, the day came when Maud knew the hurt had ended and they could once again be as they were. It was the last afternoon at their current stop, and few patrons had come calling. The crowds were waning as harvest time grew closer. Maud was taking a break in her train car while Gus broke down their tent. The air was hot, so she lounged on some pillows with her skirt bunched up around her thighs to cool herself. She didn't hear the little girl approach until a tiny voice pierced the air.

"Mama?" Lotteva called from the doorway.

"Yes, honey girl. You can come in," Maud said. She beckoned her daughter enter with one hand.

Lotteva moved closer clutching some papers to her chest and looking sheepishly at the floor. She left the boxcar door open to let the air move around the stuffiness of the room.

"Mama, I'm sorry."

"For what?" Maud asked, genuinely confused.

"For the lion. For the day I ran off."

A hard stone moved in Maud's guts as she sat up and regarded her girl. The sorrow in her eyes was enough to break any person's heart.

"Honey, we talked about that..."

"I want to make you a present," Lotteva said, holding out a stack of drawing paper to her mother. The image on the top was a crude sketch of a daisy.

"Well thank you, honey. I love it."

"No, no. I want to make it a tattoo for you. Daddy's been teaching me on animal hide, and I'm getting good. He says I'm real good. I want to make it up to you... for when I scared you."

"You want to give me a tattoo?"

Lotteva nodded. "I wanted to make you a rose like Daddy gives you. Those are pretty, but they're too hard for me. But I can still make you a flower. See?" She pointed at her sketch.

Maud regarded the doodle of the flower and then her daughter's innocent face. Every once in a while, a child will do something wholly unexpected. They are usually small gestures, and not something a person ever sees coming. Such moments change lives and alter perspectives. Nothing is more perfect than that brand of innocent giving. If one is truly lucky, he or she will see this phenomenon over and over again, for it never gets old.

Lotteva's lips pressed together, seemingly afraid of some sort of objection, but there was none coming. Maud smiled at her daughter

131

and helped her to setup the needles and ink. Lotteva's tiny hands moved around clumsily, the way children's do when tackling an adult task, but Lotteva knew the routine well. She even went so far as to add a bit of soap in with the ink solution so it wouldn't bead on the needle.

The only bare bit of skin easily accessible was Maud's outside thigh, just below her hip. After cleaning the area, Lotteva drew her simple daisy on her mother's skin so meticulously, one would have thought she were sketching a landscape.

When the girl took the needle and dipped it in the ink, Maud turned her head away and held her breath. It would hurt surely. Lotteva didn't know about how to measure her pokes so as to minimize pain. Dead hide was one thing, but a living person's skin was another.

However, it wasn't the pain that made her look away; she was going to cry. Maud turned her head to hide her tears from a girl who would misinterpret them. Lotteva would see them as tears of agony. They weren't for that, not at all.

Maud's tears were reserved for something else. Something she'd never be able to explain to Lotteva and make her understand. They were for something that could never happen, for a sentiment never expressed. If only Maud had been able to draw on her own mother, oh how things might have been different.

***

By the end of the season, everyone prepared to go their separate ways. Maud, Gus and Lotteva would depart to their winter home over the storefront in St. Louis. Some camped together in areas with dime museums or warm spots that held fairs all year round. Others rooted themselves in bigger cities where winter work was easily found. Many stuck together, traveling with the same circus every year. Dora and the Wagner's preferred the freelance style of working. As long as they paid their share, they moved from show to show as they liked without hassle.

There was always a party on the last night together before everyone parted ways. Alcohol flowed and music filled the air. Everyone ate like it was Christmas, stuffing themselves with meat and sweet bread until they groaned with the pain of it. Even Gus managed to fill all four of his stomachs.

Maud and Trixie sat by the fire, laughing at Gus trying to dance with Lotteva. He had never been a man of rhythm, but who needed it with such a charming partner? At one point, he gave up and lifted her in the air. Lotteva squealed as Gus swung her this way and that on his hips.

The firelight bounced and flickered, as if trying to dance itself. Maud breathed in the tranquil woody smell of the fire as it illuminated the various types of wings covering Trixie's skin. After months of sitting for Maud, she was indeed ready to fly.

Appearing from the darkness was an unknown figure. The moment before, there had been no one at all, and then, there she was. People gawked as she strode into the warm light of the party with the confidence of royalty. She was a lovely girl, wearing a green dress with sleeves that fell below her shoulders. Her hair was pulled up prettily into a loose knot on her head. The slightest hint of liner accentuated her large, grey eyes. Not much else was needed in the way of makeup.

Across her chest, around her back, and down her arms flew a company of dragons. Beautiful drawings of every kind of dragon one could imagine covered her delicate skin. She had worn long sleeves and pants to cover them up all season, even when the sun made her sweat underneath all her layers. Now, she could breathe properly. Now, everything was on display. How glorious they looked now that they were free.

Someone in the back whistled. The old version of Toddy might have blushed and averted her gaze, but this woman smiled grandly. She bowed to the silent crowd like royalty, making everyone laugh.

"Well, I'll be damned," Trixie said.

"Yes, indeed," Maud said.

She knew full well that beneath the long skirt of Toddy's dress lay even more dragons etched with love along her thin legs. The girl Toddy, who had been so awkward she was only good for shoveling manure, was gone from the earth. On that day, The Dragon Lady was born from her ashes.

Part Five

1924

Jazz filled the air with the ecstatic din of its nature. It roared through the thoughts of everyone as the crowd grew feverish with drink. The twenties brought with it a sense of gaiety and invincibility.

Gone were corsets and modesty. Everything was in excess. One would never guess with all the ruckus at the *Ringling Brothers Circus* that prohibition was in full swing. Maybe beer wasn't sold out in the open, but plenty of it was drunk. In fact, Maud Wagner would wager there were more drunk folks now than before the Volstead Act. Illicit behavior seemed somehow all right when done en masse.

Business was good. When the corsets came off, so did the fear of tattoos. All of the ladies, even those in high society, began to consider them chic. It was like Gus always told her about the Victorian women. Prim and polished until suddenly a small hole appeared in proper society. A hole big enough to allow them to wiggle an arm or a leg through. That's all a tattooist needed really. One free bit of flesh.

People were coming by the tents in waves. Gus had purchased a second tent just to accommodate the number of customers, and with the three Wagner's tattooing in shifts, there was rarely an empty seat.

Luckily, there was a lull during the noontime meal, giving Maud a much-needed break. She rearranged the flash on her table after a

135

whirlwind of a morning scattered pictures everywhere. There was a commotion behind her, and she spotted Gus exiting his tent with a customer. She was a pretty thing, and Maud scowled at them as Gus wrapped the fresh tattoo on her wrist.

"Now, remember, keep it clean. And no sunbathing," he said with a flirty grin.

The girl giggled, and Maud snorted. When they turned to look at her, Maud glared at Gus and the giddy thing in braids. Gus stood unphased by her scowl, but the girl hurried away clutching her bandaged wrist to her chest.

"Oh, you know that was nothing," Gus said as Maud stomped toward him. "It's not what you think."

"You and your flirting. I swear. Even if you don't mean it, they don't know that. You keep talking lovey to these farm girl idiots, and you'll have some angry beaus or fathers on our front door. How would you feel is someone talked like that about Lotteva?"

"I do love when you get testy," Gus said while planting a kiss on her cheek. "But that wasn't a farm girl. It was Emily from the cookhouse."

"*That's* Emily? Jesus, Gus, she can't be more than eighteen. How could you?" Maud said. Her stomach started to drop down into her shoes. "I know being flirty is part of the business, but she's a child..."

"I'm telling you it's not what you think. She was giggling about something else. I would never... here look," Gus said as he ducked into his tent. He reappeared a second later holding a paper box. "She was helping me with this. It was a trade. She'd make this for me, and I'd draw her a silly butterfly. Go on, see for yourself."

Maud removed the top and peered inside. There, nestled among clouds of tissue paper, was woven garland of roses. No, not a garland. More of a crown. The roses had been cleaned of thorns and preserved with oils. Maroon and black ribbons laced around the stems ending in a knot that cascaded down the back.

"Oh, Gus. It's so pretty."

"I thought you could wear it around the fair. Emily said it will last a few months if we keep it dry."

"She was laughing like that because…"

"Because she knew this was supposed to be a surprise for you. The poor thing gets way too excited about secrets," Gus said.

He removed it from the box and placed it on her head, taking care not to mess her hair. When it was positioned properly, he nodded to her as though it were her cue to move. Maud retrieved the hand mirror from under the flash and looked at her reflection. It was stunning.

"Oh, thank you. Will you forgive me for being so cranky? I'm just bone tired. The days have been so long. That reminds me. Where is Lotteva? She was supposed to come here and relieve us for lunch."

They looked up and down the main thoroughfare, but saw no sign of their precocious, teenage daughter.

"I think she was helping with the curiosities tent. The mermaid needs some repairs," Gus said.

"That shouldn't have taken this long. I'm going to go look."

Maud settled her crown, kissed her husband on the cheek, and stepped into the current of people making their way to the cookhouse. The freaks and curiosities tents were not far from where they setup camp. There had been times in the past when she and Gus posed on those stages for all the world to ogle. It was extra money when tattooing business was slow.

Of course, they hadn't need of the extra money in the last year though. Tattooing the masses had taken up all of their time and energy, but their relationships with the freakshow performers persisted. Therefore, if a mermaid needed some touch ups, the Wagner's were there to help.

Maud turned a corner away from the hungry rubes and spotted Lotteva behind the curiosities tent. Maud's color went red all over.

Her daughter wasn't fixing a mermaid statue. She was drinking with the Gunderson twins. They passed a pewter flask back and forth and laughed like conspirators. Maud glared at her daughter as she tossed her hair over one shoulder with a flirty flip and stole the flask from one of the boys.

The twins spotted Maud before Lotteva did. The sheer terror in their faces would have been comical if she wasn't so angry. Maud didn't remember telling her body to walk forward. She merely blinked, and somehow the distance had been closed.

"Lotteva Wagner, what are you doing?" Maud raged.

Lotteva whipped around in surprise, dropping the flask in the process. Maud picked it up and sniffed the cap.

"Gin. Cheap gin at that," Maud said angrily. She turned to the Gunderson twins who were stupefied under her glare. They were about two years older than Lotteva. Blond and handsome; trouble in duplicate. "I suspect this came from your older brother's bathtub. Take it back to him and keep it away from my daughter. Hear me?"

The twins nodded vehemently and dashed away, yelling behind them, "Yes, Mrs. Wagner. We promise!" as they left.

"And tell your father that Gus will be having words with him!" Maud called back, but they were already too far away. The boys were a part of an aerialist family, and they moved through the crowds with the speed and agility of someone with those skills.

"Mama, it's not that big of a deal. You and Daddy let me have wine and beer," Lotteva said tartly. She folded her arms over her chest in frustration.

"That's not the point. I don't want you drinking with those boys. Trapeze boys are nothing but trouble. I could tell you some stories," Maud said.

"I'm not stupid. I only flirt with them to nip their brother's booze."

"That's a dangerous game, Lotteva," Maud warned. "No more. I mean it. The most dangerous threat to a young girl is the combination of men and booze."

"Really?" Lotteva laughed. "Mama, you're overreacting. We've known the Gunderson boys since they were twelve."

Maud took a deep breath. A steady dread had been building in her chest since she saw Lotteva with the boys. It was anger, yes, but it was deep-rooted fear as well. Lotteva was about the age Maud had been when she ran away. Oh, was there a more delicate creature than a teenage girl? The world expected adult things and gave no protection. So many preyed on them, and it was so easy to break their tender hearts.

However, when Lotteva mentioned how long they'd known the twins, it snapped Maud back to reality a little. It was true. The Wagner's and Gunderson's had known each other for years. Despite their mischief, they weren't bad boys. And Lotteva was not a naïve girl. Maud breathed through some of her anger and faced off with her daughter again.

"You're right. You are smarter than that. Just be careful and don't lead them on. Those two aren't the brightest, and it's not fair. *And* I don't want you sneaking gin when you are meant to be working," Maud said. She pointed a finger in the girl's face. "Now, did you finish the mermaid?"

Lotteva's eyes grew wider, and she shuffled her feet in the grass. With little thought to hide her theatrical nature, she turned her attention to the crown on Maud's head.

"Oh Mama, isn't that pretty! I heard Daddy talkin' about getting Emily to make it..."

"Lotteva Wagner, did you finish the mermaid?" Maud asked in a voice meant to cut through her daughter's bullshit.

"No," Lotteva said, slumping her shoulders. "It's gross, Mama. All crusty."

"You work with animals all the time! You shovel their manure. I watched you feed a live mouse to Dora's damn snake!"

"Yeah, that's all *alive* stuff. Natural. Whatever they dried out and used for the mermaid is... well... just wrong feeling," Lotteva said while making a show of shivering up to her neck.

"You have to be kidding me. You mean to tell me you've been gone this whole time, drinking with those boys instead of doing the work you were supposed to do?"

It was one of those questions parents asked when they didn't really need an answer. Every parent asked them, nonetheless. It was more like a statement one might scribe on a ledger. A verbal note of the misdeed for all to hear.

When she was really angry with her daughter, Maud liked to think somewhere an angel wrote down everyone one of these statements in a book of Lotteva's life, so that each one might be read back to her before granted entrance to an afterlife.

"Yes, Mama. I'm sorry."

Maud gritted her teeth and pictured that angel above her daughter writing everything down right then. It made her smile and gave her the extra patience she needed. With much effort, she softened her face and said, "Go back to your father and man the tent. Tattoo only as many as you can handle alone. None unsupervised in the tent. Daddy needs a break to eat and so do I."

"Okay, Mama!" Lotteva said with much excitement. She kissed Maud on the cheek and disappeared into the crowd.

Maud knew this was a favorable outcome for Lotteva. The girl loved tattooing as much as she loved animals. She was good too. A few more years and she would surpass Maud with the birds. Lotteva drew in the rubes. The pretty, young girl hand-poking tattoos. They got every moony-eyed boy in the county when she was in the chair. Of course, Gus wouldn't allow them in a tent unchaperoned. She either tattooed in the open or under her father's careful watch.

If she were a good mother, she would have been stricter. Not a beating. No. She'd never strike Lotteva. The incident with the lion was the last time. However, she knew she should have made her stay and fix the mermaid. It was Lotteva's task to do, and she'd shirked it.

Maud just couldn't gather the strength to be strict. It would have taken an exhausting amount of effort to police the girl. Sending her away was easier, and Maud was tired. She resolved herself to trudge to the side entrance of the curiosities tent and duck inside. There was a Fiji mermaid in need of repair.

***

The group of chattering girls approached the Wagner's tents in a clump of glitter and baubles. All wore very expensive dresses with real pearls that dangled below their breasts. Iridescent bangles dropped from their ear lobes and flashed on their rings. They were far too well-dressed for a trip to the circus.

The one in the middle appeared to be the leader. She stood inches taller than the others with blond hair cut short and wavy against her head. Her earrings alone cost more than Lotteva's whole wardrobe. She wore a smile that was flirtatiously dangerous. A cat sizing up a canary. Maud glared at her.

"Hello, ladies!" Gus said, ever the showman and breaker of tension. "Are any of you interested in a tattoo?"

The blond one didn't take her eyes from Maud, seemingly amused by the older woman's scornful glare. One of her cohorts giggled and took a pull from a delicate, silver flask out in front of everyone. Another chastised her in mock horror and bade her to put it away. All the muttering and chirping sent the rest into a frenzy of laughter. They reminded Maud of a brood of chickens.

"How do we know we won't get some kind of circus disease from your needles?" asked one girl.

"My lady, I promise you all of your instruments are cleaned thoroughly with alcohol. We take all precautions," Gus said, his charming persona unwavering on his face.

"Alcohol? That's the last thing was need!"

There was more laughter as another flask was produced and passed around. All took a swig, except the blond one. She was still eyeing Mrs. Wagner.

On the surface, it looked like bemusement, but Maud sensed the girl was sizing her up. She definitely didn't like the blond. A good amount of malice silently danced in the space between them. The two women were locked in a kind of staring stalemate.

"Our tattoos are completely safe. I guarantee it!" Gus said. "In fact, we are running a special for a limited time only. Buy one tattoo get the second free."

Maud suppressed a smile. That was Gus. He was so good at charming people, much better than she. Now, the girl wouldn't back down in front of the others. She would lose her Alpha status if she declined. When Gus quoted them a price twice as high as usual, Maud couldn't contain her grin any longer.

"I'll do it if Lana's game," said the mean blond.

"I'm game, Ester. Let's do it."

The brood giggled and one hooted like a sailor. Lotteva collected their money.

"Ladies, choose your executioner," Gus said, waving his hands in front of the two tents.

Ester took a tiny flask from her purse and pulled a long swig. The other girls looked appropriately impressed. After she replaced the flask, she leveled a glare at Maud again. A deeply carved grin cut itself into her face.

"I choose the one with the roses."

***

The blond looked around Maud's tent, taking in everything. Maud had decorated it more and more over the years. Scarves were draped here and there, and a few sparkly bobbles and trinkets made the tent look more exotic, while still being easy to pack and move.

Maud sat in her chair behind the table and straightened her crown of roses. One by one, she placed her needles on a towel in front of the girl, dousing them in alcohol. Then, she brought out the well of premixed ink.

Normally, Maud would've waited until the customer was facing away from her to clean the needles. Sometimes, when there was a long line, she did it in between tattoos. People often lost their nerve when presented with the implements themselves. But with this girl, Maud made a show of cleaning each and every needle. Why not scare the spoiled brat?

Ester just grinned at her as if noting the dare. If she felt any apprehension, her face didn't show it. The girl merely flipped through the flash on the table absentmindedly.

"Have you thought about what you want?" Maud asked.

"These are a little boring. What if I want something else?" Ester clicked her tongue as though she were completely unimpressed.

"Custom is more expensive," Maid said with an unwavering gaze.

"I'm pretty sure your man out front overcharged us."

Maud smiled up at the girl, noting her keen eye. "Why on earth would he do such a thing?"

"Because you think we're rich and stupid."

Maud arched her famous eyebrow. "Well, aren't you?"

"You got some nerve, lady, talking to me like that. If I wanted to, I could..."

"You could what? Tell everyone you think the tattoo circus people charged you too much? Honey, I don't care who you think you are. I don't really care what you do. We work for ourselves and answer to no one."

Maud crossed her arms and watched Ester take a defiant stance across from her. Only a small table separated the two women. Ester leaned forward menacingly and placed her hands on the table. Maud was still sitting in her chair, and Ester starred down at her with all the malice of a bully itching to put someone in her place.

"What if I walk out that door and get a refund? You won't get any money then," Ester said.

"That's not the question at hand," Maud said, completely unmoved by Ester's theatrics.

Ester leaned over the table; her eyes lit with the impending quarrel. It was obvious this was like fuel for her. Gasoline on a fire she had no intention of dousing. "Oh really? And what is the question at hand?"

Maud stood and looked the girl in the eyes. If pressed, Maud couldn't tell why this brat rubbed her the wrong way. Something about her very being was abrasive. Ester had the air of someone who wanted a good fight. Normally, Maud wasn't so inclined, but this girl's attitude set her blood aflame.

"The question *at hand* is whether or not I'm going to agree to do your tattoo at all. My business, my rules. If you're a spoiled little shit, and I don't like you, you can turn around right now and walk out of that door."

Ester flinched a touch. Maud figured she was used to being able to lord money over working-class folks like her. The thing was Maud and Gus had already tattooed more than their quota for the season, and it was only June. She could easily walk out, retrieve the money, and throw this girl's coins back in her face. A large part of her wanted to do just that.

"But you wouldn't get your payment, and I saw the frock that girl of yours was wearing. Seems to me you need my money."

Maud slapped her face before either of them knew what had happened. Ester's menacing grin was gone, replaced by an **O** of shock. She held her hand over her now reddening cheek. Maud tried hard to compose herself. She hadn't expected such a surge of anger, but she also hadn't counted on Lotteva being a target. The blond had cut her quick and sharply.

"Get out," Maud said in a low voice.

The menace was real, and Ester's nostrils flared when she heard it. The top girl of the brood looked visibly shaken and small. No longer a predator, not in this tent.

"You... you slapped me," Ester said in disbelief.

Maud stood stoic before the girl. Her words came out in a growl. "Get out."

"But, you... can't... do that," Ester said.

"I just did."

"I paid you for a tattoo, and..."

"My tent, my rules. You are evicted. Now, move on out. You're taking up space a real customer should occupy," Maud said.

The malice in her booming voice surprised even herself, but she decided to lean into it. Maud stood up taller making Ester shrink a touch by comparison.

"I can't just *leave*. They are all expecting me to go through with this," Ester said, sounding whiny and mercurial.

Ester balled up her fists at her sides. Rage overtook the shock and frustration. Maud thought the girl's hair might catch fire with how hot her head was getting. This was a different fire altogether.

"You will tattoo me. We had a deal."

"You don't get told no very often, do you? In fact, I bet you are pretty damn used to getting your way most of the time."

"My father will..."

"Your father will be overwrought with anger when he learns his little angel was trying to get a tattoo from a bunch of dirty, circus folks."

At that, every muscle tensed on Ester's body. The girl positively shook with rage. Then, something rolled over her like a sudden wave. She loosened her grip and unclenched her jaw. Maud watched her shake off the anger and soften her gaze. The next words were ones of perfect diplomacy. She even tried for an amiable smile.

"What do I need to do to change your mind?"

Maud had to hand it to her. Ester was accomplished with masks. Maud leaned back in her chair, crossing her arms over her chest. Now in her forties, she had years of experience reading people and offered no apologies for her insights. Something in the girl's gaze whispered more to her story. A pure, spoiled brat would've probably stormed out by now. She would have given some palatable excuse to her friends and been done with the whole thing.

"You owe me an apology for insulting my daughter."

Ester stood a little straighter. It looked as though the idea of prostrating herself wasn't sitting well. Of course, Maud had no doubt she'd try to look as defiant as possible while doing so. Ester jutted out her chin and hardened her features.

"I'm sorry for insulting your daughter. Now, will you give me a tattoo like we agreed?"

Maud took a while contemplating. It was a little too much fun holding this smug child in the palm of her hand, but in the end, she relented. A few more minutes of silence, and Maud would seem just as cruel as Ester.

"All right." She gestured at the seat, and Ester tentatively walked around the table and sat.

"Now, what is it that you want? Birds or butterflies? Maybe a heart with the name of your boyfriend?"

"No, none of that," Ester said, waving off Maud's suggestions as though they were far too small for her liking.

"Then what?"

"Can you do me something pretty like that Egyptian princess in the newspapers?"

It was Maud's turn to be humbled. Ester knew more than she gave her credit. Explorers had recently unearthed a two-thousand-year-old mummy of an Egyptian Priestess named Amunet. Even though the Wagner's travelled the country, it was hard to miss the news in the papers.

The discovery was especially interesting because she had tattoos on her body. Lines, circles, and little dots and dashes. Maud and Gus had entertained a slew of customers wanting something dainty "like that Egyptian princess," but Maud would have never pegged Ester for one of them. They usually ran in the older, more intellectual circles and would never consider carrying a flask in public.

"Can you do it or not?"

"Yes. Amunet. We've been getting some requests for tattoos like hers. Normally, it's for a line or some dashes around an ankle. Something small and not easily noticeable."

"That's not exactly what I was thinking." Ester removed her gold bracelets and put her hand out to Maud. She pointed at the top part of her wrist just above where her hand met the joint.

"I want it here. A scarab. I've seen them in pictures."

Maud leveled her gaze on Ester. "That's not going to be easy to cover up."

"I don't want it covered."

There was an intensity in those words. Something more than flimsy and whimsy. Ester's eyes were resolute and defiant. Maud again raised her skeptical brow.

"What? Can't you do it? Do you even know what a scarab looks like?" Ester asked.

"Yes, I know what a scarab looks like," Maud said. She'd had about as much as she could handle of this girl's patronizing tone. "You sure about this?"

"I couldn't be surer."

Maud searched for some hint of reluctance in the girl's face and found none. "All right then. Move that chair to the other side of the table. It'll be easier to draw that way. Let's get this show popping."

Ester did as she was told. Maud cleared a spot by pushing the various pictures of flash off to the side. Once they were settled, Maud pulled out a sharpened bit of graphite and wiped Ester's wrist with alcohol. She started sketching out a perfect scarab beetle.

"Not bad. Who taught you to do this?" asked Ester.

Maud waited for a smart remark or perhaps a mocking laugh, but when she looked at her customer, there was only curiosity. "My husband."

"Your husband taught you? I gotta say, you are the first woman I've seen tattooing people."

Ester's tone was unreadable. A part of Maud wanted to relax and connect with her, but Ester had a snake's tongue. In the end, she decided to take the girl's words at face value and answer in kind. "I'm the first I ever saw too, but I guarantee you, I won't be the last."

The drawing was done, and Maud blew away the excess graphite. Now only the shadow of her drawing remained, but it was enough. The gentle woodiness of the graphite was overwhelmed by the sudden smack of ink and alcohol piercing the air. She put a bit of ink in the hollow of her hand and reached for a needle. Ester tensed almost imperceptibly.

"Does it hurt?" Ester asked.

"Are you worried?"

Ester looked Maud up and down. "I suppose it can't be too bad if you did it so many times."

It was hard to tell if this was sarcastic or meant as a compliment. Perhaps Ester, herself, didn't even know. Maybe sarcasm was second nature to her. Maybe having a real conversation was difficult without throwing up masks. Either way, Maud ignored the comment and started poking along the design. Ester winced quite a bit in the beginning, but soon got used to the sensation and relaxed into the rhythm of it. The pain was always worse around the bone where less flesh cushioned the nerves. The girl occasionally looked away or gritted her teeth, but she tried hard not to show if any of it hurt.

"Is it nice? Getting to wear clothes like that, I mean," Esther asked. "My father would skin me alive."

Maud looked down at her clothes. It was hot in June, so she was in her thigh-hugging shorts accented with black lace. Her top was little more than a shawl tied around her bosom in a strapless way that best accentuated her tattoos. She had been dressing this way for so long, Maud forgot how odd it was to other people.

"My father isn't around to disapprove," she said with a chuckle.

"A friend of mine went to Atlantic City and got arrested because her bathing suit was too short. Hers wasn't nearly as short as that."

"I'm not much of a swimmer," Maud said.

"Still... people gotta say something, right?"

Ester suddenly seemed genuinely transfixed by Maud and her attire. The questions appeared to be merely questions, and not some setup to insult. Maud decided to answer her query at face value.

"Nobody much cares what a tattoo lady wears. The ink is clothing. Besides, if I cover it up, no one will see the beautiful work we do."

"You mean the beautiful work your husband does," Ester said.

"And what I do."

"You said he taught you."

"And someone taught him, and someone taught that person. Doesn't make the student any less of an artist. Our daughter Lotteva is already surpassing me on banners and words. Her flower tattoos are just amazing. She's probably the one working on your friend."

Ester twitched suddenly with a bit of shock and pain. Luckily, the movement didn't mess the line Maud was attempting to draw.

"Don't move like that. You'll end up with a crooked beetle."

"You are teaching her to tattoo?" Ester sounded amazed.

"Yes. We have been since she was a child. Tread carefully before continuing to talk about her. I am a woman with a needle after all." Maud offered the tiniest hint of a smirk.

"You let her…" Ester began but was quickly cut short.

"There's no *letting* Lotteva do much of anything. The girl is a free spirit."

Of course, that was what Maud loved about her daughter, but it also made her fearful. She would never want to cage that bird, but it could be so frightening when it flew so high.

"But, is she tattooed? Did you do it?" Ester asked. Genuine wonder spread across her face. It softened the girl's hard edges and made her appear younger.

"No, she isn't. I won't let her," Maud said with a stiff resolve in her voice.

"Why not? I thought there was no *letting* her do anything."

"I don't think that's any of your business," Maud said, shutting her down.

Quiet settled into the tent, which suited Maud just fine. Who could get any work done with all the gabbing Ester did? Not to mention, her interest in Lotteva, which made Maud nervous.

The scarab was looking lovely. One of the finer ones Maud had done. She'd never admit it to Ester, but she hoped Gus would get a quick glance at it before she had to bandage it up. There was not much better in the world than seeing Gus smile in admiration of her work.

A gentle breeze rustled the tent, bringing with it the scent of cotton candy. Some folks still called it Fairy Floss. Either way, the air it infected smelled warm and sugary. A general sense of happiness always draped Maud when she smelled cotton candy. Perhaps it was because the smelled signaled they were on the road among friends. It also reminded her of her very first day at the circus.

"Why must everything here smell of food?" Ester asked.

She sounded irritated and wanting at the same time. The wrist Maud was holding suddenly looked a little thinner. Ester, the sturdy girl with the sharp mouth, seemed to shrink a touch. How loose her frock hung on her now. What size was it after all? Lotteva was no horse of a girl, but Maud took in some visual measurements and decided her daughter would never manage to fit into the dress that bagged on the girl before her.

"You get used to it," Maud said.

"But really, how do you stand it?"

"Stand what?"

"The moving around. The smell of food and hearing loud crowds all the time. It would drive me mad to never have a quiet moment," Ester said. She slumped under her bothersome dress as though the air was getting heavier.

"It's not so bad. I like seeing new places. The food is better at the circus than most places I've seen, and most of the time the crowds are not too bad."

"When I was outside, they seemed stifling." Ester crinkled her nose as though she smelled something putrid. Her eyebrows pinched together like had a headache.

"Well, that's because it's the *Ringling Brothers Circus*. Biggest one around. Lots of busy towns. Lots of hustle and bustle. Not my cup of tea really. I prefer the smaller shows where we don't get lost in the crowd."

"Then why join up with the large ones?"

"My family loves them."

A pregnant pause sat between them. Maud was working hard on making the scarab look beautiful now. In the beginning, it was to spite the spoiled girl. A game of wills. Now? Well, she kind of wanted it to look great for the other girl who might be hidden inside. The frail one revealing herself in the baggy dress.

Maud knew as soon as the girl left her tent, whatever glimpses she got of the real Ester would get buried right away. The ones with the heaviest masks tended to be the ones who held them up the longest.

"It's nice your husband is so good to you and your daughter."

"Well, he's a caring fellow. Smiles so I don't have to. I'm not much for them if you hadn't noticed."

"I mean, you can wear anything you want. Lotteva gets to be a free spirit and all that. I didn't figure men like that existed outside fairytale books."

Had anyone else heard this, they might mistake it for a veiled threat on Maud's husband. Perhaps she wanted him for herself. Even though Gus Wagner was aging, he was holding up quite well. Only a handful of grey hairs showed at his temples, and his smile was just as bright as always.

The heavy honeymoon period had quickly turned into a loving couple. Now, they were dear companions. Life was content and sturdy. Maud loved to think back at their romantic years with fondness. However, now, she'd take stability over passion any day. Even so, Gus still flirted with the pretty girls, and they blossomed in his sunlight. Had Ester fallen under his spell, or was she trying to dig at Maud in some way?

Suddenly, there was a flash on her face that told a different story.

A bit of black melancholy in the shadows of her eyes. Dark glimpses of holes in one's soul. Ester looked away, past Maud, and toward something else in the distance. The needle made no difference to her anymore. She was miles from that tent, looking at someone else.

"So, it's just you and your dad? Or is there a mom who will be angry at me for this beetle?" Maud asked.

"Just us two. Daddy is an investment something or other. He deals with money. Banker. Big muckity muck." Maud watched as Ester tensed up and tightened her jaw.

"I see," Maid said.

"It's a very stressful job," Ester said. The girl began to dig her nails into her leg.

"I'm sure that's so."

"He's *very* important."

Maud nodded. It sounded like something someone told Ester over and over again. Perhaps an excuse for something. Judging by the far-away stare of the teenage girl, it was probably something more than missing a birthday party or chastising her choice of friends.

Ester was still looking off into the distance when she began nervously fingering the pearl earrings dangling from her earlobes. Up close, they looked even more expensive than Maud originally thought. The girl played with them aimlessly, and Maud wondered what wrong they were intended to put right.

The girl's distant ponderings made her lazy physically. Her arm was succumbing to gravity and lolling over the side of the table. Maud struggled to hold her hand still so she might work on a stable surface. In order to right the situation, Maud grabbed the girl's elbow, lifted her sleeve as to not catch it on anything, and placed it back in the right spot.

Ester flinched and jerked her hand away. Maud didn't understand why at first. But then, she spotted the dark purple bruises on the girl's arm. Oblong, angry bruises—most likely made by rough fingers. Without an explanation, Ester pulled down her sleeve and extended the tattooed arm back to Maud.

"It's not what you think," she said after a long pause.

Maud continued poking without a word. More than anything else, she felt sorry for the girl, but saying so would be a grave insult. "I don't think anything," Maud said.

"He's sorry when he does it. It's the booze. It's only when..."

"Your father?"

"Yes, but he's hurting. He misses my mother."

"Does he touch you too?" asked Maud without looking up.

"How did you know?"

Ester had bruises, masks, and severe weight loss. She was covered head to toe in apology presents. The connection was not a hard one to make.

"I had an uncle who did the same thing to me."

"It was a rape? He raped you?" Ester asked as though the label was important.

"Not in the sense of the word. I didn't know much about those sorts of things, having grown up with god-fearing people. Whatever you call it, it was wrong, and it made me feel worthless and ashamed. I started bracing a chair against my bedroom doorknob before I went to bed. That worked for a time, but..."

"But he figured out how to knock it over by sticking a broom under the door," Ester said, supplying her own answer to finish Maud's sentence.

Maud paused before she set to finish her story. Ester's scarab was finished so she wiped it with alcohol. She decided to keep it unbandaged for the time being.

"He got bolder and bolder. Trying to pull me into the tall wheat fields when he was supposed to be fetching something. Fumbling for my skirts as I ran away. I tried to tell my mama, but I didn't have the right words to explain what was happening, and she shut me down before I could find them. Daddy didn't help either. I knew it was only a matter of time before he did something far worse to me."

"It doesn't take them long," Ester said, now looking for all intents and purposes like a child in a woman's dress. "And no one listens even if you try to tell them. What did you do?"

"I ran away with the circus," Maud said with a wide grin.

The tension broke just a little. Ester chuckled, and Maud laughed with her to ease the heavy air they were choking on together. "I wish I could do that."

"I'm afraid you might be little too refined for the circus," Maud said.

"Yeah. Yeah, I know."

"Well, this ought to get his blood boiling. A little revenge," Maud said while gesturing to the perfect scarab on Ester's tiny wrist.

The girl stared at it in wonderment. Her eyes filled with just enough water to be moving but not enough to gather into tears. Slowly, her look turned from admiration to vindictive malice. Maud figured a million angry words were moving through her at that moment. A million words the tattoo said for her.

"Yes. This outta do the trick." When she looked up at Maud, her face was not a little girl's anymore. It was the pristine face of a rich girl hell bent on putting someone in their place. Only this time, it wasn't Maud on her target list.

"Thank you. It's lovely."

"You're welcome, Ester."

She made to leave, but Maud caught her other wrist in a motion so quick, it frightened Ester and her mask faltered. Maud made sure she had the girl's attention before she spoke because every word of what she planned to say needed to take root in the girl's brain.

"You don't owe him a thing, girl. No matter how many expensive gifts, no matter what he says, no matter how it makes you feel. He has no right. Get away from him."

Ester, wide-eyed, simply nodded. Maud let go of her wrist. There was nothing else to say. Nothing more could be said.

When Ester returned to her friends, she transformed back into the rich, society girl she was before. The girls laughed and made a fuss over her beautiful tattoo as she lifted the bandage to show it to them. Lana displayed the tiny butterfly she'd gotten on her ankle, but it was Ester's scarab that won all the attention. She modeled it and basked in the praise. How bold she was to get it on her wrist. How beautiful and unique a design. Her father would simply flip.

Just before the brood departed, Ester turned and met Maud's eyes. She bowed so slightly no one would notice if not watching carefully. Maud nodded back to her. Two women had walked into the tattoo tent enemies and walked out the most unlikely of friends.

***

Later that evening, Maud found herself eating alone in the cookhouse. As the light faded, so did the ability to tattoo, so they had closed up shop for the night. Maud was exhausted from the day but needed a hot meal. Gus opted to eat some roasted peanuts and retire to bed. It was a strange evening when Gus Wagner declined a gathering.

"Are you feeling all right?" Maud asked.

"Yes, my love. Just need to rest."

"It has nothing to do with those pretty girls we saw today? You aren't on your way to meet one, are you?"

The jab was only half-hearted, even though recounting her story with her uncle had left her underbelly exposed and tender. Gus was her companion, her anchor. Yet, she felt the need for him to hold her. Maud wanted him to tell her he loved her. She knew it, but wanted it said so the air around her might know it as well.

"You know, I don't even recall their names. I just remember the pretty beetle you drew," Gus said.

He held his wife and placed a tender kiss on her forehead. Maud pressed her face into his chest and breathed in his scent of sweet hay, sweat, and sunshine.

"Are *you* all right?" he asked.

"Yes. Just a strange day. You sure you don't want to join me for dinner?"

"I'm so tired. Just thinking about hoofing it there makes all of my stomachs turn. Like I maybe I shouldn't be there or something."

That left Maud sitting at one of the long tables alone, sulking a bit in her soup and cornbread. Rows and rows of bench seats were empty around her. The patrons were wary of sitting too close to the tattooed woman. Nothing new to her. It was the way of things in the circus. Invisible lines were drawn between performers and the rubes.

She couldn't stop thinking about the spoiled girl. At least, she had seemed spoiled at first, but that impression changed with a few words and a tattoo. How had she read her so wrong in the beginning?

Ester had been, in fact, a fantastic liar. Was it a mere act of vanity to hide the truth? Did she play the princess to win the admiration and respect she never got at home? What would her father do to her behind closed doors when he saw what Maud had drawn on her wrist?

That idea made Maud shiver. When she remembered how she'd slapped Ester for mocking Lotteva's dress, she felt sudden shame. Maud drank a sip of water to wash the bad taste from her mouth.

A clanging of metal and the thud of a body shocked her back to the here and now. Maud jumped a little in her seat. When she looked up, Dora was sitting across from her. She had thrown her satchel on the table next to them and heaved herself onto the bench across from Maud in the most unlady-like fashion. Still clad in her maroon

157

costume and headdress, Dora made a show of how tired she was.

"Hey there, toots. A bit jumpy, are we? I'm about as done as a goose on Christmas."

She reached unceremoniously across the table and snatched Maud's cornbread from her hands. Dora took one very large bite and grinned with cheeks stuffed with cornbread. Maud sat completely unamused.

"Maybe I'm jumpy because your goose looks more like a loud peacock." Maud motioned at the quaff of feathers and finery on Dora's head and shoulders.

Dora let out an exacerbated sigh and removed the feathery mess. She shuffled around on the hard, wooden bench. Looking up and down the long table, Dora took in Maud's lack of company.

"Say what you want about my peacock, toots. You look about as lonely as a rooster with no legs. Where's the family?"

"Gus is tired, back at the boxcar. Lotteva is... well, I'm not sure where she is," Maud said.

As though being summoned by their conversation, Lotteva made a big show of dancing into the cook house and plopping down next to Dora and across from her mother. She wore an outlandish red and yellow outfit. Clown makeup was plastered thickly on her face. Despite all the paint, her beautiful, young smile still blazed through.

"Lotteva Wagner...what on earth?" Maud said.

"The clowns said I could help with the big top tonight." Lotteva snatched the rest of Maud's cornbread from Dora. "Extra pay if I help out."

"We don't need any extra pay," Maud said. Her manner hardened as she stared at her painted daughter.

"Mama, if I go, I get to see the elephants up close. It's fun." Lotteva swallowed a lump of cornbread and grinned.

"I don't like it," Maud said.

"You just don't like the clowns." Lotteva gave her mother an exaggerated pout.

"I'm fine with the clowns. I worry about you and large animals." An old quiver shook in Maud's chest.

"God, Mama. The lion was a long time ago," Lotteva said.

"And I don't like you wearing all that cake on your face," Maud said.

"Says the human picture gallery," Lotteva said. "Why can't I get a tattoo Mama? Maybe I wouldn't wear all this if I had a tattoo to make me special."

"I told you, no tattoos. You don't need them." Maud crossed her arms over her chest.

Lotteva stood, balled up her fists and sat them square on her hips. Her intention was to look defiant, but on a face so young and pretty, it came across like more of a child play-acting. The glare she intended was too big for her age.

"I'm going to the big top," Lotteva said before marching out of the tent.

A part of Maud wanted to go after her daughter. Perhaps she could cool her head and make things right. In the end, she stayed. Whether it was stubbornness or laziness she did not know.

"Still won't let the child get a tattoo?" Dora asked.

"No. I've told her that. She keeps pressing."

"Well, it used to be because she was just a baby. She's more or less full-grown now. Why is it still a no?" Dora was the picture of gentle sincerity. Ever the doting godmother, she would have probably given in to Lotteva's demands long ago. But she was also Maud's friend, and Dora was forever on her side.

"Because... I don't want it," Maud said.

"What about what she wants, sugar?"

"She doesn't *need* it. Her skin is too beautiful for something frivolous, and knowing Lotteva, she wouldn't go for that anyway. Maybe one day when she needs it, I'll let her."

"What do you mean if she needs it?" Dora asked .

There was a loud clang in the back of the tent that interrupted their conversation. It startled the few patrons in the cookhouse. At first, it seemed nothing more than a pan falling in among the tub of pots, but the noise continued. More clanging and movement that was soon followed by shouting and screaming. Maud and Dora stood at attention when smoke began to billow out from the back, rising to the top of the tent.

"Fire!" shouted someone in the crowd.

The circus women raced as salmon might against a stream. Patrons made for the exits, but Maud knew the cooks personally and went to see about them. If there was a way to get them out, she and Dora would do it.

By the time they reached the makeshift kitchen, fire was already licking its way up the canvas and spreading like some sort of disease. Flames danced upward and onward, sprinting faster than what seemed possible. Dark smoke collected densely around their eyes.

When Maud crouched down, she could just barely spot Betty, one of the older cooks she knew. Betty was trapped under an avalanche of pots and cutlery. She wasn't moving.

Maud got down on her hands and knees, crawling toward the unconscious woman. Smoke filled her lungs, making her cough with every breath. She tried calling Betty's name, but her words seemed to get swallowed in the murky blackness.

With every breath of smoke she took, Maud felt weaker and more terrified. She hadn't even made it to the unconscious woman before someone grabbed her ankles and yanked her backward. Maud's belly scraped against the ground, creating a wake of itchy straw around her.

"I said leave her, damn it!" Maud looked up with burning eyes. It was Dora yelling at her and pulling her to her feet. "Ain't nothin' you can do for her now, so move!"

Dora pushed Maud forward, and the two women ran. They slumped to keep their heads out of the smoke. The fire spread so quickly because the canvas was coated for weather. Circus folks used paraffin wax and gasoline to waterproof the tents. They were accounting for rain but not the idea of a kitchen fire.

Now, the rubes were both clamoring to get away from the fire and crowding around to watch the spectacle. The two exits were choked with people trying to push themselves free of the burning cookhouse tent. Maud and Dora, having lost time trying to help Dee, were in the back of the crowd. The heat was getting unbearable. Maud's flesh felt like it would curl up like bacon fat and flake away.

"This way!" Dora shouted.

She led Maud by the wrist to the opposite side of the tent. The fire was closer there, but Dora had a knife. Without hesitation, she stabbed her blade into the fabric and sawed downward to create a makeshift opening in the tent. The canvas was taut and thick, but with Maud's help, the two women opened a hole big enough to fit through. Dora climbed out first, holding out her hand to Maud, who managed to get her head and arms through the hole and breathe a glorious breath of clean air.

Before she could get much farther, there was a series of snapping sounds that popped over the roar of the rising flames. All circus folk knew that sound and feared it. It was the cracking of the suspension poles that held the giant tent up in the air. They seemed to all go at once, causing the ropes that held the canvas taut to slack and give way. The massive structure that was the cookhouse deflated like a balloon and collapsed in upon itself, still burning wild with fire.

Though the bulk of the tent's weight fell away from her and toward the weak points of the exits, Maud found herself suddenly trapped beneath a mass of heavy fabric. She only got the smallest glimpse of Dora yelping and jumping backward before the weight of the canvas knocked her to the ground.

No longer could she see the stars in the open sky. The clean air was replaced by smoke, trapped with her among the folds of fabric. Maud lifted the fold above her head, trying to make a pocket of good air she could breathe. It was useless; there was only smoke and darkness around her.

She pulled her body through the hole they had made, reaching out her hand in the direction she thought was correct, but who could tell? Her feet felt hot, so she pulled herself away from that direction. Reaching her arms out, she tried to grab a handhold outside the collapsed tent. She couldn't breathe. Everything was smoke. It filled her lungs, slowed her movements. It made her want to give up and lay there.

Somewhere in the distance, beyond the roar of fire, she heard her name. But whoever called for her sounded so far away. Was it Dora? Maybe Lotteva had circled back? Hope fluttered in her chest, but she had stopped moving. Everything was too much, too hard. Maud sunk into the ground beneath the weight of the canvas.

Another voice, an old one in her mind, told her she deserved this. This was the death of a heretic. This was the death of a runaway. This was the death of woman who abandoned her parents to the sea of wheat.

A tiny, steely hand grabbed her wrist. Then another hand grabbed it. Suddenly, Maud was being dragged across the ground, sticks and rocks scraping her underside. When she broke free from the tent, it was like being reborn. She gasped, wide-eyed, drawing in ragged breaths and grabbing blindly in a new world. A world where she was not dead.

Whoever had her wrists suddenly had help. A stronger set of arms grabbed Maud's legs, and the two carried her to a nearby grassy hill. Maud sat up and coughed up black mucous. She spat smoke to her side. Before her stood Dora, costume singed and face blackened. Her eyes were clear though and full of purpose.

"Maudie. You sit here with your friend," Dora said. "I'm gonna go see if I can help on the other side." Dora ran away from her and into the chaos of the fiery night.

It took Maud a second to process what Dora meant. What friend? She was suddenly aware that she wasn't alone. Maud turned and saw the owner of the steely hands that saved her.

"Ester?"

The girl sat beside Maud, panting and staring at the blaze in front of them. Her blond hair was a mess, and her fine dress was covered in dirt and soot. There was a rip in the shoulder, causing the frock to hang at a strange angle. The pretty bangles dripped off severed threading.

Ester looked at Maud. All pretense of superiority gone. This was just Ester, the real one. Not the mask she wore for her friends. Not the spoiled child of a wealthy banker. She was a frightened girl who was far stronger than anyone knew.

"You saved me?" Maud asked through numb lips. Her chest burned, but she tried not to cough. The moment was so strange, she was afraid one sharp noise might frighten the girl away.

Ester nodded, shock still covering her face. "I saw you go in the cookhouse."

"You followed me?"

"I just... I was just curious. My friends left, but I didn't want to go. When it caught fire, I looked for you, but the way in was blocked. When I came 'round, I saw your friend trying to help you through the rip, and that's when the tent fell."

"You went under the tent to pull me out?" Maud said. It was a stupid question because of the obvious answer. Maud was here, alive, because of Ester, but the whole thing was too unreal to comprehend.

"I saw where you were better than your friend. She was jumping to get away from the falling pieces."

Maud squinted her eyes, trying to make sense of her savior. "Why did you help me?"

Ester didn't answer. She only fidgeted with her purse and looked away. Maud reached across the void between them and took the girl's hand. It felt so small in hers.

"You saved me, honey. Thank you."

She looked so miniscule now. With a little shrug, Ester stood to leave Maud on her hill of green. Now that the girl's underbelly had been exposed, she looked like she was preparing to make a hasty retreat. "It's nothing. You helped me earlier. I gotta go come up with some story to explain why I look like this."

A stone formed in Maud's stomach like a pearl among the soft flesh of an oyster. She could only imagine what the child was in for when she returned to her father's house. Her fine dress was tattered to ribbons. There was a fresh tattoo on her wrist. What hell was waiting for her? All because she did a good deed and saved Maud's life.

Before Ester could walk away, Maud called to her. "What does your father drink in the morning?"

"What?" asked Ester, turning back around.

"Coffee or tea, which one?"

"Um... coffee."

"How does he take it? Black or with sugar?" Maud knew she was coming across like a loon.

"Cream and sugar," Ester said while still looking confused.

"That's good. Come closer."

Ester squinted, trying to read this line of questioning. She knelt down so her face was near Maud's. Maud leaned in and spoke as quietly as she could among the cries of the men dousing the flames of the tent nearby. Black smoke billowed up to the heavens and snuffed out the stars. For a moment, they felt invisible. They were safe.

"You got options, child. Just about every pharmacy carries arsenic."

"What do you mean?"

"You dose him all at once, they will see it. Got me? The doctors will know. But, if you dose his coffee a little every morning, they won't. It's a powder fine as flour. Would be nothing to add it in with his sugar. Over a few months, he'll get sicker and sicker. They will think it's a bad stomach bug or something like that."

"I... don't understand."

"That man is going to kill you one way or another."

Ester fiddled with her torn dress, her large eyes darting from Maud to the fire and back to her fingers again. "How do you even know about this?"

"Living on the road teaches a woman a few things. Not all men are as lovely as my husband."

Maud knew of arsenic, but she'd never poisoned anyone herself. She merely helped a cooch tent girl get her hands on some. They were having issues with a violent manager. An elderly palm reader gave instructions on the dosage. The girls didn't kill the man—just made him too sick to beat on them until something more permanent could be done.

"I don't know if I can do it," Ester said.

"You saved my life. I can't save yours in return, but I can give you some knowledge to help you do it yourself. They may not be good options, but honey, you've got them. You don't have to go back to living that way. Just a small amount in his sugar. A little pinch. It builds up."

"Even... even if it didn't kill him... would it make him real sick? Like he can't get out of bed? Sick enough he'd leave me alone?"

"Honey, he'd be hard pressed to make it to the bathroom let alone your bedroom."

A little light flashed across Ester's face. The doubtful child she had been moments ago slipped away. Ester's eyes reflected the dying embers among the cookhouse tent like a mirror, perfect and truthful. Her features hardened as the tiniest wisp of a smile tugged at one corner of her mouth.

She had options, oh hell yes, she had them.

Ester jutted out her chin and gave Maud a little curtsy with the blackened rags of her once fine dress. Then, she turned and strode out in the evening like she hadn't a care in the world.

Part Six

1937

With the thirties came the crash. America could have rebounded if the stock market was the only thing to die. But everything and everyone felt the hit like a slap to the face.

The thing of it was, with the crash came the dust. It was a never-ending dust that baffled the doctors and wiped out whole communities. The plague blacked out the sky and choked everything in sight. Farmers, their livestock, and their crops were all wasting away in unison. Dust storms swept in hard and fast, burying a town in a matter of hours. It was a velvet hammer of dirt and it could kill a man caught out in the open.

What place was there in this desolate desert for a band of entertainers?

Apparently, people still needed something to occupy their minds. What was the point of keeping your body fed if your mind left you in despair? The circuses became a welcomed sight, even in the worst places. For a few coins, a man could treat his family to a day of wonder. For one afternoon, they could pretend they were royalty taking in the sights.

It didn't mean they wanted tattoos though.

Maud and Gus's business faltered for the first time in their history of traveling together. They had no choice but to lower their prices. Gus was forced to sell their winter house in St. Louis to keep them fed, clothed, and on the road.

Gus began teaching himself to whittle wood and carved useful things to sell. His animal inspired canes were particularly popular. He also took up taxidermy. The dusty areas provided an endless supply of starved jack rabbits for his practice. The poor beasts, having no burrows left to call home, invaded farmland in search of food. Farmers considered them a plague from the bible and when the wretched creatures found no food, the roads grew littered with their carcasses.

Maud went back to performing to help earn money for the family. Contortions were no longer a practical sort of business. Maud was now a woman in her fifties, and the days of handstands and back bends had long passed. Though she still possessed a youthful patina, the years were wearing her joints a little thin. Often, she found herself kneeling over to pull out a stake, an action well known to her, only to be greeted with a tinge of pain in her back.

Perhaps the days of figure-hugging costumes were over, but tattooed ladies were still a marvel. She used her natural showmanship to display her body to the masses. Up on stage, she was a masterpiece.

Though her arms weren't the sinewy vines of her youth, and parts of her cheeks and belly sagged, she was a vision. People came from far and wide to marvel at the woman tattooed from head to toe. She was an art gallery all to herself. They would point and gasp in wonder after paying their penny at the door.

Maud gave them their money's worth. She wore gowns fabricated from old curtains and costume veils. They were a slapdash affair to inspect up close, but the finished product was a thing from storybooks on stage. Maud was a colorful figure from another world visiting their dull lives.

Women swooned over her birds, and men leaned in close to take in the lions on her chest. She even let the little ones come close to the stage and touch the dragon on her arm to see that the tattoos were not merely drawn on her.

The Kansas Maud knew as a child had vanished. Where there was once a sea of golden wheat, now there was only dust for miles. Secretly, she had scanned the faces of the crowd as the Harry Carry Wild West Show made its journey across her home state. Any time a circus was near her old home, she couldn't help but look and wonder.

Could her parents be among the crowd? Might an old friend recognize her? How could they? It had been so many years, and she was a completely different person. Maud had shed that skin decades ago.

She had kept up the letters to her parents, two to three a season, but the post office box Maud and Gus had in St. Louis never held news from her home. She checked with a giddy hope every time, and every time she was disappointed. Even if her mother did lay eyes on her in one of these shows, would she even know her own daughter? If she read Maud's letters, would she care about her comings and goings?

It was a blustery afternoon in Kansas when the storm hit. The canvas around Maud's stage bent and sagged with the wind as she wrapped up her show to a large standing ovation. At first, Maud thought nothing of it. The winds of Kansas were constant, always had been. However, the wind grew angrier, and the air fell in a way that sent a rush to Maud's gut.

Folks in her tent began to look around anxiously as the beams creaked. The wooden posts tried to hold solid against the strengthening wind outside. There was a look they all shared. Dread, fear, and familiarity. Somewhere in the back, a boy coughed over and over again into a handkerchief. Maud saw when he pulled it away, it was soaked in mud and spittle.

"Everyone, stay put in here," Maud said while throwing a wrap around her shoulders. "I'm going to see what's happening outside."

Grit and wind nearly toppled her as she exited the tent. The very air smelled of electricity. In the distance, a storm was raging toward their little fairground. A dark, velveteen hammer made of clouds and dust barreled down on them only a few miles away. With it came wind strong enough to beat a man to death and so thick it could block out the afternoon sun. Everywhere, people ran this way and that, trying to find shelter from the storm.

In a moment of desperate awe, Maud tried to brace herself on a nearby shovel stuck upright in the ground. An arc of electricity leapt from the metal handle to her finger. She yelped and jumped back closer to the tent.

Nothing but fear infected the world around her. It spread like a disease.

Maud couldn't seem to find the parts of her mind that told her to run, to think, to act. Shock froze her in place. All in a rush, her vision filled with her husband's face. The deep creases around his eyes pinched against the wind as he searched her face frantically. Gus shouted above the elevating roar.

"Maudie! It's coming. Can you hear me? We have to get to the train!"

She snapped to attention, searching the grounds for their daughter. "Lotteva?"

"Gregory is getting her. We are all moving to the train cars. Tents aren't going to hold. This storm is coming fast. We have to move now!"

"The rubes, the people inside. We have to get them out!" Maud shouted.

Gus and Maud dashed into the tent, looking to all the people inside like crazed lunatics. "Get out of here," Gus said. "The storm's coming! Follow us to the train cars. Hurry!"

A few of the smaller children began to wail as their parents gathered them in their arms. Older children grabbed the hands of smaller ones. Whole families linked themselves together like a length of chain before running out into the unknown. Gus held open the tent flap as Maud herded them along.

By the time everyone made it outside, the sky had already darkened considerably. The static in the air made the hair on Maud's arms stand on end. In the few short minutes it took to collect the families, the ominous wall of dust had moved less than a mile away. They didn't have much time to make it to the train cars.

"This way!" Gus yelled.

Performers and rubes alike clamored out of tents and away from the storm. Gus and Maud led the pack of people through the fairgrounds. Weaving in and out of tents, they used the quickest way to cut to the show's train cars.

A few roustabouts hammered the stakes that held the menagerie tent deeper into the ground. There was no time to move the more dangerous animals. They would have to ride out the storm in their cages. Other performers recruited the hefty men to lead their show horses toward the livestock cars. The show ponies, who were used to relying solely on the direction of their masters, fidgeted and stamped the ground.

The draft horses and mules easily broke free from their tethers and stampeded in different directions. Their hooves pounded the hard ground as they broke from the roustabouts and trampled tents to get away from the storm barreling down on them. Gus and Maud had to stop, holding their group back, to allow three mares passage in front of them. The horses raced past them, and they began again toward the train.

Winds whipped around them, dust billowing in swirls here and there. The dirt stung their eyes, making it hard to take a decent breath.

Every bite had grit in it. Meanwhile the sky grew darker and darker; when they arrived at the cars, it looked nearly midnight.

Maud led the masses to the nearest train car. The door was thrown open, and several performers were helping to hoist the families. Marvin, the strong man, and Nick, the contortionist, took children from their fathers and helped women in after them. Gus also helped to lift the multitude of children inside.

Looking up and down the long line of cars, Maud saw other groups taking shelter like theirs. Some had their animal ramps lowered, and some of the show animals were being led to safety. She scanned the darkening landscape for Lotteva. Her daughter was nowhere in sight.

"Maud, honey. We have to get in now," Gus said, suddenly standing behind her.

"Lotteva? Do you see her?"

Gus shook his head and put his hand to his brow, trying to shield his vision from the dust building up around them. It was beginning to get hard to see anything beyond three cars in each direction. Maud's costume dress flapped furiously in the wind as she stared into the darkening abyss. She knew, just knew, Lotteva was out there somewhere. Maud's heart beat for her daughter, calling to her wherever she might be.

"Maud, we don't have much time," Gus said. "Gregory is with her. They probably got in another car."

"I'm not going in until I know where she is."

"Maud, Gus, come on!" came the voices from inside the car.

They could no longer see more than six feet in front of them. Gus tried to pull his wife by her arm toward the train car. The group had closed the sliding gate almost shut with an opening only wide enough to let in a single person at a time. It couldn't stay that way for long or else everyone could suffocate in the thick dust.

Two figures emerged from the nothingness. When the pair got close enough, despite hiding their faces from the storm raging about them, Maud recognized the dark auburn mop whipping around in the wind. Maud's arms ached for her daughter, and she closed the gap between them in seconds. She wrapped Lotteva and pulled her the remaining distance toward the train car. Gregory, the wolf man from Argentina, followed close behind. His entire face was covered in hair so thick it looked like fur. The dirt blowing around had coated it with fine, brown dust.

"Where were you?" Maud shouted over the roar.

"Greg... helping... the show horses." Most of what Lotteva said was eaten by the wind.

"Enough," Gus said, moving them to the train car. "Get in. Now!"

Gus pulled himself into the small opening of the car. He hung his arm down to grab Lotteva. Gregory made a cup with his hands for her to put a foot in, and the two of them had her safely in the car in no time.

Next came Maud. Gregory made the same cup with his hands, and she braced her foot in it. The arm that jutted out to grab her was not the one she expected. She expected it would be Gus's pale, tattooed arm. Instead, a strong, brown arm appeared among the thickening dust.

Maud grabbed the lifeline as the man who owned it hauled her into the car. Gregory barely had to lift her at all the stranger was so strong. Before she knew it, she was out of the storm and in the shelter of the train car. Maud lost sight of the man who hoisted her into the car; her main focus was Lotteva and Gus. The dark fellow seemed to disappear into the shadows before she could turn to thank him.

The wolf man was the last to make it inside. Gus helped to pull in Gregory, and several men pushed the heavy, wooden door shut. In the short time the door was open to accommodate each person to enter, a triangular assemblage of dust had gathered like a cookie cut from a sheet. The lock was thrown, and everyone gathered together like so many sheep taking shelter in numbers.

The storm raged and rocked the train. Even though the boxcar was built for stock animals, it was still meant to keep out the elements. Mules and horses weren't good for much if they were beaten all night with weather. Yet, the velvet hammer rang against the walls, turning afternoon into midnight. Dust found its way in through the cracks, choking the very air around them. Everyone stood still and tried to breathe shallowly.

Folks began pulling out handkerchiefs and bandanas to cover their mouths. Anything to block out some of the dust. Maud recognized one woman from the audience of her show. She had so many little ones to protect, she held out her skirt for three of them to share together.

Maud looked down at her elaborate costume, feeling silly for the ridiculousness of her garment. She began ripping off pieces of her skirt and handing them to the other people in the car.

Lotteva was wearing men's pants, but she took the scarf from her head and ripped the bottom of her blouse. Gus followed suit and took his pocketknife to his shirt, cutting long triangles. The Amazing Wagner's, now half-dressed, handed out bits of cloth to all the people taking cover in the stock car. Each in turn thanked them with a nod. One little girl giggled and pointed at Lotteva's exposed navel.

Maud had tied a particularly long strip of veil around her head to secure the makeshift mask while she worked. It wasn't until they covered everyone in the car that she saw a dark form slumped in the corner. Perhaps she wouldn't have noticed him at all had he not coughed hard and spit out a bit of mud.

There was no mistaking the man who had pulled her to safety. He was the only Negro in the whole circus as far as she knew. Not a rube, surely. Not by himself. A fellow like him would stick out like a fly in a milk bottle.

Thinking about that, Maud tried to remember ever seeing a black family at the circus. Performers occasionally accompanied the various circus outfits. Men and women sometimes painted themselves like African tribal people; they stretched their ears and lips in strange ways for the freak shows.

Most of the rube families visiting the circus were white. There were a handful of Negro patrons she could recall in larger cities toward the north, but Kansas? What was a man like him doing there?

Just then, the man in the corner looked at her as though he was wondering that very same thing. In that locking of eyes, a sort of understanding occurred. The type that could go unspoken for years and still be there. The recognition of a fellow outsider.

It was only broken when he coughed again and spat mud into the hay. No one tended to him or asked if he was all right. Everyone seemed to agree that he was something other than them. While Maud covered herself in tattoos, ostracizing herself in plain sight, he blended with the shadows, as though he wanted to be a part of the darkness.

Maud ripped the last bit of fabric her dress could spare before it turned into a farce of a garment. It only took a few strides to reach the man. The rest of the occupants moved out of her way like Moses and the red sea.

Her savior seemed surprised when she walked up to him. Another coughing fit kept him from speaking. Maud didn't need him to talk though. She only needed him to accept. She held out the piece of her gown. At first, he looked confused. When Maud didn't blink or move, he reached up and took the veil from her.

Outside the storm raged against the little circus. Horses reared in their cars, and mules brayed. Children clung to their mothers, and babies wailed only to be drowned out in the cacophony of the roaring storm. The one quiet moment had happened between two people nodding to one another over the gift of a torn veil.

***

By the time the storm ebbed, the land left to them had been ripped apart. In a matter of hours dust was piled three feet deep on one side of the train cars.

Canvas tents flapped in the breeze, clinging to what remained of posts and bits of wood. None were left standing. Even the cookhouse and the Big Top tents were deflated to little more than giant bed sheets billowing among ragged ropes and post debris. Wagons were upended and belongings thrown about. Tumbleweed chased each other among the wreckage as if they were capable of enjoying the spectacle.

The world smelled of smoke, but there had been no fire.

Maud took only a few steps from the train car before her foot pressed down on something familiar. It was a poster—a poster she had painted. The Amazing Wagners and their tattooing family. A tattooed man and woman holding hands. The woman wore a rose in her hair. A long gash ran through the center, right in between Gus and herself. Inside, she could feel the tear as though it were a real wound running down the length of her back.

Maud picked up the poster and dusted it off. There was something altogether visceral when one looked at a piece of cherished work torn asunder. As though a piece of the artist was also mangled deep inside.

Everyone who wasn't with the circus left. Those who had been fortunate enough to take shelter with the Wagners departed with bits of their costumes still pressed to their mouths and a lot of gratitude in their eyes. After they were gone, Gus, Lotteva and Maud were left with the tattered remains of their lives. The state of their minds mirrored their state of dress. Ripped apart in tattered ribbons.

Fortunately, they had set up their tattoo shop on the other side of the Big Top. The far larger tent took the brunt of the storm's wrath, leaving the Wagners' tents still relatively intact. Underneath the wreckage,

Gus was able to salvage their tattoo tent, three posts, some rope, and most of the stakes.

Maud's spirits revived when she and Lotteva were able to retrieve their costume trunk and tools chest. The luggage was sturdy, and Maud was grateful she had held onto it instead of selling it off when money got tight.

It took all three Wagners to haul their cases and the remnants of their show back to their boxcar. Dora was already there, securing her snake and cooing sweet things to her birds. She appeared frazzled and shaken; a frightening image on such a confident woman.

"Is everything all right?" Maud asked.

"I got all my critters to safety," Dora said. "We waited out the thing in here."

The Wagners hauled in the broken pieces of their lives and joined Dora, plopping down in the car. Maud felt tired and heavy, like her bones weighed more than they had an hour before. She practically creaked when she moved. All of her attention was on her pain, so she didn't notice Dora sitting in front of her until her friend took her hand.

"Toots, we gotta talk," Dora said.

"What is it?"

"I think this is my last season."

"No," Lotteva said, suddenly appearing beside them. "You can't just go."

"Honey, I'm gettin' long in the tooth for the circus. Too much to keep on workin' this life. The dancer costumes haven't fit me in ages. Now, I'm the crazy, old coot with the pretty animals. That's not the mystique I'm wantin' to cultivate."

It was true that Dora had hung up the glitz and glamour of the sequined leotards and turbans. Rhinestones were replaced with long skirts and beaded shawls. She still acted in theatrical animal shows, but that didn't bring in the same kind of money as exotic snake dancing.

"I can't even afford my own car. Not that I mind bunkin' with you, but the circus just ain't a place for me anymore," Dora said.

"No. You can't," Lotteva said, setting her mouth in an angry line.

"What will you do? Where will you go?" Maud asked.

"I believe I'm gonna... get married," she said with a resolute breath in the space between. The words may have come across without much emotion, but a faint smile played on Dora's face.

"Married? To who?" Gus asked, suddenly interested in the conversation.

"Well, Gus, I actually have you to thank for that. Charlie Grimm is my intended."

"Charlie Grimm? The Charlie Grimm who used to rent our home in St. Louis?"

"The one and the same. We've been seein' each other so many times at your family dinners and holidays. I s'pose it was inevitable we'd make a match together. He's a fine man. We've been writing letters all season. He wants to make an honest woman of me. Can you imagine that? At my age."

Maud reached across and took her friend's hand, which was dry and calloused from so many years of hard work. Though the idea of losing her life-long friend to retirement pained Maud, she was happy for her. Dora was an extension of their family, but she was unwed and childless; she had no kin to take care of her. Dora's vocation had a significantly shorter lifespan than Maud's. This was a smart choice for Dora, and Maud knew Charlie to be a good man.

"I will miss you terribly," Maud said. "But I bless your union with everything I have in my being. I want nothing more for you than to be happy."

Dora squeezed Maud's hand, tears welling in her eyes. The two friends embraced, only to be interrupted by Lotteva's frustrated wails.

"You *can't* go! You just can't, Auntie Dora. We need you here. *I* need you here!"

Dora pulled away from Maud to face her goddaughter. "Oh sugar, I will miss you somethin' fierce, but you'll be all right. You are stronger than an ox, and you got your parents to care for you."

"But... but I need you!" Lotteva screamed.

Without another word, the girl broke from her family and bolted out of the train car. A trail of tears and dirt followed in her wake. Maud and Gus both stood to go after her, but Dora stepped in the doorway and placed a hand out to stop both of them.

"I've got this. You two are exhausted. I'm the reason she's cryin', so I have to be the reason she stops."

Though Maud wanted to rush after Lotteva, she let Dora go in her stead. Whatever was going on between her daughter and Auntie Dora needed to be sorted out between them. They had a special bond Maud tried to respect. Plus, she was a little ashamed to admit her legs were too weary to go far. This life was tough on aging bones, and she felt gravity dragging her down.

Maud took Gus's hand and pulled him down to sit with her. She laid her head in his lap while he petted her hair. She soon fell asleep dreaming of a life without Dora. What an incredibly sad life it was going to be.

Gus and Maud napped for an hour or so before they ambled to what was standing of the cook tent. Silently, they melted in with the rest of the circus workers. Everyone groaned instead of talked. Coughing replaced laughter. The circus folk needed to eat, but they walked about like people missing half of their souls.

Maud spotted Dora sitting at a far table and joined her. They plopped their bowls of stew next to hers. The cook had called it stew. It was really more broth. Maud thought she spotted a piece of potato floating hers, but that was about it.

179

"How's Lotteva?" Gus asked Dora.

"She's fine," Dora replied.

She shot a glance Maud's way that said otherwise, making Maud's stomach drop. Before she could open her mouth to press, Dora placed a finger over her lips to quiet her. When Maud looked confused, Dora tilted her head to Gus. He was too preoccupied with his stew to notice the silent conversation between the women.

Maud nodded to her friend. The message was received. Dora would tell her later when Gus was not present. She'd play along, but she needed to know a few things first.

"Where is she?" Maud asked.

"She should be in the boxcar. You guys must have just missed her," Dora said.

"What was all that hullabaloo about?" Gus asked.

"She's just tender from all the stress. Doesn't want her Auntie Dora to go away. I don't wanna leave my little one either. Listen to me. Still callin' her my little one when she's in her twenties. I forget how she's a grown woman sometimes," Dora said.

Maud sensed something else behind that statement but couldn't read what it was. She, too, felt that way. Perhaps if Lotteva had gotten married and started a family like most young women her age, they would see her as older. Of course, Maud would never want that for her daughter if she didn't choose it herself. So many were forced into it. Truth be told, Maud would be happy if Lotteva lived on the road with them for the rest of her life.

All three of them startled when a man cleared his throat behind Gus. From the shadows came a dark figure. He bowed his head and held a ratted hat in his hands. Even though he stood tall above the group, he kept his chin low, casting shadows over his neckline. None of them had seen him coming. He just appeared. Maud recognized him at once. It was the Negro man from the train car.

"Mr. and Mrs. Wagner?" he asked in a low voice.

"Yes, that's us," Gus said with some trepidation.

"I do believe there is a woman crying in your car," he said as his eyes shot to the ground. "It sounds serious."

The three of them jolted to their feet and raced out of the cook tent. Maud caught a brief glimpse of the man before he melted back into the shadows.

They raced through the destroyed campground toward their car. All of their depressed sluggishness evaporated. Maud was all adrenaline and fear. She leapt over debris and sand drifts like a woman half her age. As they drew closer, they heard Lotteva's wails. Gus threw back the train car door and found their daughter crouched over a sheet that was covered in blood.

One would have thought the air had been instantly removed from the car. Time seemed to stand still. No one made a noise—not man nor beast. Even Dora's terrible birds kept mum while everyone took in the terrifying scene.

"Lotteva!" Maud shrieked as she raced to her girl and tried to assess what was going on. The air smelled tangy and raw.

Lotteva's eyes were swollen and tears rained from them in torrents. Her skirt was pulled up around her knees, and there was blood smeared on her thighs. Her poor face had the coloring of a ghost.

"What happened!" Gus screamed. His eyes were wild with fear. "Did someone hurt you? Was it that black man?"

"What... what man?" Lotteva said through sobs. "There was no man here."

Dora was soon next to Maud, sizing up the situation. Maud didn't know what to do first. It was pretty apparent where the blood was coming from, but they both knew this was more than your average monthly. When Maud looked into her friend's eyes, she saw something: This wasn't a complete surprise to Dora. That realization cut deep.

"Gus, you go run and fetch the doctor. We will handle this," Dora said.

Gus hesitated at the door. His mustache sagged as sweat dribbled down his brow. For a man who was always well put together, he was almost-comically disheveled. He blinked hard a few times before he turned and ran away. He disappeared into the night; the sound of his voice calling for help dissipated in the wind.

"What happened? Were you pregnant?" Maud asked, pulling part of the bloody sheet from under Lotteva.

Dora grabbed a jug of water and wetted some rags. Maud held her daughter's hands while Dora began cleaning her.

"Yes!" Lotteva cried in a sudden whoosh of air. Fresh tears ran down her face.

"Honey, why didn't you tell anyone?" Maud asked.

"I did," Lotteva said, shooting a look at Dora.

Things were finally falling into place, and the truth of it stung. When Dora ran after Lotteva, she told her auntie about the pregnancy. That's why she didn't want Dora to go. A sharp pain of hurt stabbed Maud in the gut. Her daughter felt more comfortable going to Dora than her own mother. What kind of mother did that make her?

"Why didn't you... tell me?" Maud asked trying to mask her sadness. All her question accomplished was making Lotteva cry harder.

"Toots," Dora said placing a hand over Maud's. "There's some things you can't tell your mama, no matter how much you love her. I've known for a couple of weeks now. We were just trying to come up with how to tell you and Gus."

Dora always knew the perfect words to say in any hard situation. She always had answers. Maud had never met Dora's equal, but all the pretty words in the world wouldn't patch this hurt.

Maud thought about the past month and wondered how she hadn't guessed. Had Lotteva been ill in the mornings? Was she eating normally? For the life of her, she couldn't think straight. Everything had been so chaotic and hard. Her heart sank as she searched her memory and came up short. Her girl had been dealing with this terrifying thing, and Maud was oblivious to it. Maud's opinion of her mothering fell even further.

"I was going to tell you eventually. I didn't mean to get pregnant, but I didn't mean to lose it either," Lotteva said in a miniscule voice that cracked with another sob. "Daddy's gonna hate me."

"Sugar, he'd never do that," Dora said. "Do you love this boy that put you in the family way? The one you told me about?"

"I sure thought I did, but I'm not so sure now."

Seeing her daughter like this lit a fire in Maud's belly that made her want to find the boy responsible and beat him soundly, but Lotteva was in front of her. Her daughter was the one crying and rage wouldn't help matter. Not in front of Lotteva. She had to treat the patient in front of her and not the disease.

Maud scooted on the floor and placed a clean pillow on her lap. She pulled Lotteva toward her, and Lotteva rested her head in her lap. Dora wrapped a blanket around Lotteva's waist while Maud petted Lotteva's hair. It was a familiar situation Maud had been in only hours ago. This time, it was Lotteva needing the comfort. Holding the girl healed a part of her, and she squeezed Lotteva's shoulder just to feel her skin.

"Is he someone you want to marry?" Maud asked trying not to bite down on the words. This boy would hear from Maud and Gus later, but she needed to know where the relationship stood. "Honey, it's only natural…"

"No. I can't leave you and daddy. I just can't." Lotteva shook her head. "Besides, I think he's got other girlfriends. It was stupid of me to see him."

"Don't beat yourself up, honey. We all make mistakes," Maud said into Lotteva's hair. She was surely a testament to that fact.

"I'm not doing that again. Never. Ever. Again."

"All right, sugar," Dora said. "No one says you have to. Try to calm yourself. The doctor will be here soon. Tomorrow is a new day... for everyone."

"Well, not everyone." Lotteva glanced at the stack of bloodied laundry Dora had piled in the corner.

Maud took her daughter and pressed her against her breast again. They didn't say anything more. Maud was content enough in that moment to hold Lotteva close in the eerie peace of the post-storm world.

***

The next day, the circus struggled to repair its broken wing. After the doctor said Lotteva would be all right, Maud left her daughter in the loving care of her Auntie Dora as Maud and Gus opted to work. It was too difficult being all together in the cramped car. The longer Maud stayed idle, the darker her thoughts became. Gus stomped around in silence. He had a hot head of steam and barely managed to reign it in. Every time Lotteva met his eyes, she'd start bawling all over again.

After pitching her tent and patching up the torn parts, Maud sat in the shade of it, trying to paste their poster back together. It was a seemingly impossible task because the wind kept kicking up and blowing grit into the paste. After a few failed attempts, Maud threw the poster to the ground in a huff. She'd have to pick it back up later or paint a new one altogether.

Maud was startled when someone behind her cleared their throat. When she looked up, she saw the Negro fellow from the storm the day before. He bowed before her, ragged hat in hand.

"Ma'am, I was wonderin' if you was takin' customers today."

She looked at him, unsure what to say. "Who are you asking for?"

"Me. I want the tattoo," he said in a deep voice.

"You?"

"Not a chance," Gus said, suddenly at her side.

Maud turned and looked at her husband's face. His mouth was set and determined. It wasn't like him to be so course around a customer or a circus worker. She half-expected him to flash a smile as though he were kidding the man, but that didn't happen. Gus just dug his heels in deeper.

"I can oblige you if you have the money, but not my wife."

Initially, the man was taken aback, but then, his eyes got hard as stones. His chin raised ever so slightly. He didn't so much glare at Gus as visibly stand his ground. For the first time, Maud noticed the line of a scar around his neck.

"I 'spose the lady can make up her own mind. I came to get a tattoo from *her*," the man said, pointing at Maud.

"Not happening," Gus said.

Indignity rose in Maud's eyes. Rarely had Gus taken the traditional husband role with her. Had he wanted a submissive wife, he would have married a sweet, country thing instead of Maud Stevens. Perhaps it was the sudden catastrophe of the storm. Maybe it was Lotteva's news. Either way, Gus Wagner was overstepping. Maud had been through the ringer as much as he, and the idea of anyone holding her down made her want to buck all the harder.

Maud placed herself in between the two men. "You got money?" she asked the dark-skinned man.

"Yes, ma'am. Two bits for a tattoo?"

"Let's see it," she said, motioning at the little table in front of her tent.

He fumbled in his pockets, pulled out the appropriate coins, and slapped them down on the table.

"That's good enough for me. Please go inside, sir. I'll be right in."

"Maud!" Gus shouted.

She put one finger up to his mouth. A warning. Gus had been sharp and cold with Lotteva all night. Everyone else in his path got a similar treatment. Maud had reached her limit.

The man eyed Gus one more time before he walked around the table and ducked into the tent. They could hear the scraping of the chair against the ground as he sat down.

"Maudie, you can't tattoo that man."

"Why not? We could use the money. Lord only knows when this heap will get us to another town. It could be weeks."

"I'm not leaving you alone in that tent with a colored man," Gus said through gritted teeth.

Fire heated the backs of her eyes. Her hands were balled into fists and shaking from the anger of it all.

"Oh really? You won't let me? Since when do you *let* me do anything? You didn't seem to care all those times I tattooed men alone in the tent before. Their money was fine."

"It's different."

"How? How is it different?"

"Those men were white. They know better than to take advantage of a lady. Men like that…"

"Like what?"

Maud was in his face now. She raised up on her toes to even their height difference. Every bit of her was daring him to keep going. For all his free thinking, Gus was still a white man in his bones and, right then, she hated him for it.

Gus backed away a step and put up his hands in defense. "Don't be like that," he said. "They are fine people. Plenty of them a credit to their race, but they aren't civilized like we are. It's not their fault being how they were slaves so long. They just don't always know better."

"And white men do? White men know better?"

Maud had upped the ante. Old memories flashed across her eyes. Thoughts of her uncle, a white man, shown through as plain as if Gus had tattooed them there.

Gus knew her better than anyone. Many a quiet evening had been spent holding one another and spilling the contents of their lives on the pillows around them. Everything that had happened to her, and everything that had driven her away from home—he knew it all. Not only that, Gus could read her like a book. Most times, she didn't have to say a word to have a whole conversation with him.

Gus softened. The words he had used only moments before rang hard between them. His face relaxed, his jaw loosened. His battle was surely lost.

"I don't like it, honey. It worries me," he said.

"He helped us in the storm, and he got us when he heard Lotteva crying last night. Seems pretty honorable to me."

"That isn't the same. How can you trust…?"

"And women can't wear pants or tattoo folks either," she said.

"That's not what I said," Gus said. He was back peddling now and couldn't find a way forward. Maud ceded no ground.

"They can't earn their own living or want to see the world or work with animals…"

"Maudie, obviously I don't think that. Please honey, that's not what I meant. I just want you to be safe is all."

Maud settled back down on her heels but crossed her arms over her bosom.

"You ain't never had no one tell you what you can't do. Not ever in your life. Well, I have since I was born. I bet he has too, and still does today, with idiot men like you. I'm going in that tent, and I'm going to do this job."

Gus cast his eyes downward. There was no ground to win anymore.

"I can't lose you. If something were to happen... I mean to you or Lotteva... I'd just crumble. After last night, I'm already losing my baby girl, and I can't stomach something happening to you. I'm nothing without you, Maudie."

Maud softened and relaxed her shoulders. Her arms fell. Gus's eyes, normally jovial and warm, appeared hollow inside. Maud could read the sorrow and fear in his gaze. She moved closer and took his hands in hers.

"You are the great Gus Wagner. International globetrotter. Tattooist extraordinaire."

"Nothing," he said earnestly. "Nothing... without you."

She leaned in and let him wrap his arms around her. Burying her face against his shoulder, she took in his scent and hugged him back. They rarely did this anymore. The art of holding one another seemed lost to the youth. Circus days were filled with work, especially when times were so tough. Since the crash, they'd barely had time to sleep. Where did affection fit in?

In that moment, she regretted their hiatus. Maud wished she'd taken more time to hold her husband. She longed to press skin to skin and feel his heartbeat as clearly as her own. She should have made time for this. Her husband was hurting, so she squeezed him tighter.

"You aren't losing Lotteva. She wasn't going to be your baby girl forever, but she will always be your daughter."

"I know, but..."

"She thinks you are going to hate her. Go hold Lotteva the way you just held me. It will all be all right."

Gus released his wife and cast a fleeting glance over to the tattoo tent where Maud's client awaited her. Without another word, Gus turned on his heel and walked away. He left her with a lowered head and a heavy heart.

***

He stared wide-eyed at Maud when she entered the tent. A few unattended holes in the fabric still gaped open, allowing for the slightest breeze. She sat in the chair next to him and brought out her box of tools. When she opened it, he flinched a little at the sight of the needles.

"I... I didn't mean to start a fight with your husband."

Maud looked at him. After seeing the tinge of fear in his face, she closed the little box and tried for a gentle smile. "You didn't." The raw emotion of the last few days had made her abrupt. "Now, what's your name, mister?"

"Jake, ma'am. Jake Calhoun."

"All right Mr. Calhoun. Now, don't be nervous. These tools of mine, they look scary, but they don't hurt like you'd think."

He swallowed hard but put on a brave enough face. Men often tried to hide their fear in front of her. To squirm in front of a woman covered in tattoos was shameful and cowardly. It seemed to be a universal truth among the male gender, no matter age or race.

"You see all the pictures I've got on me?"

Jake looked her over, noticing each image. "Yes, ma'am. They're pretty."

"Thank you. The point I'm making is not how pretty they are, but that I sat through the making of every one of them. If a woman can do it, surely you can."

"I ain't afraid, but I reckon you a might bit braver than me."

Jake did a decent enough job of hiding his neck, but Maud caught another glimpse of his scar as a hole in the tent allowed a flash of light to illuminate it. She noticed how his head bowed naturally, especially when she looked at him. He kept to the shadows and used his chin to block what he could from people.

"I might beg to differ with you there," she said, trying not to stare at the scar.

Jake noticed her stare and raised his chin. "You want a better look, Mrs. Wagner?"

There was more of a bite in his voice and Maud flushed. "No. I didn't mean to be rude."

"It's all right," he said. "It's actually the reason I'm here." Jake leaned forward and moved his head to the right. Light touched his neck, displaying the mark in all its horror. It was a rope burn; that was for certain. Maud had seen the like before on the hands of roustabouts and workers who had let a rope get away from them. Rope burn could do a number on human flesh.

His skin, so smooth everywhere else, puckered here and there along the edges where the fibers had done their worst. In between, the flesh drew taut in bands. There was no denying what had happened to the poor soul, and Maud could understand why he worked so hard to mask it.

Jake Calhoun looked at her while she ran a finger along the scar. Her gentle touch made the hair on his neck stand up.

"It's a nasty one. But I'm not sure what you want me to do about it." she said.

"Can you cover it up? With a tattoo, I mean."

Maud stared at Jake, wondering how to respond. Kansas's constant wind had stilled in that moment as if it too were quieting long enough to hear her answer. It was the strangest request she'd had in years.

"You want me to tattoo over your scar?"

"Yes, ma'am. Can you do it?" Jake looked more than a little hopeful.

"Your neck is especially sensitive. It will hurt more."

"I don't care. Can you do it?" Jake asked with more agitation in his voice.

"Well, possibly. But why would you...?"

"Can you do it?" he asked forcibly, cutting her off.

He beat his hand on the table, and Maud jumped a little in her seat. A long silence passed between them as Jake visibly tried to compose himself. There was a lot of hurt and anger swirling around in his eyes, and Maud wasn't sure where it came from. Perhaps having a stranger examine something so intimate left him feeling exposed.

For a fearful instant, she thought about calling to Gus. Jake scared her with his sudden outburst. Then, she chastised herself for thinking that way about a man wanting to cover up his pain. It hurt her to realize that despite all her good intentions, she too was white all the way into her bones.

Maud steadied herself and packed away her small-minded thoughts. Anyone who had survived that sort of scar, no matter their color, deserved the benefit of the doubt. She kept mum until he spoke.

"I'm sorry," he said sadly. "I didn't mean to scare you."

"You're right. It's none of my business."

"Can you do it, Mrs. Wagner? Can you cover it?"

Maud motioned for him to tip his head again. She ran a slender finger over the bumps and ridges of the line of it. His skin didn't prickle this time.

"It's a harder thing. Tattooing over scarred flesh, I mean."

Jake cast his eyes downward. A lost wind seemed to leak from him like a sieve. "So, you can't do it?"

"I didn't say that. It's just harder, is all. Skin that's been injured like this isn't smooth like a canvas ought to be. It's fibrous and hard in places. It's like that tent over there. If I were to try to paint a picture on the canvas it would be harder for all the patches and stitching. The drawing would look like it has breaks. It will take more time to blend everything."

His jaw set and clenched. "I got more money if that's where you headed."

191

"That's not my meaning. It's just harder. What do you want tattooed on here?"

"I don't care really. What does it matter?"

She let go of his neck, and he relaxed back in the chair. "If you wanted something specific like a snake or a bird or something like that, it might be a problem." Maud said, as she pulled out her drawing tools. "Your scar pulls tight in places. It might make for a very peculiar face on a bird."

His brow knitted in the middle of his forehead. Confusion spread its fingers from one side of his face to the other. Maud smiled, took her finger, and pulled at the skin on one of her cheeks. The effect was that of a comedic, cock-eyed face. Jake suddenly understood but didn't laugh.

"What do you think we should do?"

"Well, I don't rightly know. I've covered scars before, but they were much smaller."

She pulled out some of the flash pages that hadn't been ruined in the storm. Jake looked over them as she laid them on the table. None seemed right.

Maud frowned at the prospect of not being able to help Jake. She couldn't help thinking about shame; how it moved people and changed their views on life. Something like a scar could make a person other and apart from everyone else. It marked you with your trauma for the world to see.

Olive Oatman flashed in front of her eyes. The statuesque woman herself, standing in front of a misfit crowd of farmers with her Indian tattoos. All that made her other was a group of lines and triangles. Maud looked at Jake with sudden inspiration in her eyes.

"We could do something unusual. Nothing like a picture. We could make a pattern of sorts around your neck. Lines and triangles the way the Indians do."

"The Indians? You could do that?"

"Yes. My husband has so many books with pictures of tattoos from people all over the world. Lots do patterns of dots and lines and triangles. It would be easier to cover that way."

Jake seemed to brighten a little at her enthusiasm. He nodded almost imperceptibly, as though it were only to himself. "So, you *can* do it?"

Maud grinned back at him. "Yes, I do believe I can."

"All right then, let's get started with your dots and lines and such."

Maud pulled up her chair close to him, and Jake tilted his head away for her to see well. Maud reached into her toolbox and retrieved a bit of charcoal to draw the pattern. When she held the stick up his neck, she saw the color wasn't much different. With a shake of her head and a slight blush, Maud replaced the charcoal and brought out a bit of white chalk instead.

Jake flinched only a little when she began drawing around his neck. The intimacy of her touch made them both silent and uneasy. She was easily twenty years older than he and doubted he found her pretty, but the moment was so tender and close. They both found themselves holding their breath for long periods of time.

Something had to give. Someone had to lighten the air, or they would both suffocate in it.

"So, there's this riverboat captain in Mississippi," she said.

"What?" he asked.

"It's a joke. There's a riverboat captain in Mississippi. And one night he calls all of his passengers to the top deck because he's got this announcement to make."

"I don't get it."

"I'm not done yet. You wanna hear the rest of the story or not?" she asked. When he nodded, she continued. "So, this riverboat captain, he calls his passengers up to the top deck in the middle of the night because he's got an announcement. Everyone's real concerned because this captain looks very grave, and he woke them up to tell them something serious."

"What'd he tell them?"

"So, he stands on the stage in front of everyone and says, 'My fair ladies and gentlemen, I'm afraid I have some bad news. Our ship has struck a tree and we are sinking as I speak.' Well, obviously, everyone starts crying and panicking. None of them knows how to swim. Turn around, please."

Suddenly realizing that last bit wasn't part of the story, Jake stood and rotated in his seat, allowing Maud access to the other side of his neck.

"Thank you. Anyways, the captain says, 'I am hoping to find among you someone who is adept with prayer. This boat needs God's help at the moment.' The folks look around, and a preacher steps forward, bible pressed to his heart. Move just a bit this way."

Jake shifted and tilted his head yet again.

"The captain beams at the preacher before him. He takes his hand and escorts him to the stage with reverence. Just before the preacher makes to pray over the masses on deck, the captain says, 'Wonderful. Thank you, father. You stand here and pray while we hand out the life vests. We're one short.'"

It was a good thing Maud had been drawing instead of poking Jake Calhoun because the man's body shook with a burst of laughter. It happened suddenly, and he couldn't contain it. Maud herself giggled, more tickled with his merriment than anything else.

Her eyes flitted over to the shadow of two feet standing just outside the tent. Slowly but surely, they moved away. She nodded to herself with approval.

"I'm not sure God would like that one, Mrs. Wagner."

"I'm sure he's heard it before, Mr. Calhoun. Besides, it's not my joke. Just repeating it."

Laughter was replaced with apprehension the moment Maud packed away her chalk and cleaned her needles. Jake watched her work with the tools and mix the ink. Her hands were stained nearly black after years of hand poking tattoos.

On her left hand, she wore the semi-permanent stain in the saucer bit of skin between her thumb and forefinger. It was the webbing that doubled as her ink well. On her right hand, circles of grey smudged over the callouses of her middle and index fingers. There was a matching circle on the tip of her thumb.

"You do this much longer, your hands be as dark as mine," he said with a joking quiver in his voice.

"That is a definite possibility. Come on, now. Up you go."

"You want me on the table?"

"It'll be easier on the both of us if you are laying down. Just try not to touch your neck on anything so you don't smear the drawing."

Jake stood but didn't get on the table right away. Instead, he stared at it like it might reach out and bite him. His fingers rubbed together in some unheard rhythm. Maud put her hands on her hips.

"Nearly thirty years. That's how long I've been doing this. You wanted a tattoo from me. Now trust me and lay down. If this scar is a testament to your past, you've seen worse pain than my needles."

Jake positioned himself on the table. He trembled a little when she sat down beside him. Maud looked over her drawing, marveling at how different it was. She had drawn one, thick line all the way around his neck and over the bulk of the scar. From there, she had sketched in small triangles pointing down. Below that were two smaller lines drawn all the way around and perfectly spaced from one another. It was very pretty and would fit the bill nicely.

"Try not to move or flinch. The first pokes are always the hardest because your skin doesn't know what to expect. After a bit, you'll get used to it. Lots of nerves in the neck. I'm going to start slow to get you used to it."

"I can handle it, Mrs. Wagner."

He didn't move when she began. Poor Jake shut his eyes and kicked his heel against the table. She could tell he wanted to cry out, but bless him, he kept his neck still. She wished she hadn't sold her old whiskey flask. Poor Jake could surely have benefited from a stiff drink.

"It's like getting stung by a bee over and over," he said through gritted teeth.

"I know. I promise it will pass. Your body will help you ease into it though. Just give it some time. This is the hardest part."

After a while, he did relax into the dull pain of the needle. The rhythm of it was constant, and thus, easy to lose oneself in. Some people compared it to a trance. It still had to be excruciating on the tender flesh of his neck, but the urge to scream seemed to abate.

Maud worked on the undamaged bits first, trying to see how well the black ink would show up in brown skin. It was a first for her. Nearly all of their patrons were white. Gus had tattooed a few Mexican fellows when they travelled through Texas, and some of the people Maud worked on were tanned almost to a blackened color. She had seen those books of Gus's with pictures of people wearing tattoos who were far darker than Jake. After getting the lines just right, she liked the look of her work.

The scarred part was next, and it was tricky. As she predicted, his skin was pulled taut in some areas and all bunched in others. It took every ounce of her skill to get an even spread of ink along the scar. Some she had to stab deeper to get it to take the ink at all. Other parts pursed and collected too much ink.

Maud checked in with her patron. Jake still tensed, but he seemed to be in less pain when she worked over the scars. She wondered if damaged skin hurt less. If so, that was a blessing for Jake. The real chore was matching the scarred ink to the unscarred flesh next to it.

Her work wasn't flawless by any means, but she was happy. A really close inspection would reveal her mistakes, but even Gus wouldn't be able to see the difference standing right next to the man.

While she worked, Maud didn't speak. Partly because she was concentrating so hard and partly because it was just too intimate. Jake laid out before her, helpless under her needle. Maud couldn't help but wonder what had happened to him.

When she told him to turn over on his stomach, she moved a chair over to the edge of the table. The backing of it was just high enough to cradle his forehead. Any other way would force Jake to turn his face one way or another, and that would make it nearly impossible to finish the tattoo. His skin would be too twisted. She folded some rags to pad the high back of the chair, and he adjusted his body until he felt comfortable.

Now that he was no longer able to look up at her, Maud felt more comfortable talking. She began poking once again, took a deep breath, and started in on a story she hoped would lead to his.

"You know, I started with the circus when I was sixteen. I was an aerialist."

"Really?"

"Yep, sure was. I will never forget the first day I met the big man. Mr. James Barlow, owner of *The Great Barlow Show*. My friend Dora already worked for him, and she made the introductions. I was nervous as anything. I'd never met a circus boss before. I expected... well... I don't know what I expected. A flashy costume, fireworks coming out of his hat, maybe a monkey on his shoulder or something. I figured he'd look like all his performers rolled into one big man."

Maud waited for him to say something to continue the story. If he didn't say anything, she figured he didn't want to talk. She would have to respect that no matter how much she wanted to hear his story.

"What was he like?" Jake asked.

"Oh, nothing at all what I thought. He was fat and short. Wore the ugliest suit I'd ever seen. That was something coming from a Kansas farm girl."

He snickered and she waited for him to stop before continuing to poke his skin. Maud took a deep breath as the next bit was tricky.

"Mr. Barlow was kind enough, I suppose. He took me in and gave me a job, so I thank him to this day for that. I'll never forget what he said though after my friend introduced me. He said, 'Honey, as long as you don't make a fuss and you ain't colored, you're welcome here.'"

Silence filled the tent. She wished she could swat it away and open the tent flap to air out its corpse. Maud hated the way things sat stale. It was a risk, saying something like that. After all, she wanted to know about Jake's trauma. Maud knew nothing about living in the circus as a Negro. But there was something about being so close to him, touching the ghost of something horrible, that made her want to know more. Maud wanted to know this man. She wanted to understand why a black man would work in a world that was overwhelmingly white. She wanted Jake Calhoun to tell his story to her. What was the history around his terrible scar?

She told herself she wouldn't pry further. The door was open. He had a right to keep this going or stop it by saying nothing at all. If was difficult, but she bit her tongue until he pressed forward.

"He said colored?" Jake asked.

"No, he didn't. He said a different word."

"I figured as much."

"When I saw you in the train car yesterday, I couldn't help but wonder why you would want to work for folks like that. I don't know how they are here to your people, but..."

"But there ain't many of us around," he said, finishing her sentence. "So probably same kind of boss here as the one you met."

"Yes," she said.

"Ain't much else out there to do unless you want to farm for the big bosses."

"You mean tenant farming?" Maud asked.

"Basically, the same as bein' a slave. Just a different package. Besides, circus food is better than most places I've seen."

Maud thought about that and agreed. In a time when bread was a luxury, the circus cookhouse was a good, constant source for hot meals.

"There's the railroads," she offered.

"They pay worse than the circus. Plus, the work's harder."

"Are you ever scared?" she asked.

"Are you?" he said.

"Not really. Not anymore. But I got my family. You look like you're all alone."

"The worst already happened to me. Not much else they can do now."

Her hand lifted as she inhaled and exhaled as quietly as possible. A silence settled between them tense and heady with intention. This was the same sensation as the impending storm. That electric foreboding.

"It was a bit ago in Duluth. Me and a few of my friends were working the James Robinson Circus. Times were better then and pay was good. Things sort of calmed, you know. Enough to let yer guard down."

Maud nodded to the back of his head, and she set her hands back to working on his tattoo.

"One night, there was this girl. Pretty girl, but I knew better than to stare too long at a white woman. She laughed too hard and drank too much with some of the fellers. Shouldn't be a reason for what happened, but it was to them."

Jake tensed a little down his back but kept his neck as still as he could.

"Anyways, sometime later I heard a scream when I went to make water by the train. There was a gunshot and another scream. I went to see and found the girl fightin' off several men in a train car. One had a gun to her head. I hollered at them, and they scattered like rats. Never did see their faces. The one with the gun though, I saw his. He walked into the light and pointed it right at me. He would'a shot too if boss man hadn't come 'round the bend. Gunman took off like a jack rabbit."

"Did they catch him? Was she okay?"

"She was messed up a bit, bruised and such, but I don't think they did what they came to do, if that's what you meant. She's so upset, poor girl couldn't talk. Just cried and cried. Boss man didn't see nothin' either. Just some boys running away, and then there I was in the car with her."

"He thought you..."

"He thought I did it. Didn't ask me or her no questions neither. Just called his boys and made a mob. Same people we'd been working next to all summer turned on us in a second. They strung up me and my friends right there in the Big Top. Hung us from the main post in the middle. Everyone cheerin' while the six of us died."

Maud had finished the tattoo. For the life of her, she wished there was more to work on, anything to keep her hands busy. She reached for a rag and found the very one she had used as a mask the day before. When she dabbed his tender flesh with the water, goose flesh spread underneath it. Whether from the cool water or the memory, she wasn't sure.

"But, you lived," she said.

"Yes, I did. The girl found her voice again enough to tell them I wasn't the one who hurt her. She say I helped to get her out. Just before I blacked out, boss man cut me loose. The crowd booed, and he told me to run away. Told them to let me alone. I was a good one, he said. I ran sure enough, and on the way, I bumped into the man I'd seen with the gun. He was in the crowd cheerin' with the rest."

"What happened to your friends?"

Jake hesitated for a moment as though a whole world of hurt lived in the next thing he said.

"I left them. I shouldn't 'ave, but I was so scared. I couldn't breathe. None of them touched that girl, but they died fer it anyway."

"There's nothing you could've done," Maud said breathlessly.

"I tell myself that sometimes. It don't sound right no matter how I say it tho."

A few tears made their way out of the corners of Maud's eyes. She couldn't help it. Not any of it. She had wanted the story, and she got it. Everything in the whole world turned ugly.

Maud finished wiping the back of his neck and brushed away her own tears in the process. She bade him to get down from the table and sit upright in the chair. Jake, for his part, averted his gaze from her red-rimmed eyes. Everyone, no matter what their heritage, knew it was rude to gape at a woman crying. Not a tear fell from his brown eyes, however. Perhaps he had relived the night enough to where it didn't hurt anymore. Or maybe he was just numb. Like tattoos, the pain of life dulls the longer you live.

She didn't hold up the mirror for him to see until she finished wiping the front of the tattoo as well. It was impossible for her to not bask in the beauty of her own design, even if it was red and swollen. The tattoo was lovely on his skin, following the natural contours of his neck perfectly and masking the terrible scar underneath. The lines looked flawless after she took a few steps back. The little triangles matched perfectly to the designs she had seen on Olive Oatman so long ago. She wished she had a camera.

When she held up the mirror for Mr. Calhoun to see, she braced herself for his reaction. Sometimes, people cried after seeing their tattoo for the first time. Some laughed. One woman she tattooed had been ecstatic to get one, and then screamed at Maud to take it off. What a hard dance that was to maneuver.

Jake stared for a good long while saying nothing at all. Maud put his hands on the mirror, forcing him to hold it steady while she grabbed the other mirror and positioned it behind him. He saw the back bit and took a deep breath.

A shiver went straight to the pit of her stomach. What if he hated it? This was a symbol that was supposed to help him heal, and what if she mucked it up?

"Is it not what you wanted? I thought I covered the scar pretty..."

"What does it mean? Them symbols you put on me."

"I got it from a white woman who lived with the Indians for a time. They tattooed her that way on her chin."

"Why'd they do that?"

"She said it was something they did for loved ones. It was so they'd be able to find their way to their ancestors after they died," Maud said.

She had a nervous lump in her throat that was hard to swallow. It made her voice lower and a little croaky. Jake still hadn't said whether or not he liked it.

"Ancestors? Like Indian heaven?"

"I suppose. I don't know enough about Indians and their idea of heaven, but that's the meaning I took from her speech. Maybe it means they find their own version of heaven."

"What's your version of heaven, Mrs. Wagner?" Jake said softly.

Maud paused a moment to think on that one. It was one of those real questions again. The kind you had to think really hard about before answering.

"I suppose it would be a circus."

"You already in a circus," he said.

"I mean the circus as it used to be. One with all my friends. There's nothing better than your first view of the circus. The colors, the music, the dancing... and cotton candy. Just loads of cotton candy. Everyone is happy to put their cares away, even if it's for a brief time. People accepting one another just as they came."

"That is a nice idea of heaven," Jake said with a smile. "I don't rightly know what my idea of heaven would be, but I guarantee it wouldn't be a circus."

"Well, I guess... I hoped maybe if this tattoo didn't help direct you to heaven, maybe it would direct you to peace," Maud said. She injected every word with her heartfelt sincerity. Her shoulders relaxed as the smallest of smiles spread across his face.

"Do you like it?" Maud asked.

"It's... it's just... I ain't got the words. Mrs. Wagner, thank you."

Maud could see his face in the mirror he held. There was a dark depth in Jake's almond eyes. When they began to water, she had to turn away. If he got her crying again, Gus would really be worried.

She bandaged his neck and told him how to properly care for the artwork. Jake thanked her again and again. Yes, he understood it would be sore for a while and to keep it clean. No, he wouldn't take the bandage off until he absolutely had to.

The sun was threatening to set in the horizon. Time spent on art was time lost to the ether. Both Maud and Jake were taken aback by the colors in the sky and what time it meant. Somewhere in the distance, some sort of stew simmered in the cookhouse, beckoning all the hungry people with the aroma of home. Anything to heal some open wounds.

Jake said his farewells and was about to leave her company when she stopped him. Maud knew it wasn't her right, but after everything they shared, she had to ask.

"Why, Mr. Calhoun?"

"Why what, Mrs. Wagner?"

"Why get the tattoo? I understand you want to cover the scar. You want to cover the bad thing that happened to you. People see you different because of it. But why the tattoo? It's bigger than your scar. People will still think you're different. They will still stare."

There was a pause where Maud genuinely couldn't tell what Jake was going to do next. His face was unreadable. Was he going to walk away or was he trying to think of an answer? Either way, she wouldn't blame him a bit. It was his answer to give or not give.

"Because, Mrs. Wagner, I'd rather have a scar I chose than one chose for me."

***

Maud spotted her family outside their boxcar. A shot of fear ran through her as she set her eyes on Gus and Lotteva hugging one another. This, in itself, wasn't a bad thing, but her daughter was weeping so hard, it startled her. Gus held her in his arms, whispering something inaudible into her wild, auburn hair.

Before she could race to them, Dora intercepted Maud and held her by the arms. Maud had been so wrapped up in her worry, she hadn't noticed her friend.

"Give them a minute, toots."

"What's happened? Is Lotteva all right?" Maud asked.

The pitch of Maud's voice was getting higher without her meaning to. Something inside her guts quivered watching Lotteva weep so. Why was Dora holding her back? Had something else happened?

"Everything is fine. Well, as fine as fine can be after last night," Dora said gently. "Gus is just bein' a good daddy. Give them a minute. The girl has plenty of tears to get through. You remember how it is."

Maud reached over and grabbed her friend's hand. They squeezed each other tightly while observing the tender scene. There was pressure in her throat that threatened to become a sob, but she pushed it down.

"Do you really have to go, Dora? I mean, I understand, but what are we going to do without you?" Maud felt her own set of tears welling up and making her voice break.

"You're gonna be just fine, sugar. I'm leaving you in capable hands."

Part Seven

1942

Somehow, someway, the Wagner family made it to San Francisco. For the first time in decades, they opted for a stationary position while the world readied itself for war. Men and women flocked to port cities to enlist, rivet, weld, and nurse. Everyone wanted to join the war effort in some way.

Maud couldn't help but wonder at the shift in her nation. One minute the entire country was on the verge of devastation, and the next, everyone was at war. An attack on the base in Pearl Harbor had turned the country upside down, and the landscape changed almost overnight.

Maud and Gus were too old to be much good to anyone, so they continued to do what they did best—tattooing. When the newly enlisted Navy boys hit the streets of San Francisco, their business boomed.

Suddenly, the city was positively teeming with men waiting for their turn to go fight the war. Dora made the call to Maud, pleading for their help. Her new husband, Charlie, could not possibly handle the demand. He had a small tattoo shop, and they were so busy he had to turn away twice as many he tattooed. Maud was eager to oblige in the hopes of earning back the money they lost during the great depression. Of course, she also wanted to see her friend again.

Off to the great city of San Francisco they went. The streets became living things. So many people moved about, it seemed the whole place might shake itself to death with the vibrations. A system of veins and arteries, and the people were blood flowing constantly through it, giving life to the jungle of buildings.

Charlie's new shop was booming. The place itself was a small affair, barely large enough to accommodate more than four people, including the artist. Therefore, the Wagner family set up shop right outside Charlie's, hastily throwing together tables and chairs. Their space could not accommodate a tent, so tattoos were drawn in the open air.

The customers were mainly sailors. Men so young Maud could scarcely believe they were out of grade school. It almost felt wrong to call them men. There were some older ones, but most looked like children.

The tantalizing colors of sin littered the streets. Everything for a price...even women. Though Gus and Maud had aged as gracefully as possible together, Maud was in her sixties. Men became distinguished as they aged, but women ripened on the vine early. Her body had held on to youth a long time, but it was surely turning as she hit her autumn years. Despite all the maturity and hardness of her age, a small part of her wallowed in the insecurity of a younger woman who didn't recognize herself in the mirror.

One day, they sat outside, calling to the sailors who paused long enough to banter with them. The days were cool, even in the hot months. The sun seemed to take a break and allowed the cool Pacific to blow its breath in between the buildings. Maud loved the weather, and she sat outside in her chair with a comfortable shawl around her shoulders. She would talk with the looky-loos if they engaged her, but she left most of the calling to Gus and Lotteva. Sailors wanted tattoos from the older man and the pretty girl, anyway.

Any worry she ever had about Lotteva and the randy sailors was quickly put to rest. She was a child of the circus and wilier than most girls. Despite her baby scare years before, Lotteva never suffered from the detrimental naiveté that had infected Maud when she was a girl. No one could pull the wool over Lotteva's eyes. No one human anyway. The girl, now in her thirties, still had an affinity for animals, and they were the only things that seemed to steal her heart completely.

Maud leaned back in her chair as a group of sailors approached. Some looked serious about getting tattoos. Most people gawked at the flash apprehensively, unwilling to make eye contact. Those were usually the ones who blushed and walked away when asked if they wanted to be daring that day.

These boys, a group of three, walked straight up and looked Gus in the eye. Most were merely kids, nineteen or twenty at most, but the ringleader was older. He hovered around forty or so, and the others looked to him for approval. He had a different patch on his sleeve from the others as well, making him a higher rank of some sort. Maud didn't understand the difference, and he gave no hints.

"This the place? Should we stop here, sir?" asked one eager naval youth.

The older man looked from Lotteva to Gus to Maud. He nodded with a smile, and the others hooted with excitement.

"I choose her. The pretty dame," said the young sailor.

His companions laughed and elbowed him in turn. Lotteva smiled courteously and motioned for him to take a seat. He did so and asked the question she got on a regular basis. After all, she was lovely, even if she still wore pants. Her dark auburn hair flowed in the breeze. It framed her round faces prettily.

"Say, you got a fella?" he asked.

"Pardon me?" she replied innocently enough.

"You got a fella? A man who claimed you, I mean."

"No, I heard you right the first time, sir. What I meant to say was pardon me, I don't see how that's any of your damn business. I've claimed myself, and that's all you need to know. Now, what tattoo would you like?"

His friends laughed as the boy's face quickly turned into surprise and then embarrassment. He blushed all over, turning him beet red all over. Maud grinned at her girl.

The other boy picked Gus to do his tattoo, which Maud expected. What she hadn't expected was for the older sailor to smile at her so—like how Gus used to look when they first met. Granted this man was bigger and didn't have the mustache, but they both were tanned from years in the open sea air.

The laugh lines around his eyes creased deeper than a man his age should. Probably from a long life laughing in the sun. When the older gentleman looked at her, his steely blue eyes shone like sea glass. After the other boy pointed to Gus, he grinned at her even wider.

"That's just fine with me boys. I was hoping to get mine from this lady anyway."

The sailor walked around her table and put out a hand in greeting. His voice had a tinge of accent to it, but not an obvious one. All the travelling had adapted Maud in the art of placing people, but he was a puzzler.

Most people she saw held the moderate tongue of the Midwest. Sort of country, sort of not. In Texas, everything sounded more cowboy than anything. Louisiana was full of French speaking folks, and the other Southern parts spoke slowly in long-winded sentences, adding syllables where there shouldn't have been any. Northeasterners were fast and spoke harshly. Folks from Boston, Chicago, and New York had a way altogether alien, and it took nothing to point them out in a crowd.

This one, though. This one was hard to peg. If she were to guess, perhaps he hailed from the southwest for they were still a hodgepodge of pioneers and Indians. A people who hadn't quite found their American voice just yet.

"Lawrence Fischer," he said with a firm handshake.

"Maud Wagner," she said.

She motioned for him to sit and gestured at the usual flash drawings before them: birds and hearts, anchors and girls, flags and snakes.

"Price is twenty-five cents today no matter what you choose."

"Well, ma'am. I reckon I could get me a haircut and a meal for nearly that."

Maud crossed her arms, raising her one skeptical eyebrow. Of all the parts that sagged on her over the years, her eyebrows hadn't been one of them.

"Mr. Fischer, you are welcome to do that instead."

Lawrence laughed and sat in the chair. "Just seeing if there was any wiggle room in the price is all," he said with a wide grin.

"Sir, does it look like I wiggle?"

He couldn't help but laugh again, and Maud softened as well. The two sat amiably next to one another on that fine day in San Francisco. A breeze blew here and there, cooling their party in the midst of the crowds. Lawrence and Maud fell easily into comfortable conversation.

"What is it you'd like today, sailor?"

"Well Mrs. Wagner, it's more like what would I like covered today."

"Pardon?"

Lawrence rolled up a sleeve to reveal a tattoo of a nude woman. Maud recognized the style at once. It was a typical icon one might see from the pacific islands. Hawaii maybe. The woman was rendered well enough, though not as well as could be. Her nipples and pubic area were a shock of black in the drawing. Something like that might have caused your average lady to avert her eyes, but Maud was no average lady. It was hard for her to see anything lewd about it. Just another drawing like any other with its strengths and faults.

"See this one here? It's a problem."

"Because she's nude?" asked Maud.

"Yeah, 'fraid so. Got this one a while back in Honolulu. I'm not shamed a bit by her, but there's rumors around the ships. Navy doesn't look too kindly on nudie girls. Don't wanna risk them not letting me go this time around. I am on the wrong side of forty as it is."

"So, you want me to dress her. Is that it?"

"Yes, ma'am. I reckon that's what I need. Still want her to look like a Hawaiian gal though. Maybe one of them hula skirts?"

Maud studied the tattoo for a few minutes and pictured how she might fix the image. Sure, adding a bra and a hula skirt was easy enough, but perhaps she could also add a bit more. Maybe a necklace or something.

No, she thought. It wasn't her drawing to fix. She would dress the woman as best she could and conserve as much of the original drawing as possible. When she met his eyes again, Lawrence was smiling a wily grin, giving the impression of effortless humility and pride at the same time. What a paradox he was and how very charming. Maud wondered if he always looked that way, or if it was just with women. A flicker of a thought entered her mind, and she waved it away before it ever had the chance to light on anything solid. Still, it danced in the distance, teasing her with silly images.

Despite fleeting thoughts, there was no danger of Maud getting carried away. Gus was a lovely man and a generous husband. She loved him, and no one could ever replace him. The flirtation was innocent enough, as long as it stayed that way. After all, Gus did it often enough with some of the ladies he drew on. It put them at ease. At least, that was his excuse. Why couldn't a woman of Maud's age play at the idea for a little fun? It's not like it happened to her often.

"You think you can dress her, Mrs. Wagner?"

"I believe so, yes."

Lawrence plunked down a quarter, and she readied her needles and ink. He marveled at the little inkwell she made of her hand and the needles sewn to wooden sticks. When Maud wiped down his arm, he playfully winced, acting like it burned.

"You aren't gonna be one of *those*, are you?" asked Maud, the beginning of a smile pulling at one edge of her mouth.

"No, ma'am. Just joshing you. Gotta say though, I haven't seen a hand-poked tattoo in years. Why is it you don't use one of those machines?"

"Don't like them," she said as she began poking his arm. "They are faster but hurt more. Plus, it feels wrong somehow. Letting a machine do it for you. Something like this ought to be done by hand like any art."

"I don't disagree with you there." He pointed the tattoo she was currently drawing a bra on. "Can you tell how this one was done?"

"Machine. Absolutely no doubt."

"How can you tell?"

"It's the hard lines. Machines make it difficult to do soft bits, so most have hard lines with not much in the way of shading."

"Sure know your stuff. How long you been at this?" he asked.

Maud looked up at him, that one eyebrow raised high. "A long time. And no, I won't give you the satisfaction of knowing my age, sir."

Lawrence laughed. The rhythm of it shaking his arm as it beat against the air around them. Maud just smiled and waited for him to still.

"Fair enough, Mrs. Wagner. Fair enough."

The bra was simple enough to manage, being that there were only a few dots representing nipples that had to be blended. The hula skirt was a bit more difficult. Maud had to incorporate the curve of the leg lines and the pubic region into the sway of the grass. To simply shade that part heavier than the rest would give it the illusion the skirt creased there, and to fill the entire thing dark would be too much for his skin to bear. His flesh would be beaten like ground meat, and it would surely scar. So, Maud used the lines of the girl's legs to further the pattern of the skirt with her finest needle, only going back over in some areas with her double pick for unification of shading.

When the deed was finished, Lawrence was dutifully impressed. "Wow. I didn't think I'd say this, but I like her better now."

Maud washed her hands and retrieved a rag to wipe the excess ink from his arm. The steely scent of alcohol drifted between them as she added a bit to her rag and dabbed at the drawing. The skin around her new work was red, but not as red as it would have been had the drawing been completely hers.

"Keep it clean and as dry as you can. Don't take the bandage off until it falls off itself. You hear me? I mean it."

Lawrence was laughing a bit, those flirty eyes never straying from her face. "I hear you, Mrs. Wagner. I'll be good."

"Somehow, I doubt that very much, Mr. Fischer."

He glanced over at his companions. Both were still under their respective artists' needle. Gus was working cheerfully on an eagle with an American flag on the chest of his sailor. The boy was sweating, his brow red from tensing in pain. Maud snorted a little to herself. Gus wasn't even working near the bone.

Lotteva worked on a pair of sparrows on the back of the other sailor's shoulder. She had nearly perfected her mother's gift of a perfect flick at the end of their tails and wings. While the drawing was coming along beautifully, the boy wasn't fairing as well. He made a good show of it though, only turning away from Lotteva to wince. Men never did want to show pain in front of a pretty lady.

"Well, Mr. Fischer, I would say you're going to have to wait a bit until your buddies are done with their torture," Maud said.

"Would you mind if I stayed a bit and talked with you?"

The look he gave her would have made Maud blush if she was still capable of such things. Something in his eyes, or maybe the shape of his jaw, reminded her of old loves. Romances from ages ago when she was still young, still turning a man's eye. Well, one man's eye at least. It was a familiar feeling, yet so far away. For an instant, just a blink in time, she could almost smell the hay that covered the ground of *The Great Barlow Show.* Her first circus back when she was so young and lovely.

"I haven't got anyone lined up," she said looking around the table. "You're welcomed to wait it out here."

"Wonderful. You know, I got me one of those hand poked tattoos like you do. Would you like to see?"

"Sure."

He turned in the chair to face the other direction. His other arm was facing her now, and he rolled up his sleeve to reveal a tattoo. It was a lovely drawing of a fully rigged ship. Maud could tell the moment she saw the drawing it was hand poked. So gentle were the lines and so soft the detail. It was unmistakable and positively lovely. She could almost hear the ocean waves crashing against the ship it depicted.

"That's a pretty one," she said.

"Yeah, it's my favorite."

Something told her to touch it, and she even reached out her finger just for a second. Realizing how rude that would be just in time, Maud quickly retracted the finger. A group of silly girls ran past giggling and taking the attention off her. They were followed by a bunch of hooting sailors, smiling and elbowing one another. They waited until the group passed before returning to the conversation.

"You can touch. I don't mind."

There was that flirty smile of his again, like he cared at all about an old lady. Nevertheless, she reached out and gently ran two fingers over the drawing. It had healed well, barely raising the skin at all.

"I'll never forget that one. I got it the first time I traversed Cape Horn. Just about didn't make it through."

"Cape Horn? That's in Chile, yes?"

"You know your geography."

"My husband was a sailor. Never did Cape Horn himself, but he spoke about it. The sailor's graveyard."

"Yeah, it was that. The Atlantic and Pacific meet there, you see. The waters are rough, kicking waves up higher than the sails at times. Strong currents and even icebergs if you aren't careful. If your crew is really unlucky, you'll catch a storm there."

"That's what happened to you? A storm?" Maud asked.

"Sure enough. Swept us out and spun us like a top. Never seen a ship bend on its side like that without capsizing entirely. Somehow, the captain helped us make it through, and we found ourselves on the Pacific side of the Horn. Got this little beauty when we docked a day later in Chile. There was this fella hand-poking tattoos. I think he got most of his business working on sailors. He did up this ship for me in no time, like he'd been doing it for years."

Lawrence rolled down his sleeve, and there was a small part of Maud that was sad for it. She couldn't remember the last time she'd been so taken by a story told by a stranger. Maybe as long ago as her roustabout friend, Jake. To her surprise, Lawrence lifted his leg and rested his foot on a nearby crate. He rolled up his pants to reveal an Asian dragon wrapped around the upper part of his ankle.

"This one wasn't hand-poked, as I'm sure you can tell being the expert you are."

Maud reached out and touched the face of the dragon gently. Lawrence's leg hair was fair and sparse, so it was easy to admire the drawing. The tattoo was a machine job, for sure, but pretty all the same. Whoever had done it, did a clean job. The lines were sharp and precise. It looked gentle and solid at the same time.

"Got this one in Hong Kong. Strangest place I ever saw."

"I can't even imagine," she said while staring at the fierce eyes of the dragon.

She had made dragons before, but never any as foreign and strange as this one. The one on her arm looked tame compared to his. She wished she'd had something like it for reference all those years ago when she turned Toddy into the Dragon Lady.

"It was like a carnival of color. I could try to describe it, but I'm no poet. Nothing I said could do any sort of justice. Hong Kong was just another world on Earth. Ever walked into a place and just marvel that such colors existed? How did I live this long without seeing this until now?"

Maud thought back to her first circus, the one she'd run away with. The colors, the vibrancy of the people. It was truly another world mere miles from the drab one she had known all her life. She nodded.

"I have, yes. It's not unlike being drunk. You're sort of drunk on the world."

By the time she came out of her own memory, Lawrence was staring at her. The grin he wore wasn't so much flirty as admiring. It was one you shared with someone who understood something you did. Something intangible but lovely all the same. A beautiful glimmer in the fabric of time.

He replaced his foot on the ground and tugged at his shirt to untuck it from his trousers. In a flash of movement, he began pulling up his shirt over his head.

"What are you doing?" Maud asked.

"Hold on, Mrs. Wagner. My story ain't done yet."

He revealed his bare chest to her and all the passing world. Maud caught a fleeting whiff of musky sweat and cologne. His chest was firm with only the beginning hints of gravity's affects.

The man clearly had no sense of modesty. Maud had little sense of it either, but there was something different about it out in the open. It was funny spending so many years on display and marveling at the prude modesty of people in general. No one she knew cared about covering up the way proper society did. But here? Out on the street? In front of her husband and daughter? Maud was surprised by how much it shocked her, as if she hadn't done similarly a million times on stage. Maud tried not to look surprised. It would have been too great a hypocrisy for her to bear otherwise.

Lawrence pointed at a mess of a tattoo on his left breast. It was barely recognizable as a swallow and not nearly half as pretty as his other tattoos.

"This hideous beauty doesn't look like much," he said.

"That's for sure."

The impulse to touch the other tattoos did not carry over to this one. Even if it hadn't been inches above a strange man's nipple, she recoiled from the hideous drawing. Years of seeking perfection in art birthed a kind of snobbery when looking at inferior work. Maud tried not to show it in her face.

"I know I know. It's no Mona Lisa by any stretch, but here's the thing about it. She's one of my most prized possessions."

"Why is that?"

"Well, I lied about my age for the Great War. Wanted to go and be a man before my time. Didn't have a clue what I was in for, much like these young fellas here."

He pointed at his companions still trying to look tough through their tattooing ordeal. The one with Lotteva had bitten his lip nearly bloody.

"I joined the Navy, and out we went. For country and glory, or so we told ourselves. My first night at sea, I was sicker than I'd ever been. I threw up things I ate a decade before, if you catch my meaning."

Maud nodded with a knowing smile, and Lawrence continued.

"Well, I never thought I'd feel good again, not ever. But like most things, it passed just before dawn. I made my way stumbling down below to find a load of my fellow crewmen waiting for me. At first, they handed me water, and I thought what swell guys they were. Then, after I took a fair amount of water and didn't throw it up, they took off my shirt and held me down on the floor. Before I knew what was happening, a fellow called Smithwick came out with one of them tattoo guns and drew a swallow on my chest."

"He forced you? *They* forced you?"

"At first, yes. When I felt the fire of that thing, I leapt up and cowered in the corner. I thought the men around me were crazy. They all smiled at me like this was fun. I knew nothing of the ways of things, but this seemed an awful lot like torture."

"I'd say so. What did you do?"

"Well, it's more what they did. Every man in that room lifted their own shirts to show me the swallows on their breasts. Each one had a version of it. Roughly the same swallow in roughly the same spot. Something clicked in my mind then, looking at all those grinning faces. They weren't mean at all. Not really. I took their outstretched hands, and they led me back to where Smithwick was waiting for me. No one had to hold me down this time. I laid on that deck while that crusty old fella drew it into my skin. The ship bucked and pitched so much, it ended up looking like this."

He pointed at the tattoo, almost petting it a little. Maud couldn't seem to hide her confusion or her incredulity.

"I don't understand. Why did they do that? Why did you let them?"

"It meant I was one of them. Your first night at sea is the hardest. Never do you feel so far from home. You make it through, you get branded with the swallow. A bird flying free from home. You are one of the crew after that. You are a part of a family."

"So why is it your favorite?"

"Because it was the first, I guess. Don't you remember your first tattoo above all others?"

Maud touched the place on her arm Gus tattooed on their first date. The eagle with the flag. Her maiden name written above it. "Yes. I suppose I do."

"To me, my tattoos mark my life. I ain't got no family left to speak of. No one is writing my name in a family bible somewhere. No one will remember me when I'm gone. But I want to remember. I want some record of the things I accomplished. I like looking at them and remembering the day I got it and the thing I did to earn it. Markers of my journey. For better or worse. Every time I look at this little, ugly bird, I remember that morning and how brave I felt. How happy to be a part of a family at last. It's nice to remember the good moments. I figure with all the tattoos you have that you must feel similarly."

"I do. I mean, I understand that. You want your journey logged somewhere. You want it to not be forgotten. You want to immortalize something."

Lawrence took her hand in his and kissed it. "I'd say that's exactly it, Mrs. Wagner."

Maud started a bit, and her heart raced just enough to show on her face. Lawrence didn't let go, even when a man clearing his throat behind her caused them both to turn and look up. Gus was standing there, looking down at the half-naked man kissing his wife's hand. The boy he had been tattooing stood just feet away with a bandage wrapped around his arm. When Gus's gaze shifted to Maud, he frowned with an incredulous glare.

The boy Lotteva had been tattooing joined the party, grinning from ear to ear at the spectacle. A little giggle signaled Lotteva's escape into the small shop behind them. The two sailors pushed at each other, laughing at their elder friend's debacle.

Lawrence's attitude didn't falter. His charming grin never wavered. He never even released Maud's hand. He merely stared back up at Gus with a sort of blind reverence.

"You have a beautiful wife, Mr. Wagner."

Gus cocked his head to the side, taking the man's measure. "I know." He looked from Lawrence to Maud and back.

"She did a lovely job dressing my girl."

"I see you saw fit to undress yourself," Gus said.

Lawrence laughed enough to be polite. "Well sir, that's because I was just about to hire her to do me the favor of another tattoo. Right here," he said, pointing to the bare breast opposite the one with the swallow.

"You were?" Maud asked, turning back to Lawrence.

He reached in his pocket and produced another quarter. The sailor slapped it on the table and looked past Maud and Gus to his comrades behind them.

"Go on now, boys. I'll catch up. Need me one more bit of torture before we set sail."

Gus looked down at his wife for an explanation. Maud honestly had none. She decided to set her jaw and turn back to her customer. After all, Gus had his flirtations along the way. Why didn't she get one too? Maud retrieved her rag and wetted it with alcohol and water. She wiped down the part of his chest Lawrence had pointed to and dried it quickly.

"Okay Mr. Fischer, what are we doing next?"

Gus raised his eyebrows, obviously confused by the whole affair. He crossed his arms, but Maud didn't address him further. She merely turned her back and went about the business of preparing the man for another drawing. Gus threw up his hands and went about cleaning his table. Lawrence leaned in when Gus turned away.

"I want you to draw me another girl," he said softly.

"Oh really? What kind of girl?"

"Well, I want a very specific girl. She's real pretty. I would like you to do a tattoo of you for me. A self portrait of sorts."

"What? Why would you want a picture of me?"

"Well Mrs. Wagner, I've had me just a red-letter day today. Been going around this fine city, living the good life with the boys. I've been sailing around the world for years, and I find myself back in my home country with a purpose again. Going to go fight the Japs for country and glory. All that plus I met a like-minded lady, a pretty one to boot, who draws better than anyone I ever met. I want to remember this day forever. Especially since I know what we're heading for. These boys don't know what's coming, but I do. I've been there. I've seen the dark days ahead of us. I sure would be grateful to have a picture of the lovely lady I met today to remind me of better days amidst the blackness of war."

Without thinking, Maud pressed her hand to her mouth. So sweet was the request, it nearly stopped the words in her throat. She turned around to see if anyone else had heard. Someone had indeed.

Gus stood just a bit behind her; his eyes wide with the weight of the confession. Though Maud was an independent woman, this was a bizarre thing to ask. Even she would feel strange drawing her picture on another man.

She looked to Gus with a question in her gaze. Was this all right? Was he okay with a strange man walking around with a picture of his wife forever marked on him?

Gus looked from Maud to Lawrence and back again. With a slight nod, Gus gave his blessing and went inside the shop. She didn't know why he acquiesced. Maybe it was because they were both sailors. Maybe he too knew what hell poor Lawrence was heading toward. Either way, Gus chose to be a kind man instead of a selfish one. Maud loved him for it.

221

She had never drawn her own portrait before. Well, other than in posters. Maud was still rather attractive comparably speaking, but the prospect of drawing her present self was not an interesting one. The parts that sagged and pooched, while not a persistent nuisance, still came as a surprise to her whenever she happened by a mirror. She often wore thin scarves or thick jewelry around her neck to hide the stretched skin that was once so smooth and springy. Was the young version of herself in her mind the real Maud? Or was it the aging woman staring back in the mirror?

Either way, Maud decided to draw herself on Lawrence as she liked to remember. Young, strong, and raising that one eyebrow as if to question the reasoning of the whole world. A smile just barely pulled at one corner of her mouth. She wore one of her contortionist costumes, but with a shawl around her shoulders. While one hand held the wrap in place, the other held a needle.

Well, at first it was a needle. When Maud sat back and looked at it a few feet away, it just looked like she was a young woman daintily standing on a man's breast and holding a stick. A tattooing needle, when drawn small like that, resembled nothing more than a twig.

She took a good amount of artistic license with the woman, might as well do the same with the instrument, she thought. On the top end of it, she brought the line out with a flourish. It didn't take much to accent the bottom to simulate the gentle waves of a feather's plumage. A bit of an exaggeration to be sure, but the drawing did look better with her holding a quill. The message and feeling were really the important parts, and she left those intact.

When she finished, she held up the mirror to Lawrence's bare chest for his inspection. His eyes lit up and he smiled grandly, showing his teeth. For the first time, she noticed he was missing one near the back. All that charming façade melted away, leaving the wonderment of that boy laying out on the deck of a ship, receiving his first tattoo ever.

They were both merely themselves at that moment. Wrinkles, missing teeth, and gravity aside.

Lawrence moved his hand to touch the drawing, much like Maud had done with his tattoos. She slapped his hand away.

"None of that. You have to keep this clean, remember? I won't have you messing up my portrait and getting her scarred up from carelessness."

"I wouldn't do that," he said with a fondness lingering in his gaze. "She's far too perfect to ever mess up."

***

A day later, the Wagner family was a great bit more tired but a good bit richer, so Maud and Gus decided to take the Sunday off to see the sights of San Francisco, leaving Lotteva to entertain Dora at the shop.

Lotteva had hinted at meeting some fancy officer for dinner sometime in the next week, but Maud had figured it would end like most of her daughter's romances. Lotteva loved and moved on, seemingly never comfortably settling down with one man. Her daughter held a self-assured nature Maud envied. Never did she seem to weigh her worth on one person's regard.

Perhaps she looked for a romance like her parents' and never found it. Maybe she was just too free-spirited to be tamed fully. It didn't matter either way to Maud. She could see Lotteva was happy being her own woman and left her alone to be just that. Let all others who thought differently be damned.

As Gus and Maud walked along the streets of the vibrant city, they took in the day. It was just as bright as when they first arrived. The sweet scent of fruit tree blossoms floated around them as bits of flowers danced in the sunlight like falling snow. As they walked, a breeze from the ocean blew gently around them, cooling their aging limbs. Surely this place had ugly days, but today wasn't one of them. They walked and walked, talking about all sorts of things. It had been ages since they had taken a walk like this with the leisure of the wealthy. They hopped on trolley cars, intent on seeing the whole city for all it was worth.

They had gotten word through the circus rumor mill that some of their old circus friends were working on a government dollar, helping immigrants assimilate around the outskirts of the city. So many farmers and ranchers had been displaced by the Dust Bowl; they moved in droves to the West coast, where prospect of work were still high. Though the immigrants hailed from all over America's breadbasket, most people labelled them all as "Oakies."

Gus and Maud were excited to see some of their old friends. They had arranged to meet up with their group near some slop shop the circus folk ran in the neighborhood. Maud had beautiful visions of warm hugs and cold liquor. It would be so nice to see everyone during a time when their fortunes had turned around.

Their light-hearted mood didn't wane until they reached the slums of the city. The cheery façade of San Francisco, with its lively people and architecture, faded into ramshackle houses and make-shift shelters. Half-naked children chased one another barefooted through the alleys. There was a sign on an old building that read, 'Okies Go Home.' The letters were sun-worn, indicating it had been painted a while ago.

"Where are we?" Maud asked.

"We aren't in the city proper anymore. At least, I don't think so," Gus said. "It's where the fellas told me to go, though. This is more of a shantytown than I was expecting. Charlie says a lot of the Okies ended up in places like this, which is why he prefers to stick to his tattoo shop in the city proper. These people are so sad, just trying to get away from the dust."

"How sad. I don't know if we should go on. I'm not sure if we should be here. How much farther is it to where we are meeting everyone?"

"I don't know. Let me go ask someone. Wait here for me," Gus said.

Maud nodded and watched Gus approach a group of men across the street. She clutched at her shawl even though it wasn't at all cold. In fact, the persistent breeze that cooled every other neighborhood of San Francisco seemed to be absent in this one.

It wasn't that she felt unsafe, more like she felt uneasy. She was a healthy woman with more money than she needed standing among the poorest of the poor who were struggling to get by. The longer she was there, the more her presence felt disrespectful and garish.

Maud couldn't really say what about the couple caught her eye. At first glance, they appeared to be stacked laundry. Nothing more than two piles of ragged clothing slumped over next to each other, sitting at the adjacent street corner. When she looked closer, she saw them for what they were: an old couple in rags, leaning against one another. They looked homeless and begged with a broken coffee tin in front of them.

Something visceral inside her body pulled at her. It was like a physical tether dug its hooks into her gut and guided her toward the couple. The feeling made no sense to her, but the urge was strong.

When she crossed the street, Maud reasoned the long day had worn on her psyche. She had no unearthly attraction to these people. She was merely a curious patron, ready to give them a few coins to ease their woes. As she approached, the man raised his eyes to her and held out his hand.

"Anything you might spare would be a blessing," he said in a dry whisper.

Maud stopped mid step, nearly tumbling over her feet. She was mere feet away from the couple, but something kept her from moving toward or away. That something was the man's voice. It rang so familiar; it was a voice she'd known as a child.

When she got a look at the man's face, really looked at it, she confirmed what her ears had told her. This ghost of a man before her was her father. She drew in a hard breath and turned to the woman next to him, immediately recognizing her as her mother.

Terror shook her body. Her heart trembled like a beaten dog. The ground seemed to spin and get wobbly underneath her feet. Maud's throat closed up tight while she tried not to vomit. After all she had done, after all she had been through in her life, seeing the specter of her parents made her feel like a girl getting swatted in church once again. Her mouth went dry, and she lost the capacity for words.

Maud shook in limbo then, unsure whether to run to her parents, stay where she was, or walk away like they were strangers. In a way, wasn't she a stranger? She was a different person now, a seasoned woman. Would they even know her?

Their skin was dust dry and cracked where it folded. Dark circles hung like hammocks from under their eyes and in the hollows of their cheeks. Ragged clothing draped over their bodies like it might a skeleton's. So dehydrated were they that the skin around her father's mouth pulled taut and away, showing more of his teeth than was normal. The faint scent of urine and excrement wafted when the air turned.

Had they met this fate the way others had in this part of town? The Okies, as they were called. Poor farmers with thirsty crops from years of blight and drought, driven to the coast looking for work. They escaped the horrible dust that covered the land, ending up in places like this.

Maud pictured the sea of wheat from her childhood as nothing but dust. It did not fit inside her mind, like a square peg in a round hole. Yet, here her parents sat, and they were starving. You do not leave a farm that is thriving.

Inside the coffee tin, there were three pennies. Maud dug in her handbag, pulled out a nickel, and flipped it into the tin. It clanged, metal against rusty metal, as it hit the bottom. Her mother's skeletal hand reached out to collect the offering without looking up.

"Thank you. God bless you," she said while hiding her face behind a dirty tumble of greying hair.

Maud reached out and grabbed the boney hand. It felt dry and brittle, but she wouldn't let go. When the woman started to protest, Maud bent down to get eye level with her. The dull pebbles in the woman's face looked nearly blind at first, wandering here and there. Her eyes were listless and struggling to find purchase on anything substantial, but when they landed on Maud's, a knowing ignited. At last, Maud saw a glimmer of the potent force that had once been her mother.

"Hi Mama," Maud said with a small smile.

For an instant, her mother's eyes grew wide with recognition. Maud thought she might even smile. Then, her mother set her mouth in a line, quickly pulled back her hand, and glared up at Maud. With everything that had happened, Maud thought her mother couldn't injure her anymore, but all it took was one scowl to puncture Maud's armor and hit bone.

Her father turned to see what the fuss was all about. When he saw Maud, he too recognized her. His was not a look of scorn, but of loss. The pitiful stare of something you lost so long ago there was no way of getting it back. It pained her to see him so removed, so she tried to believe he didn't see her. Maybe he was just in pain. Perhaps it had nothing to do with her.

"Daddy, it's me. It's Maudie," Maud said. "Don't you know me?"

He looked at her harder and saw the tattoos that covered her shoulders and arms. Her father locked on to the scene of lions across her chest. Horror filled his eyes as he struggled for the words. Just

227

then, Gus appeared at Maud's side.

"Maudie, what's happened?" he asked.

"These... these are my parents, Gus."

It was a bombshell, but one that only momentarily stalled Gus Wagner. Maud gaped at her husband, unsure what to say, or how to proceed. He rallied his composure and swooped in to try and help matters by squatting down with Maud and extending his hand to her father.

"Hello, sir. My name's Gus Wagner. I'm your daughter's husband. It's an honor to finally meet you. I've heard so much..." His voice trailed off as he took her father's boney hand.

When Maud's father saw the tattoos that covered Gus's arms, he threw away Gus's handshake like it was infected or covered with pests.

"Who are you? I don't know who you are," her father said.

He looked frightened and confused. Maud leaned in closer and tried to calm him with as soothing a tone as she could muster. All the while, her own heart attempted to beat its way free from under her rib cage.

"Daddy, it's me. You see me, don't you? Look at my face. You see your Maudie?"

He nodded peering into her eyes, just into her eyes. Maud took his hands in hers and smiled at the ghost of her father.

"It's me. It's your Maudie and this is my husband, Gus. We can help you now, both of you. We have a daughter, too. She's grown. You have a granddaughter. Her name is Lotteva. I wrote you about her..."

"We got yer letters," her mother said.

Maud let go of her father's hands and turned to the demon next to her. Rage set her mother's eyes ablaze, and she directed all her hatred at Maud. A weak and skeletal ghost she was no more; the true woman underneath had come out to speak.

"We got yer stupid letters. I burned them. Never read a one."

"But why?" Maud asked while trying to hold her composure. "Why wouldn't you read them? Why wouldn't you want to know your granddaughter? She's so... wonderful. I never forgot about you. Not ever. I hoped to come back some day."

"You left *us*!" her mother screamed. "You went galivanting off. You brought no end of shame to your family. Where were you when we lost everything?"

"But... but I had to."

"You know them Clark boys took a terrible beating for losing you at the circus that day?" her mother said. "We thought you'd been kidnapped or something worse. It wasn't until we got your first letter that we knew the truth. You ran away to go be... whatever *this* is."

She made a disgusted hand motion gesturing to the entirety that was her daughter. Maud stood up, making her parents look into the setting sun to see her properly. Her fists balled at her side as she struggled to blink back tears. Poor Gus stood by, helpless to do anything to make this better for her. As far as these people were concerned, he was less than human. A freak covered in pictures.

"This is your daughter. This is who I am. Who I always was," Maud said.

"I didn't raise no freak show whore," her mother said, as her father remained silent.

"Mother! I'm married and have a daughter. Gus and I have been married for..."

"It don't matter none what you call your life. Vern told me enough. He told us about what a whore you were."

Rage lit a fire inside Maud as she remembered her uncle and how he touched her. The anger began in her belly and stoked its way up and through her limbs. A vile thing told her to strike the decrepit woman. She wasn't a child anymore, no matter how much she felt like one in their presence, and this woman wasn't her mother. She didn't deserve to be her mother. All this time, Maud had pined for something else, something more. She had wanted love. She had wanted her mother to hold her, to protect her, to let her draw daisies on her skin. At the very least, they could draw flowers together.

This wasn't a mother. The thing before her was the backwards, ignorant trash that had always called itself her mother. No amount of Fiji mermaids could change that. What kind of mother called her daughter a whore? Maud loomed over the demon, and for the first time in her life, the demon looked a little afraid. Even though she knew it was wrong, she felt a kind of justice in that.

"I was no whore. I came to you and told you what he was doing. But you wouldn't hear it; you didn't want to know any of it. I was your daughter! You are supposed to protect your children, not leave them to the wolves. You should have protected me!"

Maud blinked back hot tears and hated herself for crying. It was a cry of anger, but tears were tears, no matter why they were birthed. So much rage welled up it seeped out in brine from her eyes. The demon cowered further, but still shot insults up at her like a cornered dog.

"You always did blame everyone else for your faults. You left us! You left us all alone."

"You left me to fend off that man by myself! That monster! I left you to get away from him and a life of living hell."

"That's how you saw our lives?" her father said in a weak voice. "We were a living hell?"

"Daddy... I..."

A hot spot inside her flinched at that. He had always been the kindest to her. There had been times, although not many, he stuck up for her or hid her from her mother's wrath. She had become quite accustomed to this one spot beneath the stairs he'd stash Maud when she'd forgotten to do her chores. The whipping would still come, but he helped her escape the brunt of it until her mother calmed a bit.

He even snuck her bits of bread while she waited out the storm. Of course, there came a time when she couldn't fit beneath the stairs any longer, when he could no longer hide her.

This skeleton of a man, who hid behind the anger of his wife. Had Maud been gripping his memory the tightest? Her life would have been a complete living hell if not for him.

Perhaps her father's question wasn't the important one. Maud was an aging woman, despite what pretty picture she drew on Mr. Fischer, yet these two made her feel sixteen all over again. She wasn't a child anymore, and it was time the real question came forward. They had nothing if her parents couldn't see her as their daughter. A grown woman of her own sound mind.

"What am I to you?" she asked them both.

Her mother practically spat at her when she answered. "You're a whore! Nothing but a filthy whore. Look at you! We don't want any help from a freak and her freak husband."

With a set jaw and a stoic manner, Maud switched her gaze back to her father. He gazed up at her as if to beg her not to do it. Please, his eyes said, please don't ask what you're about to ask. Don't make me say it.

But she had no choice.

"Daddy, do you agree with her? Is that what I am to you, too? A filthy whore?"

There had been many years of wondering. When she was younger, she fantasized about her father receiving one of her letters without her mother knowing. He would clutch the small envelope to his chest, happy to hear from her. She imagined he would take it down to the basement and hide it to read by lamplight where his wife would not notice him.

Her father would read her words and smile, knowing she was all right and happy somewhere in the big, wide world. Maybe he would write her back and store the letter away somewhere until it was safe to mail it, away from her mother's prying eyes. Perhaps even in that little space under the stairs where he used to hide her.

As the years passed, no letters came back to her. Every year that passed weakened the fantasy, making it fuzzy and translucent in her mind. But she still hoped it was true. The little girl in her begged him to make it true. It was his last chance. Right then. Right there.

Fairy tales aren't true, and fantasies often come up short.

Her father lowered his eyes, a lifetime's worth of defeat weighing them down, and nodded in agreement with her mother. To him, she was indeed a filthy whore. Whether he believed it himself or not, that's what she was to him because that's what she was to the demon. He failed as a father not because of his meanness but out of complacency. At that moment, it hurt Maud worse than any beating her mother ever doled out.

Everything in Maud tightened. Somewhere deep inside her, a door she hadn't known was open slammed shut. It would never be opened again. Never.

She dug back in her purse and pulled out a handful of coins. In a fit of rage, Maud threw the money down at the coffee tin on the ground. The coins tinkled and chimed as they danced around on the ground. Her parents flinched as some hit them.

Maud turned on her heel and marched away from the skeletons who used to be her parents. Gus hurried to follow her, a whirlwind of anger and tears in her wake. Behind her, she listened to hear the scraping of their limbs on the pavement. For all their pride, for all their bluster, they were starving. Would they take the money of a whore? Would they leave it for someone else to take instead, thus dubbing it unworthy money for them to use? The high road was awfully high when you were hungry.

She didn't dare look back, but she heard it. The tiniest clink of coins being collected and deposited in a coffee tin. It was slow and deliberate. Definitely the sluggish movements of the old and infirmed, but it was there. It was a small battle, this last one, but she had emerged the victor. For all her mother's high talk, she took the whore's money.

Gus caught up to her and grabbed her hand. He squeezed it without trying to steer her in any one direction. He was merely letting her know she wasn't alone. He was there. He wouldn't leave her.

"Maud, baby, they're your family," he whispered as she turned a corner to head for a trolley stop. "Should we rethink this? Maybe go back later?"

"No, they aren't my family. You and Lotteva, you're my family. Dora's my family. Those people? They are nothing but dust."

***

Maud paced furiously back and forth in Dora's bedroom. With every step, her foot pounded harder on the floor than before. It was beginning to rub at the soles of her feet, but Maud didn't desist. There would be a path worn in Dora's floorboards before too long.

"Hey, toots, take it easy," Dora said. "They ain't worth it. I can promise you that."

Maud waved away her friend's words as though they were gnats. "You always have an answer for everything, don't you? I don't need an answer. There aren't any answers," Maud said with a bite in her words. Of course, she regretted them the instant they came out. Maud stopped her obsessive pacing and stared at her friend. Dora sat on the bed, looking up at her with the gentle eyes she always reserved for Maud. She gave them to no one else, save Lotteva. "I'm... I'm sorry. I didn't mean to say that."

"I know," Dora said with a smile, but Maud saw a touch of hurt underneath. She shouldn't have snapped. After all, Dora wasn't the reason she was angry. Dora was the reason she had a life worth living.

"Come here, toots," Dora said as she made to get up.

Maud opened her arms to her friend, but as she stood, Dora faltered. She clutched her side suddenly and winced in pain as her knees buckled beneath her.

"Dora!" Maud exclaimed as she caught her under the arms before she landed on the hard floor. It took some effort, but she pulled her friend back onto the bed.

"I'm all right. It's fine," Dora said in a raspy voice.

"It doesn't look fine," Maud said. "What's wrong?"

Dora still held her hand to the right side of her waist. It wasn't the touch of someone rubbing away an aching muscle, nor was it the grip of a broken bone. The way Dora bent at the pain and held fast to her side meant something deeper. Something beyond muscle and tissue and bone. Terror rose in Maud's throat, and she wanted to scream at her own thoughts.

"It's cancer," Dora said with a whoosh of air. She reached out and grabbed Maud's hand. Dora's fingers were so cold they made Maud's feel like embers. "Started in my lungs. Now, it's everywhere. All those cigarettes, they think. I didn't want to tell you this way. Not after the day you had."

"No. No, that can't be right," Maud said.

"Afraid so, toots. I've known for some time. Why'd you think I was so insistent you come see me? It wasn't just to see you draw some pretty pictures."

"But you can't just… the doctors can help you," Maud said.

"They've tried," Dora said while squeezing Maud's hand. "It's too far gone."

Maud envisioned her parents then, sitting on the corner of the dingy shanty town, begging for money. They were fractions of what they'd been, but at least they were alive. Why did they get that blessing when

Dora didn't? Dora was the one who saved her, loved her, protected her. The last thing she deserved was to sit here in pain.

"But... but *you* are my family," Maud said slowly.

The pressure of the pain welled up and tears poured down Maud's face in waves. She threw her arms around Dora and wailed into her thinning hair. When they pulled apart, Dora's face was just as streaked as Maud's.

"See here, toots. There's nothin' for it. I won't have you makin' my last days on creation a sad affair. No funeral. No memorial. I want love, laughter and liquor. Do you hear me? No cryin' on my account."

Maud gazed into her friend's eyes and fully took her in. She hadn't noticed how tired and gaunt Dora appeared until that moment. She was, after all, a woman in her seventies, but Dora never appeared that way. There was always a light burning inside her that was infectious and youthful. This was the first time Maud registered that the light had dimmed.

"How long?" Maud asked.

"I don't know, and I don't want to know," Dora said. Maud pressed her lips together and raised her eyebrow. She could tell her friend was holding back. "Not long. Months maybe. The doctor says less, but he's the depressed sort, so I don't pay much attention to him." Tears began anew on Dora's face as her façade broke. "Please, do something for me."

"Anything."

Dora's face screwed into one of pure pain as she reached for Maud's hands. Every word came out as broken and squeaky as a child's tearful plea.

"Please don't leave until... the end. Please stay. I can't bear to... I am so afraid to... you are *my* family."

They embraced again and wept a fresh wave of sorrow. Maud clutched at her friend as though holding her tighter might heal her.

She pictured herself reaching inside Dora and pulling out the cancer with her bare hands. When the weeping reached its end, Dora did the most unusual thing. She laughed.

"What's so funny?"

"I just hope you know I'm bequeathin' all my old costumes to Lotteva. Your rump's gotten too big for 'em."

Grief was an odd thing. In a breath of time, it could jerk a person from tears to laughter and back again. Maud could attest to that. Over the next five months, they laughed, cried, raged, and drank. All of it was in the name of grief as they watched Dora wither away.

When the mighty woman passed into the next life, she was surrounded by loved ones. Lotteva wept at the foot of the bed, wrapped in her father's arms. Dora's husband, Charlie, stood in the corner nearest her and tried to put on a brave smile for his wife. Maud held Dora's hand all the way until the end. She felt her friend's life slip beneath her fingers.

It was one of the greatest honors of her life to be the one to mark the passing of a such a tender soul with the words, "*We* are your family... forever."

Part Eight

Gus had taken to other vocations in the years after the war. Soldiers came back with terrible stories; it was a war beyond compare in its atrocities. People no longer flocked to the Wagners' tattoo tent. Instead, they went off to make families. An entire nation was grateful for survival and wanted to move forward with life.

All that meant the Wagner family had to look to other means of support. Gus was good at sculpting from wood. He whittled on seemingly useless hunks of wood like they were marble. Suddenly, amazing things came from the useless. Bears, eagles, pretty girls. They were all beautiful, and he made it look so effortless.

After years of practicing on jack rabbits, his taxidermy improved quite a bit. It was not quite as refined as his whittling, but it was still admirable. At first, he did them to amuse himself, then, when money began to run thin, he sold his art at the fairs.

It was a clear, blue day when he presented Maud with a walking stick of roses. To say the piece was lovely would be an insult. Gus had intricately cut rose after rose into the wood weaving in tangled vines up to the top. It peaked in a curling flourish shaped perfectly to fit inside her hand. He'd taken the care to etch the fine detail of little leaves as well. The cane was sanded smooth, varnished, and polished

237

to a pristine shine. In fact, it was so beautiful that a banker offered Gus twice the normal price to give it to his mother. Maud told her husband to take the money.

"I made it for you, Maudie. It's yours and yours alone."

"But the money, Gus."

"No. I won't sell this. Not for any price."

"I'm not old enough to use a cane," she said. "I'll have you know I get around just fine. You're trying to turn me old before my time."

"Maud, you are going to be an old, grey woman someday. I know that for a fact. You'll need it then, and you'll remember me when you see this, even if your mind goes."

She accepted the cane with a scowl, but Gus was satisfied; he beamed at her.

For whatever reason, Maud grew surlier in her advancing age. It was true she had never been a flighty girl, but her countenance had grown more tired as the years moved along. Time weighed her down, pulling on her vigor. After the boom and energy of the war subsided, she struggled to find a place in this new world so tender from its global grieving.

None of it seemed to strike Gus the same way. He had his periods of sadness and of fear, but he softened in the places that grew rigid in his wife. If anything, Gus became more jovial. The man leaned into the nonsense of his own charm, choosing to belief his act more than the rubes. Maud had to give him credit, Gus appeared happier for it.

The family had been traveling with a small outfit around Kansas. No longer did the countryside loom over Maud with the threat of reopening old wounds. Everyone she knew there was dead, or at least, dead inside her. The rolling wheat sea was dust and ashes. Nothing more.

Gus sold his wares to the local rubes while Lotteva and Maud tattooed. Business was slow, even though a doctor and naturalist bought three of Gus's better taxidermy creatures. Maud handled the little bit of tattoo business that came their way while painting posters and portraits on the side. Lotteva busied herself with her exotic animals and working the stage as a snake charmer.

There was a storm brewing in the west. Nothing like the dust storms they had known in the past. A small build-up of clouds. A gentle rumble in the distance pointing to thunder. The noise was a cat's purring more than a thunderclap, truth be told. Even the animals ignored it for the most part.

The afternoon smelled of sweet hay and wildflowers as the rube families dispersed to their cars and lazily headed back to their homes. Winds started to blow a little harder and a little wetter. Lotteva went to rest in their tent complaining of a headache in between her eyes. Part of her hiding had to do with one moony-eyed suitor who had grand ideas of matrimony. He was a man who could guess your weight. Somehow, he didn't understand why that sort of talent was unappealing to a woman.

Maud sat outside among her newly painted posters, allowing the paint to dry and enjoying the cooling breeze. The world smelled calm and new the way it did after a storm rather than before. Gus went out to a nearby field to look for fallen branches that might be turned into works of art to sell.

He was standing in that field when it happened. Maud wished she could say she knew the exact moment. A bond as strong as theirs should have rippled her soul to mark the moment of his passing. As his wife and companion, Maud should have had some inkling about it, some intuition in her belly to tell him to stay behind. Even when the boss man sent a crew of roustabouts to fetch Gus, she didn't worry. It wasn't until the boys came back with a body instead of her husband that she felt his passing.

Gus Wagner hadn't been a large man in a physical sense of the word.

Size didn't matter all that much to a true performer. When in front of a crowd, he was tallest man for miles. The sheer volume of his person elevated him up and beyond everyone in sight. Men looked up to him in amazement, even if they had to physically look down to see him.

Maud imagined his passing when she viewed his body. In her mind, the clouds settled into gently rolling waves above as Gus made his way through the tall grass of the Kansas field. In his hand, he held a few decent bits of wood that might make a good piece of art. Without warning and without cause, a bolt of lightning erupted from the sky, striking Gus and killing him on the spot.

Nothing could be done about it. When looking for a place to land, lightning chooses the tallest thing in the area to strike. Gus Wagner had been the tallest thing in that field just like he was the tallest thing in Maud's life. Within a second, he was gone.

The fellows who retrieved his body did so in a wagon harnessed to a mule. Most knew Gus, so they did Maud the courtesy of covering his face when presenting her his body. After all, there was no need to see his face to recognize him. His tattooed arms sprawled lifeless at his sides, leaving little doubt as to his identity.

All of the moisture left Maud's mouth when she looked at his limp hand. She swallowed a few times trying to create some saliva, but the effort was fruitless. As if knowing her need, a light sprinkle fell from the sky, gently covering everyone in a mist. None of it soothed her.

His limbs were lifeless and moved only when the wagon rocked under the fidgety mule. At first, it didn't seem possible. This couldn't be Gus. She drew closer and made to remove the blanket covering his face.

"I wouldn't do that, Mrs. Wagner," said the older boy while grabbing her hand. "It ain't a pretty sight. No need for you to see it."

Maud took her hand back and touched her husband's arm instead. It was cold and damp. Not a bit of blood in it to warm his skin.

"I'm awful sorry, ma'am. We all liked Gus an awful lot."

She was busy staring at Gus's arm. Each tattoo she knew intimately. Every single one. So many nights they had spent curled around one another, memorizing every line, each shadow. Every bird, ship, and pretty girl.

Now, something else invaded those pictures. A red and black pattern spread down his arm reaching to his hand. It looked like a spider's web in some areas but fanned out like tree branches in others. Maud had seen patterns like this before during a world fair or at one of their bigger outfits in the anatomical diagram of the nervous system. Spider-like webbing and branches ran under the skin as veins and arteries to carry blood.

Was this Gus's webbing? The branches under his skin, singed by fire? She touched the pattern, confused and horrified.

"I seen that before," said the older boy. "A feller I knew got struck a while back. Lived and all but left him with a scar like that."

Without thinking, Maud grabbed for Gus's hand. That was a mistake. It had once been a constant source of warmth and comfort. Now, it was a cold limp thing, alien to her, and she let it go as soon as she felt the lack of life in it.

Maud thought she might wretch but didn't want to in front of the others. An hour ago, she was hungry and wondering when Gus would come back so they might eat at the cookhouse together. Now, the mere thought of food made her knees quiver.

The world sort of held its breath. Most folks expect the passing of a man to be more in some way—whether in glorious battle or in a bed surrounded by loved ones. When a man took up so much space in one's life, his quietus should be marked by something more momentous than a gentle rumble of thunder.

Maud nodded to the boys who offered to take Gus away to the funeral home down the road. No matter how small, every town had a funeral home. She watched long enough for the mule to round the corner and disappear out of sight. Then, Maud turned to do the hardest thing she'd ever had to do. She went to the tent to tell her daughter.

***

The funeral was a small affair. Most of their close friends had already passed away or given up the circuit years earlier, but enough of the younger guard wanted to attend to make a good showing. Gus had been well-liked, and the circus boss agreed to delay their departure long enough for everyone to pay their final respects.

Maud barely saw them. Some formed shapes here and there when someone took her hand or spoke to her, but they were mere shadows passing in front of her eyes. The only face she recognized was Lotteva's, and hers was a blood-shot mess of tears. The two of them sat together like twin widows, covered in brine and snot.

At one point, the boss man of the outfit hugged her. His deep voice broke the trance of her grief long enough to pay attention.

"Maud, I want you to know how sorry we are. He was a legend. You both are. He gave me my first tattoo. On my arm. Did I tell you that?"

"No, you didn't," she said numbly.

"Well, he did. What a fella your husband was. I reckon the only thing to take down a man like that would have to be an act of God."

Her lip curled involuntarily, and he changed the subject.

"Anyhow, I want you to know you are welcome here with us just as long as you want. We are family. If you want us to drop you somewhere along the way, we can do that, too. Anything you or Lotteva need, just tell me. I mean it."

His words barely registered. She barely registered. The sun hit Maud's face in a mocking sort of way. Other than the solemn event, the day was quite beautiful. It shouldn't be though, she thought. It shouldn't be beautiful. Not today. Birds shouldn't sing at all.

Maud sat in her chair while more strangers floated by, offering condolences. All she could do was clutch the last thing she had left of the man she called her husband. The last thing he touched, the last thing he made. A beautiful, rose cane.

"You can now, honey," Maud said to Lotteva.

"I can what?"

"You can have a tattoo now."

"What are you talking about? You never let me get one," Lotteva said.

Despite her grief, Lotteva sounded shocked. It was as if Maud had given her a shot in the arm. When Maud met her daughter's eyes, they were red-rimmed and huge. Swollen yet surprised.

"I didn't want you to need it," Maud said as she took her daughter's hand. "I understand if you need it now."

"I don't get it. Who needs a tattoo? What does that even mean, Mama?" Lotteva asked with genuine confusion.

"It doesn't matter. Just know that I'm fine with it now. If you want to get a tattoo, you can."

"But... I don't want one," she said.

"Why not?"

"Because it wouldn't be one of Daddy's."

***

1951

In the grand scheme, the world goes on spinning no matter who leaves it. The decade turned over, marking the end of another without much of a fuss. Life continued. Maud and Lotteva had to move on with the next circus.

The nineteen fifties brought with it a deeper lull in the public's desire for tattoos. Families sprang up everywhere settling into pristine, cookie-cutter neighborhoods. Children played games in the streets with relatively full bellies and furnished homes. The Dust Bowl and the war were quickly becoming forgotten nightmares.

Folks had the money for tattoos but not the want. Prosperity re-ignited, but so did the idea of proper etiquette and behavior. Never was the stigma more profound than in the women; Maud was again regarded as a great oddity, more so than ever before.

A tattoo now coincided with *deviance*. People would never say it to her face, surely. Still, Maud became the cautionary tale mothers told in the background, pointing at the tattooed lady and saying, "That's what happens if you drop out of school."

Women were meant to be neat, humble, and beyond reproach. They walked around the fair ushering their gaggle of children like beautiful teacakes. Each one made up and sprayed as though they were preserved mannequins from a department store. Perfectly frosted petit fours too lovely to eat.

"Think they're better than just about anyone, don't they?" Lotteva said. "I can't believe anyone would do themselves up like that for a husband."

"Oh, don't kid yourself," Maud said. "It isn't for the husbands. That act is for the other women. You don't know about regular society. Most times, women are the meanest to one another." She was having a hard time keeping her scowl in check.

"It would break my jaw to smile like that with all the powder and cake on it. Clown makeup is more comfortable. At least with that, we don't lie about how ridiculous it looks," Lotteva said with her own scowl firmly planted.

"Get up close and sniff when they're not looking," Maud said.

"Why?"

"Most smell like gin. The rest like bourbon. The ones who don't smell...well, let's just say if pills had a scent, they'd smell like that too."

Occasionally, they had outliers come calling. They women came to her for relief, for expression, and sometimes for the pain of it. Always somewhere discreet, often where not even their husbands would notice. Caged birds, no matter how gilded their accommodations, still needed to sing.

It was a windy day, near Michigan, when Maud saw a strange woman. She appeared no different than any other woman of about thirty-five. However, something about her plainly labelled her as different. Maybe foreign? Regardless, she caught Maud's eye.

Her manner was fast and to the point. She wore no makeup and her dress was of a fashion outdated by at least five years. Yet, she comported herself with her head high and her shoulders back. Strong and without hesitation, the woman moved among the tents and food stands.

As she walked by, Lotteva danced in one of Dora's old costumes. A long python named Melissa wrapped itself around her. In her forties now, some of Lotteva's costumes had to be let out to make way for her rounder hips. A life with no children and active work gave her the youthful body of her mother, but gravity was gravity. New sequins had to be sewn on and holes had to be covered with bangles, but people still lined up to watch her dance.

Maud, by comparison, felt feebler every day since Gus's passing. Never had the years burdened her so much as they did after that horrible day.

It just so happened the strange woman made her way to their area of the fair when the ruckus began. At first, she seemed to be drawn in by Lotteva's undulating dance. The woman marveled at her, taking in the snake with the wide, wondrous gaze of a child.

"You like this, you should get a tattoo. Best artists in the world right here," Lotteva said in her best show voice.

"You? You do this?" asked the woman, pointing at the tattoo sign.

Maud hadn't paid much attention at first, merely noting the woman's otherness. When she spoke though, it was with a voice heavily accented in German or Polish. Maud always had a difficult time differentiating between the two. Short and sharp and to the point. They both sounded that way.

On closer inspection, Maud noticed that the woman was wearing a green jacket even though it was summer, and the temperatures had been breaking records for weeks. At first, Maud thought she might be the type who was perpetually cold, but as she got closer, Maud noticed that the woman pulled at her collar and fanned her face, trying to get some relief.

"Yes, I do tattoos. We do only the best work," Lotteva said.

Agitation trembled around them all. A crowd ran past, shouting things that didn't make sense. It was like a stampede of people. Whatever was happening south of Maud's tent, it was drawing people to it. The crowd collected bystanders as it went.

One of the voices in the stampede called above the others. "Massarti! It's Massarti! The lion's got him!"

The message sent Lotteva into a whirlwind of motion. She unraveled the python from her shoulders and replaced her in the crate. After jumping in some slippers, Lotteva leapt down from her small stage, and took off after the sea of people.

"Wait," said the woman. "What about the tattoo?"

"Ask my mother!" Lotteva shouted over her back as she hurried away. "She's much better than me anyway."

In a flash of bangles and veils, Lotteva was gone, leaving the only two people unmoved by the frightful spectacle. Maud and the strange woman stood in the vacuum of silence looking at one another.

"You tattoo people?" she asked looking skeptically at Maud.

"I do."

"Your hands shake? With your age, I mean."

When she spoke, it was sharp and to the point. No pretense or flattery. Also, there was not any real insult in her voice, even though her words sounded hurtful.

"Not much. That is, unless you are annoying."

Maud smiled and waited for the joke to drop. It didn't. The woman just stared blankly at her. She looked almost funny with how unfunny she found the punch line.

"Am I this annoying person? I do not wish to pay for bad work," she said.

"I am merely joking. What you said a minute ago was rude, but I don't think you meant that way. I said a joke to even the score."

Maud had dealt with enough foreigners to know that idioms and jokes sometimes went over their heads. It must have been confusing if it wasn't your language. She patted the chair across the table from her, gesturing for the woman to sit.

When she took a seat, Maud got a better look at her. She had brown, serious eyes, and high prominent cheekbones. They lifted the shape of her face and made her pretty. Even without makeup, she held up well in a close inspection. There was a sort of natural hardness about her.

Inside the collar of her green jacket there was a wet ring where sweat had pooled. Once again, Maud wondered why such a woman might wear a jacket in the heat.

"I'm Maud," she said while extending a hand.

"Clara." They shook hands, and Clara took out her wallet. "I can pay. I have money. Please no bad work. I only pay for good work."

"Don't worry. I haven't done bad work a day in my life, and I've been at this longer than you've been alive."

"This is true? What you said. That is not a joke?"

"It is not a joke," Maud said with a smile.

"It's hard for me to tell."

"Well, how about we agree to not joke with one another? That way, there are no misunderstandings. Sound good?"

Clara nodded and looked around. The world seemed to go still. No ambient crowd noises. No children's laughter. Even the insects quietened. It made the meeting of the two women feel even stranger. They were alone together in the silence of the universe.

Maud caught the smallest tang on the wind. She would lay a solid bet somewhere south of them was a fair amount of blood.

"Where did the people go?" Clara asked.

"I heard someone say Massarti. I think something happened to him."

"Who is this? Massarti?"

"He is a foolish man. A one-armed lion tamer my daughter likes. I told them he wasn't careful enough with those cats."

"This is a joke. You said no jokes."

Maud snickered. "This is no joke... unfortunately. Well, nothing I can do. He's got everyone else running to help him. How may I help you, Miss Clara?"

Clara settled herself in her seat as though she needed to be sturdy for the rest of the conversation.

"I want a tattoo."

"Okay. What would you like and where on your body do you want it?"

"I like the snake. The one your daughter dances with. I want a snake like that."

"All right. Where would you like it?"

The woman faltered and flinched a little. Her stoic expression melted a bit as she looked around the fairgrounds, scouting for people who might notice her. However, they were all alone, and Maud thought about telling her so as a reassurance. Instead she waited, letting Clara decide for herself.

It looked like it pained Clara to remove the jacket. She fidgeted in her seat and leaned this way and that to shrug the garment loose from her shoulders. Underneath, the grey lining was soaked with sweat and smelled musty. Finally, free from the jacket, Clara was able to breathe, and relief flooded her face.

The blouse she wore was probably once lovely. It was silk in the palest color of blue, but the sleeves had been cut from it to create a makeshift tank top. Whomever had done the deed did a hack job and hadn't bothered to hem the edges. Fine blue threads stuck out like the legs of small, dead spiders all around her shoulders. Sweat ringed her collar and underarms.

"Here. I want the tattoo here," Clara said, holding out her arm over the table.

A weight fell into Maud's throat, and she choked it down as best she could. Her belly vibrated and threatened to shake her whole torso. Clara extended her arm to Maud with the underbelly of her forearm facing up. There on her wiry skin were a series of five numbers in a row.

This was a horror. These were the markings of madness. It wasn't easy for Maud to measure her face, but she did it as best she could.

"I see. You want me to cover the numbers?" Maud asked.

"Yes. Cover them with a snake."

"I can do that," Maud said gently.

"You know what these are, these numbers? What they mean?"

Maud forced herself to look up into Clara's eyes. They were hard and without pretense. There existed no joke or dancing bit of talking that would gloss over this one. Nothing but the truth, and nothing but the most brutal version of it.

"Yes, I know. I heard some stories."

"Okay then," Clara said. "Then we don't have to talk about it."

Maud nodded and took to setting up her tools. She didn't bother hiding the needles as she washed them and lined them on a rag. Not in front of this woman. What was the point?

The India ink mixed quickly with the bit of water and soap needed for a good consistency. Maud folded a towel and positioned it underneath Clara's arm for comfort. It wasn't until she was washing the horrific numbers that Maud thought about warning her customer about the pain. Not so much because of the physical pain, more the emotional pain that could well up.

"This area here," Maud said while touching the tender part of her skin, "It's sensitive. More so than other parts. If I am going to cover it, the snake will have to be rather thick. This might hurt a good deal more."

"Can you do this? The thick snake?"

"Yes, I can."

"Then I don't care. Do the tattoo how it covers best."

Maud took out her box of drawing utensils and began to carefully sketch the outline of a snake over the ugliest five numbers in the world. The head of the beast curled prettily just below the crease of her elbow, and the tail ended just above her wrist with a playful flick. In between, Maud moved the coils of the snake as naturally as she could in the limited space provided.

Clara had been looking away, but when she felt the gentle caress of the charcoal, she looked at her arm with an irritated glare.

"What is this? Why you do this?" she asked gesturing at her arm.

"I am drawing the tattoo on your arm."

"I thought what you did is permanent. I want it to cover forever. You understand? I want this gone. Forgotten," Clara said.

"I understand you, and this will be permanent."

"It has to be like… like when it was done first time. Must be always this."

"First, I have to draw it, so I know where to go with the needle. It will be just as permanent as these when I finish." Maud pointed to the visible tattoos on her chest and arms. They were easy to see around her minimal blouse. Clara calmed a bit and finally nodded.

"All right, I will trust you."

She turned her head away, and Maud pulled out her needles. After making her little inkwell in the cup of her hand, Maud reached for her smallest needle. The skin was so elastic and tender on the underbelly of things, so the tiny needle was a good choice. First pokes were the worst. Maud really didn't want to hurt Clara or trigger any memories, so she went as shallow as she could.

When Maud began, Clara didn't even wince. She looked stoically off to the side, fixing her gaze on some unknown thing in the distance. Her eyes never lighted on her arm nor on Maud.

Each poke deposited its ink as the skin popped back in place. Each time the flesh hung onto the needle a little longer as she pulled it away. Underbelly skin was so clingy.

"Are you married?" asked Maud, trying to break the tension of silence.

"I was. He died." Clara winced just a little as if the act of speaking softened her armor enough for her to feel the pain of the poking.

"Was it in the war?"

"Yes. It was early. He spoke out against them. He was taken," Clara said.

"The Nazis, you mean?"

"I don't want to talk about it," Clara said. She shut her mouth and nodded to no one in particular. It was though she were resolutely agreeing with an unseen ghost.

"All right. Not a problem."

Of course, this was a lie. Such an amazing woman sat in front of her. A woman who could survive whatever it was that led her here with that tattoo. It was crude and grotesque, but the urge to know sat inside Maud. It wasn't her right to pry, so she honored the temporary silence.

Oddly enough, it was Clara who broke it. "That girl is your daughter." It should have been a question, but it wasn't when she said it.

"Yes, she is. My beautiful girl."

"You have a husband?"

"I did. He passed a few years ago," Maud said.

Most people would offer condolences or at least bow their heads. Clara kept her gaze away from Maud and showed no sign of doing either. So, the quiet visited again upon the two women at opposite sides of the table. Somewhere in the distance there was the smallest sound of yelling, but neither woman said a word about it.

When Clara did speak again, it was something Maud hadn't expected. The outline of the tattoo had been done, and she had just finished the detail of the snake's tail.

"You have the twisters here?" Clara asked.

It was the first time Maud had heard a hint of wonder in the woman's voice. It wasn't much, but it was noticeable compared to all of her monotone, serious words.

"You mean the storms? Tornados?" Maud asked.

"Yes, that is the name. I have seen stories about them. In movies and books. I hear they are here."

"Well, they happen in this country. Not usually this far north, but it happens," Maud said wondering why the sudden change in topic. And why twisters?

"You have seen one?" she asked, still gazing at some unknown thing off to the left of Maud.

"I have. I'm from Kansas originally. Lots of twisters there."

Clara nodded just a little and clicked her tongue.

"You should tell me this story where you saw it. Sitting still here is boring. You should talk to make it better."

The laugh exploded like a gunshot from Maud. Of all the things for Clara to say, that was perhaps the most unexpected. Maud had been silent out of respect for Clara's privacy, yet it seemed silence was the last thing she wanted.

She didn't appear amused by Maud's sudden outburst of laughter. Clara merely waited patiently for it to subside so she might hear the story.

"I made no joke," Clara said.

"I know I know."

"Then why..."

"I will tell the story," Maud said. "Let me just refill the ink."

Using an eye dropper, Maud refilled the hollow place on her hand. As she tucked back into her work, she began to tell the most vivid memory she had of a tornado.

"I was about fourteen when the storm hit. Mother and Daddy had gone into town to run some errands, leaving me at home with my Uncle Vern. I wasn't happy about being alone with him, so I took to hiding in the tall wheat and ducking into the kitchen when he was around."

"I don't understand this," she said, still not looking at Maud. "Why did you hide from him? Was he a bad man?"

"Yes. Very bad," Maud said with a little shudder in the back of her throat.

"I see. You should explain that part when you first tell the story. It helps," Clara said in her deadpan way. If she picked up on Maud's aversion to the topic, she didn't show it.

"My apologies," Maud said. "Anyway, I was out in the fields when the storm hit. Thunderstorms with tornados in them look like walls of clouds. Big, thick, heavy things. The underneath of them can be tinged with greenish color."

"The sky can be green?" she asked with a little more of that wonder in her voice. She still didn't look Maud's way.

"It can when there's a tornado in it. Anyway, I saw the storm coming, so I made my way back to the house. It caught up to me just as I got to the clearing where our house stood. I remember how the wind whipped my hair around so hard. I could barely see."

Maud was almost to the numbers on Clara's arm now. Her gut didn't want to cover them up yet. Save them for last, it said. She moved the needle to the head of the snake and began working her way down from that direction.

"A little funnel was snaked down from the hard cloud above me like someone on the ground was pulling it on a string. I'll never forget how the twister sounded as it dropped from the sky. Like a freight train running by, screaming along the rails. One of those cattle cars, you know?"

Clara tensed suddenly. The veins and tendons under her arm made their presence known for a brief second. Her forearm twitched. Thankfully, Maud lifted the needle in time, so no damage was done to the drawing.

"Try to relax," Maud said.

"I am sorry. Please tell me more about the twister."

"Well, it was far enough away I could watch it for a minute. The second it hit the ground, dirt and pieces of trees swirled around it. The twister was pulling up anything it could find and tossing it about. The noise got louder, and I just knew it was heading straight toward me."

"What did you do?"

"I stood watching like an idiot. I can't explain why really. Everything in my body said to run, but I was sort of numb. Like the twister put a spell on me. I couldn't move at all. Then, I heard my uncle screaming at me from the house. He had opened the root cellar and was yelling at me to get inside, but I didn't want to go."

"You wanted to die?"

There was no mockery in that sentence. No judgment at all. Not even any disbelief.

"It wasn't as simple as that. I guess I would have been afraid if I'd thought about it. But in that second, I wasn't. The idea of ducking into a root cellar with my uncle repulsed me, and an undeniable urge to stay and watch the tornado won out. I stood there in the open, watching it get closer and closer through my mess of hair. I didn't want to move. I didn't want to make the choice. I just wanted it to be over."

"What happened? The twister, it didn't take you."

"No, my uncle did. He got to me and picked me up. Hauled me off to the root cellar and shut us inside before it got to the house. In the end, it wouldn't have made a difference. The tornado made a sharp turn before it got us. Didn't even touch our house. I always wondered though what would have happened if I stayed."

Maud finished the last little detail on the eye of the snake. She reached for the stick that had three needles lined up in a row to get more shading done on the body faster and used it to block out more details on the body. Clara's face flinched a little, but she continued to gaze away from the work being done on her arm, which she tried keep still.

"I know this feeling. The numb one you talk about."

"You do?"

"Yes. The day... the day we were liberated, I felt this. The English came. I think it was the English. Americans and English sound the same to me. But they came and set us free. I was numb as you say. Not really wanting to move. They put us in the train cars like the Germans did before. They say it was to take us back to our homes.

But we had no homes. Where would these cars take us? It sounds like your twister, these trains."

"But you found a home. Here in America."

"Yes, my husband's family is here. They sent for me. My husband was gone fast."

"I'm sorry," Maud said quietly.

"You did not kill him. Don't be sorry. He said stupid things. They were true things, and I was thinking he was brave back then. It didn't matter how brave. They took him. Later they came for me and my daughter."

Maud's breath caught in her throat. Dread trembled inside her. A part of her wanted Clara to continue, and a part wanted her to stop. She was standing before a tornado all over again not knowing how to move.

"She... my daughter was little when they took us. My husband's mother was living with us, so they took her too. They moved us here and there until we get on these trains. The day we get to the camps, I was separated from them. The soldiers, they yell to give the children to the old women. I didn't want to and was beaten until I did. It was the last time I saw her, my Adalie. I hoped she was okay with her grandmother there to care for her. I went on living for that hope."

Maud's hand shook a little. She was squeezing the stick too hard, making it tremble under the stress. She took a deep breath, shook out her hand, and began again. Clara did the same.

"They didn't say where the old women and children went. Some say they cooked them. Some say they gas them. Soldiers promised we'd see them again. How or when wasn't known, so I hoped for it someday. I hoped for it too long, but it helped me to live."

"You must have been brave."

"Brave, maybe not. Brave is dangerous. Me? I was angry. I wanted my husband back, my girl back. They starved us, beat us. They think we are not people. Some would rape the women, so I rubbed dirt all over me. Other women tried to stay clean however they could. Dignity they say. Not me. They think I'm animal, I act like animal. I tried to look strong for inspection, but ugly the rest of the time. I would scratch all over my body, so soldiers thought I had lice. They hate lice. They left me alone... like animal."

"That was very clever of you," Maud said.

"Not only that did I do. We worked in factories. At first, the women worked making uniforms for soldiers. Sewing and sewing, all day. I hid pins and broken needles in the seams. You could not see it, but one bend of the knee and stab."

Maud looked absently at the disheveled state of Clara's shirt. Surely, she knew how to sew, but she hadn't bothered to hem up the sleeves; she left them ragged on purpose.

"Later, after they moved us to another factory, they make us work on machine parts. For tanks or guns or planes or something. We were supposed to solder these pieces together along a line. I only did half a line, so it stayed together at first and break later. I wanted their weapons to fall apart. I had dreamed their tanks collapsed into pieces because of me."

The body of the snake was mostly shaded. Its scales blended in nicely together. The tattoo was already looking like a fine piece of art. All that was left was to cover the numbers.

The first number was an eight. If you asked her why she did it at the time, Maud wouldn't be able to say. She reached for a single needle, replacing the one she had been using for big areas. As her hand hovered over the number eight, something inside her told her again and again a message. The number eight could easily be turned into the letter A.

"We walked and walked," Clara said. "They marched us miles from the camps to new factories, new tortures. Women collapsed in the snow. More died every day around me. Every time I think, how can my Adalie find me now? The farther I go, the harder it will be to find her. But there was hope. It kept me going on and on."

"Why weren't you happy when they came to liberate you? I mean after you got off the trains and saw the war was over?"

"When I got off the train, I found friends. My husband had been wealthy and had many Christian friends who hid people and helped spy on the Nazis. They were there at the station when I got off, looking for people they knew. I could see when they saw me, they didn't expect I was alive. At first, I thought it's because my hair was shorter, or I was so thin I looked sick like a skeleton. But they recognized me, just didn't think I made it."

The next number on her arm was a zero. It wasn't much of an effort to turn that into a D.

"That day they told me I wasn't meant to live past the first day at Auschwitz. My name was assigned a number, the one on my arm. I had been marked for execution and didn't know. My husband you see, his bravery marked me. I was to be killed the first week there."

"How did you survive?"

"A clerical error, of all things. There were so many to process, so many to sort and tattoo with a number. My number got swapped for another woman's. One little number off from execution. Not all tattoos are good, you understand. Nazi's made these bad ones. The one she wore had my number, and they killed her. I wear a dead woman's number on my arm."

She fought the urge to shiver under the weight of that. A dead woman's number. Maud shook her head to clear the idea. The next in line was another zero. Maud was determined now in her quest. She filled in the space around a small letter a.

"When I asked about Adalie, none of them said a word. I had to pull it from them, drag it from them. Then, they say none of the old women and children made it past the first day. None of them. They kill them all. Only wanted the ones who could work. The slave laborers. All that time I hoped for my girl; she was already gone. It was wasted, this hope. I should have died that first day with her. It would have been better."

Maud squinted hard at her drawing to try to concentrate. This was a calling now. She had to finish this. The horrors had to bounce off her back long enough for her to finish what she started.

Clara still looked off to the side, not seeing what Maud was doing. Her voice broke and her face reddened. Clara's eyes tensed with pain and a few tears managed to escape, though she wiped at them roughly with her free hand. Maud discreetly reached into her pocket and handed her customer a handkerchief.

"But the hope kept you alive, didn't it? You survived because of her. That's gotta count for something," Maud said.

She had to keep her talking just for a bit longer. Clara couldn't look, not just yet. Another minute or two, and she would be finished.

"Nothing counts. It is like you said with your twister. I was numb. I wanted to die and be with my Adalie and my husband. I should have died. But I lived, and something kept me from killing myself after that. Something held me in place where I could not decide, could not move. Our friends packed me up and sent me here before I could choose, like your uncle did to you. Now I am here. Life chosen for me."

Maud finished the last details as gently as possible. Clara's skin was angry and red after all the work she did to it, so she patted it with a damp cloth as opposed to wiping it hard. It was a lovely snake, and she was proud of the work, but she didn't know how Clara would react to the fact that there, woven prettily in with the snake's undulating coils, was written the name *Adalie*.

"All right. It's done if you'd like to look at it."

For the first time since Maud began, Clara turned to face her. When she gazed down at the snake on her arm, shock took over her face. Then anger did. Clara stood in a flurry of movement, throwing the chair backwards. It clanged to the ground and kicked up dirt. Maud braced herself for what was sure to come next.

"You! I did not ask for this. I did not say to write her name. You have no right!"

The air electrified. For a moment, Maud thought lightning arcs might shoot from Clara's hair. Her eyes flashed bright and crazy. Maud stood too, holding her ink-stained hands out as if to calm a beast.

"I can explain," she said.

"This was not the deal. I did not say..."

"I can cover up the name if you wish," Maud said.

"You know what you did? You know what this says? I wanted this number covered. A dead woman's number. Clara Kramer died in Auschwitz! She should stay there. I want to forget. I tell you these things, so I can forget. Erase. I want it gone! All of it."

"Even Adalie?" asked Maud. "You want her to disappear, too?"

Clara's face fell as though all of the wind was taken from her. Water filled her eyes with both despair and fury. For a moment, she looked like she might punch Maud in the face.

Maud took a deep, long breath. She over-exaggerated the movement of her chest rising and falling to calm Clara. The ragged woman was panting like a dog. Sometimes miming what a person should do makes them mimic without thinking. It was like scratching your lip after watching someone else scratch theirs.

"I understand you're angry. I will honor your original request if you wish. First, I want you to look at the tattoo. Look down at the name. Please."

Despite the rage in her, she acquiesced just enough to glance down at the name on her arm. Compared to the horrid, crude numbers that

260

had been there moments before, the small letters of her daughter's name seemed as lovely and dainty as a song.

The lines around her face relaxed a small amount, and her eyes opened wide enough to see the beauty for what it was. Anger still flowed, flushing her skin with the heat of it, but she no longer sparked the air around her.

"When you look at those letters, you remember her, don't you? You remember holding her and singing her songs. The scent of her hair, you remember it."

Very slowly, Clara nodded.

"I understand all of it, Clara. I know the want to forget. Forgetting erases the pain of losing them, but you shouldn't forget her. Not her. Not your girl. You lived, and she needs to live too, if only in your memory. Please don't try to erase your daughter. There will be nothing left of her if you do that."

Tears came sudden and unbidden. Maud and Clara cried them together yet separated by one small table. The urge to reach across and hug this broken survivor swelled in Maud. Her arms twitched with the ache of it. With everything they had shared that afternoon, it felt right.

Neither woman reached out to the other, though. That table might as well have been a barbed fence.

In the end, it wasn't her place to comfort Clara. The tears Maud cried were for Clara and Adalie, but also for someone else. A good bit of her weeping was attached to the tallest man she knew, and it would be wrong to hold one woman's suffering while she wept for someone else entirely.

Maud settled for reaching across and holding Clara's hand instead. It seemed to be just the right amount of comfort, the perfect gesture to bridge the gap. Clara nodded to her and used the borrowed handkerchief to wipe her face.

Maud bandaged Clara's arm, forgetting to tell her about the aftercare instructions. It didn't matter really. This wasn't the first time the survivor cared for a tattoo on her arm. A terrible reminder but a true one, nonetheless.

They barely said goodbye. Clara dropped some money on the table in front of Maud. It was more than the agreed upon amount. Much more. Before Maud could contest it, Clara held up a hand to silence her. Clara, too, said nothing. She merely nodded to the artist and walked away. People had begun to populate the fairgrounds again, milling aimlessly. Clara, in her ridiculously frayed blouse, was lost inside the crowd and out of sight in mere second. She left only a sweat-stained jacket laying on a pile of hay as evidence she had ever been there.

By the time Lotteva returned, she found her mother bent over and weeping, a knife in her hand. She raced to her mother's side. Maud looked up to see her daughter panicked and worried, hovering over her.

Perhaps Lotteva expected blood? Maybe she worried Maud was hurting herself, and she planned to swoop in and stop her. It wasn't clear what Lotteva was frightened she'd find, but her face calmed when she saw what Maud was doing.

In her lap was a fine, rose-covered cane. It was lovely, intricate, and polished smooth. In the bare bit of the handle, just below where a hand might rest, there had been a part where no roses bloomed. It was there that Maud had just scratched in the name of her husband.

The letters were clumsy, not at all the fine ones she had made for Clara. Between the tears and her lack of capability with a knife, Maud had made his name look brutish in comparison to the delicate vines and roses Gus had carved for her.

It didn't matter. None of that did. His name mattered. It was there now. Permanent, so she would never ever forget him.

Part Nine

1957

After a woman lives long enough, there's nothing she hasn't seen. Each generation thinks they are original and special and different. They will never age like the folks withering away in front of them. Then, they grow older and see that it can happen to anyone.

It is a blessing if you are lucky enough to get the chance to grow old, but that doesn't change how feeble age makes you feel. How difficult basic things become. Your mind might still feel twenty or thirty, and it tells you your body can do twenty or thirty things. The great humiliation is the day a woman discovers she can't anymore, and her mind is a dirty liar.

It wasn't until 1957 that Maud dubbed her mind a liar. She had just celebrated her eightieth birthday, and for the first time in her life, she felt every damn year of it.

Maud sat outside in the warm afternoon air and took in everything as it came. Alone for once, her eyes shut to the world, and her mind drifted with the distant cadence of a sparse crowd. Lotteva had worried over her so often lately, always asking if she'd eaten. What was her pain like? Did she need help getting up? Lotteva meant well, but how annoying that beautiful girl could be.

"Mama, you don't eat enough," Lotteva said while pushing a bowl of stew at Maud.

"I ate plenty already." Maud pushed back the stew .

Lotteva scowled down at her mother. She never did inherit Maud's famous eyebrow, but she could definitely get her point across.

"Some broth, a cube of beef, and a piece of potato. That's not enough."

"Two pieces of potato."

"You filled up on cotton candy again, didn't you?" Lotteva asked. "For the love of God, Mama, your tongue is blue."

"Oh, don't fuss at me, girl. I'm older than dirt. I deserve to eat what I want."

Lotteva, at age forty-seven, looked the way Maud used to. That strained smile that was really meant to cover the annoyance beneath. Gus had brought it out of her more than Lotteva did, even though she gave him a run for his money. Maud stopped fighting and resigned to eating another cube of beef.

Blissful peace came when a younger man asked to take Lotteva to lunch in town. After much debate and looking fretfully at Maud, she finally agreed to the date. If she could have managed it, Maud would have kicked Lotteva out of the tent with a swing of her leg. Nothing in the world was worse than being coddled by a daughter she had once taught to use a spoon. They left Maud alone to man the tent, and that was just fine by her.

She didn't tattoo anymore. Oh, it was not for lack of want. Her hands ached to hold the chopstick handles between her fingers, but those were the same hands that betrayed her; they quivered and shook with uncertainty, thus ending her tattooing career.

Maud could barely paint anymore because of those hands. Letters were too structured and portraits too specialized. She had taken to the old woman's hobby of watercolors and flowers. It was a decent enough respite, but still didn't ebb the hunger in her to help people with her art. What had a painting of a watery sunset ever done for anyone anyway?

The circus was in Atlanta for a two-day gig. The crowd was good at first, but the second day found a smaller head count, which was one reason Lotteva thought it all right to leave.

Things were changing in the country again. The promise of revolution danced in the bouncy, spring air. Georgia was becoming a place of note. It made many people worry, but not Maud. Anything to change the repressive social scenery was fine by her.

Maud sat outside of the tent, dreaming of fantastic things to come. She was disturbed by the sound of sharp chirping and scratching of tiny feet. She glared at Lotteva's damn songbirds; certain the little green things were mocking her. They flitted about their cage as she stuck out her tongue at them.

Their tittering almost sounded like laughter. More specifically, the laughter of an old friend. Though gone many years ago, Dora still managed to come around to irritate Maud. If only she had a cigarette to share with a specter.

A middle-aged couple came close to her tent. They weren't customers, far from it. It seemed they only passed Maud's way to get to the cookhouse for some lunch. Neither of them gave the defiantly tattooed woman a second glance. The teenage girl they pushed though, she did.

It was the pain in the girl's face that stopped Maud's heart. Terror and pain shouldn't sit so comfortably on a girl no older than sixteen. Something in her eyes spoke of longing, like she was reaching out for something without moving an inch. Maud knew that look a little too well.

On further inspection, Maud noticed the girl's attire. A flowing blouse and an equally billowy skirt. Nothing fit tight, nothing was colorful as was the fashion of most teenagers. The drab colors of her clothes echoed all over in her skin and eyes and hair.

She probably once was pretty. Her hair looked like it might be a honey color if someone washed it. Her eyes were faded, almost grey. She appeared monochromatic, like she was a faded drawing of a young woman.

The girl stumbled along, occasionally hurried by rough hands. Maud had a clear line of sight to the cookhouse, and she spied on the family as they made their way there. A gust of air blew just before they made it to the entrance, filling the side of the tent with the smell of stew and cornbread. The teenager hurried to the nearest trash bin and vomited. She came up to admonishing glares, holding her stomach tenderly.

Maud's heart ached for the girl when she saw the dizzying pain on her face. Her parents tried to shield her embarrassment from the other circus goers, but not in a caring way. It looked more like they were trying to keep up appearances, and their daughter was ruining it. The girl wiped her mouth with a handkerchief but didn't try to clean herself beyond that. What a wounded bird, Maud thought.

With some effort, Maud pulled herself off her chair and made her way toward the cookhouse. Years ago, the old, rose cane had changed from a decoration to necessity, and she relied heavily on it as she hobbled toward the girl. Maud fingered the grooved outline of Gus's name absently as she walked.

The girl's parents were doing the type of shouting that was yelled in whispers. Everyone could hear it but pretended otherwise. The vague scent of vomit still lingered.

"You have got to straighten up," said the mother. "We brought you here to cheer you not to watch you be sick in a trash can. Compose yourself, Joy."

Maud moved behind them and pretended to trip. She stumbled and lurched into the girl. Joy caught her out of instinct. No one seemed to notice Maud still had the cane beneath her, bracing her body in case no one leapt to her rescue. An old trick, that one was.

"Oh my!" Maud shouted.

"Ma'am, are you okay?" Joy asked.

"No? I mean yes. My daughter? Have you seen her?"

"Your daughter, ma'am? No, I don't think so," replied Joy.

Maud looked to the parents and tried to gaze past them like she suffered from a clouded mind. She reached out in the air like she couldn't quite make out their faces. They shook their heads to her question.

"Oh, I'm so lost without her. She was supposed to care for me. I don't suppose…" She paused and addressed the next bit to Joy. "I don't suppose you'd help me back to my tent and keep me company until she returns, would you? I'm so lost."

"Me?"

"I don't think that's possible," said the father.

"I understand," Maud said. "I just get so frightened all by myself. It's just terrible when she leaves me."

She was really laying on the feeble old woman act, but it seemed to be working. She thought about drooling a little, but that might have been too much. Besides, the girl's parents were distracted by all the birds tattooed on Maud's shoulders. She let part of her shawl slip in order to scare the rubes with a glimpse of her lions.

"Is there someone we can get to help you? Anyone you else you know here? A friend or something?" asked the mother.

"No… no I'm afraid not. All my friends went to the great beyond. Just have my daughter these days."

"Well, I'm sure we can find someone…"

"I'll go with you," Joy said with sudden enthusiasm.

A spark lit in her eyes and with it, a bit of strength. Maud would have smiled at her if she wasn't so busy acting old and infirmed.

"Joy, honey, you need to come eat," her father said. "We are going to go see the trapeze show." Maud noticed he was far kinder now that a stranger was watching.

"I'm not hungry, and the food smell is making me feel sick," Joy said. "I don't want to embarrass you by going in and getting sick in front of people. I'll go with the woman and wait for her daughter. You two go have fun. I'll be fine."

Her fear had retreated, and a bit of her color returned. Her parents stuttered and looked nervously from one to the other. Though they obviously didn't want to leave Joy alone, they eventually nodded in agreement and went inside the cookhouse.

Joy put her arms around Maud to help her back to the tent. Maud, for her part, limped along. The thought had occurred to her to moan, but she decided against it. She made a real effort to act feeble until she touched the tables with all the flash. At that point, the view inside the cookhouse was obscured, allowing her to drop the charade.

Maud straightened the curve of her back, let go of Joy's hand, and walked confidently back to her seat. Joy stared at her with her small mouth hanging loose.

"All right, dear. We can cut the act."

"You? You're not crippled?" Joy said. The girl gaped at Maud in surprise.

"Well, not as much as I let on. Not going to dance with you or anything like that. I'm Maud, by the way."

She stuck out her hand and shook Joy's limp one.

"I'm Joy. But...but...what about your daughter?" she asked.

The girl seemed unsure of everything in front of her and didn't pay attention to where she stepped. She stumbled over the leg of a chair, but Maud decided to ignore it for Joy's sake. No need embarrassing the child. She might crack.

"My daughter's on a date with some fellow," Maud said.

"You don't need me to wait with you?"

"No honey, but it looked like you needed me to wait with you." Maud slumped into her chair and motioned for Joy to take a seat, but the girl didn't oblige.

"I don't understand."

Maud waved her hands in the as though it wasn't hard to comprehend. "You looked like you needed help, so I helped you."

"But... you fell. You said..." Joy said.

"Never trust anything a circus person says. Pretty much anything we do is a ruse. The way I see it, you got two choices. You can call me a fraud and go back to your parents, or you can stay here with me and get a good break from them. Either way is fine with me, dear."

It took a long moment of contemplation, but eventually, Joy nodded in agreement. Maud could almost see the beginnings of a smile on her lips. That alone was worth the theatrics.

"All right then. That's the spirit. Come on back, child. We'll go in the tent, so they can't see us when they leave the cookhouse."

Maud led the fragile girl behind the table and through the flaps of the tent. It was a funny sight. A feeble old woman escorting a fragile young girl.

When they passed the peeping birds in the cage, Joy smiled. "They're pretty."

Maud snorted. "They're a pain in the rear end."

Inside the tent, Joy took one chair and Maud sat in another. The tattooed lady let out a whoosh of air when she sat, making a show of the relief. Her shoes were kicked away quickly, and she rubbed her feet together as though she were a cricket.

"That's the most activity I've seen in weeks."

Joy looked over the drawings on the table next to them. Fascination lit a candle inside her, and for the first time, Maud realized her eyes weren't grey. They were a really lovely shade of hazel.

"You do these?" Joy asked in wonderment.

"I used to. Hands a bit shaky for it now," Maud said with more than a little dismay in her voice. It hurt to think of her tattooing days as long past.

"They are so... beautiful," Joy said.

"Yes, they are. I miss making them."

Joy's eyes grew bigger with excitement. One would think she'd never seen a tattoo before.

"Who does them now?"

"My daughter. Her daddy and I taught her when she was young. She was tattooing folks starting at about your age. Younger, even. Sixteen, are you?" Maud asked, trying to size her up. She looked pretty scrawny, so it was hard to tell.

"And a half," Joy said.

The grey blanket of depression started covering her again. Not as much as it did outside, but it was there, nonetheless. Her light dimmed just a touch. Something obviously happened to her, but what it was hadn't yet shown itself.

Then, the answer came. The evidence appeared on her large blouse, and Maud knew the source of the girl's illness. Joy hadn't seen it yet, being as distant as she was. The girl was numb all over and didn't notice what was blooming on her shirt in front of a stranger. There was no good way to tell her. No good way to ask.

There was nothing for it. That longing, that sorrow in Joy's gaunt stare, it was a reflection of her own. This girl was Maud's mirror-image when she was that tender age. She felt the compulsion to help poor, broken Joy.

The tent flap opened suddenly, and Lotteva stood in the doorway. Her unexpected appearance made Joy squeak and jump in her seat. Lotteva yelped with surprise herself. Maud sat still and waited for the two other women to get done with the hysterics.

"Mama, I'm sorry. I didn't know you had company." Lotteva looked wide-eyed from her mother to Joy and then back again.

"Well, I do. Is there something you wanted?" Maud asked.

Incredulity filled Lotteva's face as she properly took in the scene. "I was just coming by to check on you. Frank asked me to go to a movie since it's slow. Wanted to make sure you were okay first."

So much could pass between mother and daughter with just their eyes. One glance could tell a whole story, or even a joke, without the lips getting involved. In Lotteva's eyes, Maud saw a question. Lotteva wanted to know what the hell was going on with this abandoned teenager, and she suspected her mother was at fault somehow.

"Who are you trying to save now?" Lotteva asked without saying a word.

"If she were an animal, you'd try to save her too," Maud said back with her glare.

Joy stood to shake Lotteva's hand. When Lotteva's eyes lighted on the girl's blouse, recognition flashed in her eyes. Maud could see her daughter clueing in on the situation. Lotteva didn't know the whole truth, but she was getting the gist.

"Hi. My name is Joy. I was just keeping your mom company. She's been real nice to me. Telling me a story about when she was an aerialist."

Lotteva shook the girl's hand, trying to not let her eyes flash down to Joy's blouse. It was enough to see it in her periphery. Though Lotteva had never had the same experience, she knew very well what it meant. Maud leveled a look at her that told her to be discreet. She would fill her in later.

"You go on, honey. Go to your movie. Me and Joy here are having a chat."

"I see," Lotteva said shakily. "Well, you two enjoy your chat. Mama, I'll bring back some supper tonight."

"All right. Go on now. Bring me a potpie or something. I promise

I'll eat it this time."

Her daughter could always turn a smile on a dime, just like Gus. Lotteva left the tent with a wave, and Joy returned to her seat. She was all excited like a child at story time. She looked so young it hurt Maud even more.

Maud's old rib cage swelled with a heavy breath. It hurt to take in the air, and it hurt more to exhale the story. So many years had passed, yet the pain of it was still so strong and raw, even though she hadn't spoken of it in decades.

"You know, I've been in the circus since I was about your age," Maud said. "I started off as a contortionist and an aerialist."

"Really?"

"I know I look too damn old and ugly, but it's true. The trapeze show your parents are going to; that used to be me."

"I didn't mean... I wasn't trying to offend..."

"Don't stutter girl. I lived it, and I barely believe it myself. When I was just a little older than sixteen and a half, I became an aerialist."

"Did you grow up in the circus?"

"No. In fact, I barely knew anything about it. At the time, they needed a pretty, young body to fill out the costume. Said they'd teach me the rest. And while they did teach me to swing and flip and catch someone else, they didn't teach me everything I needed to know."

Joy was with her now, bright-eyed and anxious for the rest of the story. A large part of Maud didn't want to tell it. An even bigger part asked her why she was trying to tell it. Not even Lotteva knew this one. Why tell a near stranger?

"I saw the world. Well, I saw the country, which might as well been the world. I tattooed all manner of people. So many wonderful experiences, and I was pregnant two times," Maud said gently.

The girl startled, visibly swallowing a lump of something in her throat. Maud searched in the girl's eyes and saw trepidation and fear.

Her very soul seemed to quiver just beneath her eyes, but there was loneliness too. That empty feeling of living in a vacuum of sorrow. Maud knew it well and had to do something about it.

"Lotteva was the second. The first, well... the first was stillborn, the doctor said. I saw the baby. I held her, but she didn't look real to me. Like a doll. None of it felt real at all."

Joy had wrapped her arms around herself and shook her head back and forth as if begging for the story not to be true.

"Why are you telling me this?"

"I named her Sarah, after my mother, and we buried her on a Tuesday. I never liked my mother. Only loved her as far as one is supposed to. I named my girl after her because... I don't know why. Some part of me wanted her to be a Sarah so that I could feel close to my mom in a way that was impossible. When she died, I thought somehow that my mother cursed her. It was a superstitious thing to imagine, but there it was. In my heart, my mother cursed my baby."

"Why? Why are you telling me this?" Joy asked again, sounding so soft and tiny.

"Because I know your face, child. I've worn that same face myself. There's a longing there only a mother is capable of feeling. You had a baby, and now it's gone. I'm here to tell you, you're not alone."

Joy's hands twitched, opening and closing her grip on nothing at all. It was as if she were grasping at something she could never hold again. That invisible thread that held mother and child together even past death and beyond it.

"How did you know?"

"Look down, honey. Look at your shirt."

Joy turned her eyes downward and gasped in embarrassment. There were two, wet stains blooming over each breast like small flowers on an Eve painting. The right side larger than the left. Underneath, her small bosoms swelled and ached to feed a child who wasn't there. She grabbed the stained shirt and pulled it away from her body, trying to hide the evidence.

"Oh God. Oh God," she said panicking.

"Calm down, girl. Behind the partition in the back is a chest of Lotteva's clothes. There should be a shirt or two that will fit." She handed Joy a roll of gauze. "Now go back there, pad your bra, and change your shirt. You can tell your parents you got mud on your old one."

Without another word, Joy made her way behind the partition. There were some sounds of her riffling through Lotteva's trunk and sniffles to mask the sound of her crying. By the time Joy returned to her seat, she was grey all over again.

Maud wondered if she'd done the right thing sharing her tragedy with this near stranger.

"You all right?"

"Not really," Joy said with a little laugh.

It was fair enough. The question was absurd.

"I didn't mean to make things harder for you. I thought if you heard the same story from someone who survived it, you might feel better and less alone. Your folks didn't seem to be helping much," Maud said.

"They don't. They're the reason she's gone."

"They... they're the reason. Did they hurt you? Did they cause an accident?"

"No. She's not dead. My baby's alive, but they made me give her up."

Maud hadn't anticipated this. All she had read on the girl was the longing for a lost baby. She was a caged girl in need of comforting—of rescue. If anyone could relate to that, it was Maud. The parents seemed cruel, and probably had something to do with the pain, but to make a daughter give up a baby? Maud hadn't counted on that one.

Maud imagined her mother and tried very hard not to grimace at the face in her mind. What would her mother have done if Maud became pregnant while at the farm? If her uncle had managed to get her alone long enough to force the act that resulted in a child. That thing that married people did.

Maud shook her head a little at that repulsive thought. Then, a hard knowledge accompanied it. She could picture the scandal, the shame in her father's eyes, and the anger in her mother's. Not at her uncle, surely. He was never at fault. The blame would be placed squarely on Maud's shoulders, and the baby would be forfeited. No need to have the indecent bastard walking around and talking. It would forever remind the family of what occurred.

Without thinking about it, Maud reached toward the girl and grabbed her hand. Women, especially young ones, could be so little cared for and unprotected. Joy squeezed her hand back.

"I used to be a cheerleader. Would you have guessed that?" Joy asked.

"No more than you could guess I used to be an aerialist."

They both laughed a short laugh, but it was dark and hollow.

"I was very perky and jumped high," Joy said. "Those were the main qualifications for the job. My parents were so proud. Good girls ended up being cheerleaders."

"Was the boy a quarterback?"

"No. He was the pitcher on the baseball team. Henry Moore." Joy shut her eyes and smiled. She was somewhere else for a second, somewhere miles away. Somewhere happier. "He was such a square when I first met him. He transferred over freshman year and hadn't grown into his ears at all. Everyone said he looked like a truck driving down the road with both doors open."

Maud barked with laughter. She hadn't guessed the girl could be so funny.

"But that all changed?"

"Yeah, it did. He started showing up outside my classes. At first,

I didn't think anything of it, but it happened over and over again. I knew he had a class clear on the other side of school. Then, he started bulking up because of baseball practice. He grew out his hair to cover those ears. He got quite handsome. One day, he was waiting outside my algebra class with a whole bouquet of roses and asked me on a date right there in front of everyone. I was so mortified, I nearly fainted."

"But big gestures win hearts though, don't they?"

Joy nodded, still looking dreamily away.

"We started going steady. I'd never gone steady with a boy before. I didn't know what all went into making a child. The girls talked about things, but it was hard to tell if any of it was real. So much sounded like fluff. My mother hadn't even been able to talk to me about the curse, let alone babies. A school nurse had to tell me how to handle the monthly visits. What Henry and I did together felt strange and wonderful. I just thought this is what love must be like. What we were doing was love."

Maud had to blink away the pressure threatening to leak tears down her face. It was all so familiar, so innocent. No one should be punished for something like that.

"I didn't even know I was pregnant. I just thought I had a stomach virus. My mom saw me throwing up every morning and took me to the doctor. When he said I was pregnant, I knew my whole world was going to end. You hear about girls getting 'peachy' as they say around school, but you never really expect it to be you. Without saying a word about it, I could already hear the gossip and whispers about me, calling me a whore."

"Did you ever get to tell Henry?"

"Yes. We told Henry and his parents. They wanted nothing to do with it. Henry was set to get a baseball scholarship to college. Nothing could jeopardize that, especially not a wife and baby. They moved away as soon as the school year ended."

"What about Henry? Did he stand up to them? Did he try?"

"You mean, did he challenge someone to a duel to defend my honor?" Joy forced herself to smile. "No. He made a grand gesture once before he left. We weren't allowed to see each other, but he snuck out of baseball practice and met me under the bleachers. Henry got on one knee and proposed to me, using a gum wrapper he'd folded together as a ring. He said they couldn't separate us. We loved one another too much for that. He'd steal me away in the night, and we'd elope."

"But... that didn't happen?" Maud said, already knowing the answer.

"No. Henry, the king of grand gestures, went off with his parents like they'd planned. He wanted that scholarship. I never saw him again after that proposal. Grand gestures are nice, but most times, there's not much under them. I just ended up looking foolish with a baby on the way and a gum wrapper ring."

"He left you all alone with your parents?"

Joy looked down at her belly.

"Once I started showing, they shipped me off to stay with my aunt, saying I was helping a sick relative. She lives near here. Didn't want the neighbors to see and start the gossip mills chugging. I got bigger and bigger, and when it was time, my folks came up to be with me when she was born. The thing is, I didn't know I was going to have to give her up. Not until they walked into the hospital room with the adoption coordinator. I thought, stupidly I guess, I would get to keep my baby girl."

Joy's face looked pained as she tried to squint away the tears. She even pressed her fingers against her eyes to stop them from coming. In the end, it was a losing proposition, and the poor girl began to cry. Maud held both of Joy's hands as her shoulders heaved with the racking sobs that tore through her body.

She almost told the girl she didn't have to go on—she could stop the story there—but Joy continued as soon as she regained her voice.

"She already had Henry's eyes. The doctors said they would change, but I don't believe it. They were his. No question. I yelled and screamed and fought, but they took her anyway. The nurse said I was still a child in the eyes of the law, and my parents had legal guardianship over me. They signed the papers without ever asking me, without even telling me."

Another round of sobbing broke the poor thing and she collapsed into a sobbing heap at Maud's feet. She collected the girl's head and shoulders and brought her to her lap. There was nothing more healing in this world than a mother's embrace. If her foolish mother wouldn't do it, Maud sure as hell would.

"They said... they said I was evil. God was angry with me. My punishment was to give up my baby. They said no one would ever love me again if I didn't. Daddy said they were doing me a favor taking care of this for me."

"I can't attest to the will of God, sweet girl, but I can tell you one thing. A good many people fling his name around in order to make their judgments sound valid. A good many more quote him when they do despicable violence to others. Personally, I don't trust anyone who tries to tell me the will of God. Unless they know him personal, and have tea with him weekly, I'd say they don't know anything for sure. Sounds to me like your parents were passing their own judgments on you, and God was a good scapegoat."

"I hope that's true." Joy shook her head. "I didn't even get to name her. I don't even know my baby girl's name! How will I ever find her again? How will she ever find me?"

Joy grabbed Maud desperately, fighting between the need to be held and the back-breaking sobs that hurt her body. She buried her face in Maud's chest, wetting the two of them with tears and brine and snot. Joy stifled her wails with the fabric of Maud's blouse.

Maud held her just as tight and began to rock the girl gently back and forth. Somewhere unknown to her, came a gentle song. She hummed the tune in Joy's ear without really knowing the words. It had been something she learned long ago. Something she used to hum to Lotteva when she was little. The song seeped into Joy's honey hair and settled the panic enough to ease her tense body.

Eventually, Joy calmed. She breathed. With a stagger, she sat back in her own chair, using her old shirt to mop away grief on her face.

"I... I'm so sorry," Joy said.

"No need, honey. I know what it's like, or did you forget my story already?"

"It's just... I don't even know you. I shouldn't burden you like this."

"I'm the one who picked you out, remember? I saw my pain in your face at a hundred paces. We are strangers only in acquaintance, but I know you girl. And now, you know me."

Joy looked down and nodded, as if agreeing with her shoes.

"Tell me this, because I am curious," Maud said. "How are you dealing with this pain alone? When it happened to me, I had a whole circus of people there to help. My child's father was there. My best friend stayed with me the whole time. You've got no one. Unless your aunt is kind?"

"She's all right. Not someone I can talk to."

Maud's heart dropped for her and worry started to take the place of sorrow.

"Then, how are you holding up with no one to help you. You aren't taking to sneaking your aunt's whiskey, I hope. That's a slick slope."

Joy made a disgusted face.

"No, not that. I hate the taste. Ick. I do this other thing. I don't really talk about it. It helped for a while. I don't know why it helps, but it does. But I haven't been able to since the baby was born because my parents hover over me like vultures. They even make me sleep on the floor in their room."

A bit of dread vibrated in the back of Maud's mind. Pain like that with no outlet was a damaging thing. It festered like a wound turned to rot. This she knew all too well. She winced at what might be said next, what might be uncovered. A bandage removed.

It was with much trepidation that Maud asked, "What is the thing that you do?"

Joy settled herself in the chair as though she needed stability for what was to come next. Ever so slightly, she parted her thin legs. Every movement was calculated, every inch measured twice. The girl rolled up her flowing skirt, bunching it around her pelvis and tucking it in the places that might give her some semblance of modesty. Before she tucked the fabric in between her legs, Maud caught a glimpse of the padded underwear she wore; what all women wore after they had a baby and the bleeding came. She made a mental note to tell her about soaking rags in witch hazel to help with the swelling and pain.

Joy's delicate fingers traced over some lines on her upper thighs, touching them tenderly like petting a butterfly. Maud drew in closer to see better what they were. They were tiny scars, just a touch lighter than the rest of the flesh on Joy's legs. They came in rows of three or two here and there like little roads that started and stopped for no reason. The lines began higher on the top of her thigh and made their way down to stop midway to her knee. Any further, and they might be noticed.

The realization hit her like a kick in the chest. Joy had done these. The girl had been cutting on herself to ease the pain. With a new horror, Maud realized what else the lines were. Little tick marks moving down her legs. When she started them, Joy's belly hadn't gotten in the way. But the bigger she got, the further out her cuts had to be. Otherwise, how would see what she was doing over her growing belly. Something about that thought chilled Maud's bones. She wanted to hold the girl again and never let her go.

"You weren't trying to kill yourself?" Maud asked.

Joy shook her head. Her eyes looked so tired for someone so young.

"No. I learned in health class where the arteries were. I would have to cut somewhere else for that and a lot deeper."

"Then why?"

"I don't know really. It helped... somehow. I used to escape into books, romantic books. Books about princesses and knights. Jane Austen books with beautiful men who spoke like poems."

A light flickered in her when she spoke of her books, and Maud got a glimpse of the beauty she must have been when she was an innocent cheerleader.

"The thing of it is, after I started the cutting, I liked it. It was a relief somehow. It's hard to explain."

"Try honey. This is the part I don't understand."

"So much inside me hurt, but it didn't show. I got a hold of some straight razors, and the idea sort of came to me. Small cuts, little nips really, to make my pain show outside. I had no idea it would be so relieving. For a few blissful minutes, the outer pain I caused outweighed the inner pain. Sort of masked it for a time. It became a need because it never lasted. The cuts would heal, and I was left with the agony of living."

"You were transferring the pain."

"Yeah. That's a good way of saying it. As my belly grew, I had to cut farther and farther down my leg. My aunt found out when she saw up my slip one day. She told my parents. After they took the baby, they won't leave me alone. I want to hurt myself so bad. It hurts so much to live right now."

Her face flushed red again, and tears threatened to make an encore performance. Maud put both hands on Joy's knees, startling her out of her decline.

"You can't cut yourself. Not anymore."

"But... but I don't know if I can stop. Everything else hurts so much. It's the only thing that feels better," Joy said.

"I know, honey. When I lost my girl, I thought I'd never live again. There was no point to any of it. I was damned for leaving my family. But I'm here to tell you that's not true. It's a thing we're taught to think so we don't dare to live any other way. I lived. I laughed. I had another daughter. You will live past this too."

"I don't know if... if I can stop myself. When the books don't work, everything gets so dark."

An idea flashed in Maud's mind as if from some divine force. Such a brilliant idea. Now, if she could only overcome her old body long enough to make it happen. She wouldn't need it for more and a handful of minutes. This girl needed her to be *Marvelous Maud* just one last time.

"I know what we can do," Maud said.

"What?"

"I will give you a tattoo."

"A what?" asked Joy, suddenly sitting at attention.

"A tattoo. I will make you a tattoo to cover these scars. Something so beautiful, when you look down at it, you won't have the heart to cut it up."

"Oh... I don't know," Joy said putting a hand over her mouth.

"It's not a fix, mind you. It's a patch. A bandage until you manage to work through this need to hurt yourself. It will pass, honey. I promise that. You will get away from your parents, go out into the world, and live it. All that will happen but cutting will only lead to ruin. You could get carried away and really hurt yourself."

A cloud lifted enough to where Joy's true self could be seen again. Albeit it was diffused by the mist of sadness, but she was there, nonetheless. Words danced in front of her, words that painted pictures of a life beyond this. A life where she could laugh again.

"What would you tattoo?" she asked.

"You liked the birds, didn't you? Used to be my specialty. They're lovely to paint but hell to live with. I'm telling you, child, I was the best at them in my day. People came from far around to get my sparrows."

"But you said you didn't do it anymore," Joy said.

"I'll come out of retirement for one more show."

Maud allowed a sly grin to spread across her face. The thought of tattooing made her heart skip a beat, and for a moment, she was young again.

Joy looked down at her hands suddenly and blushed.

"I don't have any money to pay you. My parents don't let me carry any."

Of course not, Maud thought. It was another way to hold her in a place. Maud took Joy's hands again and brought the girl's eyes up to meet her own. "Ain't nobody should pay for a tattoo done by a crusty, old lady like me. Now, let's get to work before your folks show up and ruin the whole thing."

After a few seconds of hesitation, Joy smiled. The two women nodded to one another.

Maud fetched Lotteva's toolbox, and Joy retrieved the rags and alcohol she needed. It had been ages since Maud had mixed the India ink, even longer since she held one of these needles. That familiar tang seeped into the air when the jar of ink opened, followed by the gentle odor of the soap and water. Mixing was an art unto itself. Taking something raw and acrid and adding just enough lather to make it gorgeous. Maud took pleasure in every step. When she wiped Joy's thigh with the alcohol, the girl winced.

"You all right? Any of these cuts still open?"

"No," Joy said while shaking her head back and forth. "It's the smell of the alcohol. Reminded me of the hospital."

Maud smiled as reassuringly as she could before she swabbed the other leg. Her old hands trembled when reaching for the graphite pencil. This was the worrisome part. Somewhere, in the back of her brain, an irritating demon reminded her of her age and her uselessness. She grabbed the pencil anyway, more forcibly than was needed. A bit of it broke in the middle, and she threw it away. Dainty grains of graphite blew from her with a breath. Maud loosened her fingers, and the trembling ceased. Somehow, her old, worthless hands had a new master. For a beautiful moment, she was the mistress of her own body again.

The birds were lovely, just as she remembered drawing them. She hadn't lost a step. Each one had that perfect flip at the ends of tails and feathers that made them uniquely Maud's. Joy's right thigh had been cut more than the left, so she drew three sparrows on that one and two on the left. They would cover the oldest of the scars, the ones that had healed completely.

"I'm stopping here. I can't tattoo over these newer ones because they aren't healed enough. How do you like the ones I've drawn out?"

Joy's eyes glistened as she looked at the rough drawings.

"I promise the actual tattoo will be more refined than the drawings if that's what you're worried about," Maud said.

"No, no," Joy said hurriedly. "I think they're lovely. But they are facing me. I thought they'd face the other way."

"Listen, Joy. I don't want to do this, and you go cutting yourself around the birds or any such nonsense. I want these birds to look at you, and when you look at them, you remember."

"Remember what?"

"Remember the day you took your body back. Remember the day you decided to live. When you knew things would get better. I want you to remember your baby, and how she wouldn't want you to hurt yourself."

Joy couldn't speak. The tears stopped it in her throat, but she nodded.

Wiping her eyes with her dirtied shirt, the poor girl acquiesced to going on, to taking her body back, to living.

It's funny how a body remembers actions even if the mind hasn't thought of doing them in years. Maud's hands finished mixing the ink, dropped a pool into the well on her hand, and picked up her needle like she still did it five times a day. There wasn't much thinking necessary.

A flash of worry almost made her pull away at the last second. Despite the memory of her muscles, she hadn't done this in a long time. What if her hands shook and she botched this tattoo? This was a lifeline of sorts for this girl. It had to be perfect.

When her hand reached out, it was calm and steady. Not a quiver. Not one. Her hands knew what to do; they knew how to get this job done. Maud breathed out a lungful in relief. "It isn't as painful as you think, love. But just know the first part is the hardest. Then, it normally feels like a dull poking. Are you ready?"

Joy looked at the needle and back at Maud.

"You can't hurt me anymore than I've already hurt myself. Go ahead. I want you to do this."

Maud started without another word. Joy flinched a little at the anticipation of the poking, but once the first ones were done, her whole body stilled. The girl breathed deeper and easier than she had her entire visit.

Maud wondered if the act of tattooing was helping to transfer her pain into the physical form the way cutting did. Then, she didn't know how to feel about that. She had never thought about the pain of her work being used as therapy, but really why not? If it helped Joy move on, it had to be a good thing.

It went quickly. Her ancient hands didn't have to think about leaving the smallest unmarked highlight in the bird's dark eye to make it look wet and alive. Nothing reminded her that the lines nearest the wings, tail, and beak needed to be thickest to draw the eye all the way around. Her fingers guided the needle, knowing what to do without thinking.

Joy watched every line, every poke with a keen fascination.

It was easier tattooing skin so young and elastic. The top parts of the thighs were fleshy, making the skin taut. The needle moved in and out without clinging to the needle. Even the scarred parts were so fine they didn't corrupt the details.

The deed was done before they knew it, and Joy took in her new art. For the first time ever, Maud didn't feel the need to ask a customer if they liked their tattoo. She didn't fret over a response. Joy's smile was infectious. It was bright and lovely and as pure as the smile of an innocent child.

Joy reached out and hugged Maud. They didn't say a word about how gorgeous the birds were. There was no need. When the spell broke, Maud wiped down the birds and bandaged Joy's thighs. She told her how to properly care for the new art.

"How do I hide it?" asked Joy.

"You probably won't forever, but it's in a place I doubt your parents will see. Either way, when they ask you where you're going, just tell them to change your unmentionables. They won't argue with that. Then, you can clean your new artwork."

The two women walked out into the early evening's dim light, hand in hand like they were related. Joy stood a little taller, and Maud's hands were steady as she leaned on her rose cane. Off in the distance, they saw Joy's parents. Her mother and father craned their necks this way and that, looking for their wayward daughter.

"There they are. Not going to be too happy with me, I bet."

"Just tell them I fell asleep, and you didn't feel right leaving me alone. Can't fault a good Christian girl who wanted to help an old lady."

Her parents couldn't see them yet. A long shadow stretching from the cookhouse obscured them in darkness. When Joy looked down at herself, she realized she was still wearing Lotteva's old shirt.

"Oh God. What will I tell them about this?"

"You got mud on it remember? Helping me up or something. You borrowed my daughter's old shirt. Easy enough to believe and close enough to the truth it won't feel like lying."

Joy's shoulders relaxed, and she breathed out a little tension.

"I don't want to go. I wish I could stay here."

"Honey, I'd love for you to stay, but I think they'd sic the law on us. We wouldn't last one day on the lam." Maud chuckled.

"I know. I have to go back." Joy said.

"You don't have to stay though. As soon as you're eighteen, you go do what you want. Girls go to college all the time now. They work their own jobs. Get away. See the world. I'll tell you from experience, this world can be a beautiful place."

She tried to instill as much hope and promise as she could muster for the fragile girl. It was what Maud wanted for her.

"And you? What's your next adventure?"

"Dying I suppose." Maud snickered. When Joy didn't crack a smile, she continued. "Oh, don't look at me like that. I lived a big life, and that's all an old lady like me can hope for. I'm just glad I met you, Joy."

"And I'm glad I met you, Maud."

She reached over and hugged Maud one final time before breaking away to walk toward her parents. They still couldn't see the pair, so Maud knew it was safe to call to her one last time.

"Joy?"

"Yes, Maud," she said, turning toward the circus woman one last time.

"Name that little girl," Maud said with tears threatening her eyes. She managed to keep them down, but it wasn't easy.

"What?" Joy asked, visibly taken aback. "What do you mean? I don't know what they named her. I don't know what she's called."

"That doesn't matter. You call her something regardless what the world calls her. Give her a name so she stays real to you, not a ghost. Name her so you can talk to her at night before you go to sleep. So, you can write her letters. Name that baby, honey."

"Do you talk to your baby, Sarah? Even though you have Lotteva, I mean?"

"Every night," Maud said. Her shoulders relaxed as though finally sharing her story with someone had removed a weight from her back. "Since the day she was born. My love for her has never changed."

Joy looked down at the hay-covered floor, still streaked with the purples and blues of the approaching dusk. Her hands folded inside themselves, seeming to weave some unseen pattern. When she gazed back at Maud, she was smiling again.

"I think… I think I will name her Maud."

Without another word, Joy turned on her heel and walked back to her parents.

Part Ten

1961

For some unknown reason, no one ever thinks it gets cold in Oklahoma. To credit the state's stereotype, most months out of the year provide native Okies with a consistent barrage of heat and wind. However, in 1961, January was a terrible month everywhere, and it was even colder than usual in Lawton, Oklahoma, where Lotteva and Maud had decided to winter. It wasn't their first time to setup camp in Lawton. The town was more open than most to circus folk and performers, even if it had little in the way of charm. In times of need, a friendly home won out over the glitz and glamour of a big city.

Lotteva made a good deal with the married couple who ran a museum of curiosities in a prominent part of town. She would provide shows with some of her exotic animals, and Maud would take tickets as an extra attraction. Come buy a ticket from the ancient tattooed woman. The pay was decent, and they were given a small furnished apartment nearby.

It was an especially brisk day when the Haydren family came to visit. People described them as a good, Catholic family—a fact that was evident by the gaggle of children who followed the parents around like little ducklings. Last count put the family at nine children, but when they walked in the door of Wilson's Treasures and Curiosities, a new baby was swaddled tightly against the mother's chest. That put the family's tally at ten.

The older ones had the newer clothes. Crisper and still bright. The rest of the children wore clothes second and third hand, passed down from sibling to sibling. To view them in a row was to view the lifespan of a piece of clothing. From brand new all the way down to some glorified rags held together with patches. The patterns obscured and faded until one reached the youngest walking child at the tender age of three. That poor girl wore a coat barely held together with bits of old socks.

Mr. Haydren beamed at Maud across the ticket counter and plopped down the money for twelve tickets to see the museum. People could say what they wanted about the family's appearance, but the parents scrimped and saved in order to expose their children to something new.

Maud counted him a kind man. Not unlike Gus in some ways. She always had a soft spot for people who loved their children beyond themselves. Maud figured it was the least she could do to give him a break on the admission price since men like Mr. Haydren wouldn't take charity.

"Twelve please, Mrs. Wagner," he said, grinning proudly at the ancient ticket-taker.

Maud looked at the collection of money and then back at the family. She counted out a dollar and handed it back to Mr. Haydren.

"Here's your change, sir."

"But, there's twelve of us," he said.

"Children under four are free."

Maud pointed to the baby and the little girl staring doe-eyed at her. The tiny poppet could barely look over the desk she was so small. Why would she have to pay the same as a bigger person? A girl like her would probably miss half the show struggling to see over the sibling sitting in front of her anyway.

"Oh, all right," he said, taking back his dollar. "I hadn't heard that rule before."

"It's a new one," Maud said.

Of course, it wasn't a rule at all, but the kind Mr. Haydron didn't need to know. Her boss couldn't tell the difference anyway.

"Well, thank you all the same," Mr. Haydren said. "Kids, we can go to the Candy Counter after this now."

The middle children cheered while the older ones pretended at acting too old to be excited about candy. The ploy was shallow, and anyone could see their excitement. All looked to each other, whispering among themselves about which candy they'd choose. Some arguments and scuffles occurred as the parents herded their brood into the museum.

Somehow, one child managed to hang back. It was the little girl of three who had marveled at Maud from across the desk. In all the uproar, she managed to wiggle herself free. Now, she lifted on her toes to continue her examination of Maud.

"Hi there," Maud said.

"Hi," the girl replied.

She looked like she hadn't had a proper bath in weeks. An assemblage of grime collected under her nails and clung to her hairline. Maud had to look close to see this though, for the child's hair was neatly brushed and most of the dirt on her face had been wiped away. Her clothes were in tatters and had to be drafty in the January wind. Maud felt cold just looking at the girl.

"Did you need something, honey? Your parents are going to come looking for you."

There was the tiniest of nods, making her dirty blond braid bob up and down.

"Okay. What do you need? It's Bridgette, isn't it?" Maud remembered her name from the family's previous visits.

Bridgette nodded again, but she looked like she was having trouble finding the words. Her tiny mouth pursed and contracted as if chewing on what she wanted to say before saying it.

"You... you are all draw'd on," she said finally.

Maud smiled.

The days had been cold and the nights colder. It seemed the cold hurt her bones like it never had in previous years. It was necessary now to cover all her lovely pictures in the winter. She even wore a scarf around her neck. Maud was no fool though, and she knew most of her value to the museum wasn't in that she could count change and add admission. People wanted to see the pictures, even if they were on an old, sagging body like hers. So, even on the coldest days, she wore a lower-cut blouse that ended in a V just above her breast.

She never liked to hide her lions. Her scarf covered her neck but still allowed a sort of peep window to show the scene on her chest. Even though her coat covered her arms and shoulders, when she reached out to take money, her wrists were intentionally exposed. This gave every patron a little glimpse of the secrets she concealed underneath.

"Yes, honey. I'm all draw'd on."

"How'd you get that a-way?"

"Well, when I was only a bit older than you, some wild Indians kidnapped me away from my mean, old daddy. They took me to their teepees and made me one of their own. The squaws tattooed me this way to give me special, ancient Indian powers."

Maud's voice easily slipped back into that entrancing tone all circus people used to draw in the rubes. The story she told wasn't the only one. She adjusted her tale to fit the ears of the person asking. Sometimes she had travelled the deepest parts of the Congo where a shaman put a curse on her that magically marked her skin. Other times, she was the fiercest pirate princess to ever sail the seven seas.

Each tattoo represented a different man who challenged her and lost.

If she was feeling extra feisty, Maud said her family sent her to the Orient to learn the ways of the assassins. So deadly was she, they covered her body with pictures to warn others of her killing powers. The boys especially loved that one.

No one questioned the stories. They all just listened attentively. Occasionally, some of the children would compare notes and argue over who was right and who was lying. The whole affair only added to Maud's mystique in the town. When you were as old as Maud, mystique was a hard commodity to come by.

Little Bridgette's eyes filled the space of her face, giving very little room for her button nose and tiny mouth. When she spoke, it was barely more than a whisper.

"Did... Did it hurt?"

"Like the dickens. A small price to pay though for my magical powers."

"What powers did you get?"

"I have the power to read your thoughts," Maud said with a smile. "I'm very, very magical that way."

"You are?"

"I can prove it. I'll read your thoughts right now." Maud shut her eyes and placed her index fingers at each temple. She made a slow humming noise that got louder and louder. The little girl tensed with the anticipation of it all. "I got it!" Maud said suddenly.

Bridgette jumped a little and then smiled. The surge of fear mixed with excitement was why folks came to see the shows. It's was why they marveled at the bizarre. Close enough to touch the frightening, while maintaining safe distance.

"I know what you were thinking. You were thinking about how you wanted to touch my tattoo, but you didn't know how to ask. You're a very polite girl. Your daddy is so proud of you."

Maud didn't think it was possible, but Bridgette's eyes grew even wider. "How did you know?"

Maud tapped her head, careful not to undo her bun.

"I told you. Indian magic. To answer your question though, yes, you can touch my tattoo."

Bridgette took a deep breath and stood tall on her tippy toes. Maud pulled up the sleeve on her right arm to expose a tattoo to the cold air. It was a bird taking flight from a budding tree. The tail of a serpent that wove up her arm curled around the branch, framing the bird. When the little girl touched it, it was like being kissed by a snowflake. Her tiny hands were frozen but so gentle. A whiff of cold crept underneath the slit in the door, making the little thing tremble all over.

"Oh, you poor girl," Maud said. "You must be frozen half to death. Come 'round here. Let me give you my scarf."

The girl did as she was told and walked around the big desk to where Maud sat. She unraveled the scarf from her neck and wrapped it around the small child. It curled around her several times. Maud smelled the odor of dirt along with the tang of crisp winter air as she bundled the child. Goose flesh broke out along her now bare neck.

"But you won't have one," said Bridgette.

"I don't need one, remember? Indian powers. Now, go on and catch up to your family before your parents worry. Go on now. Don't want to miss the show."

Bridgette padded away without saying good-bye. Maud didn't notice the redness rimming the child's nose, nor did she catch that her tiny voice was due to a sore throat. As she turned the corner, the little girl sneezed into the loose bit of scarf, but Maud didn't think much of that at all. Children sneezed all the time. Nothing to worry about.

***

The illness turned bad in a matter of days. There was coughing, sneezing, and runny noses. Lotteva got it as well but recovered enough to go back to work within the week. Maud laid down in her bed from the sickness and just couldn't manage to get back up. Her head felt like it might roll off her head, and she couldn't find a decent breath to save her life.

Everyone believed she'd recover with a bit of bed rest and some extra warmth. Mrs. Wilson of Wilson's Treasures and Curiosities made a pot of chicken broth for them. The blessed woman carried the heavy, cast iron pot up the stairs daily to deliver it to Maud. Mr. Wilson doubled their coal delivery in the effort to warm their small apartment as though it were summer come early.

Despite everyone's efforts, Maud continued to languish in her bed. The illness just wouldn't subside. She coughed so often, her ribs bruised and cracked under the pressure of it. Every wheeze of breath was so wet Maud felt like she was drowning. Her thoughts swam around in her mind, barely pausing long enough for her to catch any one for very long.

Lotteva hovered over her like a mama cat, bringing her blankets and soup. Her mother's chill never seemed to leave, and after a good while, she could barely stomach even the thinnest broth. She called the doctor when Maud made no further progress.

The man was kind enough. He handled Maud's old bones with great care and a gentle hand. When he finished his examination, the doctor's face that told Lotteva and Maud all they needed to know. What had been a look of concern moments before turned grave after listening to Maud's breathing.

"Her condition has worsened to pneumonia."

"But it was just a cold. It was nothing. I had it too, and now, I'm fine," Lotteva said.

"To you, yes, it was a cold. You are young enough and healthy. We see this all the time with the very young and the very old. The flu or a simple cold? It turns serious fast. Their immune systems just can't handle it."

"Should we admit her to the hospital?"

"That will be your decision. I'll give you my opinion as best I can. Your mother has a severe case of pneumonia. We can treat her in the hospital, but it's up to you. We've had some success with people as old as her."

"I'm right here, you know," Maud said from her bed in the corner.

She didn't bother to try to look at the two of them as she said her piece. It hurt far too much to open her eyes and to try to focus on something so far away.

"Yes, Mrs. Wagner. I apologize," said the doctor.

"So, you're saying you can cure her in the hospital? She will get better there?"

"I'm afraid I can't say that. People like your mother, sometimes it's better to stay home in comfort. You can try the hospital, and we'll do anything and everything for her. Sometimes, we get lucky and they pull through."

"Lucky? You get lucky?" Lotteva said.

"Well... I didn't mean... I'm just saying with her advanced age..."

"Basically, with her advanced age, what is there worth salvaging? Why even bother?"

"That's not what I said," he said, stepping backward.

Lotteva's voice was getting louder as she worked up a good head of steam. "It's what you're implying! My mother is old, so just make her comfortable enough to die because she isn't any use to anyone anymore."

"Mrs. Wagner, I think..."

"That's *Ms.* Wagner. Mrs. Wagner is the woman over there you are so ready to throw away in the garbage. What a quack you are. I might as well take her to a veterinarian. They'd treat her more humanely."

The doctor put his hands up for protection as though her words were literal daggers. He stepped back a few more paces as Lotteva's eyebrows folded into an angry glare. Her hands balled into fists on each hip. She looked so much like her mother.

Maud turned her head. Though the daylight caused the underbelly of her eyes to burn and ache, she wouldn't have missed this sight for all the world. Lotteva was everything she had always wished she would be. The doctor had a good foot in height on Lotteva, but he only looked about two feet tall as Lotteva stared him down.

"That's my girl," Maud said to herself.

"Ms. Wagner, please. I'm just suggesting she might be more comfortable at home. I don't know that there's much more we can do for her."

"Oh, I know there's nothing you can do for her, and I suggest you'd be more comfortable outside and out of our home. I also suggest you leave before I put you there myself."

Without another word, the doctor left the apartment, hurrying away from the angry woman. He didn't even bother to collect his fee. Maud figured he'd rather eat the cost than test Lotteva's patience any further. Crazy circus people were unpredictable.

Lotteva grunted and slammed the door behind him. Maud wanted to laugh, but it came out in a slew of racking, wet coughs instead. The handkerchief was soaked with saliva and mucous by the time her daughter was at her side. She sat on the floor to be eye level with Maud.

"Don't listen to him, Mama. What an asshole."

Maud dabbed her mouth and grinned at her daughter.

"He was that. I think you made it clear to him. The problem is he's also right. Funny how assholes can also be right."

Lotteva's face fell, looking shocked. Sounds of carnival music danced somewhere on the wind. The tinkling of laughter and bangles.

"Mama don't listen. We can get you another doctor, another hospital. We can get you better..."

"Baby, I'm tired. I feel it all over. Maybe somebody could fix me, maybe they couldn't. Either way, I don't want to go in a hospital surrounded by strangers. I want to stay here with you, my girl. Please don't take me away."

***

Two nights later, the fever set in. Time passed oddly. The world through burning eyes rippled and bent in ways that didn't make sense. Maud's eyes and mind felt too hot, but the rest of her shivered from the chills. Lotteva piled mounds of blankets on top of her, but she still felt cold.

Lotteva put wet rags on Maud's forehead and felt her mother's arm every hour. Sweat meant the fever broke. It meant she was better. But every time she checked, all she found was skin so hot it could cook an egg.

An odd thing happened as the clock rounded the midnight mark. The world levelled itself. The throbbing in Maud's brain abated enough for her to think. She was still too weak to lift her head, but her vision steadied enough to see the worn bags under her daughter's eyes. Lotteva's cheeks, normally so pink and full of life, were sallow. In her hands sat a coffee mug of warm broth.

"Please, Mama. Please eat some. You haven't had much of anything in days."

Lotteva held out the spoon and blew on it. It was just like Maud had done for her as a child. She smiled at the memory of it and declined the soup with the turn of her head. Lotteva's long hair was greying in streaks around her temples, but every time it swished around her shoulders, Maud caught a whiff of warmth and flowers. Lotteva's smell.

"Please, Mama."

"I'm not hungry. Please stop, baby."

Lotteva put down the broth with an exacerbated sigh. Maud could see the helpless feeling in her daughter's eyes. It was the yearning to help, to make everything better. But Maud wasn't getting better, and there was nothing her daughter could do but watch her slip away. She ached for that. Ached for her to not have to see her this way. She wished Gus were here, so their daughter didn't have to be alone with this.

The stinging in her eyes made Maud shut them for a moment. That moment stretched into a longer moment that wove into a carefully knitted string of time. Dreams were normally next, feverish and strange, but that didn't happen. She had a sense of falling. Not really like falling from somewhere like a window or a trapeze. This felt like falling inside herself. Everything began to implode and collapse within her. The sensation jolted her, and she opened her eyes once more.

Lotteva was next to her again, looking off in the distance as though she too were collapsing in on herself. Maud knew if she couldn't help herself, she might as well help her daughter. Helpless idle hours invited the devil of depression into your heart. She couldn't have that for her girl.

"I want you to tattoo me," Maud said.

"What?" Lotteva said, stunned from her reverie.

"I want you to tattoo me. That's my wish. Final wish. Can't refuse those."

"But Mama, why?"

Maud moved her left hand until it peeked out from the pile of blankets covering her. Lotteva took it and helped her tuck the covers in around her arm, leaving her wrist and part of a forearm exposed to the unforgiving air. She presented a blank space on the top part of her wrist to Lotteva.

"Right here. Your daddy, he promised me a rose right there. Do you see? The little blank bit on the top of my wrist. He promised me for years he'd make me the most beautiful rose right there."

"Why didn't he?"

"One reason or another. He said he was always looking for the perfect rose to use as a model. Said he hadn't found any good enough. I don't know about all that. You know him with all his bluster. I think he didn't want to do it because it was the last blank part on me. Maybe a part of him never wanted to be done drawing pretty things on my body."

Then, the most peculiar thing happened. At the end of the bed stood Dora tapping at the side her own nose, as though Maud had just guessed something correctly in a game. She wasn't the Dora Maud had last seen, old and faded like newspaper left in the morning sun. The Dora in the room was how she looked when they first met. She was tall and pretty, dressed in a gaudy green costume with Morty coiled around her body.

Dora said, "See you soon, toots," and pulled a number of silly faces, trying to coax Maud to laugh.

For a spell, Maud was entranced by the image of her old friend and didn't know what to do. Then, when Dora play kissed Morty, a laugh sent Maud into a fit of coughing.

"At least you didn't bring the goddamn birds," she said in between coughs.

"What are you talking about? What birds, Mama?"

In a flash, Dora was gone, and Lotteva was looking worriedly at her mother. Maud remembered where she was and what was happening. Dora couldn't be in the room with them. That was an impossible thing. Ghosts were impossible.

"I want you to tattoo a rose there. It's important."

Lotteva looked from her mother's wrist to her face and back again. Her indecision made her face look like an actress in a bad movie. It might have even been funny if it was truly fiction. Again, Maud heard circus music somewhere in the distance.

"I don't know, Mama. It feels odd. Daddy was so good. All your tattoos were his."

Maud grinned. "Not all. Remember the daisy, honey?"

Sudden recognition flashed on Lotteva's face.

"Oh God, I almost forgot. I can't believe you let me practice on you. I was just a kid."

"You weren't practicing. Don't you remember? It was a present. You gave me a present," Maud said wistfully.

"I did?" Lotteva looked as though she were peering back through time, trying to snatch the moment from the ether.

"It was because you felt bad. For the lion... when you scared me. Such a funny girl you were. I felt horrible for slapping you, and you felt bad for scaring me. You made me a daisy because a rose was too hard to do."

"Oh my gosh, I do remember that," Lotteva said. Her face brightened as soon as the memory returned in its full form. "You were the first person I tattooed. You let me do it because I thought it was a present. I was like seven."

"Well, it was on my hip. No one but your daddy would ever see it. He was so proud of you every time he looked at it, you know. I'm not joking. Even after you got really good, I never saw him prouder than he was of that little daisy. I swear."

"But Mama, I don't know if I can do it." Lotteva nervously bit her lips.

"Honey, you are better than your daddy. Far better than me. Please, baby. Do me this last kindness. You wanted to make me a rose back then and couldn't. You can now, and I want my rose. Please. I don't think I have much time."

Lotteva let go of her mother's hand and stood quietly in the dark of the room. She returned a bit later with a lamp and her box of tools.

Maud's breath was shallow and came in short bursts. Her lungs felt like they were more water than air, and her head swam while she tried to collect her thoughts. The steely tang of antiseptic told her Lotteva was cleaning the tools. She barely felt the swab on her wrist. Everything was going numb in her hands and feet. Only the chilled wetness of the alcohol registered.

"Not much need in that, Lotteva," Maud said with an ironic chuckle. "Don't think I'll be around long enough to get infected."

Lotteva ignored her and continued the routine she knew so well. Measure the ink, mix it with water and soap, place the needles out in order of smallest to largest. Maud didn't feel the first poke or the ones following. The only way she knew it had begun was the pressure she felt from Lotteva holding her arm still. Something about it made her relax. Her breathing slowed, becoming gentler and more even.

When she gazed up again, there was another familiar face. Two, actually. In a dress far too tight to be legal, Tricky Trixie stood with her body covered in the wings of Maud's creation. Trixie's arm was slung over a much smaller pair of shoulders. Toddy, the dragon lady, nudged Trixie in the ribs as she stood tall in her statuesque green gown. Dragons flew across her back and shoulders. The two women beamed at her and waved enthusiastically.

Though Trixie's mouth didn't open, her words drifted like a melody on the wind. "Honey, I want to fly until I die."

"And you did, didn't you Trixie?" Maud said smiling back at her.

"Mama? Who are you talking to?"

In a flash, they were gone, and Lotteva was looking at her with a concerned face.

"Nobody, honey. Old memories is all. You remember Trixie, don't you?"

"Yes, a little. The dancer?"

"Yes, that's her. Travelled a bit with the girl who saved you when you were a kid. Toddy was her name. I covered her in dragons."

"I remember, Mama. Why are you thinking of them?"

"No reason, baby. No reason."

Lotteva went back to work on the rose, but Maud couldn't watch. She would have loved to see her daughter work, but every time she turned her head, it hurt so much. Besides, another visitor had joined them in the apartment.

Ester, dressed in her expensive dress and dripping with bobbles, stood at the foot of the bed. She was in blue and silver, flashing little bits of color every time the light hit something sparkly on her. She flashed her scarab daringly. She stood with a mixture of flirty aloofness and overblown confidence. All a show of course, and Maud smiled at her. Soon enough, Ester softened, putting one hand over her heart and bowing to her bed-ridden friend. Her earrings shook with the bow, and Maud nodded back at the girl.

"Mama, what do you keep looking at?" asked Lotteva.

"Old friends, coming to see me. People I've tattooed, people I helped. At least, I hope I helped them. I never minded being criticized for being kind to people."

"No one's here," Lotteva said.

"You're right, honey. Of course, you're right."

They fell back into the silence of reality. Lotteva busied herself on her mother's rose. Normally, something so simple would have been completed by now, but Lotteva wanted it to be perfect.

In the interim, more people came to see Maud. Jake, with his necklace of lines and triangles, stood in the corner with his back propped against the wall. Still hiding in the shadows, but he came out just enough to see her. He smoked a cigarette and grinned at Maud. After a respectful tip of his cap, he vanished in a blink.

Lawrence, the sailor, bent over her footboard, holding his weight up by gripping the wood with both hands. It was a flirtatious pose, and he grinned at her in a way that made old ladies giggle behind their hands. Such the seducer, he stood up and unbuttoned his shirt. He revealed the portrait Maud had drawn of herself. Lawrence kissed his hand and slapped it to the drawing and over his heart as though cupid himself had pierced it. Maud chuckled as he, too, disappeared.

The next visitors weren't happy or nostalgic.

An old couple, not more than bones and rags, appeared at the foot of her bed. Her father faced her, but her mother refused. He held his wife, trying to convince her to turn and face Maud who lay in the bed before them. Again and again he turned her, getting rougher with every try. Every tug was a battle.

No matter how hard he tried, each side of Maud's mother was her backside, refusing to turn, refusing to look, refusing to accept. After a while, they both realized she had no face. She had no front at all. A woman with a rotten soul damned forever to be walking away.

Her father gazed upon Maud with a longing that spanned decades. In the deep pools of his eyes, he reached out to her and apologized for all the lost time. All the letters unanswered. All the hugs not given. In a flash, her mother was gone, but her father stayed just long enough to say the thing Maud had longed to hear for ages.

"I love you, Maudie. I always have."

Then he, too, was gone.

Maud wanted to cry. She wanted to go after him, to hug him. Maud wanted to run after him as he followed her mother into wherever he came from and tell him that he didn't have to go. He didn't have to follow her anymore. It was a fantasy and nothing more. Apparitions of a dying mind. None of it was real.

"Mama? You okay?" Lotteva asked.

"Yes. Why?"

"You're crying." She daubed at Maud's face with a threadbare handkerchief. Her face was pinched all over with concern.

The only evidence Lotteva was telling the truth was the tiniest tingle of wetness making its way down her face in the deep valleys of her laugh lines. Maud wanted to wipe away the tears and play the whole thing off like it was no big deal, but she couldn't move her hands or her arms. She just waited for Lotteva to do it for her.

Oh yes, those lines ran deep. Despite the woman who wouldn't turn around, Maud had loved and laughed. There was proof of that. No one could say otherwise. The best thing an old woman could hope for was for her laugh lines to be the deepest ones on her face.

"Did you ever wonder why I never let you get a tattoo?" Maud asked.

Lotteva's breath caught in her throat. So sudden and deep was the question, she stopped shading the rose on her mother's wrist. After all, it was one of those questions, the kind you really had to answer. The kind that actually meant something.

Lotteva never went through with getting a tattoo on herself. All the years of drawing on other people and not a one tattoo on her own body. Aside from a scar on her left forearm where a circus lynx got the better of her, she didn't have a mark on her body. Not one. Lotteva was a blank canvas in a world of pictures.

She started asking for one as soon as she turned ten, but Maud wouldn't allow it. Again and again she begged her parents to let her have a tattoo. After all, both of them were absolutely covered with beautiful pictures. It became the thing she wanted most, and it stayed that way through her adolescence. Every time they said no.

In the beginning, they both protested on the grounds that she was too young. As she got older, a shift happened. Maud still adamantly rejected the idea, but Gus did not. She begged and begged well into her twenties, but Maud wouldn't relent. After a while, Lotteva gave up asking and resigned to her unmarked life, making her an anomaly in the tattooing world.

"I wondered all the time. You never explained in a way that made sense to me. Something about needing and wanting. I never got it. It didn't matter after Daddy died." Lotteva looked downward at her shoes. Even though Gus passed years ago, the mention of it continued to force her into silence. "He used to say I was too young for a tattoo, but when I got older, he didn't say that anymore. I wanted one of his tattoos so badly, but he always said that you didn't want it. He wouldn't do it unless you said it was okay."

"I told you that you could after he died," Maud said.

"I know, but why then? I didn't want it anymore. Somehow, it wasn't the same if Daddy couldn't draw it for me. I always wanted one of his."

Lotteva sighed, and Maud shut her eyes to hold back the tears.

"Why didn't you want me to have a tattoo, Mama? I'm not mad about it. Not anymore. Just tell me why you didn't want me to have one."

Maud did her best to squeeze her daughter's hand. "Over the long time I've walked the earth, I've run into all types. Lots of folks just want something pretty on their arm, some want to commemorate their sweetheart or what have you, but some do it for a *real* reason. In the early days, it was like a costume. You could decorate your body to earn a living and get independence from the world of men. Some did it out of defiance. Any animal, no matter how caged, will bite back however they can."

Maud felt Lotteva's gentle hand close around her exposed one. Maud couldn't guess how hard her daughter was squeezing. More of the sensation had left her extremities, so the touch felt feathery light.

"I've had people scarred by brutality who needed a tattoo to cover someone else's deed. A scar they chose as opposed to one they didn't, as a wise man once said to me. Some people use their tattoos to tell the story of their life. Each one, no matter how beautiful or ugly, depicting a meaningful day or a moment in their lives. All so that even in the darkest hour, they can look at it and remember better days."

Water obscured Maud's vision, and she blink it away with some effort. When the blur cleared, there stood a new person at the foot of her bed. Clara, her blouse hastily torn into a tank top, stood tall and brazen with her fists on her hips. She raised her chin at Maud as she held out her arm to show the snake writhing up it. The word *Adalie* was carefully etched into the shading of the scales.

Maud let out a held breath as her gaze softened. "Some wanted it to erase the past. There's a difference, you know. It's not the same as covering a scar. When you want to erase something, that's another thing entirely. It means you want to wipe the history books clean, as though it never happened. No tattoo can do that... No tattoo should try."

After only the briefest of nods, Clara disappeared in a flash. A hint of the word *Adalie* trailed on the wind that took her away. She was immediately replaced with a gaunt teenage girl. Joy clutched her baggy shirt and flowing skirt. She smiled broadly at Maud as though she had the best secret to tell her. She curled her finger at Maud, beckoning her closer. Like a burlesque dancer, she raised her skirt high and higher, pulling faces of shock and fright with every inch she showed.

Maud smiled back at her as she lifted the skirt to her waist to display the beautiful sparrows Maud had made for her. There were no scars on her legs anymore. Just a smooth, pale sky for the birds to fly in. Joy giggled like a girl and dropped the skirt.

"And some," Maud said with a sigh, "some just need it to take back their body."

"I don't understand, Mama," Lotteva said, bringing her mother back to reality. "Why are you telling me all this?"

Joy vanished, and Maud turned her head far enough to look her daughter in the eyes. Every tiny movement hurt, but she had to tell her. Maud had to see.

"I never wanted that for you, baby. I never wanted you to have a hard reason to get a tattoo. You were my rose, my perfect flower. I never wanted you to hurt so much you needed one to cope, or use it to be independent, or be in such a terrible place you needed something to remind you of better days. There's a difference between want and need. I never wanted you to *need* any of it at all. I wanted you to have a childhood you didn't have to recover from. I wanted you to grow and bloom out in the open without broken stems or wilted leaves. And you did, my girl. You did that so beautifully."

Lotteva was crying now, open and honest.

"But... but you said I could after Daddy died."

"It was the first time I thought you might need it. His passing left such a hole in our world, I couldn't deny you any longer. But you didn't need it, my rose. You never did. You are so much better than me, so much stronger."

"But what were *your* reasons? Look at you, Mama. Why did you need them?"

The tears came quickly, pouring in streams from Maud's eyes. Somewhere, in the back of her mind, she thought how funny this was. The pneumonia had flooded her body so much, she was leaking. Her mind was going, but she could still feel the pain in her daughter's question.

Why did you need them?

"I needed them for all of those reasons. Each and every one. They started off as wants, but the need took over. They were my costume, my independence, my defiance, and my pictures to cover the scars of the past. I tried to document my life and wipe away where I came from all at the same time. I used them to rediscover my own worth, my own body. I owe everything good in my life to these pictures. I needed them for all those reasons, and I'm so grateful I have them. I just wanted you to have all that on your own… without the pictures."

Lotteva threw herself against her mother, crying helplessly like a child might. Maud wanted desperately to hold her daughter. She couldn't of course. Half of her was already gone. It was the half you needed to hug someone. Age didn't matter in that moment, but where your spirit stood did. Maud already had one foot on the other side.

As the tears cleared and wails silenced, Maud saw another figure in the room. At first, it was hard to make him out. He was far away and blurry in the distance. Slowly, the man sauntered toward her wearing a white shirt and black slacks. His hands were in his pockets, but he couldn't possibly hide the picture gallery that ran up both arms. He smiled in that way that made his mustache curl.

"Hello there, gorgeous," Gus said. "I told you you'd live to be an old lady."

Maud smiled back at him. She had yearned to see his face again for a long time, and now, here he was. Gus Wagner looked like he did the day she met him, young and handsome and full of charm.

"Lotteva, honey, I need you to finish the rose," Maud said.

There was a sudden earnestness in her voice. Lotteva sat up straight and wiped her face with a rag.

"What?"

"Please honey, finish the rose. I don't have much longer."

There was a gentle urgency in the air, enough to silence any questions Lotteva might ask. Something inexplicable seemed to move her forward. She picked up her needle and continued to work away on the most beautiful rose she'd ever drawn. It had to be the best. It had to be finished before…

Gus peeked over his daughter's shoulder and smiled.

"It's looking good, real good. Better than I could do."

"Well, she learned from the best," Maud said. She spoke out loud, but Lotteva didn't seem to hear her anymore. She continued on her task, not looking up for anything.

"Don't worry, she can't hear you anymore. That part's over," Gus said.

"I don't understand. What part is over?" Maud asked.

"It's the fever, my dear. It's burning you up. You aren't actually speaking right now."

"The fever? She can't hear me?"

"Not anymore. But I can. Oh, how I've missed you, Maudie," Gus said while reaching down to take her hand.

Maud reached up to take his hand, not fully expecting to be able to. To her astonishment, her hand lifted and fit perfectly into his. She marveled at the sight of it. No longer were there wrinkles and veins pulling thin skin away from her bones. No spots to show how old she truly was. Her hands looked like they did when she was young. They weren't even stained with ink anymore.

When she touched her face, it too was the face of her younger self. The tattoos on her body were taut and new. Her hair was dark auburn again and pulled stylishly on top of her head. She could breathe without the pressure of a deluge on her chest. She sat up. It was a miracle.

From behind his back, Gus produced a single red rose. "I thought you might want this," he said as he helped her to her feet.

Without hesitation, Maud threaded the stem of the flower into the knot of her hair. It was an action she knew so well from years of practice. Gus was positively giddy, holding his elbow out for her to take as though she were a lady in one of Joy's novels.

"Where are we going? What happens now?" she asked, interlacing her arm in his.

"We've all been waiting for you, my dear."

Gus gestured in front of them at a nondescript wall. The only thing that decorated it was an old, faded poster advertising *The Amazing Wagners*. A tattooed man and woman held hands staring out at the real-life models that inspired the poster. Somehow, the stone of the wall dissolved and floated away like a fog lifting. The poster, too, dissipated as a great scene revealed itself before them.

It was a sort of doorway. One with no hinges or locks, but a doorway all the same. Beyond it was the circus as she remembered it. Jazz music and animal noises began as whispers and then blew loud enough to light her up inside. Figures turned into people she knew as the mist lifted, revealing more and more.

Before she realized it, there was no doorway left at all. The beautiful circus was the only world in front of her. Any semblance of what came before was behind her in a place she'd have to turn around to see.

Dora waved from a stage, beckoning her to step in and join her. Strong men, wolf men, lobster boys, tattooed men, bearded ladies. She knew them all, and they begged her to join the party. Trixie, Toddy, Jake and Lawrence danced with one another to the vibrant music in the air.

Clara and Joy stood near one another, spinning their baby girls by the arms so their little legs left the earth and orbited their mothers. Any time the girls almost collided, the women jerked them away, causing an uproar of giggles.

Everyone danced and sang. Vendors tossed food and drink in the air, free of charge. A woman with red hair held a torch and breathed fire among the revelers. Fireworks exploded in the sky, even though it was daytime. A man on stilts danced about the crowd, taller than anything else. He tipped his striped hat to Queen Maud.

Colors were so bright it hurt her eyes. Maud had forgotten how gorgeous the colors were the first time she saw them. Tents stretched into the sky waving flags against the clear, blue sky. Off in the distance, a metal Ferris wheel turned slowly around and around against a painting of wispy clouds.

Everything glistened and glittered. Gold was real gold. Silver, too, was real. Nothing was painted to disguise what it really was. A breeze blew gentle, carrying with it the scent of cotton candy and sweet hay.

Maud searched the crowd again, finding more people she knew. This couldn't all be real. She had to take in everything before it disappeared, and life dragged her back to the real world. The place where she laid dying under the weight of all that water. Any minute now, she'd return. It would rip her away. This was only a dream.

Off to the side, a tiny, waving hand caught her attention. It was a hand she hadn't counted on seeing, so it took her a hard minute to recognize the owner. The girl was so young, maybe seventeen, and dressed in the baggy dress of a farm girl. There was a blond, little girl perched on her hip. She smiled and played with her hair as it moved in the breeze.

Maud struggled to place who this was. She looked familiar but distant. It took the girl raising one, skeptical eyebrow to clue her in. Maud stopped breathing for an instant.

The young woman stood happy and proud. None of the fear or concealed shame that Maud had gotten used to seeing every time she looked in the mirror. This version of herself was different. She stood tall and smiled wide. It was the Maud as she would have been had she not been broken so long ago.

"It's not bad," the younger Maud said with a nod. "You still got here. It took you longer, but you still got here. Despite everything, you still made it."

When she looked back at the baby on the girl's hip, she realized who that was too.

"Sarah? My baby, Sarah?"

Part of her wanted to reach out to them, to touch the child, but she stayed in place. There was an invisible tether holding her back.

Two people came from nowhere to stand behind the farm girl and the baby. Her father, young and handsome again, put his arm around young Maud's shoulder. He hugged her close. The other was a young woman. Her face was smooth and lovely in the sunlight. Her dark hair hung prettily in a loose braid down her back. The woman stood graceful and happy, tickling baby Sarah around her belly.

It had been a lifetime since Maud had seen her mother this way. This was before the Fiji mermaid, perhaps before she stopped drawing. Her mother looked as she must have before life broke her down. Before she became the bitter thing Maud knew. She smiled and kissed her granddaughter's cheek. Baby Sarah giggled and reached for her.

The invisible tether in Maud snapped. Something behind her had changed.

"What do you say, Maudie? Are you ready?" Gus asked.

"Yes, yes I think I'm ready."

"Do you want to look back and see the rose Lotteva made for you? It's finished now. You could see it before we go."

Maud slowly shook her head, not able to take her eyes from the pristine beauty in front of her. Her circus. Her heaven. Her place of unbroken people.

"I don't need to look back. I've seen it, and she was the most beautiful rose I've ever known."

Maud took a step forward, and she was gone forever.

Afterword

When writing historical fiction, the best compliment a writer can receive is the question, "What part is true?" If you can't tell fiction from fact, it means I did my job weaving the two together. It's one of the finest ways to bring history to life, in my opinion. Engaging a modern reader enough to question historical fact and fiction is a great win.

This is a biopic inspired by the facts I found about Maud Wagner. I use the word "inspired" because a good bit of the story is invented. There were just not enough facts known about her to fill the book and tell the story I wanted to tell.

Maud Wagner, Gus Wagner, and Lotteva Wagner were all real people. However, much of the story of their lives together depicted in this book is fabricated. Nothing in my research points to Maud having an abusive family as a child. I chose to write it as such because Maud did run away to join the circus as a teenager. It stands to reason she might have been running away from something at home.

Much of the heart of the book has to deal with family, especially mothers and daughters. Being both a mother and a daughter, I injected a great deal of myself into this book. Far more than I normally do in my writing. Even though I had to manufacture much of the story, it was important to me to add as many facts as I could.

Maud was the first known female tattooist in North America. Before she became a tattooist, she was an aerialist and contortionist. The dates of her life and death are accurate. The same goes with Lotteva.

I nudged Gus' death later by a couple of years to better align with the narrative.

Olive Oatman's story is accurate.

My research proved that Gus traveled as a sailor and learned to tattoo from Alfred South. It really was rumored that South tattooed Queen Victoria with a Bengal tiger fighting a python, but I have no idea if that's factual. As a history buff, I would love that to be true.

Lotteva began tattooing at an early age and also worked as a clown, dancer, and animal trainer. She was an oddity in her profession in that she was completely unmarked. Her mother never let her get a tattoo. At age 83, Lotteva hand-poked her last tattoo on Ed Hardy during his artistic revival of the Sailor Jerry style. It was a rose.

Some of the most unique parts of this book are also true. Maud and Gus met at the World's Fair in 1904. My description of the fair is based on my research. Their first date happened because of the barter Maud suggested—one date in exchange for a tattoo and a lesson. They later married, had their daughter, and toured the country as a tattooing family with the circus.

Perhaps the most unbelievable, yet true, detail in *MAUD'S CIRCUS* is Gus's death. If I were to choose a character's death, I would never decide on a lightning strike. Most readers wouldn't believe it. Alas, this is actually how Gus Wagner met his unfortunate end.

As I researched, a larger story unfolded itself. Not just this small family. The world of tattoos and the circus. What this all meant to people over the years. I decided to weave a story around these people not only to chronicle the life of one amazing woman, but to also tell the history of tattoos and show the changing world of the circus throughout the decades.

While researching tattoos, I came upon some historical gems. Victorian society's fascination with them, Native American influences, and tattooed Egyptian princesses thousands of years old. My next step was to interview a myriad of people and discover why they got their tattoos. Aside from the ever-present "because it looked pretty," patterns formed in their stories, many of which are described in the narrative.

I'd like to thank all those who talked to me about their tattoos. It meant a lot that they shared their stories. Something about a permanent mark changes a person. Not just the way others regard them, but how they regard themselves.

I wrote a fictional tale about a real woman because I wanted people to know her. I wanted to tell her story, but also our shared history in tattoos. Maud Wagner ran away to the circus and tattooed the masses for decades, yet few people know her name. Until now.

About the Author

Michelle Rene is a creative advocate and the author of a number of published works of historical fiction and speculative fiction.

She has won multiple indie awards. Her novel, Hour Glass, won Chanticleer Review's "Best Book of the Year" award in 2018. Her experimental novella, Tattoo, was a Foreword Review's Indies finalist for fantasy. The Dodo Knight, a historical novella, placed as a finalist with the Next Gen Indie Book Awards. Her YA historical fantasy, Manufactured Witches, won the OZMA award for fantasy, the Discovery Award from the Writer's League of Texas, and was honored by the Indie Author Project as Texas's best YA novel in 2019.

When not writing, she is a professional artist, museum lover, belly dancer, and autism mom. She lives as the only female with her husband, son, and ungrateful cat in Dallas, Texas.

You can connect with me on:

◐ https://www.michellereneauthor.com
🐦 https://twitter.com/MRene_Author
f https://www.facebook.com/mrene.author

CPSIA information can be obtained
at www.ICGtesting.com
Printed in the USA
LVHW030721060222
710169LV00008B/911